THE NEW CHUSHINGURA

THE FORTY-SEVEN RONIN

EIJI YOSHIKAWA

Translated by
SHELLEY MARSHALL

DEDICATION

To Mom

CONTENTS

Books by Eiji Yoshikawa
Translated by Shelley Marshall

Kuroda Josui
Uesugi Kenshin
Taira no Masakado

www.jpopbooks.com

 Created with Vellum

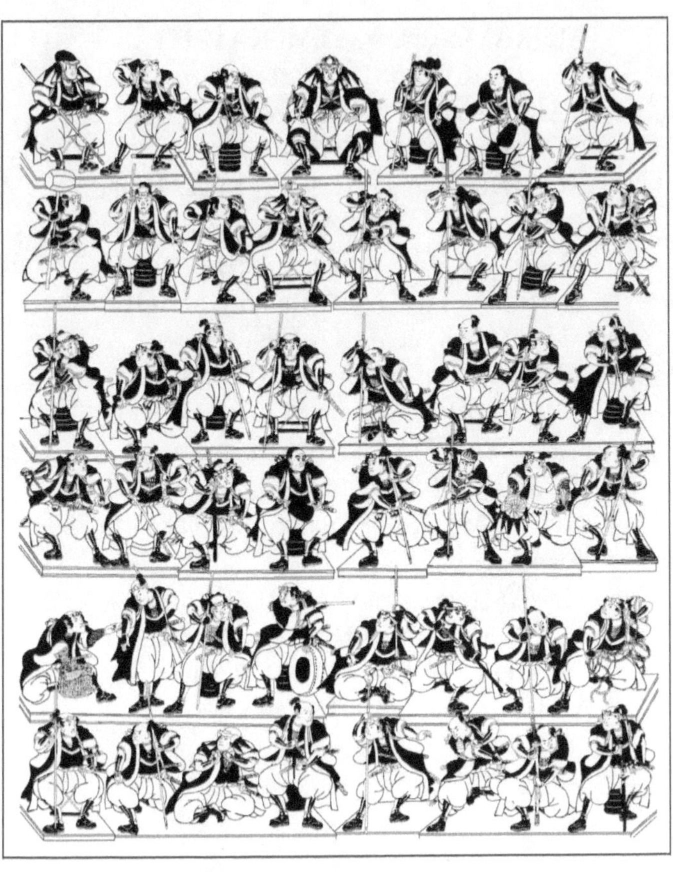

The Forty-Seven Ronin

1. ONODERA Junai OISHI Sezaemon
   HORIBE Yahei OISHI Kuranosuke
   OISHI Chikara SENBA Saburobei
   SUGAYA Hannojo
2. KANZAKI Yogoro MASE Kyudayu
   NAKAMURA Kansuke HAZAMA Kihei
   ONODERA Koemon MAEBARA Isuke
   KAIGA Yazaemon OKANO Kin'emon

3. MURAMATSU Sandayu KATSUTA
   Shinzaemon YOSHIDA Sawaemon
   TAKEBAYASHI Tadashichi OKAJIMA
   Yasoemon KURAHASHI Densuke
   SUGINO Juheiji MURAMATSU Kihei
4. OTAKA Gengo YADA Goroemon OKUDA
   Magodayu HARA Soemon FUWA
   Kazuemon HAZAMA Jujiro USHIODA
   Matanojo KATAOKA Gengoemon
5. TERASAKA Kichiemon AKABANE Genzo
   YOKOGAWA Kanbei YOSHIDA
   Chuzaemon HAZAMA Shinrokuro
   TOMINOMORI Sukeemon
   CHIKAMATSU Kanroku ISOGAI
   Jurozaemon
6. HAYAMI Tozaemon KIMURA Okaemon
   MASE Magokuro HORIBE Yasubei
   OKUDA Sadaemon MIMURA Jirozaemon
   YATO Emoshichi KAYANO Wasuke

Romanized Japanese	Sound	Sounds like	Romanized Japanese	Sound	Sounds like
a	ah	arcade	myo	myoe	
ba	bah	Bach	myu	myue	
be	bay	bay	n	n	no
bi	bee	bee	na	nah	nonsense
bo	boe	jumbo	ne	nay	neighbor
bu	bue	boohoo	ni	nee	knee
bya	byah		no	noe	no
byo	byoe		nu	new	new
byu	byue		nya	nyah	
cha	cha	cha-cha-cha	nyo	nyoe	
chi	chee	cheetah	nyu	nyue	
cho	choe	chosen	o	oh	oh
chu	chew	chew	pa	pa	papa
da	dah	dot	pe	pay	pay
de	day	day	pi	pee	peewee
di	doe	detail	po	poe	hippo
do	doe	doe	pu	poo	Pulitzer
e	ay	hay	pya	pyah	
fu	foo	fool	pyo	pyoe	
ga	gah	Lady Gaga	pyu	pyue	pupil
ge	gay	gay	ra	rah	rapport
gi	gee	guitar	re	ray	stingray
go	goe	go	ri	ree	tree
gu	goo	Google	ro	roe	row
gya	gyah		ru	rue	kangaroo
gyo	gyoe		rya	ryah	
gyu	gyue		ryo	ryoe	
ha	hah	hot	ryu	ryue	
he	hey	hey	sa	sa	samba
hi	hee	he	se	say	say
ho	hoe	hole	sha	shah	shaman
hu	hoo	who	shi	shee	sheet
hya	hyah		sho	sho	show
hyo	hyoe		shu	shoo	shoe
hyu	hyue		si	shee	sheet
i	ee	peek	so	so	so what
ja	jah	jog	su	sue	sue
ji	jee	genius	ta	tah	tonic
jo	joe	banjo	te	tay	maintain
ju	jue	June	ti	chee	cheetah
ka	kah	car	to	toe	toe
ke	kay	Mary Kay	tsu	tsoo	
ki	kee	key	u	ou	you
ko	koe	coconut	wa	wah	water
ku	koo	cuckoo	ya	yah	yacht
kya	kyah		yo	yoe	yoyo
kyo	kyoe		yu	yue	you
kyu	kyu	queue	za	zah	
ma	mah	Mama	ze	zay	
mi	mee	me	zo	zoo	Bozo
me	may	may	zu	zoo	zoo
mo	moe	moe			
mu	mue	move			
mya	myah				

Ako	ah koe	biwa	bee wah
Asano	ah sah noe	furosaki	foo row sah kee
Chushingura	chew shee n goo rah	geta	gay tah
Date	dah tay	hakama	hah kah mah
Den'emon	day n ay moe n	haori	hah oe ree
Emoshichi	ay moe shee chee	kaishakunin	kah ee shah koo nee n
Gengo	gay n go	kamishimo	kah mee shee moe
Genroku	gay n row koo	koku	koe koo
Junai	jue nah ee	kotatsu	koe tah tsoo
Kami	kah mee	sanjukkoku	sah n jue koe koo
Kazuemon	kah zoo ay moe n	tabi	tah bee
Kira	kee rah	biwa	bee wah
Kozuke	koe zoo kay	furosaki	foo row sah kee
Kuranosuke	koo rah noe sue kay	geta	gay tah
Oishi	oh ee shee	hakama	hah kah mah
Onodera	oh no day rah	haori	hah oe ree
Sengakuji	say n ga koo jee	kaishakunin	kah ee shah koo nee n
Shiroppe	shee row pay	kamishimo	kah mee shee moe
Suke	sue kay	koku	koe koo
Takumi	tah koo mee	kotatsu	koe tah tsoo
Tsunayoshi	Tsoo nah yoe shee	sanjukkoku	sah n jue koe koo
Yonezawa	yoe nay zah wah		

Japanese Pronunciation Guide

PART I

ASANO TAKUMI NO KAMI

1

———

A DIFFERENCE OF SEVEN YEARS

IDE ALONG A river brimming with spring's life processes masked the kissing sounds made by water lapping against a stonewall. The daimyo's Edo mansion in Teppouzu of the Asano clan followed the river in Tsuki-ji. A gentle breeze grazed the reddish pink plum blossoms on the fence and the willow trees. Gold- and silver-papered sliding doors blocked the odors from the sea at the mouth of the large river.

He could hear oars dipping into the water just beyond the fence and the frequent plops of white droppings from sea birds onto the large canopy.

"Home in Ako, the beaches are filled with boaters and people gathering shells at low tide," said Takumi no Kami propped on his armrest to survey the sky. His eyes recalled the smoke from salt baking on the beach in his faraway home province.

He glimpsed a refined woman of twenty-five or -six years old in the adjoining room. She was his wife sitting with elegance before a teakettle enclosed by the tea room screen. She set fine utensils on a purple tea crepe wrapper and, in time, glided over to place a teacup in front of Takumi no Kami. Her gaze followed his to the blue sky above the eaves.

He said, "Everyone in Edo takes pride in the Edo spring. But when I think of home, I become nostalgic and long for the castle keep in Ako."

"Is there a better place to live?"

He nodded. "The country is best for the country cousin."

Today, the taps from a small hand drum played in the style of the Okura School floated in from Ogasawara Hayato's mansion next door. Noh was a popular pastime but not the only popular art.

Samurai and townsmen pursued the fad of the day. Men felt unfulfilled. A large void pained many. Ruffian dandies with the flair of kabuki reached their peak. Even young ladies from good homes fancied bawdy colors. The number of abandoned babies in town grew. The parents of harlots were pompous and made good livings. Perhaps many retainers on duty in Edo played a stanza of an Edo song to a bathhouse girl. Everyone knew about Yoshiwara. At the extreme, some townsmen bragged about eating quail and took pride in sacred rohdea lilies worth fifty or one hundred gold pieces as well as their rise in the world. No one saw this as excessive in these days of the Genroku era (1688-1704).

Behind closed doors, others grumbled about the government.

"The bottom follows the example set at the top."

"During the Kan'ei era, the ways of warriors and the ways of townsmen were not corrupt as they are these days."

Many lamented in secret and vilified the consequences of the personality of Shogun Tokugawa Tsunayoshi.

Naturally, inside information about the daimyo's life stripped out the rotten parts. People on the outside only saw the extravagance and showiness of his life. In the inner circle, these times called for makeshift measures. He imposed harsh taxes on the people of his domain and borrowed money from the wealthy. He also adored the socially accomplished vassals and deemed them loyal men.

In those days, only the Asano clan was low-key and frugal. Galvanized by Confucius and the samurai philosopher Yamaga Soko, the clan's unadorned way of the warrior since its founding was out of step with the rampant overindulgence of the Genroku era.

Thus, the clan's finances boasted a surplus. The annual production of Ako salt was plentiful. In short, the absence of arrogance and the steadfast actions of the warrior in Takumi no Kami and his wife were their true fortune.

"The tea's temperature is perfect. Another, please."

"Yes."

His wife again sat in front of the *furosaki* screen.

The couple shared interests in the tea ceremony, the incense-smelling ceremony, and drawing. Vassals looked with envy at the harmony in their interests and daily lives.

Happy sun rays beamed down. This glorious day, March 3, was the peaceful festival day for the Doll's Festival.

> *Go to sleep.*
> *Now sleep.*
> *You're a good girl.*
> *What'd you buy for the festival tonight?*
> *A spool of agarwood thread.*
> *A silver needle.*
> *Don't cry. Don't worry.*
> *Good girl.*

What did you sew for the festival tonight?
An obi sash with pretty plum, cherry, and
pine trees.
A short-sleeved silk kosode kimono ...

They heard a woman singing strains of a melancholy lullaby and a crying baby. No one was outside on the grounds. The sounds must have slipped in through the fence from a boat moored below the outer stonewall. As the boatman's hoarse voice barked orders to moor the boat and other tasks, was his wife in the boathouse nursing the crying baby at her breast?

The lady of the house listened, enchanted, as she dipped the ladle into the teakettle. She glimpsed her husband's face. Also captivated, Takumi no Kami strained to listen.

Although he followed the advice for making a good marriage offered by the proverb, *Put on indestructible golden sandals and search for a bride seven years your junior*, his wife had not given him an heir.

2

A FORMAL INVITATION TO THE SHOGUN'S CASTLE

Tominomori Sukeemon was a battlefield courier in the cavalry. He strode over to a corner of the garden, opened the wooden fence gate, and poked out his head to peer toward the river.

"Hey! Boatman's wife, what are you doing there with a crying baby? Don't you realize you're bothering the people who live here? You can't moor your boat below the stonewall. Didn't you see the sign? Get out!"

A page ran up to him. "Sukeemon-dono"

"What?"

"Please come."

"Where?"

"To the tea-ceremony cottage."

"Oh no!" Sukeemon said and slapped his head like he blundered.

"He's in the tea cottage? I didn't know that. Here I am out here shouting."

Tea ceremonies were held in a cottage close to where he stood.

Sukeemon sprinted off. Two people were kneeling in

the garden of the tea room built in the style of the tea master Rikyu.

He thought Takumi no Kami had summoned him but was surprised to see the lord's wife. She quietly said, "Sukeemon."

"Yes, Ma'am."

"Please give these rice candy chicks to the boatman's child."

"Oh, candy chicks? Thank you."

As sweat of shame ran down his back, Sukeemon bowed his head to the ground instead of the boatman's wife.

With reverence, he raised the candies to his head.

Next Takumi no Kami spoke.

"When you're finished, return here."

Sukeemon bent down from atop the stonewall to hand the candy wrapped in paper to the boatman's wife. He told her the gift was from the lady of the mansion. This news made her cry with the baby. As she placed her palms together and peered inside the fence, the mooring rope was removed, and the boat floated away from Akashi Bridge.

He thought, I'm a failure and no good, nothing like a samurai. I only pretend to be tough. This is not the warrior's way. The lord and the lady didn't scold me but probably despise this lout in their hearts.

Chastened, he returned to the tea cottage garden. He berated himself with cruel words until Takumi no Kami assigned an errand.

He placed both hands in apology on the ground scattered with pine needles.

"What do you wish me to do, Lord?"

"Uh, Sukeemon? Tomorrow's the fourth. Attendance at the castle is not scheduled, but a letter signed by the shogun's Council of Elders is on its way. I've been ordered to appear at the castle. I don't know why. Have you heard about this?"

"Yes, the chief retainer informed me a little while ago."

"Asazuki is usually led, but he suffered a slight injury to a leg the other day on the equestrian grounds. Saddle another horse."

Relieved this was the errand, Sukeemon led the mount to the stable. He told his underlings and the attendants the official business would be quick work.

When he came out front the next day, he peered at the blue skies. Kanzaki Yogoro, the superintendent of foot soldiers, had assembled the retinue of attendants and was smoking beside the large brazier in the office.

"You're finished? Well done."

"I switched horses, changed the saddle, groomed him again, and am done."

"Tomorrow isn't the usual attendance day. Why is he going to the castle? Maybe, the occasion is auspicious."

"The steward Kataoka said the lord is going to receive an imperial mandate."

"An imperial mandate to do what?"

"He will host banquets for the imperial envoys visiting from the capital."

"Oh, that's quite an honor."

Tanaka Sadashiro, the personal assistant to the daimyo, seated at a desk turned his attention from updating entries in an accounting ledger to say, "You're talking nonsense. What honor? What's there to be happy about? The host of the envoys, by law, must finance the entire affair with his funds. Thus, feudal lords of clans suspected of being wealthy or disliked by the Council of Elders draw the losing numbers."

The smiling Yogoro listened in silence, but Sukeemon seethed.

"Isn't that what's expected in public service? A simple clan style is useful at those times. It's an auspicious, important mission. How can you say it's a burden?"

"Sukeemon-dono, are you angry?"

"Of course."

Looking uncomfortable, Tanaka pushed the ledger to the side. "Don't think poorly of me. I'm merely concerned about the clan's finances. Ha, ha, ha, ha. Well, it's not coming out of my pocket, so the expenses may justly be called auspicious, even fortuitous," said the assistant, then stood and left.

3

THE YOUNG GOVERNOR-GENERAL

THE CHILLY MORNING draft between the hanging scrolls in Edo Castle celebrating the deeds of emperors invigorated the feudal lords in attendance.

Deep inside the castle, the clock would soon tick nine in the morning and summon the five elders on the Council of Elders to their seats.

Tsuchiya Sagami no Kami, on duty this month, said, "Takumi no Kami, thank you for coming."

"I am honored to be here," he replied with a bow of his head.

"Now, to today's business."

Sagami no Kami's stern voice sounded like he was about to read a letter out loud.

"As a courtesy to express your gratitude at the start of this year, you are being asked to host envoys, including imperial ones. As you may know, the reception ceremony for imperial envoys is the preeminent ceremony of the shogunate. Work faithfully and with diligence on all matters."

"Yessir ..."

"However, the customary ceremonies for entertaining imperial envoys should not be too opulent because they set the example for the future."

"Yes …?"

The broad shoulders of Takumi no Kami's ceremonial *kamishimo* kimono slumped as he pondered this situation. He raised his head to reply to the row of elders.

"This mandate to carry out this important mission with your patronage is a blessing for my clan. I am honored and thank you. I would like to accept, however, given my scant knowledge, I am unable to discern the ranks of court nobles. Due to my inexperience, I humbly ask that you request another to carry out this mission."

"Wait one moment!"

Sagami no Kami pounced.

"Your concerns are of no consequence. You need not hold a distinctive ceremony for each court noble. Every year, Master of Ceremonies Kira Kozuke no Suke instructs the hosts, and the endeavor goes smoothly. You shall receive instruction on all matters from Kozuke no Suke."

To refuse again could be viewed as regret over the unexpected expense. Takumi no Kami accepted the appointment. "I look forward to his guidance," he said and left.

That same morning, Date Sakyo no Suke, the lord of Yoshida Castle in Iyo Province, received the same mandate to become a host. He accepted his charge in the antechamber.

On his way home, this most important post of his life overwhelmed Takumi no Kami. Feudal lords endeavored to complete this task each year; he had no reason to think he alone would fail. He would receive the proper training, strive for diligence, and act in good faith.

He would devise a plan with his Edo chief retainers,

Fujii Matazaemon and Yasui Hikoemon. Once again, Lord Asano Naganao of the previous generation would play a pivotal role. Those elders may know about relevant documents and have the good sense awarded by age. However, this was not his sole concern.

The moment he returned to the Teppouzu residence, he summoned his chief retainers, Fujii and Yasui.

"I have no confidence, but I believe you will be my power. This is short notice, but by order of the Council of Elders, I will visit Lord Kira, the Chief Master of Ceremonies from the distinguished *koke* family to receive instruction on all matters."

"Yessir."

This undertaking already echoed throughout the mansion. The faces of the men crammed into the business office combined visions of their future hectic lives as the hands and feet of a lord given this great responsibility and their readiness to meet this challenge.

Yasui and Fujii shut themselves inside the chief retainers' room to address the visit to the Kira residence. Sitting formally with their knees touching for a long time, they discussed every possibility. They finished and were about to leave when the grand chamberlain, Kataoka Gengoemon, happened to rush by. One asked, "Gengo-dono, where is the lord?"

Gengoemon was on urgent business. "He's almost done dressing and is speaking with his wife. Do you wish to see him?"

"Well, if his wife is there ..." one said as they raced with him through the door connecting the inner to the outer rooms.

"Forgive us, but we have another request ..."

"What is it?"

As his wife attended to Takumi no Kami, a page slid

open the partition to reveal Yasui's head of gray hair on the floor beside Fujii's head of salt-and-pepper hair.

"A short time ago, you were told to call on Lord Kira at his residence."

"Yes."

"Lord Kozuke no Suke is a major general of rank four, a member of a koke family, and an obvious lord. We advise you to call on him with a gift, but it may be viewed as a bribe and disrespectful. What shall we do for this courtesy call?"

Takumi no Kami lived life oblivious to the ways of the world.

"Yes, what should we do?"

"What do you two think?"

"Providing guidance on ceremonial matters is the rightful role of the koke clan. This is public, not private, business. The situation would be different if the visit were after the successful conclusion of this important mandate. Please understand, a symbolic gift is not a good idea at this time."

The shadow of uncertainty in his wife's eyes troubled Takumi no Kami. However, a chief retainer gave this opinion. Takumi no Kami stared at the garden greenery while listening on and off. He did not talk about the public matter but on chastity and womanly virtues.

Takumi no Kami glanced at his wife's profile. As a lord who followed the samurai code with unassailable integrity until that day, he was a man with no blemishes on his public and private behaviors. He nodded and said, "You possess true understanding. The crucial point is to avoid any breach in etiquette. That will be our plan."

4

—————

COMINGS AND GOINGS AT THE
KIRA ESTATE

TWO HOODED CRANES spread their dirty wings near the water. Large bronze lanterns and huge Izu stones surrounded the spring.

The antique dealer, a regular visitor, spread out a scroll by Chikafumi and a letter by Hon'ami. Kira Kozuke no Suke put on eyeglasses and, like a peeping bug, leaned over to inspect the works. His head shot up at the sounds of flapping wings. His white eyebrows creased from exasperation.

"Hey! Hey, Magobei!"

"Yes."

The reply from the stewards' room was accompanied by footsteps to the edge of the veranda.

"Those foul little cranes are soiling the water again. They're sullying the lanterns and the tea room windows. Insipid creatures. I can't bear the expense of feeding those pests. Call a bird merchant in town to haul them away at any cost."

"I understand, but what if Makino-sama finds out you

sold his gift? That would create ill will. And we must defer to the bothersome *Edicts on Compassion for Living Things*."

"This world has many fools. What sort of man cultivates a friendship by giving the gift of pesky creatures that must be fed, cared for, and most of all, are destined to die? How much was to curry favor in light of the shogun's law to protect domesticated animals?"

"Nevertheless, they entertain Sahyoue-sama. He's grown fond of them."

"Well, put them behind my son's room. At least, the noise will be gone."

He noticed the figure of Chief Retainer Sato Kunai behind Magobei enter the antechamber and fall prostrate.

"Lord."

"What is it?"

"The envoy of Lord Date Sakyo no Suke, who was named a host, has come to pay his respects."

"Is he here?"

Kozuke no Suke seemed to expect the envoy and took off his glasses.

"Magobei, roll up the scrolls."

"Yessir."

"Kunai, where is the envoy?"

"In the study."

"All right, I'll see him there."

Although elderly, his hip was not curved. In his younger days, Kozuke no Suke must have been a fine-looking man. Even now, he stood so tall his topknot brushed the frame of the door. He was bony and thin but maintained robust health in his old age. Despite his years, he gained the reputation of often engaging an assortment of young women through the mediation of merchants who frequently visited the residence.

He descended from the Ashikaga clan. When the

family line of Shogun Muromachi died out, the Kira clan emerged as the successor. Kozuke no Suke took pride in this history. One ancestor during the restoration was Kira Yoshiyasu, a great uncle of Lord Tokugawa Ieyasu, who possessed a distinguished lineage. Now, Kozuke no Suke was the head of an illustrious family, a major general of rank four, and granted a stipend of 4,200 *koku*. His court rank was high; his pedigree, renowned; and his authority, sanctioned by the government. Three hundred feudal lords sulked over his superiority to them.

Hand claps often rang from the drawing room.

The lord said, "Prepare food and drink."

As the envoy rose, the lord said, "Now, we will celebrate."

They rushed to provide a warm reception that offered sake instead of tea.

The tipsy envoy excused himself and was seen off by Kozuke no Suke at the entryway.

"I am grateful for your considerations. As the master of ceremonies, I will teach the ceremonies, the etiquette, and the ancient rites, as well as mete out the scoldings. Feel free to inquire about any matter. I have not yet met Sakyo no Suke-dono. Please give him my best."

On his way out, the envoy crossed paths with his counterpart from the Asano clan at the gate of the Kira residence near Gofukubashi.

Kozuke no Suke hid in the sitting room to open the friendship gift left by the envoy of Date Sakyo no Suke.

Fifty Kaga silkworms
One hundred gold nuggets
One scroll of a landscape in black ink

He checked the articles with the inventory list in his

hand. "Oh, this is as it should be ..." His narrow eyes resembling needles in his wrinkles sparkled with joy.

He told the gatekeeper to bring in the envoy from the Asano clan.

"Be courteous. The Asano clan is wealthier than Lord Sakyo no Suke. Without being coarse, change the cushions and bring out the finer tea utensils." He turned to the steward Souda. "Prepare food and drink. I am going to change my clothes. Send out Kunai to entertain him until my return."

This welcoming of guests was not a mere task of the Kira clan but the income and job of the koke clan of masters of ceremonies. The chief retainer and the steward were well aware of this reality.

More than any previous visit, Kozuke no Suke was thrilled by this visit from the lord of the affluent clan living in the Banshu-Ako castle.

He thought, If Date of Iyo Yoshida brought such exceptional gifts, the Asano who surpassed this level will send an envoy with ...

What level of lavishness would he see? Kozuke no Suke went to greet his guest with unimaginable expectations. However, the reception was short. An awkward envoy in the person of a frosty steward spoke the greeting and dashed away from the Kira estate.

After he was gone, "What was that?! The Asano clan is probably worth 53,000 koku. What is the gift of a *makiginu* plant? This is an insult to the vestibule of the Kira, the head koke family."

Kozuke no Suke spewed blatant abuse. His heavy displeasure cursed the flavors of the evening meal.

"This sake is unsavory," he sulked.

Disappointment shattered his face. The vassals by his side turned away and grumbled for some time.

"Despite an education at the private institution of Rinke, the only son of a daimyo sends one plant as the initiation fee."

"Is that how he views the important role of the shogun's envoy charged with performing the foremost imperial ceremony of the shogunate?"

"The lord of a prominent clan intends to ask us for guidance on the etiquette of a variety of traditional ceremonies, so what did he mean by today's greeting? His contempt is extraordinary."

"Look at Asano Takumi no Kami and you will see an ignorant cheapskate."

"What makes that country bumpkin fit to host court nobility?"

5

THE PRICE OF HUMANITY

WHEN OUT AND about these days to buy or sell, these comments are overheard.

"That's too much. It's ten times more expensive than before."

"In the old days, I'd go to the bathhouse and drink up. Now, I can't buy three pieces of taffy for the kids."

"People use the words *long ago* to reminisce about money. Here, *in the old days* means a change over a short four or five years. A drop in the value of money upsets ordinary people. Of course, prices rise. This year experienced another jump in prices."

Neither a natural catastrophe nor a war caused the wild jump. The people of Edo knew but did not speak of the two people to blame for this economic collapse. No one had to be told, they knew. Careless words meant the immediate loss of one's head. However, the well-informed who reflected on the matter did not automatically think of *The Two*. In short, they believed the rot had taken root in the governing authorities to which those two belonged and the system that enabled this situation.

Specifically, the current fifth-generation shogun Toku-gawa Tsunayoshi and his mother Keishoin were extraordinary spendthrifts. They did not understand the workings of money and held positions that guaranteed ignorance about the value of goods, national resources, and human labor.

A *Yanagisawa outing* was Tsunayoshi visiting the mansion in town of the judicious Grand Chamberlain Yanagisawa Yoshiyasu. This happened over fifty times. The total manpower, goods, and gold spent on amusement at Yanagisawa's residence in one outing could not be approximated in the heads of the common people.

Also, the expense of his mother Keishoin's superstitions was enormous. Her lacquered palanquin weaved its way through Edo to visit the Gokokuji Temple amid a procession of parasols. The men and horses of the guard and the temple's main gate for welcoming visitors were all adorned by human power and money. Her donations built the main gate she passed through, the Buddhist temple, and the pagoda. Several commissioners and master builders were banished to remote islands for minor errors during construction.

Her eyes saw the powerful mad monk Ryuko of Goji Temple as a living Buddha. When high-ranking officials and petty officials of the shogunate in Ryuko's orbit whispered about politics, they created the destiny of the cruel and miserable life of this generation. The politics of the shogun's harem emerged. The words of one woman were more easily rewarded with a nod from Shogun Tsunayoshi than those of any cabinet minister or assistant to the Council of Elders. A leader among them called Yanagi-sawa Yoshiyasu expanded his power. But the shogunate spent most of its gold nuggets. This stifled the progress of the clique, starting with Yoshiyasu.

The currency was recast. The old currency was withdrawn and a new currency was issued. This ploy allowed the shogunate to increase the number of coins with no denomination. Old gold and silver were salvaged from the citizenry. Low-quality money was put in circulation. An enormous difference remained in hand. Inside this misgovernment, Commissioner of the Treasury Hagiwara Shigehide was notorious. Money not spent on the Yanagisawa clique, the expenses of the shogun's harem, or for the shogun's personal affairs accumulated in the gold storehouses.

Every year, prices jumped unrelated to the previous year. This exacerbated life's hardships. The honest man's destiny was to be left behind. For nearly thirty years, starting in 1615 of the Genna era and into the Kan'ei era, in reaction to the naive ways of the warrior and the lifestyles of tradesmen and merchants, the ironclad rule of this world became the almighty power of gold. A composer wrote about this reality in a dramatic *joruri* ballad as *in the world, bribery is through gold and women.*

Men unable to follow this ironclad rule often lamented, "I can't afford to eat pricey rice." The ones who moaned and complained were the respectable men in society. The starving ones without a voice were covered in flies under bridges, behind Sensoji Temple, or in garbage dumps. The vulgar men unable to tolerate this ruled the darkness and the back alleys of the towns. They were not wicked when they committed lawless acts like burglary, extortion, robbery, and theft. They had to eat.

Vagrants, scoundrels, and down-and-out samurai focused on satisfying their wants. They were keeping up with the times. The human stimulants and temptations eroded by living for the moment and nihilism were strung together as gaudy lights. Sons and daughters from fine homes imitated whores who looked like male prostitutes in the gay teahouses. The slender figures in the shogun's harem or Yanagisawa's clique paled in color. This erosion affected the notions of human feelings, duty, and all aspects of morality. Modern people in those days began to believe their thoughts were nothing more than old-fashioned illusions of the previous generation. Society tended to reject reality and was unable to live with those feelings.

What upended fundamental human thought in this way? Even if all the structural evils like the excessive issuance of bad currency, the decay of the government, the hardships caused by the high prices of goods, the disillusionment with religion, the boisterous behavior between men and women, and the suicidal poisons of culture and art were assembled, the cause remains hard to explain.

However, society's rules, surely the primary cause, stretched across the Genroku generation.

After Ryuko or Keishoin advised Shogun Tsunayoshi, born in the Year of the Dog, he made the official announcement to the world of the strict conduct demanded by the uncommon edicts of the domesticated animal protection order, the *Edicts on Compassion for Living Things*.

Historians mark this as the genesis of *The Age of the Esteemed Dog*.

A dog kennel in Nakano and a dog mansion in Okubo were constructed on expansive grounds crowded with people unable to feed themselves. With no regard to cost, the dogs dined on polished rice and fish envied by people. Like the men who attended to the daimyo, dog magistrates, dog inspectors, dog go-betweens, and dog physicians served the dogs.

People received stipends to eat. However, ordinary people were perplexed by the handling of the esteemed dogs who barked in their faces all over town. Throwing a rock would get your head cut off. Making a dog yelp would have you dragged to the guardhouse. If you glimpsed a dog riding through in a palanquin, you had to step off the road. One time, a direct retainer merely kicked away a stray dog that had bitten him. He was ordered to commit *seppuku*, ritual suicide, and his clan was abolished. His family experienced the misery of being scattered. No one carelessly placed dog toys into children's hands but placed them on the household Shinto altar to be worshipped day and night. This exemplified the pinnacle of faith and was praised as the height of human goodness. In short, the shogun's clan was born in the Year of the Dog. This promised unfortunate lives for every living soul. In addition to currency devaluation, the price of humanity plummeted.

"The price of a human is below that of an exalted dog. Well, it's lower than that of beasts. What's going on? It's a mystery."

This was the self-mockery of the sad citizens of Edo. The underside of their mental state bloomed, that is, erupted into the sign of the times. The generation of young people in flamboyant colors, musical pieces, obscene pictures, and pornography became the lights that burned at night. The day was the day. Eyes at the crossroads followed gold.

"Gold is the world. Gold comes first. Gold comes second."

Unenlightened people from the countryside and men on duty in Edo who witnessed the changes every three years were astonished.

"Ah, Edo's prosperity is amazing. Since the Genroku era began, it evolves with each passing day and month."

6

NAIVETE AND A WICKED TONGUE

Our salutations to Lord Kira the day before yesterday went smoothly.

THIS MESSAGE CAME this morning from the two Edo chief retainers who acted as emissaries to the Kira residence. For now, Takumi no Kami met his obligations.

"All right. Today, I intend to visit him unannounced to ask for his friendship."

Accompanied by attendants, he traveled by palanquin to the Kira residence in Gofukubashi. Takumi no Kami embodied a courteous disciple to a master when he asked for guidance. His demeanor annoyed Kozuke no Suke.

Was he speaking the truth? The conversation ended with the goods brought by his vassals. Why was he blind to the importance of that act?

He viewed the honest man from the countryside as irredeemable. To him, Takumi no Kami was either too dumb to understand or only spoke politely to play a cunning trick and avoid giving the expected premium goods. He couldn't tell which it was. But Takumi no Kami's behavior convinced him he was right.

Kozuke no Suke's words held no warmth. "Are you Lord Takumi no Kami? Of course, you are young. This is an auspicious event for you. Success will bring prestige to you, the lord of a feudal domain and a castle. Well, hard work is demanded."

A faint smile covered the spiteful wrinkles around his eyes.

This first encounter troubled Takumi no Kami. This elderly man was unfriendly. However, Takumi no Kami concentrated on not showing his willfulness, the result of being raised to be a daimyo who rarely visited a stranger's home to lower his head.

"Although I've been given an imperial mandate beyond my ability, please think of me as your inexperienced junior and guide me."

"Well, I'm a humble man. Perhaps it's my age, but I've forgotten everything about bothersome ancient practices. If, however, you've brought a friendship present to receive instruction … ha, ha, ha."

Kozuke no Suke discovered his weak spot in one guess but got no reaction from Takumi no Kami. He was all seriousness and enthusiasm.

"The Council of Elders recommended I seek the counsel of Lord Kira. Young people can be pesky, but I'm sincerely asking for your guidance."

"…"

Kozuke no Suke twisted his body and rudely reached his wrinkled hand, crawling with thick blood vessels, to a bookcase. With deliberate indifference, he looked past his companion's enthusiasm.

Again, Takumi no Kami said, "Do you have any instructions for me? Please feel free to tutor me on any matter given my dearth of knowledge, even on ordinary matters of the shogunate."

"In service to the shogunate, I will not hesitate. For now, read this."

Kozuke no Suke pulled *Choku Shigeko*, the diary of an imperial envoy on a mission from the capital, off the shelf and handed it to Takumi no Kami. He studied the itinerary and returned the book.

> 11th - The imperial envoy and the temple envoy
> arrive in Edo and lodge at the Tatsunokuchi resi-
> dence for imperial envoys
> 12th - Both envoys visit the castle to present impe-
> rial gifts
> 13th - Attendance at a *sarugaku* Noh farce in the
> company of various lords
> 14th - Shogun's response to the imperial greeting
> presented in the plain wood study
> 15th - Pilgrimage to Ueno Kan'eiji Temple and
> Shiba Zojoji Temple
> 16th - Day of rest
> 17th - Envoys return to Kyoto

However, the master of ceremonies did not give him the seven-day schedule. A notice sent by the cabinet ministers had come on the day of the official appointments. He was familiar with all the information in the notice but read it as if it were new to gain Kozuke no Suke's goodwill.

He finished reading and asked, "Is there more?"

Kozuke no Suke puffed up and said, "Indeed, there is ..." and stared at Takumi no Kami.

"The envoys shall not neglect the presentation of gifts each day of their stay. These are friendship gifts. More than words, they are essential to demonstrate sincerity. Do you understand?"

Takumi no Kami did not understand.

Kozuke no Suke explained the ceremony and left. Takumi no Kami's mind obsessed over the instructions to the envoys to give gifts daily but ended up confused. As a precaution, he visited Tsuchiya Sagami no Kami, who was on monthly duty with the shogun's Council of Elders, to get answers to his questions.

He was told, "There is no precedent. Perhaps you misheard him."

Convinced his naive interpretation was the problem, Takumi no Kami nodded. "That must be it."

Sometime later, somewhere, Master of Ceremonies Kozuke no Suke caught wind of this meeting. The blue veins under the thin skin at his temples bulged.

"My goodness. That man has no sense. The incredibly stupid imbecile sought an answer from the Council of Elders for a question he asked me. Was that a deliberate attempt to anger and trap me for my brusque manner? Damn country bumpkin!"

His emotional complaint was colored by the distinctive trill of an Edo man. His favorite insults were "backwater samurai" and "on-duty country boy." He took pride in being a sophisticated city dweller.

7

———

THE INK PAINTING

PALANQUIN BEARERS WHO swept away fine gravel and visiting merchants who regularly pass through the gate of the boarding house were all wearing new work-men's *happi* coats.

Vassals assigned to the hosting duties to entertain with food and drink received the shogunate mandate of their lifetimes. They included men who cut out clean bleached cloth to wear as underwear, were determined to pray for divine protection, and carried a hidden amulet for protection.

On the morning of the eleventh, a mounted warrior dressed in a ceremonial robe was announced at the spotless gate of the Tatsunokuchi residence.

"The Gosankyo represented by the imperial envoy, Major Councilor Yanagiwara-sama; the temple envoy, Middle Councilor Kono; and the former Major Councilor Seikanji have arrived safely in Shinagawa. They will stay at the Takanawa Imperial Residence and arrive here soon."

On the morning of the eleventh, a cavalry officer dressed in an informal *noshi kamishimo* court robe made this

29

official proclamation at the gate of the immaculate Denso residence where samurai stay on visits to Edo.

The eyes of the tense Asano vassals crowded at the gate at dawn's first light. A kitchen staff member stumbled in a rush to inform the chief retainer.

"An urgent messenger from Kira-sama just came."

"From the master of ceremonies. What is it?"

"I have no idea, but he said he heard today is a day of fasting for the imperial envoy and to not serve fish or poultry."

That instruction dismayed Fujii and Yasui, the two Edo chief retainers who lacked confidence. Both looked flustered when they went to inform Takumi no Kami.

"There's no time. What should we do?"

Takumi no Kami's eyes opened in shock. Three days ago, he carefully selected today's meals and had them diligently prepared. How could they be changed on a whim?

He had neither a plan nor any ideas.

This was the first morning of a critical mission. They worked hard for several days and through sleepless nights. The immaculate lord and his vassals sitting in rows waiting for the morning's important guests lost color like they'd been plunged into the depths of hardship.

Horibe Yasubei said, "I don't know what the master of ceremonies is thinking, but I'm suspicious. This is a day of fasting, but the official formal entrance into the domain of the envoys of the Imperial Court is today. Nothing should interfere with his abstinence. Why not prepare two dishes, as a precaution?"

"Yes," interrupted the heavy silence, Takumi no Kami understood and gave a deep nod. "Yes, we'll do that."

The huge kitchen was filled with samurai in kamishimo ceremonial dress and servants wearing stiffly starched happi coats. Kitchen knives flashed like swords on a battlefield. From the back gate of the boarding house, horses galloped off and returned countless times.

The congestion eased when the procession of envoys arrived at the gate of the Tatsunokuchi residence.

After the reception, Kanzaki Yogoro was blood-red with anger.

"He lied. That raccoon dog of a master of ceremonies! That clan holds a grudge. I asked the envoy's escort about the day of fasting. It turned out to be a spiteful lie."

This news was passed on to the kitchen and the various offices. Pursued by matters at hand, both chief retainers griped while submerged in the crowded residence overflowing with the envoys' vassal attendants. The thoughtful vassals stared at Lord Takumi no Kami's face and prayed an unpleasant expression would not erupt.

However, Takumi no Kami with his usually bright eyes greeted the travel-weary envoys in fine form.

"…"

Kanzaki Yogoro and Horibe Yasubei watched from a distance.

"Ah, that is our lord."

They were happy and, guessing the lord's feelings, were overwhelmed with emotion. Kanzaki's eyelids were red, and Yasubei's eyes were hot and teary. Okuda Magodayu, the superintendent of the storehouses, and others did not sleep last night but joined them to bring furniture and utensils from the storehouse in Teppouzu.

The noon meal ended. As one empty tray after another was brought down the hall, Tsuchiya Sagami no Kami of the shogun's Council of Elders, who had come to Shinagawa to welcome the guests, arrived first. After him, a horde of lower-ranking lords exited their vehicles to pay respects. Their many horses kicked up dust clouds at the gate of the Tatsunokuchi residence.

Hatakeyama Minbu, another master of ceremonies, also made an appearance. Before leaving for home, he expressed his appreciation.

"The preparations were splendid. Seven days of hard work is not a trivial matter. Take care of Takumi no Kami."

The elderly Okuda Magodayu saw him out and said, "I am honored. The presence of our lord in the best of health encouraged our hard work. Lord Kira graciously gave him this ceremony to perform. For that, we thank him."

In a fit of sentimentality, he repeated his thanks many times, then returned to the office and joined the retainers discussing the various ceremonies of the evening. A young samurai behind him placed both hands on the ground and said, "Okuda-sama, please come with me."

He turned to see the handsome personal aide Isogai Jurozaemon, who looked splendid in his vibrant kamishimo robe.

"Isogai? What is it?"

"Lord Kira is here. He's come to conduct an inspection."

"What? Lord Kira …"

When he stood, nerves made a few men abandon their conversations and leave.

"We must greet him."

As he neared the grand entrance, Magodayu heard a hoarse, weathered voice. He looked old and a little bent at the waist of his *hakama* trousers. His unsteady feet in white *tabi* socks nervously carried his old bones to the grand entrance.

He saw Kozuke no Suke, also an older man but much taller. His wide mouth carved into hollow cheeks did not move. As Kozuke no Suke tapped his folding fan against the painted edge of the partition screen in front of the steps at the entrance, his haughty eyes glared with contempt at the Asano clan members lying prostrate.

"What is this? This!"

"Yessir."

"Did pride add this painting of the rival dragon and tiger by Gen Motonobu of the Kano school to the decor?"

"Yessir."

"Why do you always answer 'Yessir'? Do you think you're under arrest? Who ordered the display of this partition? "

Magodayu planted both hands on the wood floor and said, "I beg your pardon. Is the problem with the partition having an unsuitable design or its position?"

"Who are you?"

"I am the unrefined man called Okuda Magodayu, Superintendent of the Storehouses."

"I've heard there have been too many mistakes. Please summon your lord. What has Lord Takumi no Kami been doing?"

"He's being informed now."

"Ah ..." he said and stretched. His cold eyes glared upward.

"The dust on the ceiling has not been swept away. Do you think this vulgar entrance is suitable for welcoming imperial envoys? It is repulsive."

Takumi no Kami hurried to the feet of the grumbling man.

"If anything is amiss, please reprimand me for the carelessness that led to my vassals' errors."

"Oh, ... Lord Takumi no Kami?"

"Yes, and thank you for taking the time to conduct this inspection."

"You are the host of imperial envoys and do not need

to flatter me. Incidentally, what do you know about this partition? What is the reason for placing an ink painting in the grand entrance to a formal celebration for imperial envoys who traveled a great distance? Why didn't you set up a cheerful painting?"

"It's as you say, but I also asked the opinion of Lord Tsuchiya of the Council of Elders."

"When did Lord Tsuchiya become the master of ceremonies? Do you intend to serve as a host under the direction of Lord Tsuchiya?"

"Oh no, I never thought that."

"The Council of Elders. Well, doesn't the Council of Elders wobble when it walks? No one would know, but there is not one example of an ink painting being used on the day for welcoming important guests to an auspicious event."

"I'm so sorry. I will replace it with a colorful painting … but Lord Tsuchiya said to be austere."

"Again Lord Tsuchiya? Is the master of ceremonies a mere figurehead to him?"

"The suggestion was malicious and confused me. Without taking pity on me, please explain the level of incompetence and ineptness I've displayed."

Seeing only the pale face of their lord prostrate on the wood floor, his vassals felt danger, like sitting on ice; chests tightened from shedding hot tears.

The long silence was broken by echoes of Kozuke no Suke's raspy laughter filling the air above their heads like his false teeth were tumbling down.

"You idiot! If a figurehead teaches a living man, everything is turned upside down. Doing what you like is fine. Do whatever you wish."

His *daimon*-crested kimono sleeve decorated with a large black pattern swept over Takumi no Kami's top knot.

He listened to the fast footsteps recede as the thick cypress floorboards creaked under his knees.

"Lord ... Lord!"

The fists of Okuda Magodayu made the floor creak. The trembling man buried his face in his lord's back, gripped the pillbox hanging from the lord's belt, and didn't let go. The lord's blood boiling like his entire body would leap up to shout, "Bastard!" seemed to join with the blood of his vassals who bit down on the roots of their teeth and shut their eyes tight to concentrate on the word *patience*. They trembled and their bones rattled as they swallowed hot tears.

8

DECEPTION

A HAZY MOON shined that night. Takumi no Kami's wife sat alone. She watched the black shadows of cherry blossoms reflecting cloud-like spots on a shoji screen and heard the distant sounds of oars shrouded by a damp evening haze.

Her mind mulled over questions. Did the people envy a daimyo's life? What are his wife's hardships? The boatmen working on the Ogawa River had no idea.

She had not eaten her evening meal. Her husband's younger brother Asano Daigaku visited from Kobikicho that day. He told her that this second day of attendance of the imperial envoys at the castle likely ended without incident.

"Ah."

She didn't notice her palms line up with the setting sun in this room and bowed in prayer.

Her husband was still not home.

If he were home, around this time, she would reach for chopsticks to begin her meal. She had not slept the previous night.

If questioned, she would say defensively, "No, I'm not a fretting woman." She was oblivious to her pale, frowning face.

She struggled with the events swirling around her and tried to comfort her spirit through her feelings as a woman and her attention to detail. But the frown etched her face all day and night.

"Please guide my husband through these seven days of the imperial mandate."

The exceptional woman offered candlelight to the gods, incense to Buddha, and prayed with her whole heart in a room of anguish.

"The lord has returned!"

The lady-in-waiting was sensitive to her lady's feelings. Any noise heard out front sent her quiet steps rushing to report delightful news in a shrill voice.

"Very well."

In an instant, her heart sank like melting snow. She was joyous and wanted to weep over her husband's safe return home.

However, she was serene. Without making a sound, she pulled the hem of her long *uchikake* overgarment and sat before the mirror. One displaced strand of hair would darken her husband's mood. Her rouge had to be bright.

"..."

Her slender figure glided down the long corridor. A woman knows a woman's heart. The maids following her noticed the wife's angular shoulders getting thinner over the past several days and their likeness to a halberd. The poor lady, they sympathized and wept.

Takumi no Kami called for a meeting as he walked with sorrowful but determined, heavy steps.

He only looked back with quiet eyes at the raised eyes of his wife and went straight into the large front study.

Under brilliant lights, the vassals gathered to plan and discuss the next day's agenda. All the vassals' faces looked strained. None of them seemed to notice Takumi no Kami's pale face late that night or knew whether he had eaten.

Covertly, his wife sent a messenger with two questions.

"Will you bathe? Will you eat?"

Takumi no Kami gave one reply.

"No."

He shook his head and said, "On the fifteenth, two envoys will visit Zojoji Temple. Are the preparations satisfactory? Tomorrow, the thirteenth, the Master of Ceremonies may conduct an inspection. There can't be any mistakes."

Yasui Hikoemon said, "There's no need to worry. By this evening, we will clean the walls, shoji screens, papered sliding partitions, and ceilings."

Someone asked, "The tatami mats?"

Hikoemon stared in the voice's direction. "As a precaution, we visited Lord Kira to ask whether we should replace the tatami mats. We left them alone because he told us they are replaced every year in January and a change is unnecessary."

"All right."

Takumi no Kami looked relieved and left his seat. More than his being at ease, the vassals relaxed at the sight of their lord disappearing inside.

Kanzaki Yogoro and Horibe Yasubei leaped from their seats. On the side of the dark stable, someone was emptying water with a splash. They looked.

"Tominomori?"

"Is that you, Sukeemon?"

Sukeemon heard the voices. "I'm over here."

He had tied back his damp kimono sleeves with a *tasuki* sash and was carrying a brush to scrub a horse.

"I have a favor to ask."

"What is it?"

"Take that horse and have a look at the station of the lord's colleague, Date Sakyo no Suke."

"Look for what?"

"The tatami mats"

"Okay."

Tominomori Sukeemon and his damp sleeves galloped off.

He cracked the whip as he passed through the hazy moonlit night to the lodge for pilgrims from the Date clan at Zojoji Temple. He looked in and was hit by the scent of new tatami mats. Had they replaced every mat, including the ones in the servants' quarters?

"This is what they suspected," said Sukeemon and returned to his horse without taking a breath. After his report, Kanzaki and Horibe looked at each other.

"We knew it."

They reported to both chief retainers, who called a meeting. Soon after going to bed, Takumi no Kami was awakened with a start.

"Did Kozuke no Suke deceive our clan? The inspection is tomorrow. We must prepare tonight."

Yasui and Fujii were bewildered. The elderly Okuda's voice became raspy from barking commands. His old bones, recovered from illness, crept out of the row house as Muramatsu Kihei flew by on horseback.

Horibe Yasubei yelled, "It's gold. Accountants, this time, it's the power of gold."

He stuffed his pockets with cash and sped away on horseback to mobilize tatami-mat makers.

In no time, the area from the main temple of Zojoji

Temple to the pilgrim lodge where the Asano clan stayed was buried under paper lanterns bearing the hawk feather crest of the Asano clan. Dozens of tatami dealers made tatami needles dance like their elbows would spark fires. The men carrying out the mats, the men laying down the mats, the soldiers, and the craftsmen were equals. It was a battlefield and desperate work. As the tear-provoking night grew light, more than two hundred new tatami mats were precisely laid down. The overjoyed young samurai danced with abandon.

Around ten in the morning, Kozuke no Suke arrived to conduct the inspection. The sea of new tatami mats dazzled his eyes.

"This is fine."

His praise was empty.

"I heard quite a bit in confidence about Lord Takumi no Kami. Replacing this number of tatami mats in one night is an impressive feat. If gold and silver are not detested, matters proceed favorably."

He turned without flinching to face Takumi no Kami standing behind him, stared, and said, "We've both worked hard. I am exhausted."

While tapping his hipbone, he walked from one inspection to the next.

9

A FACE OF WATER

TAKUMI NO KAMI wanted to be gentle with his wife. He didn't want his vassals to see his face. He guessed the overwhelmed feelings of those around him.

I believe the body is born humbly. I was raised to be a daimyo and trained to be a warrior. I'm enraged, and my blood boils. But my debt of service means I must turn a blind eye for these seven days.

He lay in bed for a short time but could not sleep. The harder he tried to sleep, the more vividly Kira's face appeared in his mind and Kozuke no Suke's croaking voice pounded in his ears.

What were the teachings of Confucian philosopher Yamaga Soko-sensei, who deemed samurai *superior men*? What did Takumi no Kami's father Naganao always say? He received lessons from a benevolent mother and, from the time he was a young boy, read all the sacred scriptures. He struggled to recall them. Despite trying, he could not identify all the obstacles.

In today's society, two divergent considerations and lifestyles, one old and one new, share one world and form one society. In the same way, the lords and clan customs in the Asano clan and the Kira clan were in opposition.

I am determined and will endure. I will persevere, Takumi no Kami prayed.

An old saying warns: *If you cannot tolerate an ordeal one time, you will suffer it over a hundred times.*

He carved those words into his spirit and fell asleep. The dawn of March 14 came. This was the important ceremonial day in the response to the imperial mandate from the shogun. Both the imperial and the temple envoys would be in attendance at the castle.

His wife couldn't wait for the morning to brighten and left the bedchamber. Without the help of a lady-in-waiting, she gathered his gargle and the lacquered washbasin.

"This isn't what samurai do ..."

Takumi no Kami stared at his reflection then plunged his fingertips into the water.

This is too much, he thought and sobbed despite himself.

His palms scoured his face. As always, prayer cheered him up.

His heart persuaded him to have tea.

"Dear, is my tea ready?"

"Yes."

His wife was happy. The genuine feelings of women and his wife's soul were linked.

"If you like, I'll make another."

"No, I'm fine."

Takumi no Kami set down the teacup. Although sincerity tinted his eyes, the aroma of tea had no appeal.

A quiet voice came from beyond the shoji screen. "Please forgive us. We're terribly sorry for this unannounced visit."

"Who is it?"

"Gengoemon and Yogoro."

"Oh, Kataoka and Kanzaki? Hard at work, as always. Please, come in."

"Yessir."

Still squatting, the two slid open the screen. These men had been inseparable since boyhood. The sight of tears building in their eyes made Takumi no Kami's eyelids burn.

"What is it? An emergency?"

"No, nothing like that. With all due respect, we noticed you've looked pale, like you've been ill, for the past few days. You are surely frustrated by our bungling in carrying out these important duties day after day on your behalf. We supposed numerous unpleasant situations have arisen in the relationship with the master of ceremonies and his people. Today is the fourteenth, and we will persevere for three more days. For the sake of service, we ask for a little compassion, patience, and tolerance."

"I understand."

Takumi no Kami's eyelashes sustained a dangerous light, like dew on a flower or grass.

"Thank you for saying that, but don't worry. Yesterday, my close friend Kato Totoumi no Kami offered the same honest advice. This is not the only time reports of Kozuke no Suke's rudeness surfaced. Words cannot describe his behavior when Totoumi no Kami conducted a memorial service at Daiyu-in Temple. And on a pilgrimage to a Nikko shrine, the magistrate daimyo doesn't know how much he cried because of Kira. There's no shortage of laymen with these stories if asked. They became enraged at the thought of Kira, a major general of rank four, being judged to be a decent man because to them he is a worm.... Please, don't worry. Takumi no Kami, a descendant of Asano Mataemon Nagakatsu, has many beloved vassals at Ako Castle. I'll exchange the senility of the Master of Ceremonies for that. I understand. Say no more."

"You inspire us and … we won't speak another word."

"It would be bad luck."

Gengoemon and Yogoro looked away and automatically wiped away traces of tears.

An announcement came from outside.

"It is time."

Takumi no Kami bathed and dressed in his ceremonial garb. He felt armed with his swords. His spirit was menacing.

The master of ceremonies sent notice that he decided on the *naga-kamishimo* kimono as the ceremonial dress. That's why he wore one. One doubtful elder vassal said, "Wearing a naga-kamishimo in a public imperial ceremony is forbidden. Lord Kira's motives are always suspect. As a precaution, the trip will take some time, we should prepare an *eboshi* cap to be worn with the daimon-crested kimono."

They concealed his clothes in the scissors box.

As suspected, when he arrived at the palace, every other daimyo wore an eboshi cap. Takumi no Kami went to the business office and changed his ceremonial dress. Cold sweat trickled when he thought, What if we had not prepared the crested kimono?

He glimpsed Kozuke no Suke when he arrived. The sight of his face made the man holding down his marrow move impulsively toward him.

"Sir, Lord Kira."

"Yes. You're late."

"According to your instructions, the dress today was a naga-kamishimo, but everyone is wearing an eboshi cap and a crested kimono. I had to change. Please don't think ill of me."

"Is that so? Paying attention is a good thing. It may be my age, but my hearing has been failing. I'm very forgetful and make mistakes. It's embarrassing."

Did that voice come from a man's throat? Takumi no Kami fixed his eyes filled with disdain on him but felt nothing. Kozuke no Suke tended to close one eye and twist half of his face with his mouth. He worried about the false teeth in his upper jaw. As his tongue squirmed around his mouth, he calmly walked toward the grand entrance.

10

BREAKING UNDER PRESSURE

THE APPOINTED TIME to welcome the imperial envoys neared.

The Gosankyo, the lords of the three prominent Tokugawa branch families, would soon enter the palace. Takumi no Kami searched for Kozuke no Suke and spotted him standing in a crowd dressed in a fancy black *suou* kimono. He crept to his side and said, "Lord Kira.... I have a question."

Kozuke no Suke pretended not to hear him and walked away. On impulse, Takumi no Kami reached out and grabbed his kimono sleeve.

"Wait."

Dizziness hit Takumi no Kami in the temple like a hot iron. His voice was hoarse and, perhaps, his mouth was dry.

"Wait a minute."

"What is this?!"

Kozuke no Suke's eyes fell on his sleeve. Takumi no Kami let go.

"I have a question. Will the Gosankyo lords pray at the

imperial Buddhist altar at the grand entrance? And are they greeted after descending the stone steps? I am unfamiliar with the etiquette for seating them. I am asking for your guidance."

He spoke in one breath with both hands on the ground. He confused emotions and reason. His tongue felt pierced by needles. Searing pain in his earlobes deafened him to the sound of his voice.

Kozuke no Suke seemed to enjoy this, and a faint smile escaped. In his heart, Takumi no Kami's demeanor enraged him from the pit of his stomach. This became the opportunity to hit back. He tapped his palm with a fan.

"I know the duties and will answer a question on any matter if asked without conceit or babbling. Are you not a host? The receipt of this important duty without an understanding of the smallest of matters is astounding. And why are you befuddled and ask about etiquette just before the arrival of the envoys? Please watch and learn from your fellow host Lord Sakyo no Suke. Is the sensible man so different from the dimwitted one?"

He never addressed the questions. As he walked away, Kozuke no Suke made disparaging remarks for all to hear.

"He's absurd. If a military ceremony were being conducted, it would not be this much trouble. He's one appallingly confused samurai."

Not only Takumi no Kami and Lord Kira, everyone in attendance at this public event heard. The lords in formal dress in the area looked toward the source of the voice to watch in amazement.

The boiling blood coursing throughout his body seemed to erupt from his eyes and ears. A needle-like line etched a curse deep into the brow of Takumi no Kami glaring at Kozuke no Suke's back. He seemed to growl.

The usual tangle of jealousy and emotions of only

daimyos among daimyos was present. Slightly sympathetic men, who to their surprise felt good, stared coldly, but their hearts were pounding.

"It'd be best if young Takumi no Kami's fiery blood doesn't rise too high."

Takumi no Kami's natural coloring returned. He straightened his clothes and stood. Relieved, the daimyos, whether out of pity or for no particular reason, were looking elsewhere.

At that moment, Kajikawa Yosobei, a steward connected to the shogun's mother Keishoin, stumbled in.

"Is Lord Asano present? Has anyone seen Lord Asano?"

He asked each man he met except Kozuke no Suke. He brushed past him without asking when he saw Kozuke no Suke's stiff, lacquered-on expression.

"Lord Asano!" Kozuke no Suke called toward the entrance.

"Yes."

Takumi no Kami watched him approach.

Yosobei spoke quickly.

"The court nobles have given many gifts to Keishoin. After today's ceremony, the inner palace will express its gratitude to the envoys. Please, come to the meeting."

"Yes, I'll be there."

"Then I will see you later."

When Yosobei hurried to return, Kozuke no Suke, who had stopped a distance away, seemed to prick up his ears and called to stop him, "Oh, Kajikawa-dono. Kajikawa-dono."

Yosobei turned and said, "Aren't you the master of ceremonies?"

"If it is a ceremony, I'd like to hear about it."

"Yes, of course."

"It will be a problem if I don't understand and mistakes arise. To a country samurai with no understanding of etiquette, I must look after the daimon-crested kimono."

"Yes, I appreciate your efforts."

"What should Takumi no Kami know? Don't invite mistakes."

A shout was directed toward the waiting room where the lords had assembled to leave before the end. The inability to endure humiliation, the greatest moral value to a warrior, pierced Takumi no Kami's head like a branding iron. Over the past few days, it took all of his spiritual strength to bolster himself, but like snow falling with a thud from the highest point of a roof, everything went black before his eyes.

"Damn you! Kozuke!"

Reason finally collapsed into emotion. The sleeve of the crested kimono swept up, and light beamed from a short sword held aloft.

A shout.

The eboshi-covered head turned around; both hands were pressed to his forehead.

"You brute!"

Kozuke no Suke staggered five or six steps to the threshold of the huge Matsu-no-Ma stateroom and fell flat on the floor. He toppled over but stood right up in a daze.

"You lunatic! Takumi! …"

"Wait! You old …"

The second strike fell short and made shallow cuts from Kozuke no Suke's shoulder to his back. The sudden spray of red blood shined bright like a red flower in Takumi no Kami's days-long melancholy.

The third strike from his long sword was futile. Two tree-like arms grabbed him from behind with all their might.

"Who are you? Release me! Let me go!"

"Do you know where you are? Are you insane, Takumi no Kami-dono?"

"Kajikawa? I am a warrior. Let go!"

"I won't! Calm down!"

"Oh no. I failed. It was a mistake. I regret my actions. I'm not insane. I'm a lord with a castle and a fief worth 53,000 koku. I'm not mad."

"You're in the palace!" roared the voice of Toda, the lord of Sakura Castle. It did not penetrate Takumi no Kami's ears. As he struggled, the powerful Yosobei dragged him three or four feet away.

"Stop fighting," said Yosobei while forcing him down as he bent Takumi no Kami's arms and bloody sword. But Takumi no Kami's head still spun like water from a flash of fire.

"I'm dressed in my official clothes and being held down by your knees. That is insolence toward a superior. I'm not one to hold a grudge against a shogun family. The attack on my rival Kira was malicious but not cowardly. There's no need to worry. Please let go."

An avalanche of echoing footsteps converged from all directions to gather around him. A corner of his mind conjured the face of his wife in Teppouzu and the sad expressions of many vassals and family members living in the castle under distant skies back home in Ako.

Kajikawa Yosobei kept a tight grip. "Sir, let go of the sword. The sword ..."

They dripped sweat as the shouts continued.

The time was a little after the Hour of the Snake, around eleven in the morning. Spring was in full bloom and boasting to Heaven and Earth. A warm, gentle breeze blew that day.

PART II

EXPRESS MESSAGES TO AKO

11

BITTER ENEMIES IN A ROOM

A DIAGONAL RIP opened from the shoulder of his black suou kimono to the center of his back. In the areas gushing blood, the pain of some cuts stung him, and others were numb. When he turned, the force of the long sword was only the reaction to the metal band in his eboshi cap but left Kozuke no Suke stunned by the light striking his eyes.

He was sure his skull split in two.

"Uh. Aaah, uh, uh."

He rolled over, covered his face with his hands, and sat up.

"He, he cut me. He's … he's a madman."

Like he was stumbling in the dark, his agitated voice rose from his cheeks.

"I must see him. Takumi no Kami. Takumi no Kami did this."

He staggered down the large corridor toward the Sakura-no-Ma waiting room.

Blood spilled out, leaving splotches resembling chickens' footprints. People rushing around in a mad scramble stepped in the blood and stained the castle's floors red.

"Lord Kira, please calm down."

"Your attacker Lord Takumi no Kami has been subdued by Kajikawa Yosobei."

"Kira-dono! Kozuke-dono!"

His fellow masters of ceremonies, including Shinagawa Buzen no Kami and Otomo Oumi no Kami, ran up from behind to support him.

However, Kozuke no Suke didn't seem to recognize them and pushed them away.

He only screamed, "Get the physician! The physician."

After the people circling calmed Kozuke no Suke, Wakisaka Awaji no Kami, the lord of Tatsuno Castle in Banshu, looked as he passed by along the side.

"Were those Kira-dono's screams? I thought armor smeared with blood was a warrior's honor, but a blood-smeared suou is strange. This is a disaster for the ages."

Surprisingly cheerful voices flowed from the whirlpool of confusion resembling a boiling cauldron. That was evidence of people's opinion of Kozuke no Suke from that day on.

Okado Denpachiro was in the Tamari-no-Ma, a daimyo waiting room, packed with inspectors.

"Monk! Monk!"

He stood to question a passing tea server. "What's all the commotion about?"

"Asano Takumi no Kami-sama's sword wounded Lord Kira, the Chief Master of Ceremonies."

"What?!"

The looks changed in the eyes of the other masters of ceremonies, Kuru Juzaemon, Kondo Heihachiro, Okubo Gonzaemon, as they raced after Denpachiro.

"Bloodshed! Blood was shed by a sword!" they whispered in hot breaths into the ears they passed.

Faces stiffened by the excitement pressed together at the two places. One group stood in the large corridor at the edges of the floorboards in the Sakura-no-Ma stateroom. The others were in a corner of the Matsu-no-Ma stateroom. Odd-sounding voices flowed from both.

Okado Denpachiro ran to the Matsu-no-Ma stateroom. A head of disheveled hair and an eboshi cap missing its tie string were mercilessly pinned under the knees of Kajikawa Yosobei. Takumi no Kami's eyes reflected the sensation of blood filling his ears.

"Kajikawa! He's wearing a daimon kimono. What are you doing? That's uncalled for."

Denpachiro's hand reflexively shoved Yosobei's shoulder.

Kajikawa Yosobei came to his senses, became conscious of his rough handling caused by overexcitement, and let go of Takumi no Kami's hands.

Takumi no Kami sat up and retied the string of his eboshi cap. A huge wave slammed into his shoulder. His serene demeanor was unbelievable in a man who created pandemonium like an attempted military coup. In a voice charged with passion, he asked, "Are you the inspector?"

"I am Okado Denpachiro, the deputy inspector from the Tamari-no-Ma waiting room. Please wait until we receive instructions."

"Thank you for your consideration."

Denpachiro saw the priest Seki Kyuwa and handed him the bloody sword. Then he removed the *kougai* rod for hairdressing from the opening of the empty sheath to smooth Takumi no Kami's sidelocks. Takumi no Kami fixed his collar and sat up with eyes cast down. "I'm sorry for causing this disturbance."

Takumi no Kami sat in a corner of the Sotetsu-no-Ma room, hidden behind a large folding screen.

A crowd ushered a groaning Kira Kozuke no Suke to the north corner of the same room.

"Please sit. Kira-dono, sit there, please."

"Ah, it hurts …. Call the physician. Hurry, I beg you."

"The physician will be here soon. Please calm down."

As they placed a folding screen around him, still unable to calm himself, Kozuke no Suke's eyes darted around.

"Who's in that corner over there?"

"That's your assailant Asano Takumi no Kami."

"Eeyah!"

Unnerved, he looked like he would scramble out of the folding screen, but the attendants grabbed him like they were catching a baby turtle and scolded him.

"Where are you going? That's why we're here. Isn't your behavior unseemly given the tranquility of your rival? Please, don't invite dishonor."

12

COMPASSION OR NO MERCY

I N THE LOWEST DEPTHS of society, this world was unimaginable. The room's ceiling towered high. Sunlight shined like a rainbow through the carved open-work screen of heavenly beings in the milky white steam of hot water. A small body just five feet tall was bathing.

Tsunayoshi, the fifth-generation shogun dubbed the Dog Shogun by the people, had skin like a woman's and had laid a small rice-bran bag on the bath bed flowing with the aroma of cypress.

Shogun Tsunayoshi's peculiar nature was flamboyant, concerned with fame, and took pleasure in rituals. He appreciated life during the past several busy days, including today's functions of the shogun and the shogunate, a break from what were usually tedious days. On this day, the shogun answered to the vassals. A taste of grandeur graced this ceremonial day. He took meticulous care of his finger-tips and the edges of his sidelocks. More than whiteness and suppleness, his skin was disfigured by softness and flab, giving him curves like a woman, and painstakingly purified.

"Shogun. Shogun."

The decorative door to the adjacent changing room slammed shut.

"What is it?"

"Please excuse the intrusion," said the voice of Grand Chamberlain Yanagisawa Dewa no Kami Yoshiyasu.

"The on-duty inspectors, Okado Denpachiro and Okubo Gonzaemon, are waiting in Tamari-no-Ma for your urgent instructions."

"Oh, Dewa? Isn't it too early for the audience of the imperial envoys?"

"I'm sorry, but you will be unable to meet the envoys. I'm terribly sorry. Could you please hasten your bath?" Dewa asked with awkward hesitation.

As expected, the shogun was quick to anger. A tongue click not words was heard. Bathing sounds were heard for a short time, then the hidden skin was glimpsed going to the make-up room. Panicked by the shogun's cross expression, the bath maids dressed him and combed his hair.

When done, he didn't appear to Dewa no Kami waiting outside but went to the pavilion for relaxation.

Dewa no Kami and the two inspectors timidly entered.

"Is this matter urgent?"

"Yessir."

Okado and Okubo looked at Dewa no Kami. The shogun's emotions revealed distress, and neither could open his mouth.

"I will speak," said Dewa no Kami.

If Tsunayoshi was born in a Year of the Dog, Yanagisawa Dewa no Kami was also born in a Year of the Dog. On this point, the superstitious coincidence seemed appropriate for this lord and his vassal. Dewa possessed exhaustive knowledge of Tsunayoshi's feelings and did not fear him like his fellow vassals. He was also familiar with his displeased looks.

Dewa gave his matter-of-fact report. "A short time ago, an incident occurred involving Asano Takumi no Kami, the lord of Ako Castle. He held a grudge against Chief Master of Ceremonies Kira Kozuke no Suke that led to a sword wound. How shall they both be treated and who will take over their duties as hosts? I came right away to humbly ask for your guidance."

"What?!" said Tsunayoshi like he couldn't believe his ears. His blood after his bath rose to fill his face. "He had a malicious squabble and stabbed the chief master of ceremonies? An idiot. What kind of fool is he? More importantly, that is an extreme breach of etiquette. Summon Tajima."

"Yessir."

The page ran out. Soon an alarmed Akimoto Tajima no Kami of the shogun's Council of Elders scurried in and fell prostrate. Tajima no Kami seemed too shocked to raise his head. He only looked up at Tsunayoshi's brow. The power of Tsunayoshi's anger punched him in the gut.

The appointed time of the audiences with the envoys was fast approaching. They expressed their dark bewilderment at this predicament to each other through lips drawn tight.

"Tajima, investigate the absurd behavior of Takumi no Kami. Now!"

"Yessir."

"See whether today's ceremony for the Gosankyo envoys can be postponed."

"I understand."

"Immediately assign new hosts."

"I will do so without delay."

"Take me there now. Dewa, come with me."

"Yessir."

In the great corridor, palace attendants were wiping up blood, cleaning with water, and sweeping up the salt scattered for purification. Their faces captured their thoughts. Like the moment after a storm has passed, a still quiet from long before the incident descended.

The imperial envoys of the Gosankyo would soon be in attendance at the castle.

All five members of the shogun's Council of Elders were present to apologize.

"An unforeseen mishap has occurred. To our chagrin, we have overlooked the possibility of an improbable event such as this arising at the important welcome ceremony for imperial envoys."

Major Councilor Yanagiwara nodded.

"What is the reason for this misfortune? What offender committed this crime in the palace?"

"A man called Takumi no Kami Naganori."

"Incidents between military families and butchery do happen in castles."

"It's not unheard of, but on days when daimon-crested kimonos are worn, news like this bloody affair inside or outside the castle is an aberration since the days of the Kamakura shogun."

"What punishment is in order?"

"Even preparing to draw one's sword has led to an edict to abolish the family name. Who will carry out the duties of Takumi no Kami?"

Beginning with Akimoto Tajima no Kami, the five council elders wholeheartedly prayed Takumi no Kami's crime could be mitigated if any of the envoys of the Gosankyo, the imperial envoy or the temple envoy, spoke one word, just one word of support. But they only heard

Middle Councilor Kono and Major Councilor Seikanji express curiosity.

"As you know, samurai law is harsh."

Their responses to the postponement of the session to interview the shogun were "That's no problem," and "Well, if it must be …"

The venue of the ceremony was relocated to the Kuroki study. The ceremony proceeded smoothly.

Meanwhile, many secretly sympathized with the feelings of Takumi no Kami.

"If I were in Takumi no Kami's place, maybe … ?"

A frequent rumor was they prayed that the Gosankyo, the shogun, and even the shogun's mother Keishoin would say their thoughts out loud. What a pitiful situation. It might have been temporary madness.

However, the Gosankyo was distracted by the opulent gifts from the shogun and the inner palace and, in the end, was silent.

The people were discouraged.

"Those lords are cold-blooded …"

They whispered, "There is warrior's compassion but no lord's compassion."

13

A LINGERING GRUDGE

"**R**IGHT NOW!" WAS the urgent call.

Okado Denpachiro and Kondo Heihachiro were called to the meeting room of the Council of Elders to be told, "By order of the shogun, you two have been appointed the judicial investigators in the case of Takumi no Kami and will conduct a prompt inquiry."

Denpachiro approached and picked up the short sword used by Takumi no Kami in his bloody attack and pondered human weakness. He sympathized with Takumi no Kami's mental state in the moments before and after he drew the sword. In the rare event, Takumi no Kami was a coward who tried to evade responsibility, Denpachiro would present this sword as proof.

The two investigators waited in the Hinoki-no-Ma room, the physician's office, for Takumi no Kami to arrive. Takumi no Kami sat nearly unseen between three sturdy foot soldier officers seated to his left and right as guards.

Denpachiro stared at his brow. As expected, the hot blood that inflamed his entire body had cooled to blue.

Today's incident was not only the pent-up resentment of that day. Denpachiro sympathized with but was distressed by Takumi no Kami's inner turmoil over the past few days.

Denpachiro thought, If this had not been his duty. The pain of a warrior incapable of understanding the heart of a warrior bit into the roots of his teeth.

"Please understand your words will be examined in light of the law."

"…"

A silent Takumi no Kami lowered his head a little.

"Oblivious to where you were, you wounded Kozuke no Suke with a sword. Please explain the circumstances. Was it deliberate or insanity?"

"I am not insane."

Without thinking, Denpachiro grunted, "Uh-huh."

"Well, did you act out of malice?"

"I have no justification. All I can offer the shogun is a deep shame for my unforgivable act. Beyond submitting to the ordered punishment, I have only words of apology."

After that, Denpachiro wrested few words from him. Takumi no Kami said nothing about Kozuke no Suke's behavior or the sequence of events. Everyone knew to commit a forbidden act in the palace would end in death by seppuku. His resignation to his immutable fate was obvious in his quiet words that penetrated his rival's heart.

A flash of shame hit Denpachiro at the thought of the proof he carried and was prepared to use if needed. However, while he wanted this to be so, he worried about another man's affair. The Takumi no Kami he saw was the familiar sight of one who reached the mental state of absolute calm.

"Is there anything you'd like to say?"

"Yes, I have one question."

"What is it?"

"Was my rival Kozuke no Suke lightly wounded or …"

"Oh, his condition?"

Denpachiro lowered his chin and look straight into Takumi no Kami's eyes. Hadn't his nerves relayed Kozuke no Suke's condition to him while they were in the same room behind the folding screen a short time ago? Denpachiro sympathized.

"He was slightly wounded in two places. The one on his forehead was the strike by the long sword. Because of his age, his recovery is uncertain."

"Thank you very much."

Takumi no Kami lowered his eyes gleaming with satisfaction and traces of his grudge and placed both hands on the ground.

A little later, Kozuke no Suke was led in to take his place. His eyes showed traces of his terror. His pained face stiffened to a deathly pale.

"I haven't the slightest idea why he directed this hatred at me. I recall being thanked for my goodwill in carrying out my duties. Even in a dream, I would never imagine this bloody ending. He stabbed me in the back as I simply tried to escape the violence of a crazed assailant. It's disgraceful, but I never expected this misfortune and found it near impossible to escape."

Groans peppered his answer. His explanation had a cunning fluency.

The interrogations ended.

The shogun's two physicians Amano Ryojun and Kurizaki Doyu came to treat his wounds. A voice traveled over the folding screen.

"Kozuke-dono. This was a calamity, but the shogun is well aware of the circumstances. Don't worry, you'll recover."

He called to a man passing by and walked off. Watching him leave from behind, the man was Grand Chamberlain Yanagisawa Dewa no Kami Yoshiyasu.

14

KAJIKAWA'S CONFESSION

T**HE FACES OF** the public officials stayed tense as they went in and out of the Tokei-no-Ma room.

Starting with Abe Bungo no Kami, the dignitaries of Chief Ministers Tsuchiya, Ogasawara, and Inaba; assistants to the Council of Elders; and chief inspectors stiffened their knees and were somber.

Clouds blanketed the early afternoon sky, and the chill in the air stung. Small birds chirped in the shadows of flowers covering Fukiage Garden, but no sounds emerged.

The Gosankyo received answers from the shogun and were accommodated elsewhere. They chatted with Keishoin in the inner palace. Stealing a short break during a lull, the Council of Elders and lower-ranking officials gathered to recommend the punishment for Takumi no Kami.

"The questioning has ended," said Okado Denpachiro who came to report the results of his investigation of Takumi no Kami.

Kuru Juzaemon who questioned Kozuke no Suke was also there to give his report.

The young assistant officials informed the Council of Elders of their arrival.

The Council summoned the four inspectors to ask detailed questions to clarify certain points.

The grand chamberlain was shown in, too. Grand Chamberlain Yanagisawa Dewa no Kami stood between the Council of Elders and the shogun. He relayed the final judgment to Tsunayoshi.

"Wait in the office for his decision."

"Yessir ..."

Everyone who withdrew from the Council sat as hushed as a forest.

The tower clock in the Tokei-no-Ma chamber made them swallow saliva with every grim moment.

Eventually, the weighted chain clicked to signal four in the afternoon.

"Summon Tsuchiya Sagami no Kami-sama."

"Yessir."

The moment he stood, "And Inaba Tango no Kami-sama and Abe Bungo no Kami-sama."

"Yessir."

"Summon them! Hurry."

Next, the intermediary called, "Inoue Yamato no Kami-sama, please come forward."

The shogun's order was announced without delay.

"Tamura Ukyo-dayu will take custody of Asano Takumi no Kami until the order is announced."

"Kira Kozuke no Suke will not be punished because of his actions and passivity. He is ordered to leave the castle and recuperate."

Each situation was addressed. Otomo Oumi no Kami who tended to Kozuke no Suke at the time of the attack committed no offense. Based on precedent, Kajikawa

Yosobei who wrestled Takumi no Kami to the ground will be granted 500 koku.

For being there by chance and helping Kajikawa strip Takumi no Kami of his sword, the monk Seki Kyuwa was also rewarded with thirty silver coins.

"Kyuwa, you did a fine job."

"Kyuwa, you can live in luxury."

"Kyuwa, this is your second surprise today."

Surrounded by the envy of his fellow monks, Kyuwa was all smiles over his unexpected luck and greater honor awarded. In a leap, Kajikawa Yosobei became a much wealthier man worth 1,200 koku. Why was his crestfallen face glimpsed here and there? No one saw him in Keishoin's business office.

One of his colleagues searched and found him leaning against a pillar in the Yanagi-no-Ma room lost in thought.

"Kajikawa-dono!"

"Oh! Yes," he said startled and turned. His eyelashes sparkled with tears.

The colleague he hadn't noticed tapped his shoulder. "Congratulations!"

Kajikawa's salt-and-pepper sidelocks turned away. "I don't need this success this year."

"Isn't this sort of big luck rare in life? I can't bear my envy. You are invited to the announcement."

"…"

"Oh, you forgot about the engagement. The invitation is from Keishoin-sama. Please come soon."

"I'm coming down with a slight cold or a little chill. Please allow me to excuse myself. I'll be there soon."

His colleague ran ahead, but he stayed at the pillar. Around four in the afternoon, the shadows darkened in the surrounding trees. At that moment, the colleague saw a palanquin being carried in front of the monk's room beside the grand entrance. Several soldiers surrounded the palanquin draped with a net and noiselessly left through the Hirakawa Gate.

Ah, what is there to celebrate? What's inside of Takumi no Kami-dono's heart? thought Kajikawa as the cold evening wind skimmed his cheek. He touched the sagging skin of his palm to his cheek and smeared the tears on his old face. His sharp shoulders trembled from the chill.

"This arm is out of sorts."

Regret made him slap his arm.

"If this arm had stayed out of the way, that blade might have reached … Yes, at my age, the regrets of life remain …. Forgive me, Lord Takumi no Kami."

Kajikawa took out tissue paper tucked in his kimono and pressed it to his face as if covering it. His old, weak hips stayed stuck in his seat.

15

CLEAR AND MUDDY WATERS

His colleague Chinami called, "All inspectors, except for the four men on duty, and everyone including the assistants of the Council are to report immediately."

They filed out en masse and, overwhelmed by grief, returned to their cramped room.

Okado Denpachiro, the remaining guard on duty, asked, "What was the verdict?"

"Well …"

The entire group sat in silence.

"The communication states, 'For this outrageous act, the order is seppuku to be carried out without delay.'"

"And Kira …"

"He is ordered to withdraw promptly to rest and recuperate in Yoshida and have Kurizaki Doyu perform any needed treatment. The other koke families are ordered to provide kind and sympathetic assistance."

"What?" Denpachiro wasn't alone in this reaction.

All the spirited young inspectors with their small stipends looked surprised.

The *Edicts on Compassion for Living Things* came to mind. If Takumi no Kami were a dog, merciful tears would cascade from the shogun and Yoshiyasu born in the Year of the Dog with no hint of embarrassment. Shogun Tsunayoshi valued the life of a dog more than that of Takumi no Kami. This righteous indignation was etched in the brow of Okado Denpachiro.

Almost in defiance, he asked, "Does 'without delay' mean today?"

"Yes, it does."

"The immediate punishment of a lord worth 50,000 koku is in no way too lenient a penalty. And Kozuke no Suke's awful reputation precedes him. You can't say he's without fault."

"That's true. Regardless of the merits of the sword attack in the palace, an ancient rule says it takes two to fight. To say only Lord Kira did not resist is too one-sided."

"It's biased," said Denpachiro, staring at the ceiling. He bit his lip to control himself. However, whispers continued to swirl around him.

"The story is Grand Chamberlain Yanagisawa Dewa no Kami and Kira Kozuke no Suke are close."

"They probably get along well. Dewa no Kami who rose from humble beginnings of 350 koku to the position of grand chamberlain who presides over many lords and Chief Master of Ceremonies Kira have been on friendly terms for some time and are similar in many ways."

"Dewa no Kami's protecting him in today's incident borders on intolerable. A little while ago, he was seen talking with Kira over the folding screen."

"Do I not move politics?"

"That appears to be the case. The shogun favors no one over Dewa no Kami."

This was no surprise. In the current shogunate, the

moods of Dewa no Kami influenced the shogun and the inner palace more than the words of the five men on the Council of Elders. He expressed his sentiments through the strings attached to the shogun that he manipulated.

The close alliance of Dewa no Kami and Kozuke no Suke in their friendship and official duties was common knowledge. These two were of one mind on how to live life and their views on life. The arrogant daily behavior of Kozuke no Suke had the conscious support of powerful men like Yoshiyasu, who did not hide his encouragement of wicked behavior.

Denpachiro thought, This is not the only example. Disorder has haunted the shogunate for quite some time. Private cliques dominate. Future government administration will be unpleasant. Many times he wondered, Will they ever wake up?

His thoughts wandered between self-control and righteous indignation. But in the end, his colleagues were silent and left the crowded room.

For a time, Denpachiro's boisterous tone in the assistant officials' office carried outside through the papered sliding partition.

"Rather than not speaking, I will share my opinion on the bad faith I'm aware of and am prepared to be reprimanded. To begin with, Takumi no Kami is wealthy and powerful among daimyos. He is the lord of a castle, worth 50,000 koku, and reputed to be a gentle man with integrity. To this day, he never gained a bad reputation. Even so, he was prepared for the abolition of his clan name and able to reflect on the insufferable details leading to his audacity today to violate the ban on violence.

"Based on his formal confession we submitted in writing, the order was seppuku to be performed without delay. The public will find the news of praise of his rival Kozuke no Suke to be a strange verdict. The world wondered why and struggled to bear the heartache. I request a postponement of two or three days before carrying out the seppuku for further deliberation."

He feared nothing, given his belief in justice. His earlobes turned deep red, and tears filled his eyes. His passion took over. The council assistants Kato Etchu no Kami and Inaba Tsushima no Kami hung onto his words that made an impact. One vigorously nodded and said, "Yes, I agree."

"We will bring your opinion to the Council of Elders. Please wait a little while longer."

The two left but soon returned.

"Denpachiro, we understand your feelings but are no match for the power of the Council of Elders. Any attempt to mediate is useless."

Denpachiro crawled forward on his knees. "Given this is the shogun's will and the verdict of the Council of Elders, it can't be helped. However, if the decision is left to random men, that cannot be called proper administration. What are the views of the military clans not related to the shogun's clan? The public may also have strange ideas. I apologize for being long-winded, but again I insist on a reason for the rejection of my concerns."

Replacing the soft tone taken a short time ago, he patiently emphasized justice. They recognized his readiness to bet his stipend on justice with his quiet words.

"We hear what you've said …"

The two assistants again went to the officials' office to convey his ideas.

Some on the Council of Elders were touched by Denpachiro's opinion.

"His points are reasonable and inescapable."

They presented his unedited opinion to Yanagisawa

Dewa no Kami. As expected, Dewa no Kami's eyebrows twitched.

"It's the height of absurdity for a matter already settled by the shogun to be addressed over and over. This will never be adopted. Inform Denpachiro his request is outrageous and to show more reserve."

The elders gave their scathing reply and withdrew.

16

SPRING LIGHTNING

T HE HOUR DREW close to bright noontime.

The place was the dismounting station outside the Edo castle. There, the story takes a turn.

~

FACES STRETCHED LIKE CANDY. Sleepy eyes looked up to see wispy clouds like daytime fog sweeping by to blot out or reveal the noontime sun. Even the horses were yawning.

Since morning, the horse dismounting station at the front castle gate had been buried under unmoving horses, palanquins, and attendants. They formed a fog of over-looked humanity.

"Hey, Kanzaki, is lunch soon?"

"Hmm … It's that late?"

"Seems so," mumbled Akabane Genzo and stood to leave the attendants' shed assigned to the Asano clan.

Kataoka Gengoemon stood beside Asazuma, the beloved horse of the lord. The bored man stroked the muzzle of the horse whose eyes reflected the same boredom. Gengoemon's blank stare was not normal.

When asked, "Kataoka, are you gonna eat?" he said, "Oh … is it noon?"

"Yup. I don't see the servant boy. I'm going to the teahouse for hot water."

"I can wait until evening."

"What are you thinking about?"

"I'm not thinking about anything in particular, but Asazuma's neighs sound strange. A short time ago, I heard it four times."

"Wasn't that another horse neighing and acting up?"

"But she sounds funny. How can you be a cavalry officer and not hear it?"

"I think it's your imagination. Too much worrying on our part will stir up the lord's spirit for no reason. There's nothing we can do outside the castle, okay? Let's eat."

"In that case, let me tell you a story. I recently read a book on phonology. Its theory is the voice has sound features like a face has physical features. Lately, I've sensed a change in Asazuma's neighing. Maybe, I hear it because I can discern the five tones of the Chinese musical scale."

"Ha, ha, ha, a human's face looks nothing like a horse's face. So it makes no sense to apply human phonology to a horse."

"A cock's crowing or a dog's barking reveals a sixth sense. For example, a pheasant's crowing predicts earthquakes."

"That's interesting. You can explain that theory to me while we eat. I can't wait any longer. Now, I'm off to get a teakettle."

In the temporary shed, hot water boiled in a cauldron. The footmen and servant boys from various clans jostled each other to grab hold of earthen teapots and kettles.

The face of a servant boy of the Asano clan looked inside, and Genzo raised his hand above the crowd.

He yelled, "Hey, bring one here," but nothing came.

A voice cried out, "Something bad has happened."

People were shrieking and running all around.

The scene at the expansive horse dismounting station turned into a mass of humanity breaking like the tide.

"What is it?"

"Blood was spilled in the castle."

"You're lying."

"Lying? An express messenger left on horseback from the Hirakawa Gate and headed to the Tatsunokuchi residence."

"It's true?"

Someone handed the teakettle to Genzo who dumped the hot water on the heads of the crowd.

"Huh?! There's been bloodshed in the castle?"

"Ow, that's hot," a man shouted.

Genzo's complexion changed in a split second. "God no!" he said, … tossed away the big kettle, and ran out.

"That's hot."

"Ow, that's hot, ow, ouch."

Hot water sprayed all over as turmoil erupted.

"Bloodshed."

"Bloodshed?"

"Bloodshed."

Concern for the lord's safety struck each man's heart. They scattered in all directions like baby spiders.

"Yawata! Go guard him."

Pent-up with anxiety, Genzo ground his teeth while praying.

"Kataoka! Kataoka!"

He looked around for the samurai escort of the Asano clan.

"Kanzaki!"

Kanzaki Yogoro wasn't there. He couldn't see Kataoka Gengoemon. The other men in the clan ran around aimlessly like raging waves. Only dense yellow sand danced. The white horse Asazuma kicked the sand like it was trying to pull out the post and never stopped neighing.

"Akabane?" asked Horibe Yasubei who galloped up like he was going to ram them.

"Hey, have you heard?"

"Yes, but we don't know what's going on."

"I'm praying, just in case …"

"Where are the others?"

"I don't see them."

"They may be at the Sakurada or Hirakawa Gate. I could ask the guards what's happened."

It was a battlefield. Dust hung high in the air. The vassals of several clans galloped off like flowers shaken to the ground by spring lightning.

Both Horibe and Akabane running as sand stung their eyes could only think this must be a mistake.

The angry wave of the crowd struck the Sakurada Gate.

"Listen up guard!"

"Open the gate! Open the gate!"

"We heard a bloody attack occurred in the castle. Who violated the ban?"

"Who was the attacker?"

"Please tell us."

"We need to know about our lord's welfare as soon as possible."

"Don't you understand a warrior's feelings?"

"Guard!" someone bellowed like a madman.

The shouts ended in abuse.

"Fools!"

The guards might have been frightened by the rare riot and locked shut the gate door. No answer would come through a closed gate.

They reluctantly made their way to the Nagara Gate. It was shut, as was the Chujaku Gate.

Wild rumors flew and grew into speculation. Anxiety drew a black vortex. The storm of voices reached deep inside the castle.

"Ignore them," said Inspector Suzuki Goemon, poking up his head over the great gate.

"Quiet down! Calm down! A fight in the palace involved Asano Takumi no Kami and Kira Kozuke no Suke. Neither man's life is in danger. The investigation is underway. Quiet down!"

A white fan was waved and seemed to cry out in desperation. Voices grew hoarse in the tsunami's direction.

"This is not working," he said and ordered the inspectors to the worksite. In no time, they split several cedar planks, wrote on them in thick black strokes, and erected them at the dismounting stations at the great gate and the other gates. Finally, the crowd was silent.

Asano Takumi no Kami wounded Kira Kozuke no Suke with a sword. Both men are being questioned about the altercation in the castle.

17

BY THE FASTEST HORSE

"**O**H, NO!"

Horibe and Akabane froze below the bulletin.

A mounted warrior swept in like a strong wind to their side and looked up.

"Ah!"

The horse's hooves stood still as the warrior's teary eyes stared vacantly at the forests of autumn leaves on the mountain. The warrior was Kataoka Gengoemon.

The men who edged up and lying prone behind them were all vassals of the Asano clan.

"Hmmm," was all some said, folded their arms, and looked toward the far-off castle visible between the trees.

A limp Gengoemon slid from the horse's back.

"Men."

"…"

Sorrowful faces looked up in unison from the ground at Gengoemon. He dropped to his knees.

"What was coming, finally came. Of course, we're more than ready for the sake of the lord. Our urgent task is to send word by the fastest horse to Oishi-dono back home. Who's the fastest?"

As he looked around to gauge his colleagues, from far off Kayano Sanpei said, "I'll go."

Right after him, Hayami Tozaemon said, "Me too!"

"You two will leave at once."

"Yessir."

"Tell Oishi-dono second and third fast messengers will follow with the news as we learn more about the lord's sentence and other matters."

"Yessir," said Hayami and Kayano. Still dressed in the robes worn under the kamishimo used in the day's ceremony, they flew onto their horses, cracked the whips, and headed to town. They secured fast palanquins at the town's general administrative office at Yatsuyama depot.

"Reinforce the shoulders. We'll be traveling nonstop, all day and night, through wind and rain to Ako Castle in Banshu."

That morning, their empty bodies carrying trembling souls galloped at full speed down the Tokaido Road to the skies back home not seen in their dreams and to the people oblivious to this incident in their dreams.

After the fast horses left, Kataoka, Horibe, Kanzaki, and others stood under the great gate, motionless like straw men.

These men entered as far as the castle's waiting area at the entrance to be near their lord, Takumi no Kami. They would learn more details when their comrades inside came out and anxiously waited with a ray of hope in their gloomy hearts.

The attendants Tatebe Kiroku, Isogai Jurozaemon, and Nakamura Seiemon left the castle in despair. The eyelids of the young Isogai Jurozaemon looked red. Everyone was stricken with terrifying palpitations.

Isogai Jurozaemon clutched the two swords worn by the lord to his chest.

Their colleagues' eyes on the verge of tears greeted them with momentary silence.

Jurozaemon said, "The attendants are ordered to withdraw to the mansion to wait for news ..." and passed the lord's swords to Gengoemon. The weight of the swords sent tremors to his bones. He saw a vision of the lord's face.

"It's inevitable ..."

He placed the swords in the lord's empty palanquin and laid the attendants' tools below them. On weakened legs, the party returned to the Teppouzu mansion. Who could have imagined they'd accompany an empty palanquin on today's return home?

One said, "Don't they say, 'The world is like a twisted rope?' ... Springtime penetrates the body."

"There's more pain to come. Think about his wife's shock."

"Yes... My heart aches just thinking about that."

No one's legs moved forward. Lingering for one step shortened the lady's sorrow.

18

A DISASTROUS BATTLE

T AKUMI NO KAMI'S wife already knew.

Asano Daigaku, Takumi no Kami's younger brother who lived in a villa in Kobikicho, was the color of paper.

"Sister, a terrible thing has happened."

He staggered into her room before noon, around the time the attendants returned.

The lord's wife looked at Daigaku breathing hard and knew. She did not spend one day of her married life not knowing.

The blood of the Asano clan was strong in her, too. Until the daughter of Asano Inaba no Kami Nagaharu, the lord of Miyoshi Castle, married, she was called Princess Aguri.

The lower classes sympathized with the cloistered woman with lovely eyes and a fine mind. Her union with Takumi no Kami created a suitable couple envied within the clan.

As expected, she was shocked and trembled like the

tears in the lashes of her beautiful eyes but calmly said, "Daigaku-sama, please have a seat."

"I can't stay. Aah, my brother shed blood in the palace. He was taken into custody and confined to the residence of Tamura Ukyo-dayu."

Her face blanched to the color of ivory.

"Who did he assault?"

"We still don't know."

"What will be the lord's fate?"

"I've only heard rumors. The Council of Elders held an impromptu hearing to address this situation. I was informed to prevent misunderstandings by the family and rushed here immediately after that."

He was a bit exasperated tears did not cloud her serene eyes.

"Your brother became entangled in a serious affair. You, as the younger brother, were told neither his rival's name nor his fate to silence the family and sent home without being allowed to ask questions. Is that what happened?"

"You're right. I didn't realize that."

"That's regrettable. That kind of failure should not happen in the Asano clan, to the lord, or to the vassals."

"I apologize."

Red-faced and confused, he went out front, then returned and sat down. The entire party of attendants arrived home, barely making a sound.

Not far behind them, the inspectors Amano Denshiro and Kondo Heihachiro came as the messengers. Mizuno Kenmotsu appeared. And relatives like Toda Uneme no Sho and Asano Mino no Kami rushed there. All were envoys aware of the shogunate's intentions.

So that the family does not misunderstand ...

This was the first move, a warning. Sending relatives

like Uneme no Sho and Mino no Kami was brilliant muzzling by the shogunate. The plan was to use blood relatives to control blood relatives.

"The strict order is to vacate the daimyo's Teppouzu residence tonight. Everyone must leave," said Uneme no Sho to his cousin, Takumi no Kami's wife.

Additional conditions of the seppuku were the abolishment of the clan name and the forfeiture of its domain. The wife did not flinch and, with the vassal representatives, accepted.

Simultaneously, several of Mino no Kami's men and vassals of the Toda clan closely monitored key locations inside and outside the mansion.

A crowd formed like a tsunami rising from the ground. From the first reports of the incident, people rushed around mostly sighing. Between dismay and disorder, each moment brought dusk closer, then the sun set. The Asano vassals handled several urgent matters.

1. Transfer control of the Tatsunokuchi residence and retrieve furniture, decorations, and utensils.
2. Receive the lord's remains at the residence of Tamura Ukyo-dayu for prompt burial at Sengakuji Temple.
3. Send an express message to the lord's home province.
4. Vacate the Aoyama villa and the daimyo's main residence in Teppouzu.
5. The wife of Takumi no Kami departs the mansion.

The next order of business was disbanding the clan. In the bewildering pit of losing their lord, losing their stipends, and having no place to go, all actions had to be carried out in one night. The military public order would not allow disorder to erupt and turn them into the world's laughingstock.

The two chief retainers, Yasui Hikoemon and Fujii Matazaemon, were a problem. These two elders were advanced in age. Although they both accepted their appointments to take charge of all matters, the pair was only in charge of themselves. Their restless feet never seemed to touch the ground. They were useless.

The wife gave stern instructions to the lady's maids who served in the mansion and gained the servants' understanding. She straightened her husband's sitting room to maintain her mind's processing.

"What are the chief retainers doing?" asked an indignant Kanzaki Yogoro.

The two elders Okuda Magodayu and Muramatsu Kihei rushed in to ask, "What happened to Gengo?"

"Kataoka told us to take care of the rest and left."

"Uh-huh.... He probably went to confirm."

"Yes."

"Who else is there? Hara Soemon."

"He's here."

"Please call him."

"Hara!" called Yogoro from the corridor.

"Yes."

Soemon, the commander of the foot soldiers, ran over. Straw debris was stuck to his sweaty face. The two retainers Muramatsu and Okuda said, "Hara. Go to the Tatsunokuchi residence. You're responsible for salvaging the furnishings and surrendering the estate to the representative. Go now."

"Yessir."

Soemon ran out. He opened the back gate facing the Ogawa River and called to the foot soldiers and the sailors to pair up and grab the oars to ten small boats.

"Hurry!" he shouted and jumped in one.

Like swimming plovers, the line of boats rowed under Dosan Bridge.

Several hundred laborers, foot soldiers, and boatmen had been rounded up and formed two lines from the riverbank to inside the gate of the Denso mansion.

"Good," said Soemon. He ordered the Asano clan's furniture brought in to host the Gosankyo be successively passed out hand to hand from the government housing.

Every fixture and utensil—meal boxes, earthenware, cushions, folding screens, ornaments, partition screens, curtains, paper lanterns, umbrellas, decorative spears—passed between hands and were disgorged like a rushing stream.

Finally, dust was swept away and water sprayed. Even the ashes in the *kamado* stove were raked clean.

The retainer Toda Noto no Kami said, "I have been engaged to assume the role of host to replace Lord Takumi no Kami. With all the furniture and utensils gone, I wish to undertake his duties. I understand the hardship in assuming this role."

The mission was completed in no time.

The vassals of Noto no Kami marveled at the swift and precise withdrawal.

"It's splendid."

The evening clouds of spring were red. Soemon provided paper lanterns for the ten boats, and they rowed away like arrows down Yayosu-bori.

Around that time, envoys were selected to receive the lord's corpse: Tatebe Kipachi, Edo caretaker; Kasuya Kanemon, steward; Tanaka Sadashiro, personal assistant; Nakamura Seiemon; and Isogai Jurozaemon. Under the watchful eyes of the people of Edo who soon heard the rumors, they left the Teppouzu residence, stepped solemnly into black destruction on their way to the Shiba residence of Tamura Ukyo-dayu, and mournfully crossed a bridge somewhere.

19

———

THE TAMURA MANSION

THE EVENING CLOUDS turned a scarlet red over the flowery Mount Atago.

A palanquin draped with a net for transporting prisoners surrounded by the poles of foot soldiers and the stern samurai of a spear squad passed from the Hirakawa Gate of Edo Castle and through the Hibiya Gate and the Sakurada crossroads to arrive, close to four in the afternoon, at the Tamura mansion at the foot of Mount Atago in Shiba.

Carpenters were already at the residence and finished building a one-room, wooden plank enclosure. They carried in the netted palanquin and placed it on a dirty straw mat laid far from the entryway.

"Takumi no Kami-dono, please ..."

The lattice and the net were swept aside, Takumi no Kami's faint voice said, "I apologize for the trouble I've caused," and stepped out.

"Please ... your possessions and ceremonial dress."

"..."

He nodded then removed and handed over everything

—his crested kimono, eboshi cap, tissue paper, small sword, and fan—to a vassal of the Tamura clan.

Now, he wore only a plain short-sleeved kosode robe.

The enclosure was the jail cell for the prisoner. A bathroom was provided in a corner. Outside the papered sliding door were guards with intimidating power.

A tray of food was soon brought to him.

He picked up the chopsticks for the last time and ate three bowls of boiled rice. Evening stars were visible through the tall window, and twilight shrouded the area.

The white grains of rice stuck to the chopsticks and the stars at the edge of the eaves marked the end. Takumi no Kami could believe one hundred years separated morning from evening on that day. He was surprised by the serenity in his doomed body on the verge of oblivion, but his mind jumped to thoughts of his wife. When near any vassal, his entire body felt swamped by tears.

He felt his act was inexcusable and begged for forgiveness in his prayers.

He also consoled himself, My wife and my vassals understand!

He only regretted his inability to erase the futility of rushing and desperately flinging his long sword at his rival only to graze him.

A considerate samurai named Okado Denpachiro understood his heart and told him about Kira's condition.

"He may not recover."

While Takumi no Kami was being transferred from Edo Castle to this place, the walls of the darkened room and the sealed shut palanquin became extensions of his nervous system. He sensed the warriors' energies and listened to their whispers. He probably didn't know Kira escaped serious harm and was treated by the shogun's physician.

"It's a shame."

As long as he breathes, he could not escape that thought. He wasn't a wise or a virtuous man. He had the earthly desires of an ordinary man.

"Guard? Is anyone there?" he called from his cell.

"Yes, what do you want?" said Ikuta Magoso of the Tamura clan.

"While I'm still alive, I wish to write a letter to my vassals. Would that be a problem?"

"Wait a moment," said the guard and left. A little later, he said, "Your request requires the lord's permission. There's nothing I can do." The rejection was blunt.

"I understand …"

Takumi no Kami bit his lip. Emotions of immeasurable depth filled his face. This may be the first time in over thirty years of life he was stung by cruel words aimed at him by an undervassal escort of another clan.

In a near whisper, he said, "Excuse me, but can you pass on a message?"

"I can't speak to the shogun."

"In that case … I'd like to dictate my request to the inspectors."

The guard reluctantly picked up a writing brush, said, "Speak," and wrote what he heard.

Takumi no Kami shut his eyes and said, "Gentlemen."

"Go on …"

"This is a note on today."

"And …"

"I have not stated my reason for that inevitable incident. I understand your suspicions."

That was it.

"Please pass this on to my vassal Kataoka Gengoemon or Isogai Jurozaemon."

Later, the hands of Gengoemon would carry home

Takumi no Kami's last words, mirroring his thoughts to the heart of Oishi Kuranosuke.

"I don't know whether this is permitted, but I'll keep this."

When the guard, Ikuta Magoso, dropped the writing brush into the ink stone box, sounds of commotion flowed in from the direction of the entryway.

"Inspector!"

"Greetings."

He heard a voice as cold as wind skimming over ice.

20

THE BLUE KAMISHIMO

CHIEF INVESTIGATOR SHODA Shimousa no Kami, the lead investigator, and the two assistant investigators Okado Denpachiro and Okubo Gonzaemon were accompanied by eleven men, including the *kaishakunin* who performs the beheading during the seppuku.

"Excuse us," they said and passed directly into the grand study.

Ukyo-dayu went out to greet them.

"Everything has been prepared."

"Well then, goodbye."

The chief investigator and his retinue headed to the site. White curtains swayed in the courtyard at dusk. A rug lay over three tatami mats.

"I have reservations about these preparations," said the frowning investigator Denpachiro.

A short time ago, he was admonished in the palace and ordered to confine himself at home. Now, he was on duty and selected on purpose at the beginning. The reprimand had been lifted, and he was viewed as an assistant inspector.

"Ukyo-dayu-dono."

"Yes."

"The prisoner today is the lord of a castle. With no reason to divest him of his rank, does the man ordered to be punished according to the code of the samurai understand he will commit seppuku in the courtyard like a commoner?"

"Yes."

"I believe this handling is improper, given the etiquette of military clans. I'd like to hear your thoughts," said Denpachiro as if conducting a cross-examination.

"Wait a minute." Shimousa no Kami broke in from the side.

"It doesn't matter if it takes place in the courtyard."

"Why?" pressed the offended Denpachiro, nose flaring.

"As the chief investigator, I say it is not an impediment. Please refrain from needless talk."

He stared at Denpachiro to exert his authority as his superior. Denpachiro knew a quarrel would be foolish. Even in the shogunate, Shoda Shimousa no Kami was known as the right-hand man of Yanagisawa Dewa no Kami Yoshiyasu. This agent of Dewa no Kami, who became emotional when protecting Yoshiyasu, believed arguments should not arise because of an underling's objection.

The front gatekeeper said, "A message for the lord," approached Ukyo-dayu and whispered to him.

Ukyo-dayu looked perplexed. "I'll ask the investigator."

"What is it?"

"For some time, a man called Kataoka Gengoemon from Takumi no Kami's clan has been wandering confused outside the residence. He refuses to go home and insists on seeing his lord one more time. Our clan is at a loss on how to handle this request."

"Is that so?"

Shimousa no Kami turned away and did not answer.

Denpachiro searched his face for an answer but found nothing. At that moment, he made up his mind. Tomorrow he would give up his government stipend.

"All right. I understand the warrior's feelings. Let him see his lord."

"Yessir," said the gatekeeper and scurried away.

The camp stools and the *fuku-zori* sandals with white straps were brought out to the courtyard. The three investigators called Takumi no Kami to the small study.

The writing on thick ceremonial paper beginning with "By order of the Shogun ..." was read.

Soon everyone from the investigators on down took their positions.

After Takumi no Kami heard the shogun's order, he put on the plain blue hakama trousers of his blue kamishimo.

He retied the strap of the hakama trousers three times. It was a little unkempt, a disgrace. The vassals who would see the corpse would probably think, His spirit was confused at the end and ashamed. He wanted a knot he could show to his praiseworthy wife.

"All right."

Takumi no Kami looked at the knot. Satisfied, he sat.

Mysteriously, feelings of relief came.

Thoughts sprang to his mind of the flavor of the light tea always brewed by his wife. Now, a cup of tea would be a comfort when he returned home tired in the evening. How many years had that been the custom of this husband and his wife?

"Asano Takumi no Kami!"

The summoning voice broke the silence.

"Prepare yourself," a stern voice urged from somewhere.

He nodded in greeting to the investigators in their seats.

"Escorts, come forward."

The blue kamishimo rose like water. He was guided down the corridor of the study, five then ten steps closer with both hands placed below the hakama's strap and his eyes cast down. In the evening darkness at the edge of the veranda falling into a deep blue, a man holding a steady gaze set both hands on the ground.

Takumi no Kami trembled, shaking the joints of his legs. His spirit was as clear as a lake. He shouted, "Yes," from joy like a sudden storm.

A sharp pain surged through his entire body to the ends of the hair on his temples. He had to endure an unbearable horror.

"Lord … Lord! …" cried out a low, powerful voice, unable to control his sobbing.

For a short time, Takumi no Kami had no words. Was it joy or sorrow? Did a storm of the greatest love produced by human blood and complex emotions blow away his spirit to rob him of the ability to move his lips?

Finally, he spoke in his usual mild tone.

"Gengo?"

"Yes…. Yessir."

Darkness already cloaked the spring evening.

Scattered white flakes danced to the ground near the eaves. Were they flowers sent by the winds from Mount Atago or the Yoshino cherry blossoms nearby? A petal landed on Gengo's back.

"You asked to be here."

"…"

Gengo's cracking joints and tearful sobs could be heard. The lord gave him a final brave look.

"Goodbye."

Without a sound, Takumi no Kami expanded his chest.

From a hushed silence to the rustling of the blue hakama, like a baby, Gengo struggled with the reluctant parting. He wanted to wail with all his might.

21

SCATTERED BY THE WINDS

THE BACKDROP OF white curtains at the death platform surrounded three tatami mats on the ground in the midst of spring's impermanence and the night's sorrow. The night stars stared at the silent man seated there.

Guards, investigators, and the kaishakunin filled the grounds, but no one coughed.

The night is bright, thought Takumi no Kami.

The lanterns in the mansion and the stars in the sky seemed to greet him. I'd prefer to die smiling was another sudden thought.

He glimpsed Gengoemon's face and was elated by this chance meeting. The will he wished to convey through his eyes lifted his spirit like he imbued Gengo with this thought.

He had one regret.

If only I could convey this to my vassals, he thought and closed his eyes. He opened them and glanced to the left and right. "Excuse me, may I bother you for paper and a brush?"

Using his pinky to hold down the piece of tissue paper jostled by the wind, he wrote.

> *Like cherry blossoms scattered by inviting*
> *winds,*
> *Forever gone.*
> *With sorrow, I bid farewell in the*
> *springtime.*

He laid it down and said, "I request a final act of kindness. I wish the knife to be given to the kaishakunin. Right after I use it, I'd like the knife to be presented to him."

As usual, the lead investigator did not nod, but both assistant investigators consented to his wish.

"That will not be a problem."

The kaishakunin, Isoda Take-dayu, carried in the *tanto* knife and said, "Prepare yourself," then stood behind Takumi no Kami.

Takumi no Kami gave a courteous nod to each man present. He untied the front of his blue hakama trousers and picked up the small blade from the wooden stand beside him, and said to the kaishakunin, "I am indebted to you."

The sound of the blade leaving the sheath softly glided down his back.

A ladle knocked on the empty water pail.

"Are you ready?"

When Take-dayu spoke again, Takumi no Kami's topknot was already down, like he was biting his chest. The shoulders of his blue kamishimo trembled like the wings of a cicada.

Lights, like countless iridescent beetles, drew frightful eddies of red, blue, white, purple, and green on his black eyelids. In a moment, each speck was the face of his wife

Princess Aguri, Ako Castle, his father Nagatomo, the round smiling face of the still young Kuranosuke, the persimmon fruits that grow in the inner citadel of his castle home, and himself hugged to the bosom of his wet nurse.

A rush of wind, and the white blade dispersed into water droplets and passed between the life of the thirty-five-year-old and eternal death.

⌒

THE LEAD INVESTIGATOR, his assistants, and the shogunate authorities filed out.

"This way …"

Just as a vassal of the Tamura clan opened the door of the side gate from the inside, men from the Asano clan, who had been impatiently waiting outside since before the light dimmed, rushed to the courtyard.

"Watch your step. There are many garden stones."

Light from swaying lanterns guided them. A huge paper lantern hung from a pole above the backdrop of white curtains.

"Ah!"

"Lord!"

They fanned out inside. Isogai Jurozaemon, Tatebe Kipachi, and Kataoka Gengoemon fell prostrate and sobbed like they were eating the earth.

His corpse lay flat under a white futon. The severed head was attached sideways to the top of the left shoulder. Crying men placed the body and the head in the coffin.

They accepted the relics of the small sword, tissue paper, folding fan, and tabi socks from the Tamura residence.

Isogai Jurozaemon pushed the tabi socks into his crying

face. A page since the age of fourteen, more than serving the lord, the lord raised him. The lord scolded him.

"Stop sniveling."

"Your waistband's untied."

These tabi socks never once kicked a vassal.

Instead of returning to days long gone, Jurozaemon's crying voice cursed someone. "Damn you!"

Gengoemon again said, "It's too hard to look at," and walked out to follow the coffin led by a lantern of the Asano clan.

People might have been secretly seeing them off from the dark backstreets because fear of the shogunate kept their faces and figures out of sight.

The vassals mourned in an all-night vigil at Sengakuji Temple through the quiet reading of sutras.

22

A LOVEBIRD RETURNS HOME ALONE

"THE LORD HAD a splendid end."

When his wife heard this from the vassal who confirmed the events at the Tamura residence, she answered in a soft voice, "Thank you, that puts my mind at ease."

The mansion in Teppouzu to be vacated that night was cleaned until the evening to remove every speck of dust.

The cherry blossoms on the eaves seen by her that morning danced through the air. Last evening, she probably listened to the sounds of the river lapping against the stonewall behind the mansion. She wanted to sit there forever.

A short time ago out front, the two express messengers, Hara Soemon and Oishi Sezaemon, prepared to leave for Ako, but others were in a rush to go, too. Fewer than the usual number of people were present. The river breeze blew through the opened mansion like a thoroughfare.

"Tae ... Tae ..."

A maid around sixteen or seventeen played with her fingers in front of the lady.

"Did you call?"

"Sit behind me."

"Yes, Ma'am."

When Tae sat behind her, the lady made her pick up the knife placed at her knees.

"Please cut my hair."

"What? … But Ma'am, you'll be returning to your parents' home."

"Before then, my hair will be cut. At least, it will be cut on the evening of the lord's death.… Why did you pull back your hand?"

"Yes, Ma'am."

Tae cut the black hair as her tears fell onto the lady's back. Still gripping the hair, her weeping figure collapsed onto the tatami mat.

"Ah! …" Okuda Magodayu appeared and stared. Without saying a word, he only announced he came to pay his respects.

Her father was Asano Dosa no Kami of Nanbuzaka. She decided on a room in his home to live alone from this evening on as a lovebird with no mate.

Her heart said goodbye forever to the sounds of the river waves and the plants in the garden.

She said farewell in her heart to her home for half of her life and vanished into the palanquin from her birth family that came for her.

Under sorrowful lantern light, only on this evening, everyone from the chief retainers to the junior servants, who will soon scatter to places unknown, placed their hands on the ground to see her off.

Earlier that evening, death separated her from her husband. Now, she said goodbye to her life as a young wife.

"Take care of yourself."

"Good health to you."

As the vassals spoke these words, the bearers lifted the palanquin. A few legs trembled. As the blue door closed, for the first time, muted sobs escaped into the moonless spring night.

PART III

A DIARY OF FIVE DAYS OF LIGHTNING-FAST RUNNERS

23

─────

DANGERS AND NEGOTIATIONS

I N THE DEAD of night, sweaty, hoarse voices were raised as two fast palanquins, each carried on six shoulders, passed through the town of Odawara.

At midnight, someone opened the wicket gate and the observation window of the merchant's home of a wholesaler of front doors, and light leaked out to the sounds of fights or footsteps of passersby.

"Whoa … They look like Asano-sama's vassals."

"They were remarkable."

The rumors spread quicker than the fast palanquins. The locals in this area already knew about today's incident in Edo.

The reinforced shoulders of laborers connected post town to post town. To not waste time when switching bearers, a healthy man with sturdy legs always ran far ahead of the fast palanquins. With them, the unprecedented Edo incident passed down the Tokaido Road like a swift wind.

Inside the palanquins, Hayami Tozaemon and Kayano Sanpei, the first messengers who left Edo right after the incident, gripped the bleached white straps hanging from their palanquins' ceilings. They rode with white headbands wrapping their heads and white cloths wrapping their stomachs.

"Bearer! Bearer!"

Tozaemon called for some time from the palanquin swaying like a wave, but his voice was drowned out by the shouts of the crowd and not heard by the bearers. Everyone was excited.

"I guess they can't hear me," said Tozaemon and stomped the palanquin's floor.

"Oh, do you have to pee?"

"Don't stop. Run."

"We're running."

"I'm catching the voices of townsmen saying, 'This time, they're Asano's vassals.' Are they talking about a fast messenger who left before us?"

"Could be."

"A fast messenger from which clan?"

"Was it the Okata clan?"

"No, men from Geishu shouldn't be that fast. This is puzzling."

"Maybe it's another clan."

"We've arrived after the fast messenger from another clan. This is a disgrace to our hometown. Go faster."

"It will be hard on you, Sir."

"I know. Run faster and don't worry about the riders' bodies."

"We left the post-horse depot in Edo around two in the afternoon."

"Yes."

"I'm not kidding. The fifty miles to Odawara will take half the day and half the night. You'll still say it's too slow. We had to have been born horses to catch up."

"I don't know which clan, but someone's a step ahead of us because we're too slow. Catch up and pass them."

"Sir! Give us a break!"

"Run fast even if I fall out. I'll pay well and drinks will be on me. "

Following his lead, Kayano Sanpei stirred up his bearers from inside the palanquin.

When they arrived at the station in Yumoto, news of their coming preceded them. Close to twenty helpers were waiting to switch the shoulders carrying the palanquins.

"Ready?"

The substitutes answered, "Yes!"

Never touching the ground, the palanquins moved from the shoulders of the current bearers to the new ones. In no time, they dashed off.

The mountain road began at Sammai-bashi Bridge.

They reached the first perilous spot on the road. The number of men grew. By lifting more than carrying, they climbed the dark, steep road, an extraordinary but not rare situation, even on Mount Hakone. The voices of sweat and hard work echoed in the valley.

A large paper lantern hung from the pole set up outside the post-horse inn in Hatajuku where the two messengers were eating meals of gruel.

A chicken somewhere cackled though dawn was hours away. Now in the blackness of the universe, distant ears heard only the roaring waters of the Sukumo River.

As they slurped gruel from wooden bowls, Tozaemon's and Sanpei's chests tightened at thoughts of the grave events of the day. Every moment of the day swirled around in their heads like a revolving lantern. A few moments later in the dead of night on Mount Hakone, cold spring winds not felt in the capital penetrated their bodies. They never shook the notion of being in a dream.

"Go men!"

Before the gruel settled, their bodies were whipped around again. The road got steeper from the Wariishizaka and Onakorobizaka passes, but three miles separated Hatajuku and the Hakone Inn at the peak.

"Keep going. Don't give up."

The bearers drove themselves.

Tozaemon's head hit the back of the palanquin and the ceiling many times. The paper cord tying his hair broke. His loose hair fell down disheveled.

They climbed the final steep pass of Gongenzaka and saw the light of the lake water across the roof of the Hakone Inn.

"We made it."

"We've reached the summit."

They cheered and danced on the flat ground until in front of the checkpoint barrier.

From sundown to sunrise, checkpoints were closed by law. It was still dark, and the gate was shut.

The bearers came up to the edge of the gate with force as if they were going to crash. All at once, they grunted and removed the loads from their shoulders.

"Sir, we have a little time until the road opens. You can walk around a bit," said a bearer. Tozaemon thought that was reasonable. He encouraged Sanpei to get out and stretch. But when Sanpei tried to stand, he felt the ground wobble like a wave. His stumbling when he let go alerted him to his dizziness.

"Oh? The Hayami clan is here."

While clinging to the palanquin, Sanpei discreetly pointed his chin to the side. Tozaemon wondered what he was thinking when he turned to look beside the fence ten to twelve feet away. The lanterns were out. Five thuggish palanquin bearers were squatting and hugging their bare shins. Their fast palanquin arrived earlier and, like them, was waiting for the gate to open.

24

HALFWAY THERE

"Which clan is that?"

The pair grew tired of thinking.

A cousin of Takumi no Kami is the lord of Ogaki Castle in Mino. Is it them? Or is it a Geishu clan? If not, is he a fast messenger from the shogunate heading to Kyoto disturbed by the rudeness toward the imperial envoy?

But Tozaemon found those explanations too simple. An envoy of the imperial court or a daimyo would not be alone. This clan is fast. He couldn't think of a clan that wanted to alert the home province about an incident involving the Asano clan.

"He may be a traveler not connected to our urgent business."

"True. We may be crossing paths with this fast messenger by chance."

If so, there was nothing to worry about. The two closed their mouths and looked at the sky. The daybreak they were awaiting did not grow bright. They wanted to sleep but did not. They were aware of the futility of knocking on the gate to awaken the checkpoint keeper.

The two seemed to walk a short distance, as in a walking meditation. On their way back, they strolled past the side of the suspicious palanquin and heard soft snoring coming from inside. Someone was enjoying a pleasant sleep.

Then the snoring stopped. The man inside shook his body and shouted, "Bearers, hoist up."

The bearers leaped up and positioned their staffs. Inside the fence, the footsteps of the checkpoint official approached. They noticed the light brighten in a flash around the lake in the still morning.

"Ah, it's open."

Tozaemon and Sanpei were soon in their palanquins. They were probably hypersensitive and quick. The palanquin carrying the snoring, sleepy burden ran through first when the gate opened. In the palanquin, a clear, resonant voice directed at the government office said, "You've probably heard that yesterday morning around eleven, Asano Takumi no Kami wounded Lord Kira Kozuke no Suke with a sword in Edo Castle. I have been dispatched by emergency order to Lord Kira's domain in the Hazu district of Mikawa. I am Shimizu Ichigaku, a guard in the Kira clan, and request permission to travel by palanquin."

His voice struck the ears of Sanpei and Tozaemon entering behind him. They knew Kira's domain was worth 1,000 koku in the Usui district in Joshu and 3,300 koku in the Hazu district in Mikawa. Above all, Mikawa is the territory of Kira Hassho and the native province of the Kira clan. A domain populated for generations would have a magistrate's office.

After the lead palanquin passed through, Tozaemon, thinking he misheard, advanced to the front of the government office. His request was identical but told from the opposite standpoint. The checkpoint officials said, "Pass." Compassion filled their eyes.

They resumed their journey home. Hearing the name Kira heightened the men's emotions. They persisted in scolding the bearers but did not catch up until Mishima.

They arrived at the post-horse depot during the morning hustle and bustle and spotted the other palanquin. They were surprised the man from the Kira clan called Shimizu Ichigaku was not in the palanquin but sitting on a stool in the depot's teahouse sipping tea. His dress was ordinary. Nothing about him suggested urgency.

He might have been in his thirties or older. A curve appeared in the high bridge of his nose. His stern lips were closed in a thick line. He wore zori sandals. He said to the proprietress of the tea store, "Granny, spicy riceballs, please, a little extra salt."

In front of the depot, men were buried in the changing of shoulders for the two recently arrived palanquins. Travelers and officials of the post town probably knew a little of the truth of the sword attack and noisily surrounded the men they heard were from the Asano clan. Shimizu Ichigaku watched the scene with cold eyes as he gulped tea and ate riceballs.

"Master, I don't see the men you're looking for. They may be sleeping in their palanquins or eating."

The bearer froze, amazed by the tip received from his passenger Ichigaku.

Tozaemon and Sanpei were pressed for time in front of the depot.

"I don't want gruel. Soup will be fine. Hurry, please."

Their fast palanquins overtook Ichigaku and left white dust on the row of trees. However, the upset Tozaemon couldn't help feeling the calm-looking Shimizu Ichigaku saw through his panic. He was amazed a lord like Kozuke no Suke had a samurai with such a defiant, hateful look.

The second and third days were said to be the most trying for a messenger in a fast palanquin traveling a long distance. Fog envelops the brain and thinking becomes impossible. The shaking worsens and aggravates feelings of nausea. From time to time, Sanpei stuffed smelling salts in his cheek. Tozaemon in the first palanquin asked, "Sanpei, are you all right?"

"I'm fine," he answered in a cheerful tone, but his face had been pale since the afternoon of the second day and looked pained.

At sunset when the bronze waters of the Fujikawa River were visible between the pine trees, a man on horseback rode with his whip raised from the direction of Yoshiwara.

He shouted, "Pardon me," as he shot past them.

Watching him from behind, they recognized Shimizu Ichigaku. They knew the reason for his speed. When going by palanquin or by horse or, depending on the situation, by foot, he might have set out at the time of the incident to travel nonstop the nearly 205 miles from Edo to the territory of Yokosuka village in the Hazu district in Mikawa.

The distance from Ako in Banshu to be covered by Hayami and Kayano was twice as long. Nonetheless, Ichigaku's drive was fearless. This would be too hard for anyone but a samurai with extensive training in horsemanship and walking, and a disciplined body. Hayami Tozaemon respected this rival who left them in the dust.

When they reached the ferryboat crossing at the Fujikawa River, the gap after being overtaken could not be closed. The fast palanquins depended on the ferryboat; Shimizu Ichigaku picked a shallow sandbank to cross with ease on horseback to the opposite shore.

"This is too much. We should have dumped the palanquins and switched to horses at the depot," said Sanpei, his
pale, fatigued brow filled with impatience. However, Tozaemon, older by one year, sensibly advised him to rest during
the ferry trip.

He said, "A 195-mile-long road lay ahead. We must
think about the number of days and our health on our
journey longer than 400 miles. Besides, he's already won,"
and chuckled.

25

UNDER THE PROTECTION OF
LORD KIRA

Gloom cloaked the dawn of the sixteenth. They had been without rest or sleep for the thirty-seven or -eight hours since leaving Edo. The fast palanquins carrying the messengers rushed past rows of pine trees between the post town Fujikawa in the Nukada district in Mikawa and the castle town Okazaki.

They climbed Azukizaka and glimpsed Okazaki Castle through the dense morning fog at daybreak.

"Do it."

"I'll do it. I'll do it."

The bearers were talking in front of the still shuttered teahouse. The palanquins were on the ground, and they stood with arms folded.

Kayano Sanpei on a razor's edge swept aside the straw curtain to yell at the bearers.

"Dammit, what are you doing? Hurry up, let's go."

"We're taking a break and having a smoke."

"This is outrageous. Don't you know the rules of fast palanquins between post towns? No breaks until the next depot."

117

"You'll get your reward. It's my body. I can't stand hearing complaints while I'm resting my body."

"Why I'll …" he clutched his sword. "You're slowing us down on purpose."

"I'm not interested in going slow. I don't think they'll let us through."

"What?" asked Sanpei and jumped out of his palanquin.

This surprised Tozaemon. "Wait. Don't be rash. We're in the middle of an important mission."

"I know … but … their impudence."

"There's probably some detail we're missing. I'll find out. Hey fellows, is it money you want?" Tozaemon calmly asked while scrutinizing the bearers' faces. Meanwhile, forty to fifty men, peasants who weren't bearers, old men, townsmen, and provincial samurai, gathered around them. Tozaemon knew his careless words were inappropriate and rushed to clarify.

"Weren't a lot of folks in the post town saying these samurai were Asano vassals?" an old man asked the bearers while wagging a dirty cane at Tozaemon and Sanpei.

The bearers in one voice said, "Yeah, these guys are going to Ako."

The motley crowd targeted the two with bold stares. The crowd babbled the news from mouth to mouth in an almost incomprehensible dialect. One of them, a barefoot youth with a face like a water sprite, cursed them. "You fools." Then he flung a handful of dirt at Sanpei's face and ran to hide behind the adults. The boy's abuse lit a fire. Men and women with eyes burning with hate ganged up to block the road.

"Those Ako samurai sure do look like fools."

"What are you looking at? Vassals of a jackass daimyo who cut a man in the palace."

"Takumi no Kami is a lunatic, a madman."

"He stabbed Kozuke no Suke-sama."

"He's our lord's rival."

"You mean his enemy."

"If we let them pass down this road, we'll be ridiculed in the other provinces."

"They won't pass. Not through here."

"You're too bold saying you're going to pass through here."

"They're fools!"

"Beat them up!"

A violent storm of foul abuse pelted them from all sides. The peasants joined in. The townsmen screamed. Even women and snot-nosed kids let loose and cursed them to their faces.

As the crowd grew excited, so did Sanpei. He gripped the hilt of his sword and set a terrifying look in his eyes. Not by chance, Tozaemon grabbed his wrist and pushed himself out front to be abused.

"Citizens, please quiet down."

"What citizens? We've never eaten one grain of rice of the Asano clan."

"Well, please calm down and listen. Where are you from?"

The old man clutching the cane stood tall and said, "We hail from the domain of the Kira clan."

He looked like a teacher from a temple school. He raised his cane again and poked the air.

"I'll tell you since you don't know. A little over three and a half miles south of here, the Hazu district, and the seven villages of Otokawa, Komiyata, Yokosuka, Toba,

Okayama, Aiba, and Miyahazama have been the domain of the Kira clan since the days of the Ashikaga clan.

"Mount Yatsuomote is north of the district. This region produces mica, has been called Kira's domain for ages, and is cheered as *Kira's Villages*.

"In eighteen generations until this generation's Kozuke no Suke Yoshinaka-sama, over seven hundred years, the people living in this Kira clan domain never changed the domain head. They're nothing like the branch families of new daimyos created in the warring states. Do you understand?"

"Yes ... and so?"

"Since you're asking, a shallow man like your lord Takumi no Kami ..."

Unable to bear his words, Sanpei's knuckles holding the handle whitened, and his elbow was as taut as a bowstring.

"Not another word, old man!"

Tozaemon said, "Stop it, Sanpei. Instead of objecting, be tolerant and listen to the simple voices of the people."

The old temple schoolteacher, in an agitated tone unlike an elder, said, "Last night around midnight, we heard the sword of an idiot attacked the lord of our domain in Edo Castle and severely wounded him. These people of the domain are showing their distress ... no, their sorrow ... no, it's neither."

Just as his halting, pained words reflected some force acting on him, the same grief over this wretched event experienced by these rivals stabbed Tozaemon standing in the rubble of his lord's house.

"Our lord is an old man. I've heard the wounds in the middle of his forehead and on his back were shallow, but will he recover? At that time, his samurai attendant Kobayashi Heihachiro-sama had accompanied the lord's wife Tomiko-sama from Edo to the ancestral memorial service in the family cemetery in Yokosuka and Kezouin Temple and was still there. They heard the sorrowful news there. This uproar at dawn was to show you the lady's shock and the anger of the peasants and the townspeople."

Sanpei shut his parched mouth. Tozaemon listened in silence to the old man's explanation.

"You may understand that, but others don't know. We think of the lord of our domain as our father. For the eternity of seven hundred years, the people did not change nor did the lord of the domain. The ruler and his subjects were connected to the earth. Power laid in the benevolent rule of Kozuke no Suke-sama over them.

"The things he has done for us include repairing the water damage to Yahagidaira; making immense investments in private property; filling in Yoroigafuchi to develop fine fields; building the Ougon embankment; saving the peasants in Atsumi worth 8,000 koku from the fear of crop failures; and encouraging work in the salt fields. You don't know how he's done his damnedest for the lives of the people.

"And when the reign of Kozuke no Suke-sama began, he repaired destroyed temples, did not levy heavy taxes like they do in other domains, and was charitable to the poor. He cast bells for the Buddhist temples; bells that had been silent for a long time rang again in the villages.

"The peasants responded to his kindness. When news came about the horrible incident in Edo during the night, they visited the guardian gods at Kezouin Temple. They prayed to the wooden statues of the ancestors of the Kira family to bless and care for Kozuke no Suke-sama. The entire domain grieved and was enraged."

The old man did not run out of words, which sounded sincere.

"From the Hazu district in turmoil mixing worry with

anger, villagers heard Asano's fast palanquins would pass through the streets before their eyes and noses. How could they watch in silence? Villagers always went to the post town of Fujikawa in the Suke district to work as carriers and horse drivers. Although wretched, they would swing their arms to stop the vassals of Kira-sama's rival. You began as valuable envoys but will be hurt and unable to fulfill your duties. It'd be best if you return home by the back streets."

The crowd had been silent as the old man explained their reasoning but broke in.

"No. That's not good enough."

"Our hated enemy is gonna get a beating."

The wild-eyed mob closed in. They carried broken sticks and grabbed rocks.

26

ZEN WITHOUT A SWORD

Hayami Tozaemon raised his hand to the indignant faces and said, "I understand your grievance, but please let me speak."

"There's nothing for you to say. You vassal of a coward! Who sneak attacks in the palace? If he had a grudge, he should have fought like a man in another place. He has no manners. He's lower than a dog. A dog. A beast. That's your lord."

No one looked more wounded than Kayano Sanpei. He raised his bloodshot eyes and said, "What … what did you say?"

"I said he's a beast. Am I wrong?"

"Dammit! What do any of you know? My lord had compelling reasons to shed your lord's blood. Everyone knows Kozuke no Suke is a cruel and greedy man."

"Shut up!"

Straw sandals for cows flew toward Sanpei. Muck stuck to his chest. The crowd was livid and shot back.

"You bastards!"

"Fools!"

Sanpei, covered in dirt and wrought with emotion, said, "You ignorant bumpkins. You can try my patience, but I will not allow insults."

When Tozaemon waved his hands to control the crowd and seemed to step forward, the trembling mob shrunk back.

A spirited dissenter shouted, "Knock them down!"

In an instant, rocks, pieces of wood, and straw sandals battered the two. Tozaemon was alarmed by the storm engulfing him. Although unnerved, he managed to speak.

"Wait, quiet down. Both sides have reasons, but the Asano side had valid reasons for the bloodshed. You and I share similar feelings toward our lords. For us, news of the seppuku of Takumi no Kami-sama and the seizure of the castle and the lands cannot be avoided. This moment in my life is to pass on this sad news without a second's delay to the people back home who know nothing."

All around them, furious voices spat out their words.

"He got what he deserved."

"It had to be."

Tozaemon froze. Like an ignorant man, he believed in genuine innocence. He gauged the faces in the crowd and spoke to persuade them.

"The shogun alone will pass judgment on the punishment. If the vassals and the people of the domains engage in personal struggles, blood will be washed with blood forever. If this were any other situation, I'd follow your wishes. If told to return by this road, I would return, or if told to place both hands on the ground and apologize, I would.

"However, we carry this calamity striking our lord in our bodies and take on this important task for our clan. We heard the people in our rival's domain were preparing to block the roads and took a detour. We will face the world and the people in our home province. The Ako clan will also lose face.

"Even at risk to my life as a warrior, I will not take one step back. If we're not allowed to pass, our only way to pass will be by the sword. However, this misfortune is growing and will only sow the seeds of laughter in the world. Please hear me out."

"Self-serving nonsense."

"You will suffer needless injuries."

"You're threatening us. No matter what you say, you're not getting through. Come on! Everybody!"

The clouds brightened and cleared away at dawn. The roads were growing livelier. They were losing time. A safe ending was becoming harder to imagine. Tozaemon eventually came to this inescapable conclusion. But his expression remained calm to the end.

"In that case, summon the town official. Or come with us to Okazaki to request a hearing. If anything, I have no problem ending this battle of words a moment sooner."

"Fool. Do you think this is an ordinary fight you meet with a government official to resolve?"

"So you won't listen to reason?"

Tozaemon, who had been quiet, stood a little taller and glared with his sharp eyes. Kayano Sanpei appeared to tighten his grip on the handle of his sword. The crowd hesitated.

"You're not passing! Not here!"

Rocks flew out with the shouts. The fast palanquin bearers swung their staffs.

"You bastards!"

A cane came from behind Sanpei. His elbow had been grabbed by Tozaemon, and the cane slammed down on his shoulder.

Tozaemon let go of Sanpei's arm and said, "Don't kill them. Throw them back!" and dodged the attack.

Rods, staffs, bamboo spears, and rocks formed a whirlwind that raised grass and dust. Tozaemon and Sanpei charged in. If pushed ten steps, they pushed back ten steps. They tried to toss, kick, or shove anyone they touched but were outnumbered. Curious onlookers found out about the melee and swelled the crowd.

He thought brandishing a bare sword as a threat might scatter the crowd with little resistance. But this population held sincere feelings about the lord of their domain. He'd be surprised if that weren't so. He had no idea when to use force if their stubborn resistance did not stop.

27

AZUKIZAKA

NOT ONE DROP of blood will flow here, Tozaemon pledged. If they see blood, the crowd, better called a mob, will violate the regulations of the post road. If government officials supported by the Kira clan come out, more problems will arise. Besides being late, we might be delayed for several days. The people of this domain are honest, stubborn, and care about their lord. We should be able to chase them away without the sight of blood. The body withers like cotton in a fast palanquin over a long distance. We'll be in danger if it gets any worse.

He struggled to swim the eddy of obstacles. Now, Tozaemon's sole conviction in the meditation point below his navel was "to do my best then stop" in the way of the samurai. Life and death posed another problem.

If he and Sanpei struck down the crowd in desperation, simplicity and honesty would revert to savagery. The crowd turned ferocious and reckless.

"Kill them."

"Beat them to death."

Then from one spot in the black mass of people came these words.

"Run away! Or don't! But if you stay, I will become your rival! Silence!"

A hulk of a man yelled as he forced his way to the center of the scuffle. He spread his arms wide before Tozaemon and Sanpei and glared with menace at the faces in the mob.

The crowd looked at the samurai and pulled back like flustered game. The samurai gave one command. "Go home!"

He said, "I understand your feelings, but you have no reason to be upset. If this territory of the Kira clan is safe, the lord's life will not be harmed. You should pity the Asano vassals. Why should you torment these messengers here? They will pass. For my sake, let them pass."

The crowd did not budge.

"Do you understand? Don't spend half the day away from cultivating the fields and your other tasks. The lord of the fief is the lord of farmers. If you toss aside your hoes and spend a day on this distraction, the world will perish. Leave this to me and go home.... Please go home."

At first, his words were severe, but his last words admonished them with gentle gratitude. The crowd dropped their heads and abandoned their sticks and bamboo spears. They whispered to each other, bowed to the samurai, and scattered.

As he watched them go, the samurai said to himself, "They're good people."

He gave a brief bow and said to Tozaemon and Sanpei, "For a daimyo having such fine men, the action of Asano Takumi no Kami is regrettable. I understand the feelings of those in your clan."

Tozaemon stared at this man and remembered in his heart.

"Aren't you Shimizu Ichigaku?"

"Excuse my rudeness along this journey."

"Uh-huh," Tozaemon moaned without thinking.

He envied the people of this domain and this samurai but couldn't reconcile the man called Kira Kozuke no Suke he knew in his head after thinking about him over and over.

Shimizu Ichigaku acknowledged them, looked toward the fast palanquins, and said, "I blundered. Not thinking, I drove them all away. Even the depot workers left. Would you like something to eat?"

"Thanks to you there's no longer any reason to walk or run to the administrative office in Okazaki."

"Well, you're probably in a hurry."

"In that case, are we free to pass?"

"The highway is public."

Ichigaku raised his head and smiled brightly. A row of healthy teeth was visible inside the bluish stubble of chin hair. Sanpei studied that face and with deep emotion introduced himself.

"I am Kayano Sanpei, a petty samurai in the Asano clan. Thank you for coming to our aid."

Hayami Tozaemon gave his name and said, "Well, our business is urgent."

He took an object from the empty palanquin and held it to his side.

"So it is. Don't waste another moment," said Ichigaku in encouragement.

"We'll probably not meet again …"

"No," said Ichigaku and faintly smiled. "We may have another chance."

"With your permission," they said and ran off.

"Kayano-san, Kayano-san."

Ichigaku called him back.

"Yes, what is it?"

"The belt of your hakama trousers is untied," Ichigaku advised, turned on his heels, and briskly walked toward Azukizaka.

28

———

THE CROSSROADS OF THIS WORLD

T HEY SPENT ALL day and night in fast palanquins, being shaken in spaces with no food, sleep, or will.

Both acquired sickly tints. It was no surprise that on the third day the knowing Tozaemon kept his eyes shut with his hand clinging to the bleached strap.

Wherever they ran, they heard people say, "Those are Asano's, Asano's fast palanquins."

The public offered this opinion in castle towns and only showed interest in the eruption of bloodshed in Edo.

Some thought Takumi no Kami was justified in his action as a samurai. Many laid blame on a fiery temper and a tantrum thrown by a privileged son who knew little of the world. Especially when they crossed Kyoto, hurtful voices stabbed their ears.

"They're the vassals of a disrespectful man."

They believed a host of imperial envoys spilled blood because a modern daimyo knows all about the shogunate and forgot about the Imperial Court.

Kira also stirred up ill feelings.

"He was accustomed to being treated as a powerful court noble and chafed."

The criticism of who was being disrespectful leaned toward the one who harmed another, Takumi no Kami.

Tozaemon passed through, astonished.

Accurate rumors were fine, but outrageous false reports in circulation prompted some people out and about to hurl rocks at the palanquins. Others spread rumors like war was about to break out. Many theories came from the dissatisfied or vagrants waiting for some sort of upheaval in the nation.

This singular interest consumed the world. Eyes strained to see off the two fast palanquins. The duo shut their eyes and sped past the public's gaze.

From time to time, Sanpei sounded like he would vomit in his palanquin. He seemed unhealthy, beyond his usual nervous nature. Passion won in his slender body. He was a refined young man and loved by Takumi no Kami as a page from around the age of thirteen and liked him as a friend. Tozaemon worried constantly about him in this role as an express messenger.

Kayano Sanpei was born in a house in the village of Kayano in Sesshu. He came from generations of provincial samurai. The old gate of an earthen wall sprouting grassy flowers on its roof was built parallel to the traffic traveling the Tokaido Road.

"Ah ... it's good to be home."

When the fast palanquin started down the Tokaido Road, a multitude of feelings struck Sanpei.

He saw the familiar persimmon trees. The shop curtains of the storehouse of the miso shop and the cotton dealer, all unchanged from his boyhood, seemed to be blowing in the peaceful spring winds.

Around this time thirteen years ago, he went to Ako to perform his government service at the recommendation of Oshima Dewa no Kami. The town changed little over the years.

His father was spending his remaining years in his birthplace. He probably did not know his son was passing through his hometown by fast palanquin on a day in ten years of a sudden change in his lord's house. His mother did not know either.

As he chaotically sketched the incident in his giddy head, he glimpsed an earthen fence of coarse dirt along a small gully outside the palanquin.

I'm home!

He raised the straw curtain and surprised himself when he stuck his head out. He watched the precious dark brown wall flow by and soon saw the front gate. Fake lotus flowers and white paper lanterns were set out before the gate. A large group of peasants wearing fine-patterned *haori* half coats and men in kimonos with the family crest and donning braided straw hats stood in a sunny spot on the road.

"What's going on?"

The scents of incense and flowers brushed past Sanpei's face. He could see crying figures dressed in pure white in the shadow of the dark gate. Bearers were about to lift a funeral palanquin onto their shoulders.

"Fast palanquin coming through!"

"Watch out!"

The mourners stepped back and fled the road. Behind the priest, a young woman dressed in pure white and wiping away tears said, "Oh, it's Sanpei!"

The mourners were surprised.

The young woman leaped at his palanquin and broke

down crying as if no one was watching. The others might have wondered if she had gone mad.

Sounding surprised, Sanpei said, "Sis?"

"Sanpei! … Sanpei! … Please stop."

"Who died?"

"Mother …"

"What?! Mother?"

His younger sister trembled as her tears poured down.

An elderly samurai bent at the waist like a bow but still strong in his bony shoulders came carrying a pair of zori sandals with paper cords.

"Sanpei?" he said and looked.

"Father?"

"Why did you come?"

"I've come this way on official business and not for rest."

"The undeniable fact is your mother's wake took place last night. This year she turned fifty-two, too young to die. But she was slender like you and died after an illness."

"I can't say I'm here as a devoted son."

"Well, she died content. You became a page to Takumi no Kami-sama. We heard you were a good learner."

"Yes. Yes."

"But this fast palanquin worries me. Your face tells me this is not a simple matter. What has happened?"

"You haven't heard?"

The rumors should have reached this area. Presumably, the relatives thought the serious incident in the clan served by the son would be too distressing to the elderly father who lost his wife and kept quiet.

"I'll send you a letter with more details about this matter. I'm on my way back to the home province with no time to spare. I ache because I can't help with my mother's coffin."

"Your service is important. Go."

"Yessir."

Sanpei did not leave the palanquin but reached out to touch his mother's coffin. Tozaemon in the lead palanquin placed his hands together.

29

THE GUNPOWDER GUARD

THEY SAY YOU can be carefree in the mountains, and guests often came. Last evening, younger samurai in the clan arrived with a half-gallon bottle of sake. A noisy party unfolded in this guard hut amid the plucking of the strings of a Heike *biwa* lute and the recitation of poems about battles. In time, Yokogawa Kanpei's spirit was refreshed and his boredom relieved.

"It's cold," he said, noticing his shivering. He looked around the hut. The oil in the bright lamp had not run out. The half-gallon bottle of liquor was sleeping on its side. No one tended to the fire in the hearth. He had dozed off in his clothes, and drool moistened his elbow.

"Ah, I'm thirsty."

He jumped up and stretched. His fists sprouting hair seemed to punch through the hut's ceiling. Yokogawa Kanpei was six feet tall. People guessed he had the strength of ten men, but that probably was not true. He wedged his physique into the guard's hut. His round face sported eyes with a childish twinkle and was topped with thick hair. When he shaved, blood spots often dotted his chin.

"I slept and slept," he said with delight and went into the room with the dirt floor.

His feet searched for and finally slipped into his *geta* sandals. He opened the door wide.

"What is this? Why is it still dark?"

Stars filled the new dawn skies. However, the air touching his face felt like daybreak.

He stood on the peak of Wakiyama behind Ako Castle. Guards were stationed there to protect the clan's gunpowder storehouse. Yokogawa Kanpei was a rank-and-file soldier with a stipend of five *ryo* with rice rations for three. He was a gunpowder guard.

The cliff beside the hut was chiseled away when the hut was built. An open water pipe drew the gushing cold spring water into the kitchen. Kanpei removed the bamboo spout to let the water spray into his mouth.

"Aaaah."

He gargled and spat out the water like a rainbow. Then he stood at the edge of the cliff in front of the guardhouse and pressed both hands to his huge sides. He bent over repeatedly and shook his head. What was he doing?

A gap in the clouds shone blue like the scales of a bonito fish.

Many lines gradually emerged from the depths of darkness to white. They were the salt fields on the Ako shore, and the smoke from salt being cooked. From there, a snaking whiteness ended near the provincial border with Bizen. He was scanning the coastline.

"Hey what's that?"

Kanpei's round face discovered something.

"What could that be this time of the morning?"

Ako Road was the main road that branched from Banshu Road, passed through the Takatori mountain pass, crossed on the ferries on the Chikusa River, and entered the castle town. The sight of a cluster of lamps rushing down this road through the moonless dawn was not unusual. However, he often stood at this spot in the evening or the dead of night and had never seen a sight like this.

"There are at least twelve or thirteen lanterns … What's going on?"

He closed one eye and raised a finger in front of the other. With this technique, he measured the speed of the advancing light. They were not simply walking. They were heading for the castle town at the fastest speed possible by human legs.

He strained to listen as they approached. He could hear the faint grunts of exertion during lulls in the wind.

"Those are fast palanquins!" said Kanpei and ran inside the hut.

He yanked the futon off a man sleeping in a corner.

"Hey, wake up!"

"Huh? Yokogawa? Let me sleep."

"You're on duty!"

"What? Right now?"

"I'm going to the castle."

"See you later."

"Get up now. You're on duty! The castle's not open. I'm going to wake up the daimyo's keeper of the castle, Oishi-sama."

"Did something happen?"

"Today is the nineteenth. Right?"

"So it is."

"…"

Kanpei counted the number of days on his fingers and said, "The important mission of the lord in Edo lasted five days—the twelfth, thirteenth, fourteenth, fifteenth, and sixteenth. Everyone is praying it ended without incident. It's strange to use fast palanquins."

"Did you say fast palanquins?"

"That's not a good sign."

"Hey, are they carrying lanterns?"

"You dope. It's already light out. Wouldn't it be Chief Retainer Oishi?"

Kanpei slipped on his zori sandals, put on his long sword suited to his large physique, and flew down the familiar trail through the bamboo grass thicket he walked daily.

A TALE OF RED SMARTWEED

30

A SERMON ON GOOD AND PLENTIFUL WATER

O N THIS SPRING dawn, sleeping was comfortable. The castle town of Ako was still in shadows.

Near the ocean where muffled waves noises could be heard, the castle tower of Kariya Castle bathed in the sea light from the bay soared above the pines. The previous night's darkness lingered over every street corner in the castle town. Lights were put out leisurely in the lanterns on the eaves of meeting houses. The distant barks of stray dogs noisily echoed. The Livestock Protection Order was not restricted to Edo. Infestations of the exalted dogs were horrible in castle towns throughout the nation. People ranked below these dogs in Ako, too.

"Kamiya. I'm all right. I'm fine," a loud voice shouted with delight at a street corner in Hashimotocho. The good-spirited shouter, a man wearing priestly attire and zori sandals, tottered dangerously while a townsman supported the center of his back.

A closer look revealed he was Priest Ryousetsu from Niihama. He was a refined man on the path of Zen. The always-lighthearted man enjoyed life. His tipsy stumbles created a parade of children to mock him.

The priest from Shofukuji Temple
Is good at drinking but bad at Go.
He licks salt, sips sake, and loses at Go.

Many laughed at him, but many merchants in town and clansmen would trade places. Something in Ryousetsu's personality allowed others to forget all worries when in his company. He taught others how to enjoy life as it is.

Last night, he visited the home of the inn proprietor Kamiya Shiroemon to play Go and drink until dawn. The proprietor held back and, feeling responsible, became his minder. He pushed Ryousetsu's back like he was supporting a fragile object.

"Just a little more. A little further. Walk straight ahead."

"I can't."

"Why not?"

"Someone's talking, so if I walk straight ahead, I'll crash into him. Anyway, it's best for the world to stumble along."

"But no one will pass by."

"Dogs will pass by. Oh no, great and honorable dogs will pass by."

They roared with laughter and went to the well at the roadside teahouse.

"Kamiya, I want to sober up."

"You are talking quite a lot. Are you thirsty?"

"Please draw me a cup. This well gives us the water of gratitude. It's one of the wells dug at every street corner in the castle town for the domain's population when the founder Naga Naoko was transferred from the post of the daimyo of Hitachi to Kasama.

"My father joined the Ako clan, followed Naga Naoko from Hitachi, and joined in the efforts to supply water. Above all, during the development of the salt fields, the lord and his subjects worked so hard they forgot to eat and sleep.

"Both the daimyo and the imperial era changed. The lands growing staple grains were productive. Salt production grew. The climate and natural features were outstanding. Blessings were abundant in material goods and nature. People today, particularly townsmen but also farmers and retainers, do not know poverty, and life's a little too easy. At first, this country was not plentiful. Today, we enjoy the fruits of the hard work of Naga Naoko and the gift of the tribulations experienced by our forefathers who moved here from Hitachi.... When you drink this well water, the favor of the homeland is the taste penetrating the tongue and the spirit."

"Priest, was that a sermon? Well, here's the water, drink up."

"No, you drink."

"I'm fine."

"It seems so. As I've said, compared to the Hitachi region in Kanto, today, Ako has abundant natural blessings in the beautiful scenery of Setouchi, nature's production, and an excellent climate. Therefore, the families in your homes are extravagant, apathetic, selfish, and can't dream of the hardships of your forbearers. From time to time, it's nice to bring the family along for a drink."

"You're still drunk. That sermon was too long. Look way over there. Is something coming this way? Please, don't drink so fast."

"What's coming?"

Ryousetsu turned to look where Kamiya was pointing.

He was silent for a short time as he strained to see. "Ah!" he said and tugged on Kamiya's sleeve.

The light from lanterns held aloft by the tired arms of a dozen shadows crossed the Chikusa River. They collided with the moonless dawn drifting to white as if choked by the salty air of the tide. Their rhythmic grunts of "Ay! Ay!" encouraged them as they entered the castle town.

"Kamiya, aren't those fast palanquins?"

"They could be."

"I wonder what's happened …"

The mass of sweaty, tired, and dirty men and gruff shouts passed in front of them to a corner of the crossroads.

"Water! Water!" voices about to give out echoed from inside the two fast palanquins.

The bottoms of the palanquins landed with thuds on the roadside. Everyone was panting and dropped where they stood.

"Ah, this is Ako."

"We're here."

As they talked, they scanned the town and looked up at the faintly bright skies.

The six palanquin bearers came running and took over the well. They drew cold water with their waist ladles and carried it back to the palanquins' sides.

"Aah, delicious," they heard a voice say.

One after another, the laborers wetted their faces from the bucket, quenched their thirst, wrung out the hand towels that wrapped their heads, then went back, hoisted the palanquins, and sprinted from the town to the castle.

Ryousetsu left the shade of the tree to see them off in silence. A huge sigh escaped.

"That was a momentous arrival," he mumbled.

Kamiya watched his face and said, "Priest, what on Earth has happened?"

"You don't know?"

"Why should I?"

"It's like something sung about by Toshibi …"

> *Lacquer trees are divided according to use.*
> *Oils are brewed according to brightness.*
> *Orchids scatter in white fog.*
> *Katsura trees bend before the autumn*
> *winds.*

Ryousetsu went alone to the corner where the fast palanquins turned like they forgot they were carrying passengers.

Just then, a burly vassal flew out shoulders first through the air. His power and massive physique collided with Ryousetsu who crossed his path. The vassal heavily breathed out an apology, "I'm sorry," and ran off.

The staggering Ryousetsu called out, "Aren't you Yoko-gawa-san from Gunpowder Mountain? Hey, Kanpei-dono, Kanpei-dono."

But the man already ran up to the moat and never looked back. Eventually, with the tip of his sheath raised, he took long strides through the gate of the *nagayamon* row house barracks of the residence of the daimyo's chief retainer, Oishi Kuranosuke.

31

AFTER A NATIONAL CRISIS

A T THIS TIME, the door to the inner sleeping chamber of the lord was not normally open, but all the doors on both wings of the nagayamon were wide open but not for cleaning the main building and the drawing room.

After five in the morning on the fourteenth, Hayami Tozaemon and Kayano Sanpei left Edo and traveled the long distance of 427 miles with no rest or sleep.

Now in the last twenty minutes of the five o'clock hour, their journey endured for four and a half days ended. Of course, the two men looked to be on the brink of death.

A little before the palanquins arrived at Oishi's home, the bearer running in front knocked on the gate to report the arrival of the express messengers from Edo. Every member of the family was awake and anxiously awaited their arrival while they wondered what happened.

In the kitchen, gruel was cooking. His wife Riku, son Chikara, and the servants all came out to the entryway steps. They saw the palanquins and recognized the men.

"Aren't they Hayami-sama and Kayano-sama?"

The men were offered medicated baths. The cords of

their straw sandals were untied. They were taken by the hand and led up the steps. The compassion shown was sincere, but Kuranosuke's voice was not heard and he was not seen.

"I'm sorry, but my father will formally greet you in a few moments."

Tozaemon gave a slight bow to Chikara and assured Riku of his courage as he staggered past them. In his condition, Sanpei only breathed. A servant carried him on his back to the tatami mats. His hands dropped to the tatami.

"Aaah ..."

He looked like he was about to faint.

Tozaemon raised his voice to lift Sanpei's spirit.

"Did the chief retainer wake up early?"

Riku answered, "Yes, he's been waiting in the study for a little while."

Sanpei raised his chest like a plucked string and removed the metal kougai rod from his short sword sheath. His hands nimbly combed his hair tousled over four and a half days. He pulled the wrinkles out of the clothes from his neck down to the hem of his hakama trousers, then spoke for the first time.

"May we be shown in?"

This morning, like every morning, the light of dawn and quiet energy enlivened the inner study. However, the two messengers passed inside by sidling in on their knees and looked up at the intimidating face of the seated Kuranosuke. A foreboding of a serious rebuke awakened their spirits.

Without altering his expression, Kuranosuke said, "What is it? Don't speak on extraneous matters. Fast palanquins make me uneasy. Please, get to the point."

"On the fourteenth, the lord wounded a man with his

sword in Edo Castle. This letter from Kataoka Gengoemon describes the incident. We left Edo when the commotion began. News about the lord, his punishment, and other details will arrive later by some unknown number of fast messengers."

Kuranosuke took the paper held out by Tozaemon and read it in silence. Blood settled in his expression with each line. Like a heat wave drifting into the depths of calm, excitement was not visible anywhere on his pudgy body.

He finished reading and only said, "Uh-huh."

A low sigh resembling a moan could be heard behind his closed lips. He directed his dark, bushy eyebrows toward the garden and looked far into the distance.

Brightness shined in the chirps of small birds and in the colors of dawn beyond the eaves. The big drooping cherry blossom tree he cherished was in full bloom like the queen of the garden. Unlike a typical morning, each white blossom reflected in Kuranosuke's pupils like a throng of unlucky larvae.

"This is a troublesome matter. Please go rest."

Kuranosuke rose when he spoke these kind words to the two men and went into his sitting room. The breakfast attended by the entire family would soon start. A short time after six in the morning rang out in the castle, he was dressed for an appearance at the castle, stepped out of the entryway, and seen off by the alarmed faces of his wife Chikara.

The gunpowder guard Yokogawa Kanpei standing to the side in the entryway spotted Kuranosuke and gave a wobbly bow.

Kuranosuke's displeased eyes glanced at his face.

"Aren't you Yokogawa?"

"Yessir …"

"Why have you come down the mountain?"

"Last night, from Wakiyama I saw the unusual lights of fast palanquins crossing Chikusa River and entering the castle town. It bothered me and I ran to the mansion. It was a premonition because a little while ago Chikara-dono said a report came of the lord drawing blood in Edo. I was worried about the chief retainer's heartache and the clan's surprise. I'm stunned and stand here a bit confused."

"Isn't your vital duty to guard the gunpowder storehouse on Wakiyama?"

"Yessir."

"Why did you leave your post without permission? If you thought it was that sort of emergency, that's all the more reason to stay at your post. Return to the mountain now."

This was not his usual scolding. It echoed in Chikara's and Riku's ears. The servants were cut to the quick like he was upbraiding them.

Before a moment passed, official notice was sent to the vassals to appear in the castle.

Given the unexpected summons, everyone was asking, "What happened?"

More than two hundred resident vassals arrived one after another at the front castle gate of Kariya Castle.

Fast post horses and express messengers dashed to district magistrates and government officials in regions outside the castle town. Around the time the sun was at its height, day fog resembling an ominous cloud swept grayness over the castle keep of Kariya Castle. A fraught atmosphere shrouded the entire clan.

The serious incident in Edo from the mouths of the express messengers became the talk among the townsmen in the castle town.

Like samurai reminded of an oncoming war, instinctively, the townsmen were anxious and in an uproar.

"If the shogunate confiscates the clan's domain, what'll we do with the clan's money we hold?"

"If the lord is ruined, won't the clan's scrip become worthless scraps of paper?"

The tradesmen, merchants, and peasants stampeded to the homes of the town elders, but they made little progress. Crowds gathered at each crossroad and barged into the office of the currency magistrate that prints the clan's scrip.

"Please exchange this scrip for gold."

"Why are you handing in the clan's scrip?"

"Please exchange it. Please change it to gold that I can use."

Of course, the magistrate and the inspector were at the castle. A servant closed the gate to the government office and silenced them. With each moment, the townsmen in the run on the treasury grew in number.

"Exchange the scrip for gold!"

A force emerged that risked becoming thrown rocks, torn down fences, and a riot.

32

ROCKS IN THE WAVES

T HE NUMBER OF men gathered in one room in the castle, from the senior ranks of the chief retainer and the keeper of the castle down to the rank-and-file soldiers, gave the appearance of war.

Over three hundred men were affiliated with the clan as Ako soldiers. A proclamation ordering the soldiers to appear at the castle this morning surprised the more than two hundred men not stationed in Edo. An anxious light filled their eyes as they assembled in the castle keep.

Eventually, heavy footsteps from the business office brought five men: Head of the Chief Retainers Oishi Kuranosuke, Keeper of the Castle Ono Kurobei, Steward Tanaka Seibei, and Inspectors Mase Kyudayu and Uemura Yogoemon. Their faces were hardened like wood carvings.

They sat, and Kuranosuke told the gathering about the incident in Edo. With great sorrow, he read the letter brought by the express messengers.

"We still have no confirmation about what happened next. I believe that news will come with the next messenger. Given the situation, brace for the worst. Each of you will prepare yourself as usual. Do not take this lightly."

Countless stunned faces froze and gulped saliva. For a short time, no one spoke.

"The lord, the lord ... shed blood?" someone asked incredulously. Eventually, the indisputable fact crushed them from the depths of their hearts.

"But ... seppuku takes place on the same day."

Heavy breaths were drawn like a nightmare in a bad dream. The eyes of some faces despaired, and the shock paled other faces.

"Why did he attack Kira?" asked one with shoulders shaking.

"Chief Retainer!"

Parched voices from the seats didn't stop talking.

"Not one word in the letter mentioned his rival Kozuke no Suke. The messengers said nothing about the judgment?"

All eyes bombarded Kuranosuke with looks saying we want to know!

Kuranosuke opened his eyes to answer without words. Kurobei beside him unfolded his arms stuck deep into his sleeves to compensate for his opaque demeanor.

"After this morning's first fast palanquins carrying Hayami and Kayano, another express messenger has probably left Edo and will soon appear. The skies of Edo are far away. We will only know in time."

Before he finished, the racket of whispering voices disrupted the gathering. Although asked to quiet down and wait for the next report, that request was unreasonable to passionate, red-blooded men like Kurobei and Kuranosuke, who left it to the individual hearts of the silent men, the whispering men, the resentful men, the men moving their eyes restlessly, and the men groaning in melancholy. Kurobei and Kuranosuke placed themselves like rocks among the waves of the huge shock to all the vassals.

Mimura Jirozaemon, who did not attend because he was helping in the kitchen, peeked into the adjacent room from the tatami corridor but saw no one and shouted, "Keeper of the Castle! Keeper of the Castle!"

Kurobei turned his wrinkled face around and stood. His already stooped waist bent further. However, he took pride in being an old man favored with good health and promptly passed into the next room.

"Mimura, what's going on?"

Jirozaemon kneeled and said, "There's unrest in the castle town. It's not just one group. Please look from the tower."

"Unrest. What sort of unrest? I have nothing to do with the business of the townsmen."

He put his face through the gap in the tower and, with no one telling him, he was staring at the clan's vassals who had been in the hall now gathered in clusters of four or five in the castle town.

Yellow dust rose above the town. Huge lines resembling columns of ants were visible at the crossroads and centered on the gate of the scrip printing mansion. They formed a boisterous circle around the fence. Small scuffles filled with violent menace were breaking out with the town elders and the meeting hall officials attempting to block them.

"Those townsmen heard the rumors of the calamity visited on this house and are fighting to exchange their clan scrip. This is bad!"

Not just Kurobei, several frowning vassals witnessing this returned to the hall as this bitter experience sank in.

"Despite living many tranquil years under the protection of the lord, they descend into this despicable behavior.

They've forgotten their obligations, consider only personal losses and gains, and shove their way through to exchange the scrip."

The vassals were upset and encouraged action from the clan.

"They must be arrested. The town elders and the meeting hall officials have lost control of this situation."

"It's difficult to forgive the townsmen. They're probably the ringleaders. If five or six of them are tied up now, they'll quiet down."

The effect was far-reaching. A portion of the Earth's crust collapsed in Edo over four hundred miles away and seemed to emerge in this madness far from Edo and boil up in the earth of Ako.

The Edo shock was a tremor in the system. This reality sent a shudder through life. If the lord committed seppuku, the castle will be confiscated, and the vassals will scatter. The scrip issued by the Asano clan will lose value and become scrap paper.

If the accumulated gold for eating awful food, sweating and working, lowering your head one hundred times for profit and a small amount of money only for nurturing parents, wives, and children are reduced to worthless paper, a townsman may go crazy. This fire was the substance that becomes a riot.

Kuranosuke scanned in amazement the gathered faces.

"Okajima! Katsuta! Sugino!" he called and watched each one stand in turn. "Maebara!"

The four men came forward, stood before him, and stared at the tension in his stern brow. Like he already guessed the mission to be ordered, Maebara Isuke asked, "Chief Retainer, are we going to the castle town?"

"Yes, but ..." Kuranosuke stopped and stared at the

four and thought all were too young. Turning to the side, Senba Saburobei was seated nearby.

"Saburobei, you'll be good. There's the potential for a riot. Go now and calm them, boost their faith in the lord."

"Yessir."

"Fuwa, you go, too," he said, pointing to Fuwa Kazuemon behind him.

"The uproar created by the townsmen is not unreasonable. They must be reassured. After spotting any disturbance, they run there. We've already erred. Don't try to browbeat them to convince them. Tell them they'll be able to exchange the clan scrip tomorrow and to go home."

"Yessir."

Senba Saburobei was a sensible man nearing fifty. Fuwa Kazuemon was the coastal magistrate, possessed ample knowledge of public sentiment, and was friendly with the townsmen. With confidence, Kuranosuke sent the pair off, then he turned back to the other four.

"We are going to the business office," he said and stood.

33

TWO CHIEF RETAINERS

C OUNTLESS LEDGERS SUCH as the clan scrip ledgers, the treasury ledgers, and the loan notes to businesses on the shore were stacked before Kuranosuke.

"I'd like Ono-san to be present."

Ono Kurobei saw the mountain of ledgers and said nothing, then asked, "What is the urgent matter?"

"We don't have a moment to waste. The clan's scrip will be exchanged."

"Oh, will the total value of the scrip be exchanged for gold?"

"Probably not."

Katsuta Shinzaemon, an assistant in the scrip printing office, set up a desk, tallied the thick account books, entered the amounts in key places, and stacked them beside Kuranosuke.

Okajima Yasoemon, the magistrate of accounts, accompanied by Sugino and Maebara entered the treasury with ledgers in hand and returned to the business office.

"I finished copying them," he said while reviewing the report.

"The clan's total gold reserve is 7,000 ryo. Up to today, the outstanding scrip totaled 12,000 ryo. I calculate a difference of 5,000 ryo."

"All right …"

From the side, Kurobei groaned, looked at Kuranosuke, and said with a sense of defeat, "In no way does the current gold reserves of 7,000 ryo cover 12,000 ryo."

Kuranosuke watched the abacus operated by Shinzaemon and read the result.

He brightened and said, "We can use a 60% exchange rate."

"A 60% exchange rate?" Kurobei had doubts. "Well, not leaving out one ryo, how do you intend to use the clan's gold reserves for future activities and miscellaneous expenses of the clan?"

"I'll worry about that later. More than that, there's no other way to handle this situation. If you consider the future, what's in store for their pitiful lives?"

"It's difficult to do something that's rarely done."

As his elder, Kurobei's attitude toward the younger Kuranosuke among the senior retainers was always admiration. In human terms, their association was neither love nor hate. They conducted clan business smoothly. However, Kurobei couldn't help thinking Kuranosuke lacked experience. Kurobei's view of Kuranosuke was pragmatic. Although his usual working behavior was mindless and his demeanor somewhat dull, he had seniority because of his family lineage. Common sense said that without him, no other man could oversee 53,000 koku.

Kuranosuke's high-strung nature probably made him dogmatic and place power into the ends of his words not spoken to challenge a rival. While Kurobei thought Kuranosuke was unpopular, for the first time, he felt hostile toward him.

"Oishi-dono, this is not normal. How will you explain this later? What will you do? Money funds the reorganization of the clan and the withdrawal fee within the clan. Also, if irresponsibly imitated in some future calamity, it will not work."

Given his tendency to talk as old men do, when he flew into a rage, he upbraided an underling. However, Kuranosuke nodded in agreement with his words.

"You are absolutely right. However, this is not on my authority. My guide is the lord's spirit and to do as he would."

"When did the lord leave a message on this matter? Your reasoning is faulty!"

"…"

"This is not a laughing matter! Oishi-dono, this time, as the chief retainer, you must take on this formidable duty."

"Of course."

"Paying everyone with the cash reserves in the treasury without careful consideration is the lord's will. How do I make sense of that?"

"You have given this careful consideration. Excuse me, Ono-san, you have held the critical post of providing counsel since the time of the previous lord and throughout the childhood of Takumi no Kami-sama until today and are well acquainted with the lord's character. If the lord were here, what would he say? Do you know his heart?"

"If the lord were here? … If the lord were here, this wouldn't be happening, would it?"

Sugino, Maebara, and Okajima around them said nothing and stared at the profiles of the two chief retainers. A huge gap in humanity was evident between Kuranosuke who said to do what's in the lord's spirit and Ono Kurobei who objected to Kuranosuke's claim of knowing the views of the absent lord.

The spectators knew these two chief retainers usually worked amicably but had clashing personalities and could not look away.

Kuranosuke had always been unpopular even among the young samurai who were not devoted to Ono. They'd say, "Kuranosuke can't make up his mind."

At worst, they'd say he's as useless as a lantern in the daylight. If he seemed to be persuaded by Kurobei's opinion and about to back down, amazingly, Kuranosuke would persist and rebel with an emphatic "No!"

However, his complexion did not change. Earlier, he showed his smile to rebuke Kurobei.

Kuranosuke said, "You do not understand the consequences. I'd like you to leave it to me."

Before his rival objected, he said, "Shinzaemon, put up notice boards at the crossroads. Have the carpenters make ten."

He took a writing brush and wrote a draft announcement of the 60% exchange rate for the clan scrip and handed it to Okajima Yasoemon.

"Write this on the notice boards and erect them at the usual places. Be quick." He gave the order like there was no time to spare.

They were notified when the boards were finished. As Okajima and the others rushed out, they passed Yoshida Chuzaemon, the district magistrate of Kato-gun who came by horse. He was late because he began his journey far from the castle town. He entered the business office with dirt stuck to his sweaty face.

"I'm here." He greeted Kuranosuke who turned his head to look.

"Ah, … Yoshida-san?"

The sight of Chuzaemon moved Kuranosuke's heart with an emotion he had forgotten, and hot tears welled up.

34

THE DEPTHS OF TWILIGHT

YOSHIDA CHUZAEMON'S BONY build made him look around sixty years old. His waist was straight, and he stood six feet tall. His lips were plump and deep red like an old man's. His gray hair resembled corn silk. Were his skin darker than any peasant's and his muscular build the results of being posted only in the countryside?

However, his spirit was gentle like a woman's. The peasants where he was posted came to love him like a loving father. When he came to the castle town, he wore a soldier's camp helmet and rode a horse. Potatoes and ginseng burdocks were tied to the horse's back as gifts for Kuranosuke's home where he always stayed.

On the nights he visited, the two forgot about their posts and talked. Kuranosuke had a taste for sake, and Chuzaemon was a drinker. They couldn't be called close confidantes, but Chuzaemon glimpsed some of Kuranosuke's personality. No one probed deeper into Chuzaemon's intelligence as a rural magistrate in Kato-gun than Kuranosuke.

They were so-called best friends who indulged each

other. That may have been why vague emotions moved Kuranosuke the moment he saw Chuzaemon.

"I've been waiting for you," said Chief Retainer Kuranosuke, burdened by a great crisis and sitting like a rock or a man.

Chuzaemon said, "I don't know what to say … Not a word …" and stared at a spot on the tatami.

"More than anything, I know the clan's disaster will not become a disaster to the people of the domain. I just established an emergency plan to exchange the clan's scrip."

"You've done well. From the start of my journey in Kato-gun to the castle town on the shore, the looks on the faces of the peasants and the townspeople weighed on me. What you're doing is what the lord would have wished."

Chuzaemon and Kuranosuke were men of few words, but these words expressed a thousand emotions. Apparently on business, Kurobei went out to the hall swathed in the colors of twilight. In anticipation of night, the kitchen servants moved between the scattered groups standing or walking to serve hand-rolled rice on sushi trays, but not one hand reached out.

A monk lit the mesh lanterns on the *bonbori* lamp stands and placed the paper lanterns in the hall. This failed to lift the day's gloom.

Unable to do anything, each one speculated or pondered with varying degrees of desperation over the steps to take. The air became stagnant and blackened like sediment muddying a swamp. All around Kuranosuke in the business office abacuses clicked, ledger pages rustled when turned, and accountants' tense faces flickered red under the candlelight. No one noticed the sun go down.

Eventually, a relieved-sounding Kuranosuke said, "Very good."

For the time being, the uncollected land taxes, the total

loans to be returned to the salt makers on the beach, and the current total rice stores of the clan were thoroughly assessed.

He held warm tea in his mouth, then asked, "Where's Ono?"

"He's with some samurai."

Kuranosuke left and invited Kurobei to another room, but after some time, he didn't appear. The others watched the pine door where the two chief retainers deliberated over critical matters.

"Sotomura-dono, the chief retainer would like to see you."

Troop Leader Sotomura Genzaemon was nervous as he passed from a corner of the hall through the pine door. Soon he reappeared and raced to the front gate, apparently with urgent orders.

He was going to request 4,500 ryo from Lord Asano Geishu in Hiroshima.

Kuranosuke said that amount was the collection of unpaid land taxes in the domain and outstanding loans from that region. He used numbers to explain the detailed solution established over half a day. Kurobei began to come around.

"In that case, at the 60% exchange rate, exchanging the scrip will probably not be a burden."

After nine that evening, the downcast faces of the samurai in the ink dark hall colored by firelight were awakened by a report from the front gate.

"The second fast messenger has arrived!"

Both chief retainers Oishi and Ono rushed to the front of the group. The clan samurai still clung to a ray of hope, despite the first report of the lord's seppuku on the same day.

With a judgment viewed by the imperial envoy as a

rightful judgment of the shogunate, an escape route may have been provided just in time to save one life. But that was unlikely. Any chance to spare his life would have ruled out the singular judgment of seppuku on the same day.

This thought came to anyone's mind, but no one dared speak it. Each man contradicted his common sense. Only one man, the second messenger, thought, Is there any chance? He prayed with all his might for that ray of hope as he waited impatiently.

35

THE MANY SHAPES OF FALLEN
LEAVES

WHILE THEY STUDIED the expressions of Kuranosuke and Kurobei who soon returned from the front, foreboding stabbed the men's hearts.

It was seppuku.

A mysteriously chilly moment flowed over the hardened faces of the samurai. In the light of several candles, deep breaths were drawn.

Their intuition knew. The document read by Kuranosuke and the second report relayed by the messenger pushed the fate of the Ako clan into the darkness of despair.

At the end of Kuranosuke's stream of words explaining the report to over two hundred heads bowed and listening, the outburst began.

"I ... I don't understand his punishment."

"It takes two to fight. Isn't that an ironclad rule in the castle of the Edo shogunate?!"

"But Kira! Kira's life was spared. And he received gracious words from the shogun and was allowed to leave ..."

"That's not fair."

Excited voices erupted all around. When they thought about the lord's resentment, they could not keep quiet, wailed, and sunk into sobbing human shadows.

"Chief Retainer! Keeper of the Castle! The vital matter has already been decided. What have you decided to do?"

A young samurai already eased closer on his knees.

A voice from the back shouted to condemn the foolishness of his colleague.

"Idiot. Do you have to ask? The way of the samurai does not have two paths. Isn't a hero's death defending the castle the only way?"

This torrent resembled an armload of leaves falling into swirling rapids. The astonishment, action, and intention differed for each leaf. Faces flushed with blood, faces devoid of blood, vacant and dazed looks, expressions thinking only of themselves, and emotional looks thinking about nothing but anger were out of control and taking on the form of rising and falling leaves spiraling in swirling rapids.

"An envoy will come to take possession of the castle. But we will not step one foot outside of the castle. If we leave, the name of Ako will be disgraced."

"We will die! We will follow the lord!"

"If we are to die the same death, we should confront the enemy, who will come to take the castle, and fight a battle of vengeance to our satisfaction. There are men with backbone in Ako who will die."

"Well said. Objectors speak out."

The words of the agitated young samurai drowned out the nearby elders and the silent men. The hot-bloodied among them were no longer aware of Kuranosuke and Kurobei.

An anxious Kurobei attempted to speak but stayed silent. He only repeated to himself, This can't be allowed. Kuranosuke looked vacant and didn't seem to have a plan. Will he sink, float away, or hang onto a rock in the rapids? He looked like a fallen leaf caught by an eddy, at the mercy of the water. Only he looked like a bystander, a kingfisher perched on a tree branch sticking out of the water to scan the water.

His face revealed his concern over the endless turmoil.

"Ono-san, further deliberation would be too much. It's getting late. From here on, we must watch out for each other."

Kurobei gave a sharp nod and said, "Both of us should keep quiet. This grave clan matter is not a personal grudge. I wish to be careful about personal attacks and uncalled-for stubbornness on my part. Now, the clan will become one, act with restraint, and gain the admiration of others. Each willful controversy in the lord's absence will bring quick smiles to other clans. Tonight, everyone, except the fire lookouts and the storehouse workers, go home until the announcement to return to the castle. On that day, we will discuss everything."

He saw their reluctance and said, "You may go."

Kurobei stood; others stood wherever they wanted in the hall. Kuranosuke was talking to Yoshida Chuzaemon in the next room. Chuzaemon would stay in the castle, light the fires, and be on the night watch. They talked until they reached the entrance and parted.

Kuranosuke exited the front gate into a beautiful starry night.

36

FEAR IN IMPERIAL LANDS

K URANOSUKE WATCHED THE clan samurai scatter from the edge of the moat down the road to home. His heart ached for each shadow when he thought about the families, relatives, and followers they nurtured.

Oh, the lord … His gentle nature … Was he tempted by a demon?

He struggled to understand the lord's feelings but failed. No tears came. He was jolted by sorrow and wanted to cry for the innocent families of the rank-and-file who cared for aged mothers, sick people, and wives and children on tiny stipends of seven or ten koku.

When he gathered more details from the third and fourth reports and information coming from Edo, he would better understand the lord's feelings and his relationship with his rival, Kira. But first, he would view the lord's actions from his absolute sense of justice and common sense in the way of the samurai. In the lord's place, he wanted to apologize to the world, especially to the wives and children of the poor lower-ranking samurai and the foot soldiers, for the lord's inexcusable act.

More than anything, cowering before the imperial envoy would be disrespectful. That alone is no defense. He feared offering the life of the Ako clan and burying Kariya Castle as the tombstone would be insufficient as compensation for the crime.

"This matter will not be settled until I meet with Onodera Junai. I must see him soon."

He stood on Karahashi Bridge over the moat, staring at the water. A foamy tide rose from the water gate. He walked along the shore like the water was pushing him. Few mansions were in this area.

Since the young age of twenty-two, Kira Kozuke no Suke frequently went to the capital in Kyoto. He had been an envoy of the shogunate connected to the construction of Sento Imperial Palace. He also worked with his father Yoshifuyu as an intermediary between the Imperial Court and the shogunate on the abdication of Emperor Go-Sai and stood as an official greeter in the accession. And now, at sixty years old, he was an acquaintance or a relative of countless powerful court nobles. Naturally, Kira believed taking the initiative and carrying out a plan in that realm would bring him success. In the world of the Imperial Court moved only by superficial truths and emotions, and court nobles who grumble about the crime of disrespect, without Kira's influence, could the Ako clan be vindicated and apologize for the grave offense?

These thoughts sent a shudder down Kuranosuke's backbone.

"Hold the castle—Fall on your sword—Scatter— I'm worried about what to do, but after I meet with Junai ..."

This realization startled him and he stopped. In time, he was back at the nagayamon gate of his mansion. A human shadow black like a bat nimbly went back to the skirt of the earthen wall.

"..."

Kuranosuke turned and glimpsed the brazen man clinging to the fence. Unable to stay there, he moved from the corner and hid on the side. The man had been following him since the edge of the moat.

Kuranosuke had a hunch why the man was following him.

When an imperial mandate was issued to receive Matsuyama Castle eight years earlier, Kuranosuke played this petty trick. In no time, his spies entered the rival clan's domain.

"Everything on Earth and in Heaven goes around and comes around. What I did to others is now being done to me."

His entire family appeared to be kept awake by anxiety, and lights burned in the main building.

Kuranosuke feared the lights in his home. However, his gait changed to that of the head of the household. At the threshold of the entryway, the man leaped from his hiding place and said, "Master?"

He was an elderly farmer from Oseki village named Hachisuke. He had served faithfully as a servant in the mansion from Kuranosuke's youth. His body had endured the burden of water pails.

"This is wrong," said the elderly servant who returned to his son's home in Oseki a few years earlier.

"Oh, Uncle? ..."

His face brought back memories. After his parents died, Kuranosuke came to always think of this modest older man as a parent.

"Are you in town for amusement? It's good you came."

"What are you saying? The master's heart shouldn't worry about that.... This year will be disastrous. I could never imagine seeing the domain in this pitiful state."

Hachisuke pressed a hand towel into his face, forgot he was a man and cried.

Knowing the master would return home, light from standing paper-covered lanterns lit the entryway. His wife Riku cradling the suckling baby, his oldest son Chikara, and his second son Kichichiyo came out to greet him. The father and mother were not their usual selves, and the innocent children seemed joyless.

37

CLOUDS OF DUST

THE GLARING DIVISION caused by this blow was the difference in the positions of the samurai and the townspeople. The incident exposed the difference in their two ways of life and forced the conflict to the surface. Some had absolutely no life outside of the castle, the land, and the clan name. Others made calculations for themselves, carried their personal lives into the commotion in town, and bluntly and shrewdly asserted their interests.

The townsmen feared the scrip they clutched would turn into wastepaper. Later, they looked calmer and a little embarrassed. Notice boards announcing the 60% exchange rate for the clan scrip were erected at the crossroads. The townsmen's rival was the currency magistrate who readied the piles of cash.

Under the orders of Kuranosuke, the accountant Okajima Yasoemon anxiously spent yesterday and today in the mansion and assessed the situation. He observed the inactivity and asked, "Won't a 60% exchange rate upset the townsmen?"

From his desk, Katsuta Shinzaemon, an auditor of the

currency office, said, "No, that's not happening. Everyone who came to exchange his script apologized and returned home crying. The handling by Oishi-dono should be praised. The ones not coming to exchange their scrip have nothing to worry about."

"To the contrary, Oishi-dono said the problem is the delay in handling unfinished business. We will inform the town headman of the time limit. With a push from our office, the accounts for the clan scrip will be settled in two or three days."

"If that's not done, nothing will be settled before the return of the envoy who went to appeal to the members of the main family."

"No, the envoy on the way to ask Lord Geishu for cooperation was called back. All of a sudden, unpaid salt taxes and other levies were steadily collected. Oishi-dono's worried look over this will disappear."

"Well, the town headman will come under pressure soon."

The minds of the townsmen in the castle town perceived the calm surrounding the economic strength of the clan's treasury and, on that day, were already nimbly working in other directions. The smuggling of weapons exploded. Where was the demand coming from? Everything from the smaller *shu* or *bu* denominations of old eternal coins buried under dust in antique shops to blunt swords and rusty spears with no buyers disappeared in the blink of an eye.

On this morning's steamers, dozens of buyers from the Osaka-Kyoto region with cash attached to their necks came ashore, probably looking for sacrifice sales in the Ako castle town. Merchants with loud voices colored by Kyoto and Osaka accents and specialized knowledge of paintings and calligraphy, secondhand clothes, hand tools, curios, armor and weapons, and even paper scraps wandered the back streets of the residential parts of town. One group bought a cannon rumored to have been used during the Shimabara Rebellion and passed through town with their cannon loaded onto a cart. People out and about did not give the sight a second look.

"I'll buy a horse and pay any price for a good one."

Even horse dealers who rarely bought field horses bragged as they walked around full of confidence. They went to the mansions of the poor samurai of the clan and engaged the wives and women hungry for money. They pulled out and waved around unseemly amounts of money from their neck wallets. Even the bit of a purchased saddle rattled with pride as it was hauled through town. If that was viewed as the delightfulness of human nature and freedom in society, it was the same as inexhaustible interest. When they looked at the people at the beach, they claimed shortages of lighters and barges. Shipping agents frantically played tug-of-war with boatmen. The wages of workmen and porters soared thirty percent. Nevertheless, laborers ready to work could not be found.

The power of demand drew in unimaginable objects and people. The drastic changes in the economy centered on the collapse of one clan were unmistakable. The shrewd speculative spirits of the townsmen riding the wave and seizing opportunities bet on never-ending action. They seemed to lament the trip to the currency office to exchange the clan scrip.

38

———

THE TASTE OF SMARTWEED

DURING THE SHORT seven days from the nineteenth when news came of the incident to the twenty-fifth, the situation of the common people was apparent in the mental workings of the townsmen and their ability to live prosperous lives. The parts of town where the clan's samurai lived were the opposite, soundless swamps. The shadows of samurai walking or riding horses to settle unfinished business looked pitiful to the townspeople. They, who were not samurai, appreciated the opposite of ordinary.

Later, two more express messengers arrived from Edo. They only reported the closed gate at Asano Daigaku's residence and the completion of the eviction from the clan residence. Also, a call never came to gather in the castle. The men assigned to settle unfinished business persevered. The ones with little work closed the doors of the gate and did nothing other than mourn the lord. Musical performances were rumored to have been suspended by the Miyoshi branch of the same Asano clan as well as in

Hiroshima in Geishu, and sounds for enjoyment were no longer heard.

All the sounds in the world seemed to transform, as did the human heart. The farmers on the path of farmers and the townsmen on the path of townsmen did not drift aimlessly through life. In the end, this test was for the warriors. The current backbone of society and the power of government were neither in the shogun's clan nor in the lords of the domains. Power was held by the warriors wearing coarse clothing and eating crude food but still faithful to the old system.

They supported the men synonymous with brutishness, such as the samurai on duty in Edo and the low-ranking country samurai. The way of the samurai still lived in those men who were trusted by the common people. If the samurai seemed to betray their customary pledge or behavior, the common people might ridicule them.

In the backstreets or the alleys behind the mansions close to the main road, the ears of wheat, the flowers of vegetables, and the peaches on ridges in the fields grew unseen in places brightened by a fine sun far from the world. The backs of insects soaked in the sun; this made their bellies swell.

Several streams like veins flowed from Mount Uneyama through the castle town and stitched the cultivated land to the sea. Fourteen-year-old Oishi Chikara and his younger brother were walking along one water vein. Kichichiyo, an eleven-year-old, plunged both hands into the rice paddy turning them black and placed something into a straw wrapper.

"Please throw that out," Chikara said many times.

"No," said Kichichiyo as he shook the wrapping.

"Father is not going to eat that thing. So won't bringing it home be a waste?"

"Liar. Father likes them. Old Man Yoshida said so."

"He always used to eat them, but not anymore."

"Why?"

"After all that talking, and you still don't understand? The lord of the domain Takumi no Kami committed seppuku."

"I know that, but why can't he eat mud snails because the lord died?"

"You're a clueless child. Even on the anniversaries of the deaths of Grandfather and Grandmother, didn't we abstain for purification?"

"Well, mud snails aren't the same as fish."

"They're living creatures."

"Vegetables and radishes are living creatures, too."

"That makes no sense. Be a good boy. Throw them out and wash your hands in that stream over there."

A disappointed Kichichiyo tossed away the package of mud snails, washed his hands, and wiped them on his hakama trousers.

"Oh, it's the priest from Shofukuji Temple."

The two brothers took long strides for about sixty feet then stopped. The soiled sacred robe the color of dried leaves was so worn out it no longer held the shape of a sacred robe. He was the familiar Priest Ryousetsu. Oblivious to the boys standing behind him, he picked young grass along the shore of the stream and put it in his robe's sleeve.

"Ryousetsu-san, what are you doing?" called out Kichichiyo.

"Oh ..."

He looked back and understood the youths' hearts at a glance. It felt like the bright spring wind drifting by them blew from the breast of the baby-faced man.

"Where have you been?" asked Ryousetsu.

Kichichiyo pointed to the shadow of the mountain surrounding the back of the castle town.

"Ogaya."

"What were you doing there?"

"We heard a lot of soldiers from many provinces, Himeji, Okayama, and Takamatsu, were coming to launch attacks at Hosaka Cliffs and Takatori Pass. So me and Chikara went to see."

"Ha, ha, sightseers?"

"We saw the ocean, too."

"You probably did. Military boats are lined up on the sea such as the Kyougoku from Marugame in Sanshu, the Hachisuka from Tokushima in Awa, the Honda from Himeji, and the Matsuhira from Iyo. Many troops are being sent to the border to surround this Ako territory like a long castle wall. Arrows and gun barrels are pointing at your clan."

"It's war, Priest."

"Well, this situation is ever changing."

While his brother chatted with Ryousetsu, a silent Chikara smiled. He glanced at Ryousetsu's hand and asked, "Priest, what were you picking over there?"

"Me?"

Ryousetsu stared at the dirt under his fingernails and said, "I'm picking dropwort, but only smartweed grows around here."

"If you want, we can help."

"No, no, I'm fine. I don't need them that much. Chief Retainer Oishi is probably home."

"Father is home but ..."

Ryousetsu straightened up and said, "I'd been thinking about visiting and at long last I've come. It always becomes a feast. Today, I'm only bringing a side dish and began picking dropwort, but there's not much dropwort only smartweed. Look, there's red smartweed here and over there."

He walked off and said, "Here's some red smartweed. Do you know why there's so much red smartweed in Ako?"

"No."

"I'm sorry. I mixed up the question. There's been a lot of red smartweed in this area since ancient times. That's why this region is called Ako, which means red plant ears."

"I never heard that before."

"Not knowing that sort of thing is fine, but there is something you must know."

"What's that?"

"Service."

"I'm learning about that from Father."

"Did you ask about the physician? He probably delves in with his heart and soul. To be a samurai is service. There is no other work. Have you read *The Code of the Samurai* by Yamaga Soko-sensei?"

"Yes."

"He writes about that plant. It's as useless as a lantern or the moon during the day. Even horses don't eat smartweed, but it's a clear sign of the goodness of the soil and the sun. When it's time to fish for sweetfish in the Chikusa River, isn't it a necessary garnish for sweetfish grilled in miso sauce? Its flavor is sharp and stings the tongue. It provides a fine service that purges bugs in the stomach and becomes medicine for hot weather. Usually, it looks like a worthless weed, but every man to his taste."

Ryousetsu played with the flower of the smartweed with his lips and bit it to release its sweet flavor.

"Ako samurai are red smartweed samurai. That's what I want to be. From its start, the nature of a clan warrior was not the result of rich harvests and beautiful scenery or created from the gentle sea breeze of Setonouchi or the soil of Chugoku. That essence from my grandfathers and great-grandfathers unable to fight the nature of men in the clan is still embedded deep inside me. Now three generations later, it's probably become diluted in me. Do you know where that's from?"

"It's probably a teaching of Yamaga Soko-sensei."

"Of course, I'm inspired by Yamaga-sensei. However, I question the inspiration that reaches the natural human, the land, and humanity. Yamaga-sensei was not a man of this province but from Aizu."

"Until the middle of the imperial era of Prince Naganao, the lord was in Kasama Castle in Hitachi. I heard our grandfather Yoshikane and great-grandfather Yoshikatsu both came from Hitachi. So when Father looks at me, he always says with a smile, 'You carry the bones of Kanto.'"

"Kuranosuke-dono was born in Ako, but he already possessed the backbone of Kanto to add to the benevolence of Ako. The lands west of Kyoto are rich in natural products. The scenery is beautiful, and the culture is enlightened. Therefore, great winds lazily blow there, but the light of wisdom brightens humanity. Hitachi is whipped by winds, and has rough terrain and unrefined but grows stouthearted and resolute people. I believe a man like Chief Retainer Oishi embodies the middle path between these two."

Chikara vaguely wondered why Priest Ryousetsu was quick to assess with a critical eye his father who has been a good friend for many years and dissected his character. The reason was Ryousetsu liked his father and relied on him. Chikara thought Ryousetsu was guiding him more than anyone else about the importance of his father's position in this crisis.

39

ONE DIRECTION

EW WORDS ARE needed between friends. If one says, "A game?" and the response is "Okay," everything has been said.

Ryousetsu always said this to get someone to take out the Go board. A household member would set up the board and the stones between the two. The clacking sounds of the black and white stones soon leaked from the room. Sensitive to Kuranosuke's feelings, a household member brought tea but could not detect any dust at the positions that differed each time of the host and guest sandwiching the Go board set up to the side in the southern part of the library.

Kuranosuke laughed sometimes. Ryousetsu's cheerful voice was especially loud. Occasionally, the scratching sounds of moving stones were heard.

"Ma'am. Ma'am," Ryousetsu would call to Kuranosuke's wife.

"Yes," Riku answered and appeared after a short time.

Ryousetsu looked at her pale face, and Riku cast down her eyes. Not one hair was out of place.

"Ma'am, …"

"Yes."

"Earlier, I left some dropwort in the kitchen. Could I trouble you to make boiled greens or sesame spinach?"

"As you wish."

"And I probably don't have to tell you, my usual drink."

"Of course," said Riku but glanced at her husband who looked uncertain.

Ryousetsu caught her eye and asked, "Chief Retainer, wouldn't you like sake?"

Kuranosuke turned his bright eyes as if to repel Ryousetsu's eyes pressuring him. Next, he turned his glum face to the flowers of the drooping cherry tree that faded entirely over four or five days and drew his lips into a line.

"Would you? I know the chief retainer has been dressed for mourning from the start. If you do not drink, I, a humble priest, will not drink."

Kuranosuke touched the Go stones and said, "Another game."

"All right …"

"Riku, bring what you've prepared. The usual fish will be fine."

Ryousetsu placed his stone with a clack. He asked, "Do you approve?"

"I do," Kuranosuke said with no particular meaning.

The days were long in the spring. Patient eyes were buried in the black and white on the board made from evergreen. The lingering aroma of dropwort from the trays went unnoticed and was forgotten.

"Chief Retainer, are you going to eat?"

"Wait."

"I'll wait, but around this time my stomach …"

"Wait."

"Will we hold the castle?"

"Well …"

"Will we surrender the castle?"

"That would be rash."

"You will move slowly at first."

"Something like that."

Ryousetsu snapped his head around to the bowl smelling of dogwort. He picked up a goblet and pushed it in front of Kuranosuke's pensive face to show him the space in the cup.

"Breathe."

"I'll eat."

"Will you have a drink? A cup?" asked Ryousetsu holding up the sake bottle for emphasis. When he gave up prodding and trying to pour the sake, it came out.

"If you drink this while mourning for your lord, is that bad or good?"

"I'll pour."

"Is that okay?"

"My body is fine. The life of a samurai is vast."

Ryousetsu stretched his thick throat and tapped his knees. His pleasant laughing voice seemed to come from the ceiling to fill the room. He did not pour the sake from the bottle into Kuranosuke's cup but into his own empty teacup and drank.

"That's it. A wide path for the monk and a vast path for the warrior are fine."

What use is a game of Go? His sleeve had already scattered the stones. Kuranosuke picked up the ones that had fallen to the foot of the board and ended the game with no regrets. Then he repeated several times, "It's vast. That's it. What a relief. Now, I have peace of mind."

Ryousetsu put his dirty heels in his zori sandals and

exited the back garden with a light heart to go home. Kuranosuke stood with his back to the edge of the veranda to see him off. With an odd feeling of distant wild voices at his back, he turned around.

40

THE FLOWERS NEVER SEEN

YESTERDAY, A RONIN wearing straw sandals and hakama trousers hiked up and ready for a fight visited the nagayamon gate holding a nine-foot spear as a cane. He carried an armor storage box on his back. Today again, a ronin with a sparse beard on a sunburned face and similarly dressed came using a spear as his cane. His severe eyes shined when he soundlessly entered the gate of Oishi's mansion.

A ronin faced the entryway and stuck out his chest. "I'm at your service!"

No response came from inside the mansion. Startled by the voice, a figure in the shadows of the inner shrubbery shook the leaves of a tree.

Beneath the window near the guest drawing room, the movements were not simply those of a man bending in like a sly cat burglar. When the eyes separated by some distance seemed to meet, the figure ran at a diagonal through the shrubbery and escaped outside the nagayamon gate.

He wore navy leggings on his shins and a currency scale at his waist. He was a townsman and looked like a traveler who arrived not too long ago. Just as the ronin placed his spear on his side, he walked sideways in pursuit of the shadow of a man running between the trees.

"Pow!"

He punched the nose of his opponent who leaped out, knocking him out.

The townsman with a ghastly pale face cowered. As the ronin raised his spear in one hand, his other hand grabbed the man's collar. He glared and said, "You're from another province."

"Yes, yes. I'm a merchant from Kyoto. I'm not some weirdo."

"Liar."

"Why would I lie? I'm telling you, I'm Hikobei, a secondhand goods dealer, go ask at any established shop in Junkeibori. I have a license and walk to many provinces to buy goods."

While he screamed and struggled against the hand clamped to the back of his neck, the elderly servant Hachisuke was turning the earth in the forty-square-yard field beside the row house.

"Huh?" He turned and came running, gripping the hoe.

The man jumped up, but the hoe whacked his leg hard. Hachisuke swung again and cursed, "This bastard's a spy."

"A spy?"

The ronin let go of his neck. The man said, "Ouch," and fell flat on his face.

"Listen, he sounds like he's from Shikoku."

The man's hip bone was worn out by the butt end of the spear making him tumble over three times. His nose was scraped to a bright strawberry red. He jumped up and escaped outside the gate like a tossed-out cat.

"Uncle, do guys like him come often?"

"Just when we're careless or there are gaps. Well, that's how it is. Yatanojo-sama, it's good you came."

"Is the chief retainer home?"

"He is. Izeki Monzaemon-sama, a ronin of this clan; Tokubei-sama; Okano Jidayu-sama, and Ooka Seikuro-sama visited him yesterday."

"Did they rush here?"

"I'm just a ronin but I will never forget the kindness of the Asano clan," said Hachisuke, his eyes welling up with tears.

"Uncle, are you tilling the field?"

"The chief retainer ordered me to divide the roots of the chrysanthemums for transplanting."

"That's a strange thing to do. Maybe, the chief retainer intends to see the chrysanthemums bloom at this mansion this fall?"

"It sounded odd so I asked again. The chief retainer said that no matter which clan receives the fief after the Asano clan, the people of any clan must have the pleasure of seeing the flowers in bloom every fall, and to not leave shriveled flowers behind. I think that's proper, but it's not only about the chrysanthemums. I think it was to sow seeds, prune, and burn fallen leaves."

Hachisuke kept talking as he went to the gate to announce the visitor. Meanwhile, Yatanojo ladled water from the well into the washbasin for feet. The call from inside was to come right in. Nakamura Yatanojo placed his spear and armor box on the entryway steps and passed through.

"It's been a while."

A man of few words, Yatanojo said only that and placed both hands on the ground. Of the men formerly in the clan and now distant memories to those now in the clan, he was the fifth to come after hearing of the incident. Kuranosuke was delighted they reassessed the virtue of the late lord and came.

"I've come prepared and have no regrets over leaving my wife and child. I think I'm useless, but I'm a ronin. Even while sleeping, I couldn't forget the kindness of my former clan. Please, use this body as you wish. On my way here, two or three thousand soldiers from different clans hardened the peaks at the provincial borders with Takatori and Hotate.

"I wondered why horses and weapons in the domain haven't been taken quickly to where the enemy lies. The rumors in the streets are the Ako people will hold the castle with all their might and surely unify with other provinces. Please understand the innermost thoughts of a man who came running, dressed in old armor and carrying a rusty spear, and let one more man join the castle siege. Even if I'm a fool, I wish to repay the favors of the late lord with my life."

What core human truth did his faltering words strike? How could Kuranosuke refuse him? He was troubled. Hands on his knees, he slumped and fidgeted. When his companion finished speaking, he bowed his head, feeling unworthy of the man's sincerity. He said in a soft voice, "You're a man of high principles."

"What can I say? I have no words but am overjoyed. Every man is not a samurai in the Asano clan, but each one values justice. And the law of the world says to gather ronin and rise in revolt against the shogunate. I am grateful for your wish to not sully the previous lord's name. However, I will announce the farewell to the castle. Yesterday, I said as much to Okano, Izeki, and Ooka."

For half the day yesterday, they struggled with that, but Kuranosuke did not budge. No matter which direction he was viewed from, his troubled look, like a rock, never changed.

"Tonight, I must get a good night's sleep," said Kuranosuke. He ordered an evening meal for Yatanojo and then retreated to his bedroom. He mulled over a plan for a grand meeting in the castle to bring consensus to the clan's samurai to be held on the twenty-seventh, the following day.

PART V

THE RECORD OF BIRDS FLYING AWAY

41

A RIVER TO CROSS

S WEAT ROLLED DOWN the back of the lined kimono. White splotches drawn on the kimono's solid brown front resembled smudges on old paper.

Muramatsu Sandayu looked at his father's back and thought a halo glowed from the salt in the sweat. He pondered how much sweat could be wrung from a sixty-year-old body and was moved to tears.

"Father, you can see Mount Shosha from here."

"Yes, I see it."

They panted and gasped for air in the ascent to the peak, but on the descent, the elderly Kihei hurried down with the young Sandayu behind him. In this way, he hated being beaten.

On Taketori Pass they were crossing, nearly four hundred soldiers from the Himeji clan set up camp and established wartime checkpoints. They lined up their spears and guns and menaced travelers on the roads. The father and son passed through but stared right at the soldiers, never lowering their heads.

"Muramatsu Kihei and Muramatsu Sandayu stationed in Edo."

A guard called out their names and waved them through.

"Are you returning to your home province from Edo?" asked a commander in the Himeji clan wearing armor suited to his rank. He empathized with their weariness from a long journey.

"Goodbye." Kihei gave a brusque farewell. "I see the dispatch of troops. Since there's no trouble in the area, each one is working hard. If we're at the brink of war, we may meet on the battlefield."

They swiftly passed through the enemy's encampment. His ears still rang with the amused-sounding voice of the Himeji clan's commander.

"I see it! There it is."

This time, Kihei was pointing. He saw the Ako castle town, the Chikusa River, and the Onzaki shore. Their pace quickened. They came out at the foot of the mountain and eventually reached the banks of the river.

"Son, let's rest."

Kihei sat on a rock. He sighed with relief over the distance they traveled stretching 390 miles. He grabbed his hand towel to wipe the sweat off his chest.

"Well, Sandayu."

"Yes."

"You will go home from here."

"What?"

"Return to Edo."

Sandayu looked dejected, bent his knees, and inched closer to his father. "But that wasn't the promise."

"The reason I let you come was to defeat your enthusiasm. We've traveled this far together, but once you enter the castle town on foot, you will not be able to return home. This river is the boundary. Reconsider and go back to Edo. In my place, you will be a good son and care for your old mother. And watch for problems with your weak younger brother."

"Your words surprise me. Haven't mother and my brother said their goodbyes to us in this world? How can I abandon my father to death and turn around here? I'm not going back."

"Your intentions alone for a warrior's justice and a father and son's journey are splendid. If you step on the ground of the castle town, death is certain either by holding the castle or following the lord to the grave. Before you reach that point, you can escape. Go home now."

"No, that's no good. I won't."

"Your father is ordering you." Kihei's clouded eyes turned away. "Why won't you obey?"

The father's heart well understood Sandayu. His family taught their children to be this way. Despite the disagreement with his father, he decided not to go home. In contrast to the hardening of his fierce spirit, his eyes poured tears non-stop onto the grass like a child.

Someone was tying up a horse in the tree shade behind them. Kihei turned and in a disciplined voice said, "Good day."

An armor box was loaded on one side of the horse's back and a wicker trunk on the other. An elderly warrior with gray hair and a smiling, ruddy face came toward them. He was wearing a soldier's camp helmet and wrapped in traveling clothes with rigid hand protectors and leggings. He was Onodera Junai, the daimyo's attendant living in Kyoto.

Junai asked, "Why didn't you stop by my home in Kyoto on your way back to the home province?"

"We heard you already left," Kihei answered.

"Did you hear that those living in the city of the Imperial Court fled in the night in confusion? I rushed here only after settling everything, paid respect to the court nobles, and tied up all loose ends. Why are you yelling at young Sandayu?"

"He must go back," said his fellow old soldier. Kihei told the tale leading to this fortunate meeting. After listening, Junai said, "The father's position is regrettable. I'm siding with Sandayu. Please take him with you."

Junai and Kihei were both sixty years old. Onodera Koemon, Junai's adopted son, was twenty-eight years old, a year difference from Sandayu, and still lived with his parents. Depending on the clan's situation, he said he would follow the lord to his grave or hold the castle. Kihei could no longer be stubborn.

"Kihei-dono, you have a fine son who can face the people of the clan. Well, let's go, Sandayu-dono. The young are useful. Please take my horse's muzzle. If you enter the castle town with a tearstained face, everyone will laugh."

When they crossed the Chikusa River, the minds of the father and son were already open. They thought rationally about falling side by side in battle.

42

THE CLEVER WARRIOR

O N THE TWENTY-SEVENTH, twenty-eighth, and twenty-ninth, the men of the clan held a general meeting in the grand hall of the castle. Over these three days, a lifetimes' worth of feelings burned up in a crucible of excitement.

In the second discussion, the desires of the clan's warriors split apart.

Two factions arose. One faction consisted of the pacifists who adopted the reasonable plan of peacefully surrendering the castle based on the following premise: What is the benefit of sharpening arrows in the Imperial Court? That would pointlessly disgrace a traitor and dishonor the lord after his death.

The other faction did not budge from their hardcore stance: If the lord is disgraced, the retainers will die. The code of samurai does not have two paths. There is only death for us. Hold the castle or follow the lord into death? Even if we request the appointment of Daigaku-sama as the head of the clan, we have no reason to surrender this castle.

Between them stood the worldly, intelligent men, who despite their personal beliefs, deftly averted their preferred positions to mediate the trivial side issues that arose. But their masks were soon penetrated in this passionate environment, and both factions ignored them.

Ono Kurobei led the reasonable faction that advocated surrendering the castle and not causing trouble for the shogunate.

"Why don't we try to cool down a little? Both sides have lost their heads over this. Isn't it best to step back from the flames?"

Accustomed to worldly affairs, his words seemed to throw water on those wearing grim expressions.

"Sir, your words make sense," said Kuranosuke, who did not oppose his sensible view.

However, the side with no intention of agreeing was the passionate faction, but obstinate heads turned. Veins appeared on their foreheads. They cursed Ono's cunning, cowardice, or despicable warrior's attitude. The entire group overflowed with a sense of despair.

"Why are we so frenzied? Our inability to be impassive when faced with this calamity, this curse on our clan, is not shameful. We have no views other than holding ourselves responsible to the enemy who will receive the castle and be repaid for three generations of the clan's favor. Cowards, leave now."

Kuranosuke's face showed approval. Which side was the chief retainer on? Doubters wondered whether he held a solid belief. Many favored Kurobei's straightforward attitude. The majority of the attendees belonged to this faction.

"Please quiet down," said Kurobei to the howling crowd that responded with louder howls. He never thought his opinion lacked righteousness. He intended to take to heart the lessons of his heavy responsibility as the keeper of the castle and his perspective as a warrior from the young rank-and-file soldiers.

The intense emotions of the young only faded in him. Also, a disagreeable trait he had from the old days was to engage in fiery confrontations. For now, if any matter, such as his hard-and-fast rules summed up by the words *the way of the samurai*, is not viewed through wisdom and theory, it would not gain approval or appear in the actions taken.

On this point, Kurobei was usually described as eloquent and sociable, and seen as far more capable than Kuranosuke. And during this time, Kurobei never thought he was inferior to the much younger Kuranosuke.

Kurobei was enraged.

"Why a castle siege? Is this loyalty? What kind of malice does the Honda clan, the Matsudaira clan, or another advancing enemy have towards this clan? Are they savages who battle guileless people? More importantly, the domain's population will suffer; starting with this clan, the main clan will be involved and disgraced as traitors. How can you not understand my loyalty to the late lord? I will not join. If I took part in that sort of silly undertaking, I should leave this seat. But as the keeper of the castle, I will not. And I forbid a reckless siege of the castle."

"You rat!"

A man in the back seats jumped up. He looked enraged like he was about to grip the hilt of his sword and leap at him.

"Wait!"

The surrounding men held him back.

Not looking like a typical old man, Kurobei stared at him. The men in both factions formed silent battle formations. A chill swept over them.

"But —"

Kuranosuke looked at Kurobei who looked him in the eyes and asked, "Am I wrong?"

"Your reasoning is masterful, but what about justice?"

"What about it?"

"The Ako clan is small, but for three generations since Joshu Kasama, it has nurtured samurai, and more than three hundred samurai received its favor. Now, will the castle be surrendered without disgrace? How do you justify that morally in a military family?"

"Well, do you think a castle siege is a good idea?"

"I don't think it's good. I think it's necessary. However, my true opinion is to follow the lord to the grave. In the best plan, everyone lines up inside the main gate of the castle and follows the lord."

"What? Follow him to the grave?"

Kurobei stared at Kuranosuke's face. Did this man think of such things?

"How should we die?"

"With integrity, I will petition for Daigaku-sama's appointment. The shogunate does not know how to account for the vassals' innermost feelings."

Kurobei said nothing. He could not challenge him because he agreed. However, those who criticized the plan to follow the lord to the grave came from all sides of the hardcore faction.

In the end, they planned to send an envoy to appeal to the chief inspector. In the rare event that proved futile, they would hold the castle. This decision came in the final consultation at the close of March, a month of ill omens.

April came. The castle fell silent as if plunged into gloom. Even during the day, he saw the samurai quarter in the castle town suspended in desolation, like after a rain shower.

Look at that, thought Kurobei with a frosty smile.

43

THE OATH

IT WAS THE fifth. On this day, an assembly was announced to distribute the remaining stores in the granary and the gold nuggets to the clan samurai.

The faces not seen for seven days gathered. Their states of mind possibly changed. Particular awareness of money entered their minds. Many times that day Kurobei noticed silent but animated faces among the men in heated discussions.

Kurobei walked around to exchange civilities and speak to each man.

"Well, do you think dying is loyalty? If the chance arises, who will die?"

Some couldn't answer, but today, he was surprised to find others who agreed with him.

Many clashes erupted over the distribution of public funds.

The funds were allocated following Kuranosuke's intention.

"The division will be equal among the men, not by status."

Beginning with Kurobei, the faction leaders, Tomura Genzaemon, Okabayashi Bokunosuke, Ito Goemon, and Tamamushi Shichiroemon, did not insist on "division according to the rice stipend."

Kuranosuke argued they could sell weapons and household goods to the men of rank. He adopted the reasoning that superiors were obligated to be considerate of the ordinary men in times like these. Kurobei placed the burdens of the entire clan on the men of rank. Unable to provide immediate measures as they had done for the rank-and-file, they had to consider the honor of the former clan in society and provide counterarguments but failed. In the end, a compromise called the Kochi Reduction was reached.

In the division by stipend, if 100 koku received an allotment of 18 ryo, then 1,000 koku would receive 180 ryo. However, the Kochi Reduction deducts 2 ryo from the distribution for every 100 koku increase in the stipend. Sixteen ryo were calculated for 200 koku and 14 ryo for 300 koku. The more one had the less one got. Until the end, Kuranosuke stressed more for those at the bottom and less for those at the top.

Also, he did not touch the allotment for the Asano clan cemetery and the money for personal use brought by the lord's widow Yozen'in when she married .

Kuranosuke took no notice of his share. He said to himself, "Now, they've mostly been sorted out."

How much change was apparent in the men who went home today holding money? He didn't seem to have an active plan, but in no time, close to twenty men pressed oaths sealed with blood into his hand.

In these written vows to god, they did not promise to follow the lord to the grave or hold the castle. They simply agreed to take a course of action. They recognized the evolution in Kuranosuke's intention.

He soon spoke about the oath, and the men who knew the oath had been placed in his hand reached out to him.

Some men should still be here, thought Kuranosuke and went to look.

However, men are hard to judge. A clever man like Kurobei doesn't say much. Many men are only theorists because they don't understand people with passion and believe it's dangerous to show too much emotion. Few like that will come. This serious matter should be difficult to carelessly leak. What looked like dullness in his eyes was patience.

On the eleventh, the envoy sent to appeal the judgment returned. The entire appeal was rejected. Instead, he returned with written instructions from the Toda family in the main clan to surrender the castle.

Given this ending, under the pretext of discussing preparations for the castle siege, they announced another meeting the next day. Fewer than half the number that came the previous day attended.

Oh, him, too, he thought, surprised by the missing men.

Of course, Kurobei came.

Around this time, the men who agreed with him sat around him and created one color. As if they held a meeting the previous night, everyone agreed for the first time. They countered the foolishness of a castle siege coming from the other faction.

Kurobei said, "It's the same problem no matter how often I say it. As the keeper of the castle and an elder, I will speak until the end. Even now, each man is having trouble throwing away his status. That is scandalous in the way of the samurai.

Isn't this the same as trampling down the name of the defunct clan and causing confusion all around to satisfy oneself? I am heartbroken over the final days of the lord's clan. But what is the point of setting fires and spilling blood over ruins? The world will laugh and say it was foolish and sheer insanity. Stop saying harmful things. No, I must persuade you, and today, I was prepared to come to the castle."

His shouting voice did not lie and only expressed his conviction. He believed in the way of the warrior. He explained if others held the castle and died in battle, he believed to continue living would bring him sorrow. Today, Kurobei's eyes were not bloodshot.

In contrast, most of the men determined to hold the castle were silent and paid no attention. The silent battle line seemed to laugh away his ideas.

"Shut up!"

A voice burst from the crowd. Onodera Junai not seen in the earlier meetings was beside Muramatsu Kihei.

The old man stood and, without hesitating, came forward and sat in front.

"Ono-san."

"What?" said a trembling Ono Kurobei. Tears filled his eyes. The sense of justice believed only by him saddened and angered him.

"Please leave. Cowards are useless here. Only those who stay will stay. That would be good."

An indignant Kurobei stood erect. He addressed Kura-nosuke but was tongue-tied and could not make himself understood.

"Excuse me."

Next, Sotomura Genzaemon left followed by Tama-mushi Shichirouemon.

One after another, men left the room. The empty seats increased at a brisk pace. More than half left, but no one lamented their departure any more than having a tooth pulled.

"It's nice and airy now," said Yoshida Chuzaemon beside Kuranosuke, smiling and exposing his large front teeth.

Are any more going to leave? Kuranosuke wondered and turned away to give them time. The men who remained had a settled feeling.

Kuranosuke said to the men behind him, "Night has come. Where are the candle stands?"

As he waited for the stands, Kuranosuke took the group into his confidence and gave them a glimpse into his thoughts. He said, "I will not die here."

Although not repeated for the men who already signed the written oath, this serious action was whispered for the first time to the men who remained after the winnowing.

I will not die here.

This unspoken intention came to anyone's heart. A flushed face swallowed saliva and looked at Kuranosuke's face.

Kuranosuke said, "Until the end, as long as it's within our power, we will cling to the shogunate as if Daigaku-sama were appointed to head the clan. Divine will decides that outcome. But after that, the samurai who serves will walk only one path. There can be no wavering. If you are born a samurai, you will die a samurai. That is the only way. For now, I ask you to leave the place of death to me. Does anyone object?"

About fifty men were present. Their shadows pressed in closer. The candle stands were set up nearby.

Ink stones were brought in. Each one wrote the same oath, sealed it with blood, and held it out before Kuranosuke. Among them was the name Mimura Jirozaemon, a kitchen servant. Another youngster who wore bangs, fifteen-year-old Yato Emoshichi, also wrote and presented an oath.

Kuranosuke set those two papers aside. He called over the two to scold them, but the tearful dissent by the boys moved the men.

"To say this much and not act is miserable. Chief Retainer, please accept their oaths."

The others expressed support for their inclusion.

With few words, Kuranosuke gave his permission. Emoshichi lit up with a smile. He was a handsome youth with bright, round eyes. No one would want to kill this young man; he was overjoyed.

The kitchen servant Mimura Jirozaemon was a low-ranking member with a stipend of only 7 koku with a rice stipend for two people. He did not have a seat at the conference until today. But perfection in the way of the warrior was not unique to men with high stipends. A study of the remaining force on the last day revealed that rather than the high-ranking samurai, many of the men who lived this truth belonged to the group with small stipends.

"It's nothing, but I prepared a simple gift to celebrate my joy with all who took this oath.

Jirozaemon carried in cold sake and cups.

"Ah, you know me well."

Kuranosuke raised a cup and turned to each man. The word *joy* may not have been heard for several days. The men had changed over these long twenty days.

44

THE GETAWAY PACKAGES

"H ey! aren't you Otsuya?" someone called out.

The merchant Otsuya Juemon with business at the castle stopped his restless, long strides and turned to see a face with a toothy smile approaching from the darkness at the edge of the moat.

"Ah, Yasoemon-sama?"

"Where are you going?"

"I have urgent business at the beach."

"You fellows are busy making money. The townsmen will be just fine."

Okajima Yasoemon, his jaw marked by a blue trace missed by a razor, parted moments earlier from his older brother Hara Soemon and his colleagues Sugino Juheiji and Maebara Isuke at the front castle gate.

"Oh no, I would never think the inexcusable thought of profiting off the lord's tragedy."

"You're a liar."

The smell of the sake he drank with his colleagues in the castle lingered in Yasoemon's laughing voice.

"It's better to not hold back. During an emergency like

this in a province, goods move. That means profits for the merchants. Is it better to hold back? A soldier is a soldier; a merchant is a merchant. These are natural positions. To take the right path means never to sway from that stance or to cheat."

"That's true …"

"In this situation, merchants should abide by the path of the merchant. And warriors behave like warriors. That's what I think. Whether a farmer or a merchant, the man who embodies his work will become a great man, the greatest."

"Well, is it all right for merchants to profit?"

"As long as the profits aren't made immorally or unfairly. Profits must be made honestly. In the future, you will enter the province of another lord. It will be a celebration. The public mind will be renewed. The people there will be in good humor."

"I feel you're being sarcastic."

"Ha, ha, ha. You are an unusually upright man. A trip to the beach is probably for business."

"But because of tedious requests and many years of relationships, I can't say no. Merchants are simply carrying out a public service during this challenging time."

"Is it clan business?"

"Only if clan business is an order from that stingy Ono-sama, but I'm not grousing even if I take a loss or have to work my fingers to the bone."

"What's Ono's order?"

"I will pack up seventy pieces of household goods and furniture and load over twenty loads in boxes and straw mats onto a ship within the night and head to Osaka. Isn't that an unreasonable order? Not only that, there's a shortage of cargo ships. I had to negotiate with a shipping agent and will load nearly half on board tonight. The rest will be loaded tomorrow. I thought telling him would cause the imperious shoulders of that old body to shake with rage and vent unchecked, so I lost heart and went home."

"Does Kurobei intend to leave Osaka? Where is that half of the cargo?"

"Well, those fifty packages belong to his son Gun'emon, I intend to store them for one night in the dirt-floor room and in the storehouse at my store."

"Please show me?"

"Even if I showed you, wouldn't you be unimpressed?"

"No, I want to see. Kurobei amassed wealth until his hair turned gray. How much dirt accumulated under his fingernails? I'd like to see that become a topic of conversation."

He could not refuse this tag-along. Otsuya guided him to his home and offered tea at the storefront.

"It's been a long time since the warm sake served to me cooled down. Cool sake would be nice. One cup please." Yasoemon remained seated on the wooden steps at the entrance and stared at the packages piled like a mountain on the large dirt floor.

"As expected, he's a man with a different mindset. It's a shame Ono Kurobei wasn't born a merchant."

Yasoemon drank up the sake in the teacup. "Ah, that was good. Otsuya."

"Yes."

"You see this package. Don't load this one on the ship. No matter what you say, the transfer of the son Gun'emon's wealth in the storehouse should be prohibited."

"You can't insist merchants do something so ridiculous."

"Relax. Excuse Hara's younger brother for asking, but if you wish, ask Oishi-dono for permission."

"That's a problem. First of all, he's the chief retainer,

and that sort of son Gun'emon-sama … if I say that sort of thing, as a samurai, he may be insulted and kill me," said Otsuya reflecting on *burei-uchi*, the samurai's right to kill a commoner.

"Ha, ha, ha. Before that happens, I'll come and kill Kurobei. His behavior today and this shrewd preparation diverge from the path of samurai. He's a despicable man.… And I can't stand his gall, he forgets his wrongdoing. On the strength of a slight discrepancy between the funds in the treasury and the account ledgers, he has spread rumors of embezzlement by me. We'll visit him, I will cast a spell so that complaints do not come this way."

Propped up in the center of the packages, about ten spears with hilts made from blue shellfish, oak, and red handles were bundled together and sheathed by a straw wrapper. Yasoemon went to the side while wiping his face dirtied in his drinking bout and cut the rope. He removed one spear with a nine-foot-long red oak handle.

"Otsuya, that was an order."

Otsuya opened the latticed shoji screen and walked out to the street at the tip of a spear.

45

THE EMPTY HOUSE WHERE
PEOPLE LIVE

"YOU'RE A HOPELESS fool. You have both types of stupid, the visible stupid and the invisible stupid."

None of the main household furnishings were inside the mansion. Only lamp stands, dining tables, and cheap utensils remained in the servants' rooms. Ono Kurobei's family was dressed and gathered inside.

"Nanny, don't cry."

As he passed a cup to his son Gun'emon, Kurobei looked at the head of his fussy grandchild on the knees of his wet nurse.

He smiled and said, "He's like me with that red hair."

Gun'emon poured his father a drink. "A grandson mostly takes after the grandfather."

"If he's like me, that would be great. I don't know how many years I will continue as a ronin. When it's over, the Ono clan will probably have peaked during my generation."

"Does that happen?"

"Even confronting this situation, what is the point of dying? I was careful not to be pressured by money and lose my mind. I will leave for Kyoto to spend my last years without a care in the world. At first, I wondered in my heart about Daigaku-sama's future. Until the lord perished, I wanted the family name and the obligations to the neighboring regions to be fulfilled and took on a hated role. However, today is today, and I want to laugh inside the castle.

"Oishi is a considerate and generous man. For a time, he was distraught over the poverty-stricken underlings and the young samurai with no way to eat if separated from the lord. Even I wondered for an instant, What is the way of the samurai? This way of thinking put him in danger. His leg was trapped in a crevice. He's called Chief Retainer or Commander and looked on with favor. Because I'm not gullible and was prepared from the beginning, I'm able to escape being haunted by the angel of death. Tonight, Oishi is probably in bed wondering how death will come."

"Aren't they saying Okajima's followers have scattered in confusion after misappropriating funds from the treasury?"

"Yes, the account balance is far off. However, this happens on the battlefield, too. Don't say too much."

"He's a man with foresight."

"There's no reason to praise him."

Gun'emon raised the bottle. "The sake's gone."

"Wait. Wait."

"Are you finished?"

"No." Kurobei strained to listen. "Is someone knocking on the front gate?"

"It's probably Otsuya."

"But he would come by the back gate."

"..."

Tonight's departure was top secret to the people in the

house and in town. The disgrace was Kurobei's timidity. Gun'emon was also unnerved.

The tapping at the gate gradually became furious. They knew this was no ordinary visitor. The large bar shook.

"Open up! I know you're in there! I want to see you, Ono Kurobei!"

That was certainly the voice of Hara's younger brother he gossiped about, Okajima Yasoemon. A drunk-looking Kurobei left the room.

"Please stop, Father," said Gun'emon and rushed to grab his sleeve. Kurobei squinted and mumbled, "I'm not going out to see him … Who's out there?"

The father and son went to the bay window in the corridor and peered outside. Perhaps they believed he already scaled the wall and was hiding.

Yasoemon shouted in a voice that sounded like it was echoing off the mansion next door.

"From the lantern light, I can see the house is not empty. I know Kurobei and Gun'emon are inside. If you have ears, listen. As the keeper of the castle, your character is despicable. You forget generations of favor bestowed on your family and will slip away in the darkness of night like two ordinary men. What do you men called samurai in the castle have to say? You will soil the name of the late lord. I will spare your lives, but, for the second time, come out where we can see you, or we won't leave you alone. All right? I've warned you."

A spear flew over the gate's roof and pierced the shutter box at the side entrance.

Kurobei swallowed painfully. Yasoemon's laughter echoed for a time outside the gate.

46

———

A CHAT OVER TEA AT ENRINJI TEMPLE

SINCE YESTERDAY, ALL clan business moved to the prayer hall of Enrinji Temple that would also serve as the meeting place for the remaining clan samurai and the place to address unfinished business. Kuranosuke sat in front of the disorganized mass of desks and boxes filled with documents.

Yoshida Chuzaemon and the veterans Onodera and Hara remained in the castle and, from this day, would organize the castle keep, the inner citadel, and the clan storehouses.

"We're separated from the castle and will probably see the castle only in our dreams."

As they griped, the faces of the clan's samurai were mysteriously brighter than yesterday. The reason was the siege of the castle turned into its surrender.

The plan had been to die either by following the lord to the grave or by dying in battle, but they decided to surrender the castle. However, absolutely no one delighted in living here even for several more days. If life were a man's primary consideration, he could abandon his seat at any time during the assembly. No barriers prevented them from leaving Ako.

On the last day, they concluded the pact. The first words from Kuranosuke's mouth to reveal an ulterior motive for *surrendering the castle* were "Could you please leave the planning to me?"

They agreed to add this line to the written oath: I understand the life not discarded at this moment will not last a long time.

Each man would die soon!

Although they could not see the future, the unquenchable brightness shining on each face had to reflect a big change of heart.

Despair transformed into hope.

Their position changed from miserable defeat to victory.

Beginning yesterday, the life force of not dying appeared on the lively brows of the clan's samurai.

Kuranosuke was among men who changed like they stripped off black mourning clothes worn until the day before yesterday. However, from the time of the first council until today, he could not see the change no matter how hard he looked.

Despite being busy, he chatted about the world with the priest envoy from Kagakuji Temple before he left. Then the chief priest from Takamitsu Temple arrived.

He appeared out of politeness after the delivery of the donation list. Similar greetings came from Dairenji Temple.

"Katsuta, a strange thing has happened. Have you heard?" shouted Sugino Juheiji, who came back inside and made his way over to a crowd of younger men gathered in a corner of the main temple. Katsuta Shinzaemon, Yato, Mase, and a few others were talking.

"What? What happened?"

"The night before last, Ono Kurobei ran off in the night."

"Are you talking about Ono again? Yesterday, we were laughing about Ono."

"But there was another chat over tea. Yasoemon's threat was too effective, so Ono lost his nerve and forgot the nursing grandchild still in the arms of the wet nurse who was not on the steamer."

"Impossible."

"I just saw the kid."

"Where?"

"It looks like the wet nurse abandoned the child in town and went into hiding. The baby was crying weakly in the alley of storehouses near the merchants' homes. People gathered, curious about whose child it was. The wife of a local merchant nursed the baby."

"If the master is the master, and the wet nurse is a wet nurse. Yasoemon was wrong, too."

Kuranosuke overheard and turned from the room to say, "Sugino, bring the child to the temple to be cared for."

"It's Kurobei's grandson."

"I know. That infant is one person favored by the late lord."

He thought Sugino had descended the stairs of the main temple and was gone, but he was soon back and agitated.

"Chief Retainer, Chief Retainer. I saw men from Edo."

"Who?"

Kuranosuke looked toward the main gate from a side room of the inner temple.

Three darkish faces lined up sturdy shoulder to shoulder and were heading to the main temple. Horibe Yasubei was on the right; Okuda Magodayu, in the center;

and Takata Gunbei, on the left. He gasped at the sight of the familiar faces and rushed down the stairs.

Kuranosuke's expression registered relief at their arrival.

An expressionless voice spoke to the gatekeeper Emoshichi. "Pass them through."

Muramatsu Kihei, Kataoka, and Isogai came earlier from Edo and brought news about these three. A few days earlier, they received a stern letter from Yasubei's adoptive father, the elder Horibe Yahei who remained in Edo.

The trio shook off the dust and entered the room where Kuranosuke was waiting. Sunlight cast a blue tint on the large cycad plant in the garden.

47

LATER IMPLICATIONS

"**Y**OU JUST ARRIVED?" Kuranosuke greeted them.

"No, late last night."

Gunbei gulped down the tea brought by a novice. The eyes of all three men were grim. These three were the top pupils of Horiuchi Genzaemon, a famous master swordsman in Edo. Above all, Yasubei's sword was deemed more important in Kanto than in the clan's territory. A unique characteristic among the many low-ranking samurai stationed in Edo and possessing refined tastes was the inclusion of unrefined country bumpkins.

Based on the news reported after the incident, the three samurai said to their leader, the elderly Horibe Yahei, "Not one of the many wise opinions was adopted. Kira is alive and well. It's enough to ask for the head of this sworn enemy of the late lord."

The ringleaders of the radicals wanting to act were only among the men resident in the prefecture.

No one knew how much this event pained Kuranosuke's heart until this day.

Many of the aloof men like Ono's faction in Edo were

happy in a way that resembled unhappiness. These men were led by the senior vassals in Edo, Yasui Hikoemon and Fujii Matazaemon.

No matter how much they ground their teeth or how convinced they were in their hearts, with just three men, the problem was no longer how many dozen steps would it take to race inside Kira's gate.

They traveled over 450 miles to join with Ako and die in defense of the castle. Kuranosuke was troubled by the intensity visible in the trio's eyes. For a time, his behavior and expressions were uncertain, and he did not speak. Bored, he picked up his pipe and lightly tapped it. He picked up a slip of paper at the edge of the desk and twisted it into a paper string.

"Chief Retainer, I've heard the shogunate's envoy, Chief Inspector Araki Juzaemon, accepted the surrender of the castle. But is that a lie or the truth?"

"So you've heard?"

"Yes, from Yoshida Chuzaemon-dono at the castle."

"Then there's no need for me to go into detail. It is true."

The long eyebrows of salt-and-pepper hair of Okuda Magodayu at the edges trembled above his hollow eyes.

"Chief Retainer," he said in a defiant voice.

While they waited for an explosion of thunder, the backs of Magodayu's hands pressed his eyes streaming tears. This fifty-six-year-old man—a warrior—was crying.

Kuranosuke shifted his eyes to the leaves of the cycad and watched a large black butterfly flutter by.

"Are you ... a warrior?"

Takata Gunbei's lips parted; a little later, his voice emerged. His shoulders were shaking. His long sword bound tightly to his side rustled.

"Why surrender the castle? You, as the most senior

vassal, often said to return to the home province to be around men with backbone. Did the soldiers in neighboring provinces flinch? Is life disappointing? What is going on here? Desks are set up in a temple, and documents are being thumbed through. Is this the behavior of a warrior who watches his lord's house perish?"

Yasubei scooted closer on his knees and said, "My father Yahei claimed Kuranosuke was the man to depend on at this time. That surprised me. I thought nothing could be more absurd than that. We were told the plea to appoint Daigaku-sama was out of the question. Shouldn't we be more reluctant to surrender the castle dishonorably? I wish to understand. Depending on your answer, we three will know whether this return to Ako was worth it."

Kuranosuke's fingers tightly twisted the paper string. He set his lips in an unpleasant shape to answer without words. He probably thought, This overly emotional man presents more problems than clansmen like Ono or Tamamushi. First of all, Kuranosuke despised being resentful and did not carelessly evoke tears. Because of his susceptibility to them, inevitably, he assumed a stern attitude. If his companions raised their voices or their eyes became bloodshot, he would maintain his composure. Deep in his heart, he thought, This will die down. His look of uncertainty concealed his true self.

After a long pause, he answered with a customary phrase.

"You are quite right ... but ... both of you said to surrender the castle; therefore, there is no reason to end this matter. There are later implications. Didn't we have to provide a reason for acceptance to the shogunate and Toda Uneme no Kami-sama?"

Okuda Magodayu's head cast down between his

pointed shoulders looked up. "What do you mean by later implications?"

"Well," Kuranosuke held a metal-tipped *kiseru* pipe but was playing with it on his knee and not packing tobacco. "I have to see to the safety of Daigaku-sama."

"That's all?"

"Yes, will you leave that to me?"

He was evasive but not flush with anger. Yasubei gave a signal with his eyes and stood. When he left, his eyes reflected contempt, like his actions were worthless and he had given up. The backs of the three men sat side by side on the porch of the main temple and whispered as they tied the cords of their straw sandals.

"We should sound out the court adviser Secretary Okuno. If tapped, the secretary's chest should ring."

They went out in a rage. Outside the main temple gate, Sugino Juheiji returned cradling a baby. As he walked, he rocked the frantically crying baby in his awkward arms.

"You're leaving?" asked the charmingly youthful, round-faced Juheiji.

"Whose baby is that?"

Gunbei's tone sounded like an attack on Juheiji's care-free nature because he was carrying the baby.

"This is the grandson of Ono Kurobei. His grandfather and father are terrible. They left in a hurry, forgetting about the pitiful child and the nanny."

Gunbei peeked at the baby. "Looks like him."

Gunbei followed Yasubei, and let out a great sigh. He grumbled, "Dammit. The way of the samurai is not part of the Genroku era," and spat on the ground.

48

CLEANING UP

THE SOUNDS OF carpenters' chisels bounced off the waters in the moat. They were mending rotting sections of the drawbridge at the front gate of the castle. Clusters of sedge hats worn by the women weeding grass dotted the embankment of the outer citadel. A gardener had climbed a pine tree. A foot soldier at the road was giving orders and raking.

Preparations in the castle were done; the cleaning would be finished soon.

Everything from the weapons and utensils and various account ledgers of the civilian government to provincial maps was cataloged and placed at designated locations. Then they waited for the shogunate's envoy.

The two deputy envoys Araki Juzaemon and Sakakibara Uneme ordered by the shogunate to receive the castle arrived at an Ako inn. On the day before the formal surrender, they conducted a preliminary inspection of the castle's interior.

They walked over a vast area and down sparkling long corridors to inspect the inner and outer citadels. The bottoms of their white tabi socks remained spotless. The adornments of weapons dazzled. Taxation account ledgers, salt field maps, and land tax ledgers were arranged to be identified at a glance.

"We have tea," offered Kuranosuke.

"Thank you."

The envoys were graciously guided to the room used as a sitting room during Takumi no Kami's life. The fragrance of the tea wafting in brought the lord's figure to the eyes of the row of seated clan samurai.

Kuranosuke prostrated himself before the two envoys to make this heartfelt appeal with his usual fervor.

"Because of the affair of Lord Takumi no Kami and the breach of manners, I respectfully accept the order to confiscate the castle and the lands. Today, the lord is already dead and the province ruined, but his rival Lord Kira is safe. We vassals should follow the path of suicide.

"However, while Takumi no Kami's younger brother Daigaku waits, he lives in hiding. He only waits with a loyal heart for your final gracious command. If a ray of hope shines for the earlier appeal or intervention with the help of Toda Uneme no Kami, we are unified in achieving the justice of the vassals before the shrine of our late lord. We apologize first to the shogunate and then to the wider world for our crime. Our bones useless in the next world will be buried. We seek your sympathy."

"…"

The envoys were speechless. Each envoy met the other's gaze, and they left. They walked through several rooms and came to a large banquet hall.

Sunlight moved like shimmering heat to the black lattice ceiling.

Araki Juzaemon looked up and again Kuranosuke fell prostrate at his feet.

"Please understand. I spent the years of three generations in the inner citadel of this small clan. This castle built by a vassal clan to the Tokugawa received favor because of the meritorious service of the clan founder Asano Unemenosho over many years and the loyalty of later generations. Even while asleep, the late lord Takumi no Kami never forgot, always encouraged hard work from the vassals, and possessed single-minded devotion to service. His unexpected impudence was a shattering disgrace. If goodness exists to show a modicum of pity and forgiveness to Daigaku-sama, that great favor will not be forgotten for thousands of years. Please excuse my transgression with this wearisome plea, but if you could keep it in your hearts …"

Struck by Kuranosuke's quiet voice and bowing with both hands on the ground in apology, the clan's retainers escorted to the area could not hold back their tears.

The two envoys said nothing. After walking out, one whispered, "As a vassal, Kuranosuke said what had to be said."

That night, however, Juzaemon summoned Kuranosuke.

"Today, the inspection was conducted with integrity and painstaking care. Everything was excellent. After I return to the capital, an imperial hearing will be held."

He did not mention Daigaku by name, but Kuranosuke's words touched Juzaemon's heart.

Finally, the nineteenth, the day to depart the castle, came. Kuranosuke left the inn where Araki Juzaemon was staying and returned to the castle. He spent the night walking around to encourage the clan's vassals at their guard posts.

"This evening, the castle is still our late lord's. Be careful with fire at the front gate."

As dawn approached, he could hear the sounds of distant shells. When he climbed the castle tower to look, the stars filling the sky twinkled. The castle town was cloaked by darkness. The rooftops did not float into view. A line of approaching torchlights resembled stitches in the immense lacquer-like darkness and crossed the Chikusa River from Takatori Peak. Of course, for several weeks, the soldiers of clans like the Himeji and the Okayama readied guns at the provincial border to prepare for some incident.

A hard look revealed a battle line running along a road to the castle town. The procession was probably the senior envoy and Wakisaka Awaji no Kami from Tatsuno in Banshu coming to take possession of the castle.

When he turned to look at the sea, faint white waves already glowed. Military ships, like pods of whales, drew the battle line of the navy and hugged the back of the Ako region.

Kuranosuke stood as a chilling wind brushed his whiskers, never tiring, no matter how long he stood. He never imagined he would wait for this kind of dawn in his generation. He pondered the darkness deep in his heart he had to explore and believed he could close his eyes and recall this darkness if his spirit became careless.

He did not believe in pointless Buddhist teachings but was guided by conviction. On that evening, the soul of the deceased lord Takumi no Kami surely came. He believed the soul of his lord placed one hand on his shoulder and looked hard at the world with great sorrow.

A flock of ravens beat their wings and took flight from the forests of the outer citadel. Their cries infused with meaning struck his heart.

Conch shells sounded. Finally, a rumble of drums flowed down the envoys' procession. Each moment, the sea and the sky awkwardly split in two. Deep red sun rays skimmed the ocean to dye the stonewalls, flickered among the trees, and brightened every corner of the castle's roofs.

This morning when the castle would pass to another's hand was dazzling.

"It's six now."

The squad of soldiers guarding the path of the senior envoy formed a line at the edge of the moat near the opened front gate of the castle.

This is goodbye, Ako Castle …

Kuranosuke's heart announced as he took one last look around. The cleanliness wherever he looked invigorated him and gratified his heart.

PART VI

THE DEFENSE IN YONEZAWA

49

—————

YELLOWISH GREEN ARABESQUE

HE NOW HAD nothing to do other than cast a fishing line. When he thought about his high stipend, he sometimes recalled his heartbreak over the peasants planting rice for land taxes in the fields rather than for the lord.

Without a sound, Shimizu Ichigaku stretched a pole from the banks of the Kirara River.

The flowers of the vegetables blackened. During this time, the fields, the mountains, and Atsumi Plains turned green. Over the two months from the middle of March when he arrived in Yokosuka village in Sanshu nothing seemed to change but the calendar.

However, at the time of the incident in Edo, Tomiko, Lord Kozuke's wife, was at Kezoji Temple and left for Edo at once. For a time, the villagers trembled, indignant about the harm inflicted on the domain's lord. She was at a loss on how to calm them. They quieted down after hearing about the punishment of the Asano clan. Ichigaku already thought it best to return to Edo and was eager to go home, too. The letter was a command from Chisaka

Hyobu, the Edo chief retainer of Uesugi Danjo no Taihitsu of Yonezawa and related in flesh and spirit to the Kira clan.

The attendant Kimura Johachi will soon leave to meet you in the domain. When circumstances are favorable, you shall accompany him back to the capital.

Ichigaku had no idea what business his colleague Kimura Johachi had, where he was going, or on what day he would arrive. However, he could almost guess the intentions of Chisaka Hyobu, rumored to be staying in the domain. Ichigaku wondered how did his meticulous brain for governing view the evolution of the incident. He, like Ichigaku, was certain the reaction would be an attack.

"Oh, it's pulling! Sir, they're biting."

These unexpected words came from behind. The silhouette of a townsman carrying a pack on his back dropped down beside the fish basket on the embankment.

Ichigaku noticed debris sinking into the water surface and jerked up the pole.

The bait was gone.

Glistening droplets on the string traveled to his hand. He scooped up the hook and attached the bait. He flung the line that rode the wind to land with a plop on the water surface.

"Fishing?" asked the townsman squatting beside him

"…"

Whirligig beetles and river shrimps cut through gentle ripples between the reeds and etched small wavelets in every direction. The white bellies of fish flickered at the river bottom.

"There they are."

The townsman drew on his pipe and peeked into the

fish basket. Not even one fish scale touched the bottom of the basket.

"Sir, isn't the tip of your rod a little too long?"

"…"

Ichigaku silently mused over this annoying man. The tobacco he was smoking seemed to be from Shikoku. It wasn't tobacco from Awa or Satsuma but made in Chugoku. While pondering that, he lost interest in the fishing line.

"Ah! You caught one!"

The townsman craned his neck to see. Ichigaku clicked his tongue and looked over his shoulder. He saw a lightly sunburned peddler around thirty-four or -five years old. When their eyes met, the peddler's face transformed into a simpering smile.

"Sir, try to raise the line a little faster. You're a bit too slow."

Like he was talking to himself, Ichigaku said, "I'm going home." He raised the pole to see that one puny dace had swallowed the bait.

The townsman laughed again.

Ichigaku did not look amused, let the dace fall onto a grassy spot, wound the line, and stood.

His elderly parents' home was nearby. The old farm was one of the first in Yokosuka village and stood here for generations. The two large main buildings, the thatched-roof gate, hedge fence, and windbreak of zelkova trees had changed little since his boyhood.

During the busy planting season, the entire household went out to the fields. Only one person, his elderly mother sitting on the edge of the veranda and sewing for the grandchildren, saw Ichigaku.

"Shirobei, did you catch any fish today?"

Shirobei was Ichigaku's boyhood name. His mother

gave birth to a samurai with a 100-koku stipend because of her pluck from peasant beginnings, but she wasn't prideful. No matter how old he got, he remained Shirobei, the runny-nosed boy.

Ichigaku in his country dialect said, "It was no good. Nothing bit. I got bored and came home."

"You know how to handle a sword but have been no good at fishing since you were a boy."

"Ha, ha, ha. You're right."

"It's your impatience. You love riding wild horses or fighting with sticks. Your late father always told me you were no good at anything demanding patience."

"I must have changed a lot since my young days, but Mother, you still see that boy."

"You can only suppress it, but your nature at birth won't change unless you're reborn."

"Well, that's a problem."

"The body of a serving samurai must not take on extra burdens. Asano Takumi no Kami is a good example."

Pale persimmon flowers filled the tracks left by his zori sandals in front of the veranda. Ichigaku leaned the fishing pole against the side of the storage shed.

"Mother, whose is this?" he asked as he picked up a package beside her.

A small wrapping cloth with a light yellowish-green arabesque design bundled three or four account ledgers. An antique brush-and-ink case was inserted in the knot.

50

***

A SECRET GUEST COMES AND GOES

"A YARN SELLER forgot it. I bought needles."

"A peddler?"

"Yes."

"The talking nonsense never stops."

"Who?"

"You, Mother."

"Who talks nonsense? The villagers talk about being silenced by you."

Outside the windbreak trees beside the house, a fleeting human figure came around the gate. Ichigaku nodded at the whiteness of the sedge hat worn by the man coming to retrieve the item forgotten by the yarn seller. He was probably the peddler Ichigaku met earlier on the riverbank.

The sedge hat peeked in from outside the gate. He was a peddler but not the man from before. He was missing the sword worn for protection by travelers, was shorter, and had sharp eyes.

Oh, is this the house? the man asked himself. He noticed Ichigaku and took long strides inside. Ichigaku barely recognized him.

"What is this, Kimura Johachi?"

"Why are you surprised?"

"Those clothes?"

"This?" Johachi's scanned down his cotton striped kimono.

"I have more information."

"You probably do, but you can't just pop up without warning."

"Meeting with you is a problem. Anyway, I want to wipe off this sweat. Where's the well?"

Ichigaku pointed. "Over there."

Kimura Johachi held a zori sandal in one hand at the edge of the veranda.

"I'll wash my feet, too."

He set down his hat and the packages slung over his shoulder and headed for the stone well in a corner of the garden.

The melodies of rice-planting songs flowed in from the backfields. His elderly mother burned stray threads off her sleeve as she boiled water in the darkened tea room. The bucket on the well's pulley rattled a few times in a corner of the garden.

Not long after, the yarn seller turned up again. He looked surprised when he saw Ichigaku he met on the embankment but gave a slight bow and said, "Excuse me, I think I left a brush-and-ink case and a package of ledger books here. Have you seen them?"

"This?"

"Thank you so much."

After he wrapped the small wrapping cloth in the bundle on his back, tied the knot at his neck, and was about to leave, Kimura Johachi returned from the stone well. His muscles tensed.

"Ah?"

His legs weakened.

The yarn seller answered with "Huh?" turned and bolted out the gate.

"Damn it!"

A scary-looking Johachi took off after him. Ichigaku surprised by what he saw jumped into his zori sandals. By the time he was outside the fence, Johachi had caught up to the yarn seller along a path between the fields. He watched the two men unsheathe their traveling swords and furiously cross them.

Shocked shouts rose from the men and women planting in the fields. Ichigaku folded his arms and watched.

Few men among the attendants in the Kira clan could hold a spear or a long sword and challenge a full-fledged samurai from any clan.

Only two men, Kimura Johachi and Kobayashi Heihachiro, could be held up as outliers in the Kira clan and above average even among the line-up of their fellow Edo swordsmen.

That's Johachi. He's doing fine. Ichigaku smiled and waited for him to finish his business and return. As the spirited Johachi was driving back his rival, he slipped. A splash shot up as his leg slid into the river near the ridge.

"Eeyaah! ..."

Ichigaku knew it was already too late and didn't move.

The yarn seller lost interest in Johachi, who had probably been cut, and abandoned him to escape at top speed. When Johachi, covered in mud, stood, the yarn seller was far away.

Johachi's disgusted lips tightened. He gave up and came back.

"Who was that?"

Johachi tried to stifle his mild amusement when he answered, "An Ako samurai," and headed back to the well.

"Oh, an Ako man?"

"I'm sure he was Chikamatsu Kanroku, a cavalry officer. He has a face I've seen but can't quite remember. I will guard my pocket."

"It looks like you know him."

"I should know him. Last February, I ran into him often in the towns in Ako and entered his family's mansion as a secondhand goods dealer."

"So you went to Ako?"

"Yes."

"On whose order?"

"On a secret order from Chisaka Hyobu-sama."

"Of course, he was quick …"

Ichigaku stepped on the persimmon flowers on the way to the house. He gave Johachi one of his *yukata* summer kimonos from the main house.

They talked while he changed.

"It's a shame. Although he's an enemy, I see he's a true man. Was he stealing documents delivered to this house?"

"That's impossible. But some Ako men have a little spirit."

"That's true."

Johachi's lips tightened, and he stared at Ichigaku who stepped one foot onto the veranda and said, "We'll have a leisurely talk. How's your stomach?"

"I'm hungry. Soba would be nice."

"That sounds good. Mother, can you please prepare soba? My friend from Edo would like noodles," said Ichigaku and hid away with Johachi in the back room converted into a retirement room by his late father.

51

SHIROPPE FROM THE VILLAGE

"I HEARD THE surrender of the castle and disbanding of the Ako clan went smoothly. But where did the ronin go?" asked Ichigaku, the moment he sat down.

Johachi gave a detailed account, beginning with his impersonation of a secondhand goods dealer.

"After the castle was surrendered to the envoy Wakizaka Awaji no Kami, some went to Edo; others planned to rely on relatives in nearby districts. All of Ako has paused, but perhaps from now on, the fall will be the time to watch that clan."

"Do they intend to become embroiled in plots swirling around in the world?"

"That's what I saw. On the surface, they are obedient."

"Do you think unity will continue after forfeiture of the clan's land, and their interests are uncoupled?"

"After that, the only bonds will be between men. When I saw the skill in surrendering the castle, I knew a lone great man lived among the more than three hundred ronin. Despite the death of Takumi no Kami and the confiscation of the clan's lands, as long as he's alive, no one can say Ako has perished."

"An Ako man? Is he Okano Shogen or Ono Kurobei? Or Hara Soemon?"

"Anyone would think that. However, when you see the result, everything came from the power of the man called Oishi Kuranosuke, who is said to be unremarkable. Chisaka Hyobu told me to keep an eye on him. Everyone knows he's the man to watch from now on."

"Where did Kuranosuke retreat to?"

"He was preparing to move to Yamashina in Kyoto. But last month, carbuncles erupted on his left arm, and he came down with a high fever. He's still recuperating at the home of Hachiro in Ozeki village not far from the Ako castle town. My first thought was to report this to Chisaka-sama, and I left Ako and am on my way there."

His mother called from outside the room.

"Shirobe, the soba's ready. I'll bring it in."

Ichigaku turned and said, "Johachi, put it in the hearth room. We'll eat there. Mother, please join us. He's a friend you can relax around."

"We have sake. Do you drink?" his mother asked.

Johachi answered with only, "Yes, I do. Thank you."

Ichigaku joined him in a big laugh.

The next morning, Johachi and Ichigaku were dressed in their traveling clothes before breakfast. Johachi forced his expression to change from that of a townsman with a shaven head and topknot to the look of a samurai. It was a little funny.

After the meal, Ichigaku entered the room housing the Buddhist altar and sat for a short time. When he left, tears moistened his elderly mother's eyes.

"Shirobe. I don't know if I'll die this year, but I am ill. Until the lord's business is settled, neither of you need to visit here again. I will never forget the kindness of the lord."

The elderly mother blew her nose as she watched her son put on his straw sandals. Johachi left first.

"You have been very kind. Goodbye," he said, then bowed and left while tying the cord of his hat.

As the two figures walked along the ridge between the green rice fields, the people planting rice stood and waved. Ichigaku raised his bamboo hat high.

All the workers in the fields were relatives—nieces, nephews, brothers, and sisters. He took responsibility for this good and honest family under a patriarch of the Kira clan.

When the two men descended from Kezoji Temple, the family cemetery for successive generations of the Kira clan, they removed their bamboo hats and bowed to the stone steps. Ichigaku held many memories of this temple.

As a boy, he spent his summer days in play somersaulting and obsessed with catching beetles until night fell. Noblemen often came to this temple to escape the summer heat. This was the territory of Lord Kira Kozuke no Suke and his wife.

Kozuke no Suke harbored the desire to have three stone images created: one of the founder of the Kira clan, one of the restorer, and one of himself, and install them in this temple. The man who placed himself in the center and the man who returned to his hometown this time were two different men. Kozuke no Suke kept an eye on the boy Shiroppe he often saw running around inside the compound and on the nearby hills.

"That boy shows promise. I'd like to take him to Edo," he once revealed to the chief priest.

He encouraged Shiroppe from the village to become a samurai. On this fourth time returning home after becoming Shimizu Ichigaku, he had an inkling this may be his last. At any rate, he could not believe that his lord's body in this situation was peaceful and safe. If the worst happens, as a man who will strike at the enemy with his body, he discovered his own existence this time.

Even among the followers in the same Kira clan, Kimura Johachi had a somewhat unconventional upbringing.

He was a samurai by nature and a vassal of the Uesugi clan in Yonezawa. After Tomiko, the daughter of a daimyo, married Kozuke no Suke, her status as a subject was transferred to the Kira family. Consequently, she continuously went in and out of the Uesugi clan, her birth family. He was backed by Hyobu, a hereditary vassal the world observed was the Uesugi clan's Chisaka or Chisaka's Uesugi clan.

The two were secretly proud of being without rival in the Kira clan, as long as Kobayashi Heihachiro remained in Edo. How would the Ako ronin move? These three crows surrounding the lord made a secret vow: No one would lay a finger on him.

52

THE STONE SPEAKS

EDO SMOTHERED UNDER the June heat. When they left the Shinagawa inn for Takanawa, the sea breezes warmed them. The roads were dried white. Each time a horse, an ox, or a packhorse passed by, flies like sesame seeds chased the dust.

"It's too hot!" said Kimura Johachi, as he fanned his face burned bright red.

"Shimizu," he said and looked back.

Ichigaku came from behind, wiping off his chest hair with a hand towel wrung out in a roadside well.

"Is this because we've been in the countryside for a short time? I can't stand this damn heat."

"Today is pretty bad. Are we going to Chisaka-sama's place like this?"

"You're too impatient."

"But we're both sweaty messes."

"Don't worry. More than getting clean and going slowly, if I say we're here, you'd feel differently."

"Well."

His legs turned to point straight down Takanawa

Road. When he began the climb up Isaragozaka, dust flew down from a stone being split by a chisel from the construction site of stonemasons at the corner.

Four or five masons worked without looking to the right or left. One mason inserted a chisel in the face of a stone fashioned into a tombstone.

Ichigaku stopped in front of him.

"…"

Johachi stared at the characters carved by the worker. A fine tombstone, he thought. The workman's style looked different from the carving on a simple stone monument.

Lord Reiko

> *Former Junior Fifth Rank, Lower Grade*
> *Suimogenwadai*

A queer feeling swept over the two men reading these characters upside-down. This tombstone would mark the grave of Asano Takumi no Kami. Sengakuji Temple was nearby. They remembered the twenty-fourth of this month would mark exactly one hundred days since the sword attack in the palace.

"Mason."

"Yes." The stonemason raised his surprised eyes and stopped chiseling.

"Who ordered this tombstone?"

"Assistant Vice-Minister Asano Shikibu of Imaicho."

"Uh-huh … From the mansion of Yozen'in, the widow of Takumi no Kami-sama."

"Yessir."

"Did you see the messenger?"

"Yes, he was the steward."

"Was anyone else with him?"

"Horibe-sama and Okuda-sama, now ronin, and another man sometimes came."

"Were they all healthy?"

"And sir, you are?"

"I'm also from Ako but have relatives in Edo and am coming from my home province. Just as I step foot in Edo, seeing the tombstone of my lord I'm connected to eternally brings on tears."

"So you're from Ako?" the stonemason asked, then without a pause, said, "It's hot out. Please come in and have a drink of barley water."

"There's no need. You're busy."

"What? I'm thinking about your hardship. I'm taking it too easy and don't deserve it. Hey, Katsuhiro."

"Yes."

"Are there any mint candies? Tell Grandma to bring tea. Cool yourself with the well water over there and wipe off that sweat. You should have a smoke, too."

"Well then, I guess we'll go cool off."

Continuing their impersonations of Ako samurai, Shimizu Ichigaku and Kimura Johachi sat beneath the reed-screen shelf at the edge of the veranda.

The stonemason Tatsuzo revealed his spirit as an Edo man. He sat in front of the bench where the two sat to take his smoking break.

"You've worked hard. A long trip from Ako under a scorching sun is too much. I've heard a lot of rumors about Ako. The man Oishi-sama did a fine job handling the envoy when the castle was surrendered. The courage of the Ako samurai was on full display."

"Is that what they're saying in Edo?"

"To tell you the truth, some guys are insulting. Hey, Katsuhiro, didn't you hear talk at the public bath? How does that comic poem go? "

The workman hesitated and didn't answer. The stone-mason Tatsuzo looked stumped until he recalled the word-play on the name Oishi that means 'big rock.'

"Oh yes, it goes 'If you step on the big rock, surprise, surprise, a pumice stone flies.' ... But I don't believe that. How do you go to battle with the shogunate's envoy? It would be death without honor, a dog's death. Oishi-sama wouldn't act so stupidly, he would be clever. People are feeling this now. I suspect they're lies. Well, that's what the townsmen think, and I pray that's so."

"Did you say Horibe and Okuda came here?"

"I'm sorry, I was wrong to let a word about that slip out.... But earlier I heard from the netting boatman that first Horibe-sama and sometimes seven or eight or even more than ten men rented a boat and went out to sea, probably for a secret meeting. That's the rumor. I'm not sure about anything, so please take what I say lightly."

"Ha, ha, ha. You're a great supporter of the Asano clan."

"Not just the Asano clan. To be honest, I favor the weak.... I received the order for the tombstone and was told to engrave the grave marker for Takumi no Kami. While I was etching, I felt sorrow because of the lord's spirit, the feelings of Yozen'in-sama, or whatever the many people of the Ako clan were feeling. I started crying and whacked my hand with the hammer."

Kimura Johachi's pained expression lasted a while, but he said nothing. No longer able to stand it, without thinking, he snapped, "Shimizu!"

"Shouldn't we be going?" he said and walked away from the front of the house.

He climbed Isaragozaka in long strides. The smiling Ichigaku followed but took him to task.

"Kimura, you slipped up."

"What?"

"Didn't you call me Shimizu?"

"Who'd know?"

"There's something else. Didn't you take off and put your sweaty hat on Lord Reiko's tombstone? I snatched it off and put it elsewhere, but if that mason has any brains, he doesn't believe we're Ako ronin at all."

"You're right. That was a mistake."

"If that happens too often, we'll risk failing our mission to find out what's happening in Ako."

"My feelings about returning to Edo made me careless."

"We have to be more vigilant in Edo."

"As we search for future movements, everything we do will be scrutinized. If the three clans of the Kira, Uesugi, and Asano create praying mantises versus cicadas, then our aim is to become wild birds versus cicadas. If you understand, you understand. We must be ready."

53

CHISAKA HYOBU

BEFORE ONE HUNDRED days passed, he discovered sprouting gray hairs. When he washed his hands and face each morning, he feared looking in the mirror.

Chisaka Hyobu released an uncommon sigh.

"The vassals of the Asano clan do not carry this much suffering. Their lord's deed is done, and that must bring relief."

This thought penetrated his heart alone.

The anguish from last spring heavily burdened his old bones nearing sixty. As a member of the Uesugi clan, he thought about the great calamity of his forefather Uesugi Kenshin. Until his fragile bones are crushed, he would bear this burden and help Governor-General Noritsuna and, at any cost, guard the sovereign clan with rice fields worth 300,000 koku in Yonezawa.

Governor-General Danjo Taihitsu Noritsuna was adopted at the age of two from the Kira clan and sat as the heir of the Uesugi clan. His biological parents, Kozuke no Suke and his wife, Tomiko, both descended from Uesugi Harima no Kami. By blood and by justice, all eyes saw the Kira and Uesugi clans joined by an unbreakable bond.

Noritsuna's biological father sparked the grave incident in the palace. More than the wound received by Kozuke no Suke or the terror he felt, an enormous blow struck the Uesugi clan. The elderly vassal Chisaka Hyobu took on his burden as the massive rock of that sovereign clan.

As he left Yonezawa for the capital after hearing about the incident, the hairs in every pore on his body stood on end. Hyobu thought, Is this the end of a family prominent since the days of Kenshin?

Fortunately, Kozuke no Suke was the defender and related to powerful clans like the Shimazu and the Sakai. The plan from behind the scenes was effective; this side settled on *indifference*. That did not bring peace of mind to Hyobu. He thought a greater role in the incident for the Uesugi clan lay in the future.

"The old man is a problem ..."

Hyobu's worried expression faced the trees damp from the evening watering. He was sitting at the edge of the tea room falling into shadow and without thinking grumbled, "A disgraceful incident. That old man withdrawing and taking refuge here in Shirokane mansion is the same as me opening the door and shouting fire."

A little while ago, Sawane Ihei, a chief retainer stationed in Edo, visited from the daimyo's main mansion outside of Sakuradamon Gate to broach the subject.

Soon after his return, Ihei explained, "Kozuke no Suke's personal affairs are precarious. He felt an attack is imminent. In the event, Kozuke-sama moves into the Shirokane mansion, shouldn't the mansion be secured even if roads are constructed between the six storehouses? The old man seems to want that, too."

"That will not happen," said Hyobu and withdrew,

almost certain the proposal was not Ihei's but came from Kozuke's mind. Gripped by unbearable emotions, he rejected the suggestion.

But he was troubled. Hyobu was also human.

Hyobu sketched vivid memories of Lord Noritsuna as a child who was driven by impatience and a challenge to transform into the lord worth 300,000 koku. Now, he fretted over the health of his father Kozuke no Suke in the faraway land of Yonezawa.

"They may call me heartless and think of me as a demon, but I came to Edo on a vital mission."

A column of mosquitoes swarmed to breed in the dark eaves. Behind them, a petty samurai slid open a small papered partition.

"Elder."

"What is it?"

"Shimizu Ichigaku-dono and Kimura Johachi-dono are here to see you."

"They're back? Show them in."

His words reflected his impatience as he waited.

"The study will be fine," Hyobu said and jumped up to leave.

In no time, he was sitting in the study. Ichigaku and Johachi were ushered in and sat before him. Their hands and feet were free of dirt after washing at the well inside the compound, but their faces were reddened by the heat of the scorching weather.

"You undertook a critical task. Was there unusual activity in the three provinces?"

"They were peaceful."

Next, he questioned Johachi about the state of affairs in Ako. Hyobu knew most of what he reported. He focused on Kuranosuke as the main enemy and discovered Kuranosuke contracted and paid a deposit to buy land and a house in Saen in Nishinoyama, Yamashima Ward.

"You look tired and should rest."

"I saw the tragic state of the people of Ako."

"I understand, but I'd like you to leave early tomorrow for Yonezawa."

"What is my assignment?"

"I sent a letter ahead. This matter will take time to settle, so I'm sending you. I wrote to request the dispatch of around twenty able men from Yonezawa to be attendants for Kira-sama. I will hear about any roadblocks to progress through an unfavorable reputation in the world. Also, the young men back home will not consider being attendants to Lord Kira a heroic mission."

"That's not so."

"I have no doubt it's true. As warriors with compassion, support for the people of Asano comes naturally to anyone's heart. But that reasoning is wrong. Protecting Lord Kira is protecting the sovereign family of the Uesugi clan. I intend for true swordsmen to be by his side until the middle of August."

"What happens in mid-August?"

Chisaka Hyobu said nothing but pricked up his ears to determine whether the people in the garden and at the end of the corridor were busy at work. Eventually, in a low voice, he said, "Kira-sama will move his residence. He must vacate his home in Gofukubashi and move to Matsuzakacho in Honjo by August 20. Until that time, we must stay vigilant."

54

A LIVING WARRIOR OF OLD

S EVERAL DAYS EARLIER, Tatsuzo's workers pulled the tombstone into Sengakuji Temple and erected the foundation stone and the tombstone.

June 24 was the one-hundredth day after the death of Takumi no Kami Naganori. Early in the morning, a simple woman's palanquin and several attendants slipped into the temple. The hair of Takumi no Kami's wife was shaven off. A few people glimpsed her altered appearance when she slipped into the palanquin.

All morning, visitors from the Geishu clan and the people from the Toda clan returned home from the temples they visited on behalf of Asano Daigaku still confined to his home and wary of the shogunate but in sorrow on this one-hundredth day for the daimyo worth 50,000 koku.

Five in the afternoon neared. A party of more than twenty ronin finished chanting sutras and visiting the shrines then solemnly left the main temple. They appeared to be from the Asano clan, here to mark the one-hundredth day.

The faces of Horibe Yahei and his son Yasubei appeared, as did another father and son, Muramatsu Kihei and Sandayu. Kurahashi Densuke, Okuda Magodayu, Isogai Juroza, Akabane Genzo, Takata Gunbei, and Tanaka Sadashiro were also seen. Becoming ronin had not diminished the men's fortitude. Rather, each man displayed high spirits that surpassed their previous levels.

"When will we see these faces again? The life of a ronin is precarious. This is a wretched parting," said Kataoka Gengoemon. "Where will we go?"

Muramatsu Kihei called Horibe Yahei, "Elder."

Yahei turned and said, "An elder calling another elder is kind of funny."

"Ha, ha, ha. These days, a dislike of elders is the least of my worries."

"I think we'll be rejuvenated."

"I agree," Kihei said and nodded.

"However, for that rejuvenation, I propose we go somewhere and hold a memorial service."

"Very well. Where?"

"Our usual teahouse would be a problem"

"If we walk to the coast, there should be a nice restaurant. The well-behaved young ones will be a touching sight. Usually, the late lord was stern, but if given sake, he showed lenience toward any transgression by the young samurai. Today, we will drink."

"Look there. When you say that, the young bunch in back seem ready to make merry."

"It will be a memorial service."

"Yes, Elder."

From the back, Tanaka Sadashiro said, "Well, what about the bill?"

"We'll split it."

"Ha, ha, ha. We have no elder benefactor."

"As a ronin, I've become thrifty."

To look at them, these men did not seem to be in adverse circumstances. They never showed the slightest notion of revenge. The monks of Sengakuji Temple viewed them as men whose descent in the world occurred with open hearts and an air of tomorrow is tomorrow.

When they went out the main gate of the temple, only one, an elderly samurai laid down his sword in a long, red-lacquered sheath unsuitable to his bowed hip and nervously gasped for air.

"Oh, there's Bunin-dono."

Everyone looked and saw a man close to seventy years old. He wore his hair in a topknot, green leather tabi socks, workman's hakama trousers, and wiped off sweat as he approached. The ronin's home was in Nakanogou, Honjo, a distance from this place. He was a robust man. He was a distant relative of Kuranosuke and called Oishi Bunin.

"Is it over?" Bunin asked the party. "I'm sorry. But if I came sooner, a lower seat could have been added."

"Don't worry, you're not late. The memorial service is starting now. Wait until the graveside worship ends."

"Then excuse me, please go ahead."

"No, I'll find a house for you to rest in. Please wait here while someone looks."

"All right, I'll wait. Oh, Yasubei-dono."

"Yes."

"Is there someone who can escort me to the grave?"

"Of course, they've made a fine tombstone. I'll take you there."

Horibe Yasubei escorted Bunin and returned a second time to the graveyard.

Bunin sat before the new stone and bowed deeply for a long time. The chirps of cicadas soaked into countless graves. Cool breezes moved through the shade of the trees.

"Yasubei-dono."

Finally, Bunin raised his head and squared his shoulders.

"Sit there, please," he said, pointing to the ground in front of him.

"What is it?"

"I'd like to broach a minor matter. What is before you is awe-inspiring."

"I'm listening."

"It's an example."

Bunin's penetrating eyes shot a look at Yasubei's face. The full grievance burned from the bottom of his light brown eyes.

"It seems the men from Ako are missing. Today is the one-hundredth day since the lord's death. You all are good young men and have shown up. What are you planning to do?"

"…"

Yasubei dropped his head. Two or three short hairs of his side locks trembled in the breeze.

"Some time ago, ignoring cowards like Yasui and Fujii, five or ten tried. Where is that spirit?"

"I have not forgotten this situation for one day. However, a huge rift exists among us about the situation back home and Lord Kuranosuke's intentions. We believe this situation is difficult to resolve."

"That's natural. I heard from Elder Okuda that one hundred and twenty men in Ako centered around Kuranosuke made a pact. What single objective was decided by so many men? If we ask the masses, doing nothing is fine. There's always a breakdown along the way and that's frustrating. Kuranosuke's handling is soft. He lacks an objective."

The old man's spirit was amazing. He made one

wonder if this sort of samurai of long ago still lived in the Edo of the Genroku era. He scolded as he thrust an iron fan into his left knee and bathed in the blazing sun from his head.

"It's hard to hear the laughing voices in the world. I'm not an Asano vassal but, as a samurai, it's difficult to stand by and watch. Why can't you decide? Was the head of Kozuke no Suke offered in today's memorial service? What about time? When will the clever things being talked about be achieved? I don't understand why a day must be chosen to kill Kozuke no Suke. If delayed by one day, the strategic importance of just one day becomes central."

"Okuda, Takata, and I cosigned your opinion and repeated it many times to Kuranosuke. Now, however, Kuranosuke appears to be putting all his strength into pleading for Daigaku-sama's appointment."

"He's wasting time. Even if the 53,000 koku passed intact to the younger brother, would Daigaku-sama lazily take the family name with Kozuke no Suke in this state?"

"You understand that, too. Looking at Kuranosuke's tepid writings, even Elder Okuda loses his patience. Yet, there's a chance of things going wrong if a few men attack Kira. That will look like failure to future generations, and the Ako men will be laughed at as men who lost their minds. Only a day has passed, but what are the intentions of the men back home? Our original objective must be carried out within the year. Don't make this old man worry. Show me soon."

"Listening to you reassures me. But where is this fine opportunity?"

"Well, it's this —"

"There is something, Yasubei-dono."

Bunin slid one knee forward. "Do you know the shogunate ordered Kira to relocate his household?"

"What? He's moving out of Gofukubashi."

"I heard it from a reliable source. He was certain Kira will move to the location of the direct retainer Matsudaira Nobori no Suke in Matsuzakacho in Honjo. Will this chance come again? This is a golden opportunity because Kozuke no Suke must leave the estate to go."

"Bunin-dono, are you sure?"

"I even know the day. I was told by someone who regularly goes in and out of the Matsudaira mansion. He said the Kira household will move by August 20."

"Thank you."

Yasubei grabbed the weeds in the graveyard. His entire body swelled with blood. Bunin rejoiced to find a young man having the pluck of their spirited times.

"Do it. You will try. Is there anything you won't do? The right man can rouse spineless cowards to act. How many of our comrades in Edo will act? No one but you, Okuda, and Takata Gunbei."

"I would be honored."

"If we miss this chance, we'll have one more. I heard a rumor about Kozuke no Suke's request to retire. But it's hard to see him being taken care of by the Uesugi clan and sheltered until death in a secluded part of the far-off Yonezawa Castle. If that happened, one hundred or one thousand men could not succeed. Even if that doesn't happen, at his age, a sudden cold and he's dead. Do you men have honor and can walk around in broad daylight? Will I see your faces a second time before this grave?"

They were taking too long and several men came to see what was going on. Faces emerged from the shade of the trees, and one shouted, "Horibe, is Bunin-dono there?"

Bunin struggled to stand.

"I'm finished and will go now."

"The group is growing impatient."

"Should we remind them that waiting is good?"
In the end, he was an old man with strong bones.

PART VII

TAKATA GUNBEI

55

THE SHORT BOW

A RED BENKEI crab plodded across the bridge over the gurgling waters in the outer moat. A little after noon, a lively mix of pedestrians and vehicles made the day on Gofukubashi Bridge look like a holiday.

At the same time every day, a young man from the grilled eel shop clutching the handle of a small wooden bucket ran like what he carried was melting and entered the kitchen gate of the Kira mansion in Gofukubashi.

"I've brought the eels. Hanaki-san, where should I put them? I don't want the cat to get them again," he shouted. The kitchen foot soldier Hanaki Ichibei was at work with his sleeves rolled up.

"Hey, hey, don't put them there. This bundle can go outside."

"It's crowded in here. Are you moving?"

"Useless utensils are being put in the storehouse."

"You're lying. Out on the streets, they're saying the mansion is moving to Matsuzakacho in Honjo."

"So you know?"

"Yesterday, didn't a flat-bottomed barge filled with ten bundles go back and forth?"

"Shut up about that."

"Should I bring eels in a few days?"

"Yes."

"I guess I'll be bringing them to an empty house."

"I won't pay that charge.... We're placing the order to keep the moving date secret from outsiders. It's my duty not to blab. Don't go yet."

Ichibei took a toolbox off the shelf and climbed down the stepladder. He peeked into the room of the kitchen officer Nakazato Niemon.

He whispered something to Niemon who came out.

"Eel merchant."

"Yes."

"Your shop has dealt honestly with us for many years and never betrayed a confidence."

"Nothing good comes from talking about matters that don't benefit the mansion."

"That's true. This mansion will be moved within the day. So starting tomorrow, we will no longer need the eels."

"Oh ... so soon?"

"Don't tell the other merchants."

"What do you mean?"

"Do me a favor and give those eels to the hooded cranes at the lake? We have to pack up the kitchen utensils before dusk and load them onto the boat. That's why we've rolled up our sleeves."

"Should I go around to the garden?"

"Just today, it's okay."

The eel shopboy carried the bucket of eels through the middle gate. Long poles and trunks brought out to the garden were stacked into mountains on straw mats. Straw waste collected at the extravagant large lanterns and the garden trees. The sadness of a home being left drifted chaotically.

"Who are you?" A sharp man's voice came from the lake's edge. The eel shopboy almost dropped the bucket as he set it down.

"I bring eels here every day from the shop and am going to feed them to the cranes."

"Who let you in here?"

This question came from a young princely samurai wearing garden clogs, greenish-brown hakama trousers, and a plain but high-quality hemp short-sleeved kimono. The shopboy looked up to see a frail, slender face scowling at him. His hands grasped a short bow and an arrow. The eel shopboy sat with a plop, knocked back by the realization he was looking at Sahyoue no Suke, who was Kozuke no Suke's son and heir.

"Stop!" the young man ordered. "You have no business here. Leave!"

"Ye … yes. I'll just leave the eels here for the cranes."

"Eels? I don't need them. Take them and go."

"Yessir."

Sahyoue no Suke looked wary but went back inside the mansion.

"Magobei! Magobei! There's a questionable fellow in the garden. Chase him off now. And if you must, beat him."

As he called out, he fit the arrow to the short bow and aimed in the direction of the garden. The eel shopboy leaped up and tumbled out the middle gate.

56

CHASING CRANES

"**W**HAT'S GOING ON?"

"Young lord."

The clan elder Souda Magobei raced over, accompanied by the attendants Matsubara Tachu and Iwase Toneri.

Sahyoue's pallid face surprised them. And the short bow fitted with an arrow made their eyes dart around and peer into the shadows of the garden trees.

"He's gone. Good."

"What did he look like?"

"He said he came to feed the cranes."

"He was probably the eel shopboy I see every day going to the kitchen. In that case, he's not important. Please don't concern yourself.

"Is that so?"

Sahyoue no Suke's shoulders dropped, and he released a huge sigh. He shouted for Tachu and passed the short bow to the attendant. "Tachu, now, go shoot those hooded cranes," and pointed his chin to the three cranes leaning over the lake.

"What, the cranes?"

"Yes, the cranes."

"You want me to shoot them? Shouldn't I ask the lord?"

"It's all right. I already informed my father. I was thinking about shooting them myself."

"The mansion we're moving to in Honjo has an expansive spring. Can't the cranes be moved there?"

"Cranes have no goodwill. The Chinese say they are unlucky birds. And unlucky they are. Some daimyo brought those parasites as a gift to build friendship. That was January 14 of this year. Then on March 14, Asano Takumi no Kami stabbed Father in the palace. Also, didn't the order to relocate arrive on September 14?"

"Those dates are a coincidence. Why are the cranes at fault?"

The clan elder Souda Magobei suppressed a smile.

"They're horrid!" said Sahyoue no Suke, shaking his head.

"By nature, Father hates living creatures. Since he received them, he hasn't been happy. Particularly since the incident, this is not a place for cranes. I feel miserable when I see them. Sometimes the flapping of their huge wings at night is frightening."

"In that case, why not leave the cranes here or give them to relatives as gifts?"

"If those creatures are received as gifts, some scandalous event would befall that household. Shooting them is best."

"Then leave it to me. I will dispose of them so there is no trouble."

Placated by Magobei, Sahyoue said, "They will no longer be cared for by this mansion," and entered the study.

The bare room had been emptied of all the hanging scroll paintings, flower vases, and bookshelves. Sahyoue no Suke looked up at the new horizontal timber at the edges and the ceiling. During this construction, his father Kozuke no Suke was finicky. The construction budget was inadequate. He borrowed immense sums of money for the end pieces, 5,000 or 10,000 ryo from the Uesugi clan. Sahyoue no Suke recalled his mother's disappointment, and the difficult position he put her in each time.

How many tens of ryo does it cost for one cap to hide nails in the inlay work? The insane extravagance of covering them with gold coins received fawning praise but appeared to be mocked by everyone.

The thought, Others will live here, brought unbearable sadness and anger to Sahyoue no Suke.

"After I've enjoyed my old age, this mansion is where you'll spend the rest of your life. I'll bet money on that."

His father Kozuke no Suke often repeated this favorite saying about this estate to his mother. Sahyoue no Suke could not bear to think about his father's feelings. He came to resent the world that criticized his father as if he were a cold-blooded demon filled with greed.

"I don't care what people say, my father is a noble man. Despite the verbal attacks on the household, deep down his character never changed from the time before Edo. A pure, cultured man like my father can't help having contempt for all brutes, a characteristic well known to the masters of the tea ceremony, the gardeners, and the fishmongers patronized by him.

"They say he's selfish and greedy, but he shares that characteristic with all old men. They say he puts on airs or acts imperiously when in the palace or when an imperial envoy visits, but isn't that justified given Father's experience and the status of the Kira clan? He wasn't domineering only with the Asano clan.

"Takumi no Kami had no experience carrying out an important role in the shogunate and possessed a narrow samurai's disposition. Therefore, Father became cranky when Takumi no Kami defied him, a man old enough to be his father. Those of us familiar with Father's character cannot fathom the reason for Asano's rage. For some reason, the world reserves its spite only for my father and me. I don't understand that either."

Sahyoue no Suke grumbled like this incessantly and was wracked with anxiety. His father displayed the impudence naturally reached by mature men but never experienced fighting a formidable opponent in the world. Because he was born a hereditary heir in a distinguished koke family, he never dreamed of encountering this situation in his lifetime.

"Ah, he's getting away! Over there!"

In the garden, Matsubara Tachu and Iwase Toneri called over a foot soldier to catch a crane and put him into a large palanquin.

Sahyoue no Suke clicked his tongue in disgust and headed to his room. Sudden concerns about the workers busy packing up the tools made him cross the covered bridge and enter a temporary inner room behind a storehouse with two doors.

In a small room on the side of the storehouse, and the rooms on the left and right sides of the back veranda, usually, seven or eight samurai sat and kept their minds on the mouths of their sword sheaths. When they heard Sahyoue no Suke's footsteps crossing the covered bridge, the men gripped their swords, and several heads poked out.

"…"

Sahyoue no Suke made an uneasy bow and entered a

dark room that looked like a box inside a box where his aged father and mother lived their lives in hiding. The twelve-tatami room had a dismal air in the shadows of the leaves from the narrow eaves facing north.

His melancholy face poked in to see the lean shoulders of his elderly father sitting in a timid silence and the curved back of his elderly mother. Sahyoue no Suke's chest tightened. He did not understand why did this spineless father act to enrage another in the palace and is viewed by the world as an arrogant man. Back home, the people who carried out the first offerings of crops from the Mikawa domain every year respected his father like a guardian god. The father admired by those people and the father reviled by the citizens of Edo are the same man. The world should not doubt these words of his son.

57

___

THIS FAMILY

"**I**s **that you**, Sahyoue no Suke?"

Kozuke no Suke recognized his spirit. He turned his clouded face to his wife Tomiko and said, "This conversation is a bit involved. You are going to live there."

Both parents looked ready to argue. Since the incident, Sahyoue no Suke was most disappointed in the large fissure that opened between his parents already in their sixties. As their son, he often looked away.

"If I'm going to be in the way—"

"You won't be in the way. There's no point in asking."

"All right …" she said and rose.

"Have you finished packing?" he asked his son.

"I'm ready to move at any time."

"Is that so? Stop worrying."

"I will."

"Live life with courage! Few matters are worth worrying about! Your mother also says you look pale and worried. In any case, I have a few days left. Aren't you the heir to the Kira clan? Take care of yourself. How does a young man just twenty years old have such a weak constitution? The gossip in a petty world sickens your spirit."

"Yessir."

"I will not live with such a weak spirit. No matter what anyone says, I will always be faithful to my duty. The shogunate knows this. The court nobles are aware of my forty years of service since the age of nineteen. A know-nothing minor daimyo made a fool of the Chief Master of Ceremonies. I'll no longer be able to fulfill my duties as the master of ceremonies. By having daimyos at my beck and call, I conducted the annual ceremonies without mistakes by the court nobles."

He repeated this explanation dozens of times to relatives, vassals, and friends. At the root, he seemed to be an honest but faint-hearted man. He spoke up immediately on any matter, but Kozuke no Suke's voice came out high pitched, and his complexion reddened alarmingly from anger. Lately, he recognized his recent warped mindset and, as expected, was a touch embarrassed.

"Well … speaking of that now changes nothing. The only one who believes me appears to be you.… That's all I have to say."

"I understand."

"Of course, you're a child. Sahyoue, when night comes, you'll move to the new residence by boat. Home moves the spirit. Your spirit will change, and you will live."

The father was always like this with his son. Sahyoue no Suke averted his tear-filled eyes, bowed, and left.

Alone again, the old couple remained silent. One mosquito incense stick burned on an incense burner. A narrow line like the couple's feelings tied the two together. After a while, Kozuke no Suke broke the silence.

"Tomiko, why are you talking about returning to the Uesugi clan and leaving me?"

"Let me go back to my family."

"Don't you think a separation is scandalous for a couple in their sixties?"

"The disgraceful incident is known. I cannot bear any more than that."

"What do you mean?"

"I've already told you, this is pointless. I will not scold you. Rather than staying by your side, because there is nothing left to say, I will return to my family today."

"Go," he said.

"They say a man who descends from the Uesugi clan can be cold-hearted. Like Chisaka Hyobu and ... you."

"Hyobu is a vassal," he said. "That man exhibits the favorable trait of the coldness of a Yonezawa samurai. Look, am I lying? The Lord of Yonezawa is my flesh and blood. If he got wind of an alarming scheme by the Ako ronin, he would first think of my well-being, and tell me to shelter in the mansion in Shirokane or move to the castle in Yonezawa. In contrast to the concern for me shown in my faraway home, doesn't Chisaka Hyobu demolish each word of his lord and expose me to danger by not providing shelter and deeming withdrawal to Yonezawa unreasonable?"

"…"

"All right."

His voice lost its color, and his breathing became raspy. He gulped down tea.

"Hyobu's behavior reflects his emotions, and hate is reasonable. However, you have been with me for forty years. What would it mean for you to return to your home village at this age? My guess is you have embraced Hyobu's opinion."

"…"

"Great! Husbands and wives, as well as relatives,

become unreliable sometimes, but that is a common occurrence in this world. Go! Leave! Have the Uesugi clan cut all ties to me. You can tell Hyobu that. He's a vassal. Won't his status as a vassal rise?"

"Lord."

Tomiko drew her knees closer to his and stared into his face. From the time she was twenty and came as his bride from the Uesugi clan, the wife had the sterner personality. She was a helpful partner who relied on ingenuity and influence, looked out for extremely dangerous gains, arrogantly watched people because of her timidity, and properly chided her husband whose temperament amused the world. Consequently, Kozuke no Suke, like a cat, could not look at his wife. Before March, this mutual bickering never happened.

"What?" asked Kozuke no Suke with an expression he reserved for enemies.

"This is the end. I am warning you for the last time. If you treasure our sons, please consider it."

"You say such stupid things."

"Can't you make up your mind?"

"I have no intention of dying. Why should I kill myself?"

"It is not logic. I'm appealing to emotion."

"To emotion? The wife who recommends suicide to her husband speaks of emotion."

"I will speak for the sake of our sons. By chance, if revenge is taken by an unexpected blade from the Ako ronin, what will become of Sahyoue? Will the Kira clan continue to be secure? If things go bad for the lord in Yonezawa, the disasters he'll suffer will be endless. The imperial title of governor-general of another clan will be passed to the adopted child, but isn't Danjo Daihitsu-sama our son, our blood? The Kira clan and the Uesugi clan may be destroyed in your heart. I don't know whether they'll be saved."

"Enough. Stop saying this over and over."

"No, this is the end. I will talk. As your wife, I can't listen to the wild rumors. I'm bathed in abusive blame. Day and night, my spirit is threatened even by the sound of the wind. I'd like to enjoy my few remaining years. We haven't passed the normal lifespan of people? For both clans and for both of our sons—"

"Shut up!"

"…"

"If there is death, only you will die."

"If my life ends, I will die smiling."

"If the world blames me, I will not die. If the Ako ronin come for me, I will live with pride. I've always been stubborn. If I take my own life, all of them will clap their hands and sneer. That would be awful. Regrettable."

"Perhaps you're a coward."

"What did you say?!"

The sound of a slapped cheek echoed. Tomiko's quiet sobbing and crying lasted for a time.

The room was already dark. Not one candle was lit that night. A column of mosquitoes groaned around Kozuke no Suke's face hardened like a mask.

Light from outside flowed into the room. Attendants carrying paper lanterns and the clan elder Souda Magobei kneeled and said, "The time to move has come."

58

ELEVEN SHADOWS

A **FLAT-BOTTOMED BARGE** on the dark surface of the outer moat was moored to the shore under flickering lantern light.

A samurai soon ran out from the side service gate of the Kira residence near the shore and gave a muted call.

"They're coming out."

Four or five samurai clustered together on the stern began patrolling both shores.

Twenty vassals formed a human fence for the short distance from the gate to the boat. Between them, the father and the son, Kozuke no Suke and Sahyoue no Suke, both dressed in subdued clothes, walked out. Tomiko was not seen. Sahyoue no Suke took his father's hand to guide him from the gangplank onto the barge. The samurai nodded in greeting, and the father and son sat on seats provided in the hull.

"Now ..."

"Now."

This hushed exchange between the ship and the shore

scattered the vassals. The barge slid over the bottom of the narrow moat.

Kozuke no Suke gazing at the lights onshore and the stars said, "It's been several days since I felt outside winds."

That evening, Sahyoue no Suke thought only about his mother returning to the Uesugi clan. Listening to his mother's words, she seemed right. But his father's claims were also well grounded. As the son, however, no matter who was right, he thought it impossible to follow his mother. Until the end, he would harden the core of his heart and stay by the side of his isolated father.

"What's that?" exclaimed the vassals guarding the stern and the bow. The frightened eyes of the father and son darted all around the boat.

"What is it?" asked Kozuke no Suke.

A vassal whispered to the men around him and eventually into Sahyoue no Suke's ear.

"About ten suspicious ronin are walking along the shore and trailing this boat. Be on the alert."

"Where … where are they?"

Without uttering a word, a vassal nodded toward the shore on the left side. They were trailing the boats, six men in front were followed by five more. The two groups formed one party and were soon acting like they knew they were spotted. Sahyoue no Suke's alarmed eyes only turned to the two barges rowing behind them. If the worst happened, four vassals were onboard each of those barges. They had around twenty vassals. Their adversaries were eleven mysterious figures on the shore.

"We'll probably be all right?" Sahyoue no Suke whispered to the vassals.

"Don't worry. Attacks on the shore and the river are rare."

"But …"

The hair of Sahyoue no Suke's side locks stood up in the river breeze. He heard superior men were among the Ako ronin. The names Takata Gunbei, an expert spearman, and Horibe Yasubei, an expert fencer, echoed. A fight of twenty men versus eleven might not be an equal match. They lost their lord and their stipends. Now they would sacrifice their bodies.

"Row faster," Sahyoue no Suke urged the men with the oars.

Kozuke no Suke turned his head to ask, "Why are you saying that?"

"If they catch up in this area, row to the guard station. Once we get to the Ogawa River, a man will go ahead and mobilize men from the estate. But until then, don't rush. Have you thought about what will become of Takumi no Kami's younger brother Daigaku if those men blunder? Or what will be the implications for the Asano clans in Geishu and Tosa?

Sahyoue no Suke chose to stay by his father's side to protect him, instead, he found himself being protected by his father. He calmed down after observing his father's calm demeanor.

Petty officials usually viewed his father as a worldly man. From the age of nineteen, he interacted in the company of powerful court officials and aristocrats and enjoyed tanka poetry and incense-smelling ceremonies. From middle age, he turned his contemplative eyes to Buddhism. These days, he devoted himself to the tea ceremony, in particular, and often said, "The tastes of tea and Zen are one." The father, seen through his son's eyes, found his practice useful in this sort of situation and dependable in all ways.

When they rowed out to Ogawa River, the figures

shadowing them on the riverbank scattered and disappeared. For the first time, Kozuke no Suke smiled.

"What can a scrawny dog do without an owner? Why do they work with no stipend with the sole aim to make my head fly? While they walk blasted by the river breeze, cold numbed their heads, and they recognized their stupidity."

Before long, his boat and the guard boats entered Yokobori below Ryogoku. On the first bridge, the eleven men stood at the handrail in a line.

They're here.

When spotted, they scattered and scrambled over the bridge.

Between the first and second bridges somewhere near Uragashi in Matsuzakacho, those same eleven shadows stood in a line.

59

THE ZEALOTS

Earlier under the afternoon sun, a samurai drenched in sweat restlessly placed his chest in the breeze of a fan. "Good afternoon," he said as he passed through the doorway of Miyatogawa, a grilled eel shop in Hakuyacho. This man was Horibe Yasubei.

"Welcome."

"Has a party come?"

"They're upstairs."

He climbed to the second floor. The flowers of the Simon bamboo in the courtyard provided a moving, lush green wall on the back railing. The voices of a dozen men flowed from the room. Okuda, Kataoka, Akabane, Muramatsu Kihei and his son Sandayu, Takebayashi Tadashichi, and Yada Gorozaemon were present.

Takata Gunbei noticed him. "Ah, Horibe."

"I apologize for being late," said Yasubei and sat.

"We're still waiting for Isogai Juroza and Tominomori Sukeemon."

"Isogai sent word. He ate watermelon, got diarrhea,

and has been confined to bed since yesterday. Sukeemon went on a trip. Both sent their regards."

"I don't understand why a young man like Isogai is always sick. It makes no sense," said Takata Gunbei then whispered, "But an old body like Kozuke no Suke's may be struck down by illness at any time." The elder Okuda nodded in agreement.

"I'm not counting on that."

Gunbei had a bump on his shoulder like all expert spearman.

"He probably won't do that," he said and looked at the faces seated around him.

Yasubei took out a letter from his pocket.

"I received this reply the other day from the chief retainer in Yamashina. Please pass it around."

The elder Okuda read it and passed it to Gunbei. Next, Tanaka, Kataoka, and Takebayashi read the letter.

"Horibe!" said Gunbei. He was furious. Unable to bear the harsh tone of the note, he spat out his words with his usual resentment.

"A meeting with the group in Kyoto is fine, but how long are we going to go back and forth over the same complaint? Letters from Kuranosuke-dono cling to compassion from the shogunate. He considers the appointment of Daigaku-sama to be the fundamental principle and quashes reckless acts."

"Hmm," said Yasubei, lowering his chin.

From the side, Muramatsu Sandayu said, "But first," and pushed a cup into his hand.

Gunbei took the cup and said, "Looking at today's letter, Yukai of Enrinji Temple is pushing for the appointment of Daigaku-sama. Shouldn't we seek an intermediary in the Yanagisawa clan, take an active interest in the relationships with the inner palace, evaluate the results, and request emphasis on the importance of a spiteful plan as women do? There's too much perpetual indecision. Oishi-dono's mind easily sees all of that. I believe he's not a man who engages in serious tasks."

Okuda Magodayu leaned over to pull the skewer out of the grilled eel.

"Exchanging letters between Edo and Kyoto resolves nothing. Someone must go one time."

"The previous letter said Hara Soemon will leave Kyoto soon," said Kataoka Gengoemon.

Gunbei spoke with contempt. "That's like giving candy to a crying child, he'll end up holding us back. We revere the lord's name and will follow him to the grave, the first principle of the warrior. Only Oishi-dono considers this to be a reckless and wild undertaking. In the end, the difference in opinion concerns the way of the samurai. No matter how many letters are exchanged in this debate, it will never end. Even if we have to ignore the Kyoto faction, we will carry out our original aim."

They all shared Gunbei's resentment. No one saw him as a shallow man driven by the smell of sake but as a master of the spear. Others overlooked some of his shortcomings, and so did he. His transfer from the Ogasawara clan to the Asano clan brought a high stipend. He earned fame through his spearsmanship. Gunbei always spoke of the clan's hospitality. Since the catastrophe visited on Takumi no Kami, Gunbei championed the faction living in the province. Whether right or wrong, he argued if they were not resolute in carrying out their will by the one-hundredth day after the lord's death, they would not take that road.

Two men, Horibe Yasubei and Okuda Magodayu, fully agreed with him. These three men became the leaders of the faction of former clan retainers posted in the province but remained in Edo. Their position was to take immediate action.

As with the faction back home, men with differing opinions emerged, men who should have easily come together in Edo did not unite at all. Many of the clan elders holding important posts like Fujii Matazaemon and Yasui Hikoemon vanished. The particularly jumpy Horibe and Takata became unpleasant. However, a characteristic of the men here was to take no notice of these dissenters.

They were inclined to say, "Stay away from those awful men. The indecisive man watches. I'll do it alone if I must."

From behind, the elders encouraged the younger men. "We must do it."

The elder Horibe Yahei, who did not attend, was the first to say that. The ronin Oishi Bunin in Nakanojo in Honjo condemned the excessive caution and the limited ability to act by today's young men.

Yasubei moaned, "I'm sick of arguments. Indignation is good. In short, do it or don't do it."

"Of course, we'll do it," said Gunbei. "Today, we push on."

"When?" asked Takebayashi Tadashichi under his breath.

"I don't know what's going on, but packages are being sent little by little to Honjo. But it looks like Kira and his son have not moved yet."

"That will come later, within three or four days."

"Maebara Isuke never stops watching that neighborhood. If he sees anything, he'll notify us right away."

"Will he move during the day or night?"

"They say Kozuke no Suke shies away from the world and has not taken one step outside. He'll choose the night."

"He'll come out when we least expect it. When word comes from Maebara, can we get there on time?"

"For the next four or five days, he'll be in certain locations. And they probably have emergency measures," someone said quietly.

Even after the one-hundredth day of Takumi no Kami's death passed, given Kuranosuke's indecisiveness and the view that Kozuke no Suke will move to Yonezawa this coming spring, the men impatient for quick decisive action did not want to delay by one more day. They understood that Kira's change of residence was a perfect opportunity to achieve their great desire. For a short time, they conspired in secret.

Tanaka Sadashiro left his seat to go to the bathroom downstairs. He didn't return after some time. The men's cautious eyes glanced uneasily at his empty seat.

"What is Tanaka up to?"

"It's been a little long for the bathroom."

Akabane Genzo stood and said, "I'll check," and went downstairs.

60

ATTENDANTS ON THE SHORE

A FAN FANNING the smoke of grilling eel sent flapping sounds from the kitchen. Men were fast at work, ripping open and steaming eels. Tanaka Tadashiro stood under the ladder steps beside the window, peered into the kitchen, and strained to hear.

Genzo started to speak.

"Shh!" Tadashiro waved the fan touching his chest to the side to silence him.

They cupped their hands to listen to the raised voices of the delivery shopboy and the cook. The counterman also butted into their exchange.

"What's going on? Why didn't you bill them for the eels brought today?"

"He said they weren't needed."

"If they didn't need them, why didn't you bring them back?"

"Here's what happened. I'm sure the young Lord Kira was carrying a short bow and aimed an arrow at me. I was not going to get shot and die, so I left them and ran off."

"If you go to that mansion, they're arrogant and stingy

about paying. He aims that short bow as a threat and makes fools of the merchants. Go settle the bill."

"I can't go back."

"You can't? Isn't that mansion moving to Honjo today? After today, you'll have to go all the way to Matsuzakacho to get paid. If they don't pay the bill, bring back the eels."

"Will anyone go for me?"

"Scaredy cat."

"To me, my life is precious."

"You're ridiculous. Get the money for those eels. Do you think you'll be killed? That young lord knows nothing. Any samurai who'd point a bow at you is insane."

"He's a fine-looking young master. His oval face resembles Kozuke no Suke's in places."

"A cheapskate living in a mansion is sickening."

"All right, I can probably get it."

"Don't say something arrogant like that's my master's property."

"Instead, act like the kitchen foot soldier Hanaki-san leaked a secret you happened to hear."

"What secret?!"

"What? For example, the date the lord and the young lord will move to Honjo, they stupidly hid from the public."

"Of course."

"Other merchants are being told to come in four or five days, but the truth is everyone will leave the mansion today."

"You dope. How long have you been going around saying that? Is that your idea of revenge? The eels will spoil. Will someone go beg for the eels and bring them back?"

Genzo and Tadashichi locked eyes under the ladder steps. The two sensed a maid coming and went back upstairs.

In a short time, hands clapped on the second floor with the request "Please, bring the food."

After the food came, Kurahashi Densuke stopped by with nervous eyes. Meanwhile, dusk fell over the streets.

"Well, we'll talk another time."

"Regards to your wife."

Everyone made a point to exchange pleasantries at the Miyadogawa gate before leaving, but none went home.

Human figures strolled in the evening cool at the *tokoroten* jellied noodle shop in a gravel area, an empty grassy lot, and the end of the bridge. Soon the vassals of Kozuke no Suke docked the barge with little noise at the side on the shore of the outer moat visible from the side service gate of the Kira residence.

While that happened, Kurahashi Densuke said, "The fan dropped," and passed behind the men scattered there.

When they heard the whisper, "The fan dropped," the eyes of several flickered in the darkness on the opposite shore. They could see the figures of Kozuke no Suke and his son. Vassals surrounded them to conceal even their shadows as they boarded.

The creaking barge left the shore.

In no time, the group assembled in an empty lot.

Swift actions, like the wind, began. The pledge was decided. This was the place. They had not anticipated their opponents coming by boat.

"Go around and get ahead of them," said Akabane Genzo.

"To Matsuzakacho?"

"If he gets off the boat, it will be near the second bridge."

"All right," said Genzo too eagerly.

"Slow down," cautioned the elder Okuda.

"You can't get there before them. Matsuzakacho is not

the only destination for Kozuke no Suke. Other places of refuge are the daimyo's emergency residence or an annex mansion of the Uesugi clan."

"Thank you," said Muramatsu Sandayu with a nod.

"In that case …" said Gunbei, "We'll trail the boat by foot along the shore."

"You'll attract attention."

"No, we'll scatter."

"Excellent."

No one objected.

Immediately, a first, a second, and a third man began his lone chase along the shore.

But after walking four or five blocks, human figures walking along the shore ahead of them and trailing the boat carrying Kira Kozuke no Suke appeared before their eyes as a dignified union. There were eleven men. The men wore straw sandals, hiked up their hakama trousers to prepare for a fight, and were ready to cross long swords. Several held spears by their sides.

"Huh?"

"Who are they?"

Yasubei and Gunbei were suspicious.

They weren't allies but probably vassals of the Kira clan in strange disguises. Wearing straw sandals and dusty work hakama trousers and carrying backpacks exposed them as country samurai. Not one of the eleven men of frightening power let down his guard with each step forward. The tension seen would not crumble into disgraceful confusion, even if an ancient cannon shot at them. They resembled an iron fence doggedly accompanying the boat.

Gunbei ran up to Horibe Yasubei to whisper, "Shimizu Ichigaku is here!"

"…"

Yasubei's cold eyes gleamed. "Who's behind you?"

He was the elder Okuda.

He blurted out, "I know who they are! Shimizu Ichigaku went to Yonezawa. Those samurai are from his hometown! He selected them from the Uesugi clan. That's it. I'm sure of it."

"Yonezawa swordsmen?"

"They came as attendants to accompany the man hiding out."

"Crap!" said someone in a quiet but powerful tone carried off by the wind.

61

GARDEN SHEARS

SHIMIZU ICHIGAKU RECEIVED the order from Chisaka Hyobu to select ten swordsmen from his hometown of Yonezawa and return with them to Edo. They arrived this morning.

Hyobu told them, "Until the lord hiding away moves …" as today's deadline loomed.

After receiving word from Hyobu, Kozuke no Suke and his son would move to the new residence. Soon after their party untied their travel gear, they received the order from Hyobu to accompany Shimizu Ichigaku and quickly go to Edo, carry out the night's mission, and stay in Matsuzakacho.

"As expected, Hyobu-sama, your insight is keen. Skinny Ako ronin trailed us here and there," said Ichigaku. He warned his swordsmen, "Never turn around to look."

The swordsmen walked as instructed. They risked their lives with each step, and tense nerves strained their backs.

"I recognized two of them: Horibe and Takata. Those two are formidable. If they attack, I will battle those two because I named them. Even if our rivals attack from the sides and the back, those two will die in front. In time ..."

However, the chance never came.

The Ako side was impatient, but the Yonezawa samurai would not be their rivals. Shimizu Ichigaku was not the enemy. They crossed Ryogoku Bridge and stopped at the first field on a corner. Elder Okuda was there and said, "Not now."

Muramatsu Kihei also moaned, "Ah! The time has come."

Takata Gunbei, with a hint of disapproval, said, "If the elder doesn't interfere, we will attack where Kozuke no Suke disembarks. What should we do about Shimizu Ichigaku?"

The always-agitated Yasubei, whatever he was thinking, said "Takata, forget about that," and calmed down.

"Why have you come here? Are you having second thoughts?"

Gunbei got angry. "Akabane, Kataoka, you two will—"

"Will obey the elder."

Most of the men had reconsidered and headed home. Gunbei looked daggers at the backs of his departing comrades.

"Horibe, are you leaving?"

"I have to."

"Can you and Elder Okuda stay a little longer?" he asked and grabbed both men's sleeves. "I'd like to talk to you."

"What is it?"

"The three of us shouldn't leave."

"Why not?"

"Wasn't the pledge different? What was our original pledge? It was inevitable some would lose heart at a critical moment. But should we, the only three left, pledge to strengthen the iron wall and to kill Kira even when down to the last man? Have you forgotten those words?"

As he spoke, Gunbei tightened the grips of his shaking hands on the wrists of Yasubei and the elder. His anger boiling up from his passion made tears glisten in his eyes. Surprisingly, Yasubei and Okuda sensed trembling in their spirits. They thought it was respect for his passion but found beauty in his naked stubbornness.

"Takata.... Calm down, don't get so mad. We have no reason to look at tonight and cringe."

"No, even if they call us cowards, there is no room for excuses. Today's words are already—"

"Listen, you're in a hurry to die, but will you die smiling without taking Kozuke no Suke's head?"

"I am confident. I intend to make use of Shimizu Ichigaku's skill."

"Isn't Ichigaku a rival?"

"That doesn't matter."

"What the elder and I want has not changed at all tonight. But the enemy's prepared. Whatever clash occurs, I can't see us winning. Anyone with the barest knowledge of military tactics senses that immediately. No matter how many attendants and vassals we kill, neither I nor anyone else has any chance of killing Kozuke no Suke.

"First, look at the geographical advantage, a small guardhouse and many homes on the shoreline are close to Kira's residence. If one voice shouts, shrieks would break out from many lowlifes. Using a firearm or a projectile would probably be difficult. Any mistakes would bring candid advice in a letter patiently written by Oishi-dono, and the faction back home would laugh at us. As Oishi-dono said, being mocked in the world would compound the disgrace to the lord's house. Be patient, for tonight, say nothing and go home."

Okuda Magodayu soothed the bitter taste in Gunbei's mouth. He forced himself to leave but remained irate. Glum and silent, he crossed back over Ryogoku Bridge.

Still evening, Gunbei harbored tangled emotions and struggled to pass the night with his close friends, then Yasubei tapped his shoulder.

"Takata, why don't we go to the teahouse and have a taste?"

"I don't want to drink," he snapped while shaking his head.

"Don't say that."

Like an elder, Okuda Magodayu with half a smile said, "I'll go, too. Please join us."

He went along like a spoiled brat being humored. When he calmed down and drank, Gunbei's mood lightened. He drank heavily. Perhaps he decided that the life to be discarded would sleep soundly only that night. The high spirits from drinking were awful. The party of Kataoka, Takebayashi, and Muramatsu denounced the lack of commitment to wholehearted revenge. But their teary voices pledged to act until the end. Gunbei grasped the hands of the elder and Yasubei, and asked, "Will you two be going to Kamakura in a few days?"

The three had been discussing an excursion from Enoshima to Kamakura to sign a blood oath for revenge before the altar at the Tsurugaoka Hachimangu shrine, and, on this foundation, form a pact as comrades. But with no spare time, only an implicit agreement of courage existed to that day. That hope spoken by Gunbei provided them sufficient reason to trust him. Yasubei promptly said, "Very good. We'll be there."

They made a promise to meet there on the designated day and went their separate ways.

Early one morning several days later, Gunbei called

out, "Horibe, are you ready?" He showed up at his ronin house to fetch Yasubei.

The sound of garden shears came from the garden. A gray-haired old man held garden shears across the fence of morning glories revealing small flowers each morning.

"Takata-san, come in," said the gardener and opened the gate.

He was Horibe Yahei, Yasubei's father, who led him inside.

"Sachi, bring tea," he said and set the shears on the veranda.

62

SEALED IN BLOOD IN KAMAKURA

S ACHI OFFERED THEIR guest a sitting rug.

"I'll leave it here, inside the door," she looked at her father's face as she greeted Gunbei.

"Just leave it at the edge of the veranda and finish untying the sandals."

"My, my, only selfish requests …"

"It's the civility of the ronin. Am I right, Gunbei?"

"You always say something funny."

Gunbei raised the tea in the palm of his hand.

"Is Yasubei-dono still here?"

"He woke up a while ago. Sachi, what is my son doing?"

"I'm so sorry, but this morning, I believe Okuda-sama came to visit. Please wait a little longer."

"See if he's coming."

"Uh … He's working on his daily lesson."

"Oh, all right. Gunbei-dono, please excuse the delay."

"What is his daily lesson?"

"What? Oh, a trivial thing …"

The old man who often talked only about his son forced a smile but looked proud.

"Since becoming a ronin, he's been having trouble with so much free time. This summer, he took out a calligraphy book of masters' works and copies sutras every day as his writing practice," he said and chuckled.

"Oh, calligraphy is his daily lesson?"

"Yes, it is."

Gunbei raised an eyebrow. Why would someone preparing to die sooner or later than an autumn cicada learn characters?

"Well, I'm ready."

The elder Okuda, a frequent visitor, wore a light traveling outfit. He pushed open the garden gate and entered.

He encouraged Yahei by asking, "Are you going, too?"

"No, it's better if I don't."

Yahei picked up the shears to continue trimming the garden bushes with their thick growth during the dog days of summer. He could not stomach men zealous for revenge. When they scattered, he moved to this rented house. The shadows of darkness or tragedy did not dim the brightness in the faces of the people who kept the house in order or Sachijo, Yasubei's wife.

What's going on here? wondered Gunbei, dismayed. He was still a man without a wife. Eventually, Yasubei came out to greet him. When Gunbei saw the short-sleeved kosode kimono handed to him by Sachi from an inner room and the meticulous care given to his traveling gear by Sachi's hands, he felt a tinge of envy and stabbed in the heart by his lonely life.

"I'm sorry to keep you waiting."

Yasubei said he'd be gone for four or five days and wore new straw sandals. He donned a bamboo hat. Sachi walked around to the outside. Yahei also saw him off at the gate.

"Are you carrying travel medications?"

"No, that's a portable brush-and-ink case."

Their careful consideration made him reflect on Yasubei's daily life with his father and wife. Oddly, Gunbei didn't notice married women on that day's trip but strangely noticed the farmers' homes, merchants' shops, and homes of various classes he spied from the road. He fixated on the happy family circle in each home, life, or himself, and said little as he walked.

Two days later, he was praying at the Tsurugaoka Hachiman Shrine.

Okuda Magodayu came with a scroll mounted with paper stored in his sleeve.

This was the oath. Before the altar, the three men signed their names and sealed their oath with blood.

"Takata."

"What?" asked Yasubei as he dropped down in front of a large ginkgo tree.

"Are you tired? You look a little under the weather."

"It may be the water."

"That's no good." Yasubei opened a medicine case and shook out medicinal herbs into the palm of his hand. "Here, take this."

Gunbei took it in his hand and attempted to swallow it but spilled it. He seemed dissatisfied and at the tea shop, said, "Maybe, we should go home?"

"We went to a lot of trouble to come here," said the elder Okuda. He meant Gunbei had to be dragged there.

They walked around the island and saw women divers catching abalone. In front of a souvenir shop selling shell work, the father and daughter from a samurai family in a party of young samurai watched the three men from behind.

"That's strange."

"It looks like him."

They paid particular attention to Gunbei. When the three came around from the top of the rocks sprayed by crashing waves and passed in front of the souvenir shop and the samurai and his daughter, who had been watching them for some time, the father exclaimed, "Oh," and caught his breath.

Gunbei turned his head toward their voices. "Oh, you're …"

He stopped.

63

THE LINGERING SCENT OF AUTUMN

"**T**his is a strange place to meet. Will you join us later for a meal?" asked the samurai as he approached, leaving his attendant and daughter.

"I'm sorry for not keeping in touch. You haven't changed."

"I feel the same. But you had a terrible experience. The Asano clan enticed you with an exceptionally high stipend. Thinking about it now, that was unfortunate. If you had remained in the Ogasawara clan, none of this would have happened. Well, a man's fortune is unknown. Since that horrible incident, the rumors have upset poor Sayo."

From the father's greeting, Gunbei guessed Sayo was his daughter. Their conversation was often animated. The father seemed reasonable and the daughter, capable.

Horibe and Okuda walked ahead in their usual relaxed gaits and loitered at the roadside when Gunbei did not return right away.

At long last, Gunbei caught up to them and said, "Eeyah, I was weak."

However, his expression, which favored glumness since Tsurugaoka, was brighter.

"He's a talkative old fellow. We hadn't seen or heard from each other in five or six years, so I can't run off. Go to the inn. I'll see you this evening."

"Who is he?"

"He's the vassal Uchida Kageyu-dono who is a great help to my older brother and recommended me to the Osagawara clan."

"Well, we'll go ahead."

The two went to the inn and shed their sandals.

They didn't think they'd see him until after sunset, but Gunbei returned in good spirits.

He had eaten at another inn with Uchida and his daughter. After that, Gunbei's conversations were often lively. For the first time on this trip, the trio enjoyed a cheerful evening.

His cheerfulness lasted the entire journey to Edo. But after arriving in Edo, Gunbei showed his face to no one.

A short time later, Kuranosuke in Yamashina ordered Hara Soemon to leave the capital.

Soemon's mission was to go to Kyoto and extinguish the flames that erupted since the downfall of his lord's house. From a distance, Kuranosuke watched the agitated spirit of the faction residing in the province and feared a growing fire if neglected. He worried if he entrusted an ordinary man to put out that fire, it may grow and become an inferno. Therefore, Kuranosuke assigned that task to the popular veteran Soemon.

Horibe sent a message to Takata Gunbei. He replied he was ill but reluctantly visited Soemon's lodging with Okuda Magodayu.

"How worried is Oishi-dono about the men losing their hot-blooded spirit?"

Soemon's question was the heaviest blow to the two men's hearts.

Was only Soemon still uncertain? Otaka Gengo and Shindo Genshiro followed him from Yamashina.

They met several times at different locations. Because Takata Gunbei never appeared, Horibe Yasubei made a forthright appeal to rein in delegates like Hara Soemon and Otaka Gengo.

Yasubei was not alone. Many elders like Horibe Yahei, Okuda Magodayu, and Muramatsu Kihei understood the uncompromising position of not backing down and argued for swift revenge. Soemon realized this split was simply the difference between those who lacked the passion and intensity and understood the political realities of Edo and those who observed great power from the environs of Kyoto.

When he sent updates by a fast messenger, Kuranosuke promptly replied.

In the middle of October, I will visit Edo again.

"Oishi-dono is coming here!"

His voice was quietly strangled by the spirit of the provincial faction trapped in arguments and impatience.

"We'll wait for orders from the chief retainer."

This is what everyone expected.

A short time later on October 20, a letter left Yamashina. Around November 2, he sent advance notice during the trip to announce his expected arrival date in Edo.

In the letter, Oishi stated his intention to stay in a home in Shibamatsumoto-cho rented from Maekawa Kyudayu, the former head of the day laborers of the Asano clan. As a precaution, he wanted the men from the province to visit him.

Winter came. He saw frost on some mornings. In a forgotten corner of the garden or on a crude bamboo fence along the road, he smelled late-blooming chrysanthemums, like the lingering scent of autumn.

64

TWO ROADS

THE FOLLOWING NIGHT, three or four men met with Oishi-dono in Shinagawa and then dispersed.

When Horibe Yasubei returned home, his wife Sachi told him a guest had been waiting inside since the evening.

"Who is it?"

"Takata-sama."

"Gunbei?"

He had no desire to see him immediately.

Notices were sent out about today's meeting. Yasubei didn't understand why Gunbei never showed up. Instead, he came here and waited a long time. What had he been up to since they signed the compact in Kamakura?

"Tea, please," he said and planted himself in the sitting room.

"But he's been waiting a very long time."

"It's all right. I'll see him later."

While he drank his tea alone, Yasubei sensed why Gunbei came. He only thought, That may be it.

He quietly rose and opened the sliding partition to the parlor. In deep thought beside the flames, Gunbei's face looked weary from sitting. Startled, he looked up and left his seat.

As usual, he did not smile, and both men's faces were veiled. Gunbei cast down his eyes in the light beaming from Yasubei's.

No one spoke for a long time. Yasubei relied on silence. Sachi's sleeve brushed the tatami as she left the tea.

Tears rolled down Gunbei's face and scattered. He swiftly moved his fist to his face that gradually disappeared into his shoulder.

"Horibe! Forgive me," Gunbei pleaded, his elbows stuck to the tatami mat.

"The truth is I didn't want to come here and look you in the face, but I had to put on a mask and cross the threshold. Nothing in this world is as painful as duty, but I have nowhere else to turn. I fell under the spell of Uchida Kageyu we met the other day in Enoshima. He even persuaded my older brother and uncle. He will allow me to become his son-in-law."

"…"

"Of course, I declined. I was determined and stubborn. But when I went to explain my reasons to my brother and uncle, I could not find any excuse. Most of all, my brother is obligated to the Uchida clan and shouldn't have a different opinion than me before speaking with me. Until my brother persuades me to marry, won't he take responsibility? He will plead tearfully for seppuku … so I must—"

"Give me a moment," said Yasubei, averting his eyes. He looked pained by what he heard. He could not get used to the cold-bloodedness as he listened to the voice heaving with heavy breaths from this friend joined by blood.

"I understand, Takata!"

"Please listen to me."

"No!"

This refusal was blunt.

"Do I need to hear any more? Enough. Tomorrow, I will inform Elder Okuda."

"Please put yourself in my position."

"We've been friends for many years. You and I are friends from before our public service in the Asano clan. You are called Gunbei of the Spear. I've been your friend from the times you were known as The Red Sheath or The Cheap Drunk."

"…"

"But there is no honor in ending together because we are friends. We were friends until now. I will stop on the road you hope to travel. If I don't ask questions, how can I understand your feelings?"

"…"

"If the other signers of the pact find out, maybe, one of them would come out and stab you. But as long as I'm alive, he would never try…. For the sake of our friendship, please tell the others about the secret pact."

"Why would I leak something so unfavorable to them? It may be leaked, but I will not be put in that predicament."

"I should be going. How about a drink?"

"No."

He almost toppled over when he stood and said, "Goodnight. We'll talk another time."

"Will we? … Sachi, our guest is leaving."

Yasubei carrying a lantern saw his guest off at the entryway.

"Goodnight," said Gunbei and put on his zori sandals.

"What do you want?"

"At least see me off at the crossroads."

Yasubei walked outside, shoulder to shoulder, with

Gunbei. The stars were beautiful like the sky had been renewed.

The sounds of the sandals broke the silence in harmony with the evening dew.

Gunbei inched toward Yasubei's left. His body hardened like a crane spreading its wings. He kept his eyes fixed on Yasubei's body as his mind quaked to prepare for a sword attack.

If Gunbei had not been a world-renowned expert spearman, Yasubei would not be saying to himself, Don't worry. He doesn't want to kill. He was reassured by the knowledge he too was a first-class warrior. The man Gunbei was an expert with a spear, and he didn't want to take that lightly.

They came to a field of weeds coated white with frost and a row of houses on one side of the road with shutters pulled down.

"Well, Takata, goodbye."

"I'm sorry."

Gunbei bowed like a worm. When Yasubei tapped his back and told him to go in good health, Gunbei did not raise his head.

"I pray for the day you achieve your cherished wish. For everyone."

Gunbei choked when he said, "Thank you," and the words faded away. He only bowed his head.

Gunbei rose to a slouch and rushed into the dark town.

"There goes a man with a weak spirit."

Yasubei was keenly aware of the uselessness of the spear, the sword, or any other military art in making a strong man. His only conceit was his swordsmanship, and he did not reflect on a stranger's business. No, this is the plain figure of a man. After a short time, the departing figure looked like a stranger's problem.

Looking up at the chilly sky on the clear night on his way home, a stronger traveling companion replaced the sorrow of losing a friend of many years in Yasubei's heart. He muttered to himself, "He's all right. An easily broken man retreats alone. Only this last quality is true."

The next day Kuranosuke would arrive in Edo. Thinking about it now, Yasubei was gaining a dim understanding of the spirit not easily awakened by Kuranosuke.

The hardest part is failure to achieve the objective. The actions of the human heart are indecipherable.

PART VIII

BUILDING IN YAMASHINA

65

——————

THE PURPLE HOOD

DID A YOUNG court lady live in the apartment? There were no flowery aromas or deep red colors. The noises of the world were absent on this frigid morning in the middle of November.

The only furnishings were a simple alcove in the style of the artist Kobori Enshu on the cold white *torinoko*-papered sliding door, a small desk, and a buckwheat noodle jar filled with a camellia bouquet.

After shutting herself away deep inside the residence of Asano Tosa no Kami in Nanbuzaka in Akasaka, her parent's home, Yozen'in derived the most comfort by sitting formally in the altar room all day long, kept company by her enjoyable memories of the bygone days with her late husband Takumi no Kami, or turning to the desk to copy the Lotus Sutra. Only one time, she secretly shut herself in a painted palanquin to visit Sengakuji Temple. Apart from that, she almost never went outside.

The unusual sounds of short, quick steps carried down the center corridor between the family altar room and the tea room. Tae, who served for a long time in the daimyo's

Edo mansion in Teppouzu, breathed out a white mist in the cold when she spoke into the altar room.

"Madam. Madam."

"Oishi-sama is here. Uh, he's the Kuranosuke-sama people are always talking about."

"Oh. Kuranosuke has come?"

"Yes."

Tae was happy, too.

In the room next to the study, Kuranosuke was prostrate. He left the province for Edo on the third of the month and met several times with former retainers there. He did his best to calm radicals like Horibe and Okuda. Today, on the fourteenth of the month, he visited the grave of his late lord. He described the situation in the home province and expressed gratitude for the allowances given to the scattered retainers. With a tragic heart and no place in the world, how cold and heartbreaking was her life in the early winter wearing the cut hair of a widow. He sympathized for a long time in his heart for her and today came on foot to visit Sengakuji Temple to fulfill his long-cherished hope.

"What have you come to say?"

As expected, Yozen'in was a woman with trembling lips. She could not stifle her tears at the sight of Kuranosuke.

"Please forgive me."

Her tears continued for some time. Kuranosuke could not raise his head. In silence, the mistress and the follower resigned themselves to tears. With no words spoken, indescribable strong emotions were communicated.

In time, she said, "Kuranosuke, are you chilly?"

"Yes."

"Please, move closer to the brazier."

"You are too kind."

"In early summer, I heard rumors that you had fallen ill. Are you better?"

"I've nearly forgotten about that minor bump. Do not worry. For now, I'm healthy. More than that, the vassals of our disbanded clan have been concerned about the lady's heart and well-being. Unlike when the lord was alive, we do not see each other daily. Meetings and partings are endless in life. Please take care of yourself."

"I'm content, Kuranosuke, but ..."

"Yes."

"If a child is born, I would like to have a son. That is my only thought."

"..."

"The thought of a boy does not leave my heart in the morning or the evening. The path of the samurai may be arduous."

"I understand and can guess what is in your heart."

"I'm simply asking for your strength. I hear rumors about the home province and from far away, I put my hands together in support of your work."

"You are too kind."

"No, it must be said. The link between the lord and a follower is fragile. Although commonplace in this world, the scattering of men to unknown places is awful. Kuranosuke, you still think of yourself as a vassal to your lord."

"Your words embarrass me. My public service is not finished. I am inept but intend to serve Takumi no Kami when I go to the next world."

"Listening to you, I realize life is worth living. My late husband would also be delighted."

Yozen'in called over Tae. The object she placed in Tae's hand to set before Kuranosuke was a round hood worn by old men made of purple silk crepe.

"You have traveled a long way while busy with pressing

matters but took the time to visit me. I sewed this during the long hours. Given your habit of complaining about the cold, please wear this to protect yourself from the night's cold."

Most frightening, this may be the only parting. Kuranosuke lifted his eyes to peer into Yozen'in's cold eyes.

"Well, I must leave now," he said, feeling pained. However, a long stay in this place would not comfort her. Kuranosuke reluctantly left the mansion of Tosa no Kami.

Unlike his previous visit, he was a solitary ronin with neither a palanquin nor attendants. Kuranosuke stood on the road to Nanbuzaka in gusts of dry wind and searched for a town palanquin.

A sedge bamboo hat snatched by the wind tumbled past him down the hill. This hat belonged to the man standing, for no reason, below the kitchen gate of Tosa no Kami's mansion. As the man scampered after the hat, Kuranosuke's eyes focused on the man's forehead and watched him turn his back and move away.

"Palanquin!"

Kuranosuke boarded a passing palanquin. He seemed untroubled. The man with the flying hat was a compact, sturdy townsman. On fast legs, he pursued the shadow of the palanquin slipping down the slope.

66

A SPY'S JOURNEYS

KIMURA JOHACHI, A man from the Kira clan, a vassal of the Uesugi clan, and the man eating up Chisaka Hyobu's stipend, mysteriously appeared and disappeared at this place so often he lost count.

Hyobu allowed him to slip past the tea-ceremony cottage's gate at any time and through the courtyard to the edge of his sitting room's veranda. And he frequently appeared without notice, particularly, since Oishi Kuranosuke came east to Edo.

A townsman resembling a traveling peddler wearing leggings sat on the edge of the veranda. His straw sandals rested on the foundation stones. He lowered his voice when he spoke to Hyobu seated in the room. This was the man whose hat flew past Kuranosuke at Nanbuzaka. To carry out Hyobu's orders, Kimura Johachi leaped around like a ninja day and night.

"Yesterday, Kuranosuke left Sengakuji Temple and visited Yozen'in. Then he went by palanquin to the mansion of Superintendent Araki Juzaemon. Unable to plead for the restoration of the main house, he expressed

311

gratitude for the administration at Ako. That same day, he called on Matsuhira Aki no Kami and Asano Mino no Kami to pay respects. Both visits were brief."

Hyobu looked to the side as he listened to Johachi's report. Seemingly talking to himself, he said, "So he's moving carefully."

His words revealed his respect for his rival. Hyobu understood Kuranosuke's feelings. Despite having never met him, he understood the difference between a powerful clan and a minor clan and knew Kuranosuke was the man who protected the sovereign family as its most important vassal. Hyobu was an elder vassal who carried the burden of the fate of the Uesugi clan and did his best for his sovereign family. By changing places with Kuranosuke and considering how he would act, he read Kuranosuke's actions and intentions like a reflection in a mirror.

"Chief Retainer," said Johachi, he stood and straightened his squat frame. "I'd like to see seven or eight men promptly dispatched to the Kyoto area."

"Has something happened?"

"Nothing happened during Kuranosuke's stay in this province, but he looks ready to return to Yamashina. I think we should take the initiative to get ahead of his party without attracting attention."

"Five men are on their way to Yamashina. Why so many?"

"Should I choose five comrades from the residence in Honjo to accompany me?"

"No, not one of Lord Kira's men will be selected. Even after Kuranosuke returns to Kyoto, there's no shortage of rash men who would launch a solo attack. I'll dispatch the men. I want you to work with complete freedom."

"I understand. Depending on the circumstances, I may leave without announcing my departure."

"Occasional incidents can be reported in writing. That won't be noticed. It would be a mistake to believe only our spies are at work. A man like Kuranosuke will be shrewd. His maneuvers will be elaborate. Be careful, an informer may be in my residence."

Hyobu gave him traveling expenses and added, "But Johachi …"

"Yes."

"Any challenge to former Ako vassals must be discreet."

"I understand."

"Find out whether the rumors about ideas attributed to Kuranosuke are true. If you emphasize the importance of the ronins' movements, an understanding of their movements will emerge naturally."

"I agree," said Johachi.

"Both the Uesugi and Kira clans will be watching them. The rumors circulating are bad. This inflames the public's resentment, which is not good for Lord Kira. I believe I would like to help Kuranosuke and see Takumi no Kami's younger brother Asano Daigaku elevated and the clan's name restored. I'm annoyed I can't do so as an elder vassal in the Uesugi clan. How much fury would come with the restoration of the Asano clan? I think the spirit of the ronin would change dramatically. This is me thinking too much. The fact is I can't meddle. If this hazard is easily resolved, Banzai! to the clan."

"Be well."

Johachi left Hyobu's mansion.

Since the incident, agitation in the Kira clan was not surpassed by that of the Asano ronin. Beginning with Kimura Johachi, the desire of trusted attendants to fight the Asano ronin strained to the breaking point. Of course, Johachi was one of them. But whenever he approached the elder Chisaka Hyobu, he kept his fighting spirit in check. Hyobu did not want to meet Kuranosuke and his men as enemies and wanted to avoid a violent confrontation. An attack by the ronin would not crush them. Would the Uesugi home engulfed by this typhoon emerge without one damaged tile? The elder focused on that sole thought.

It's going to be tricky, thought Johachi. How passive will he be? ...

Why hasn't he ordered the assassination of Kuranosuke? The presence of Horibe, Okuda, Yoshida, and Hara killed that idea. He could not wrap his mind around the extreme difficulty of assassination but always supported it despite his doubts about whether it was the best course.

If this becomes the position, it made sense when he considered how much Chisaka Hyobu wanted to assist Kuranosuke and promote Asano Daigaku.

"Of course."

Johachi was struck by the difference between a so-called low-ranking vassal and a high-ranking vassal and agreed with the popular comment that few men were like Hyobu.

Johachi soon left for Edo. Close to the end of the month, he briefly appeared near Yamashina then returned to the shadows. About four days later, a party made up of Oishi Kuranosuke, Ushioda Matanojo, Nakamura Kansuke, Nakamura Seiemon, and Shindo Genshiro returned home. After the ronin left Ako and scattered, the public saw a Kuranosuke who found land in Yamashina for his permanent home and, for a time, took off his traveling clothes and settled down to live in Kyoto.

On the surface, all was calm. Each man was preoccupied with his fate.

67

THE NIGHT BIRD IS SHOT

THE YEAR CAME to an end. The new year was year 15 of Genroku.

Kuranosuke changed his name to Ikeda Kyuemon and spent the winter under the quilt of a *kotatsu* heater. He summoned his wife Riku, Kichichiyo, and Daisaburo from Tajima to his side. His oldest son Chikara was, as always, the center of the happy family circle. At the start of the year, the youth turned sixteen and was tall at five feet, seven inches. He was bigger than his father Kuranosuke, which was an unfailing source of laughter.

The younger brother Kichichiyo pestered his big brother. "Make my kite. My kite—"

"Later. Be a good boy."

"No, now!" whined Kichichiyo.

Chikara said, "You get into trouble because you never study and only play. Go ask Father."

Kichichiyo began his search.

Kuranosuke was in the garden on the grounds. The February sun was bright and warm. Many rocks and timber were piled on the level field. Carpenters inked lines and swung axes in an area buried in wood shavings from planing wood.

Kuranosuke sat near a bonfire watching the carpenters work and frequently fussed about the chiseling of the wood ends.

"Hey, workman, you, chiseler, stop being so careless. Aren't you building the tea-ceremony room? Sloppy work like the cheap construction of that exposed column is a problem."

The foreman came running over.

"I'm so sorry. You! Go do something else."

"Foreman."

"Yes."

"Keep on them so the work is meticulous."

"I try to keep an eye on them, but my eyes are a little weak."

"The cost of the day laborers isn't a problem. I'm building my home with the aim of enjoying the rest of my life in peace and quiet."

"That makes sense."

"Has the lumber dealer delivered the ceiling planks?"

"Yes, they're here. Would you like to see them? Here they are, Master."

"What is this? Is this plain straight-grained pine?"

"There are a few planks like this."

"These are a little rougher than the other cut ends of horizontal pieces of timber and columns. You will paste on Kamiyo cedar in the ten-tatami-mat room."

"Kamiyo cedar in there. All right?" said the foreman staring at Kuranosuke. He seemed to think like a merchant forever carrying a carpenter's square. This construction will benefit his descendants and not be the least bit wasteful.

"Now, the ten-tatami room will be Kamiyo cedar.

When that is done, please paste the finest Yoshino cedar in the four-and-a-half tatami room because the ordinary product of red cedar will not match well. I would never think of letting guests see such frugality."

The foreman believed this vain client would become a steady customer. After hearing this, he called the clerk from the lumber dealer and returned the planks.

He was persnickety about the walls, ordered the garden stones from Kii Province but continued to be half satisfied. He said to find better stones and not to worry about the freight cost. How much money was there? When Ako Castle was surrendered, one rumor claimed an elder vassal hid ten thousand ryo in another place to undertake major construction work and enjoy a pleasant future life. The carpenter's subcontractor and the plasterer talked about this on their way home from work.

"Well? I don't think so," said the plasterer's assistant Tatsuzo.

The carpenter Tomekichi said, "What do you mean?"

"I'm saying Ikeda Kyuemon is an Ako elder vassal and has the courage for revenge. I see it."

"You say he's a great man. But a man set on revenge has no reason for so much building."

"His strategy is to divide the enemy by inciting rebellion from within."

"So that strategy looks like construction? He's fussy, bothers us all the time, and wastes money."

"That is a military tactic, a counterplot to outwit the enemy."

"You sure know a lot. But where's your proof?"

"Who hasn't seen the signs?"

"You idiot. Is that what you're saying or going around asking?"

"That's what I think, but I'm asking to find someone with proof?"

"Ah, ha, ha, ha, you amaze me. You'll persist even when you know nothing."

"You're probably right," said Tatsuzo feigning ignorance and stared at the distant crossroads. "I have to make a stop, so I'll be going. See ya."

He made a quick turn at the servants' teahouse in front of the gate of Bishamondo Temple.

A townsman standing in the shadows of the trees at the crossroads trailed Tatsuzo. After he looked up and down the road, he called out, "Sekiguchi."

"Oh, Kimura?"

The plasterer's helper Tatsuzo was Sekiguchi Sakubei from the Kira clan ordered by Chisaka Hyobu to leave Edo and come to Kyoto. Kimura Johachi approached his side.

"Did something happen?"

"No nothing."

"Any visitors?"

"Yesterday, I saw Terai Genkei who's living in Yanaginobaba."

"He was the physician in the Asano clan."

"Sometimes, he makes house calls and has visited Kuranosuke a few times."

"Aren't some of them, including Onodera, Nakamura, and Ushioda, holding secret meetings in Genkei's home?"

"They may be. A little while ago, they leased Shusuian on the grounds of Zuiko-in Temple in northern Kyoto to give the impression their gatherings were for songs and poetry. They also hold meetings there."

"Shusuian is next to Asano Inari's land."

"Yes, the ancestor of the Asano clan called Asano Inari enshrined the god of harvests and donated the land for the temple. When they hold meetings, I'll dress like I'm coming to visit the god of harvests to get closer."

"Will they hold a meeting soon?"

"In the middle of next month, Otaka Gengo and Hara Soemon will leave for Edo and along the way visit Ise no Taibyo shrine. Hara is living in a rented house in Osaka, and Otaka is in one in Kyoto. They meet often in Yamashina and Shusuian, but I think there are disagreements and confusion."

"That's good, but you can't get careless."

"Of course."

"How's the construction in Yamashina going?"

"Fine."

"Oishi's strategy may be an attempt to trick our eyes."

"That's what I'm thinking, but sometimes I don't believe that's the case. His work is painstaking. And Kuranosuke seems to love construction and the cut ends of the wood. He's spending so much money, starting with a sturdy foundation. This makes the work noisy and the craftsmen overworked."

"Uh-huh. So he's going that far."

"The zealous faction of young fellows like Fuwa Kazuemon and Takebayashi Tadashichi distanced themselves from Oishi after seeing that construction site. Many now question Oishi's courage."

"So that created the rift between the comrades."

"It's a matter of time."

"Time?"

"One faction is ready to act right away, and the comrades surrounding Oishi are indecisive."

"Yup, there's that, but do you think Kuranosuke intends to act?"

"It's seventy percent or thirty percent."

"Which one?"

"Let's see. Kuranosuke's a man. Seventy percent of the world and the men around him would say he doesn't want to die."

"We'll meet again soon. If there's an emergency, I'll nail the signal to the north column in the shrine for hanging votive tablets here at Bishamondo Temple. It'll be a letter hidden behind one of the tablets in the shrine, so check there from time to time."

"All right."

The two parted in the darkness of dusk.

Soon after the month ended, the figure of Kuranosuke was no longer seen at the house in Yamashina. He wasn't seen for five or six days at the construction site. No matter who he asked, no one knew. Sekiguchi Sakubei's Tatsuzo was at a loss. On the way home from work one evening, he remembered Johachi's words and headed to Bishamondo Temple.

When he looked at the north column in the votive tablet shrine, a nail fastened a note scribbled with *The night bird is shot.* He looked up and saw several votive plaques. One frame was the writings of the poet and warrior Genzan Miyorimasa. He retrieved a stepping stone and reached up. He untied a piece of paper attached to a butterfly and recognized Kimura Johachi's handwriting.

The lord in Yamashina will make a surprise trip to Ako. Go with him. Regards.

Juhachishaku

"He went to Ako?" muttered Sekiguchi Sakubei and left the shrine. Around the time the stars twinkled white in the twilight air, he let his guard down in the compound devoid of visitors and was shocked to discover two young ronin beneath him closely watching his actions.

Sekiguchi Sakubei's clenched hand swiftly went to his mouth to devour Johachi's note. However, faster than the motion of his hand, a ronin grabbed his wrist.

"Damn you!"

Giving no hint of the martial training in his body, Sekiguchi Sakubei's power burst out. He dropped his grabbed wrist with dynamic force. The ronin's back slammed into the ground.

The hurled man grabbed his leg. "Gotcha!"

Sakubei knew that face and voice from the construction site. He was Koemon, the son of Onodera Junai. The other slender ronin, Ushioda Matanojo, wrestled him from behind.

Dammit!

The second move tried by the sweating Sakubei failed. His leg sprung into Koemon sending his side slamming into the ground with enough force to cause tremors. Stung by having been thrown, Koemon mounted him like a horse and choked him.

68

HUNT DOWN AND KILL

"**K**OEMON, NOT SO rough, you'll kill him."

"He's a big one," said Koemon, nearly out of breath. "I never believed he was a plasterer's helper. Ushioda, give me your sword strap."

"You're tying him up?"

"Of course ..."

He tied Sekiguchi Sakubei's hands tight.

"Now, where's that paper he had in the shrine?"

"I got it." Ushioda Matanojo flattened out the wrinkled scrap of paper and read it under the starlight.

"Look, Koemon."

"Uh-huh ... A spy," he said and glared at Sakubei's forehead.

"Who sent you to Yamashina?"

"..."

Sakubei smirked. He sat cross-legged on the ground, indifferent.

"You won't talk."

Koemon raised a leg and kicked the side of Sakubei's face.

"Stop. He won't talk." Matanojo held him back.

"Was it Kira? Chisaka Hyobu? It's strange to feel fear because of doubts. Deep down, we know we're to blame, but what should we do? He came a long way and survived many trials to spy on us."

The young Matanojo had abundant good sense. After becoming a ronin, his daily contact with Kuranosuke had a profound effect on him. He best understood the reason for Kuranosuke's hesitation and fears.

"I didn't know who was using the fake name Juhachishaku, but he seems to have trailed Oishi-dono to Ako. This guy looks like a man of leisure who does nothing useful. Apparently the chief retainer went to collect the rest of the money loaned to men living on the Ako beaches. He had to have another reason to go. March 14 was the first anniversary of the late lord's death, and a memorial service was held. Aha, ha, ha. That dope trailed him, but the world sees a busy ne'er-do-well."

Koemon understood why Matanojo was saying this.

"I don't care that he put on a disguise and snuck onto the chief retainer's construction site. This is unpleasant business, but he can't live."

"Don't say that. What can he report to Kira? Nothing he knows can hurt us. Well, we better not find you wandering around here again. What do you think, plasterer?"

"…"

Sakubei looked down.

"Problem solved."

"Solved?"

"Yes … However, as a warrior, out of respect, what is your full name?"

"Please give me a pass on that alone," moaned Sakubei.

Koemon was indignant.

"A pass on your name and your life is magnanimous. You are taking advantage of our kindness."

Matanojo was gentle to the end. "If it's disagreeable, then I won't ask. You and your confederates are elusive, like trying to grab a cloud. Who's coming here to Kyoto?"

"..."

"You're probably here on Chisaka Hyobu-dono's orders."

For the first time, Sakubei spoke. "Ushioda."

"I was sure I wouldn't say a word, but I'm defeated by your kindness. As you've guessed, I'm employed by the Yonezawa elder vassal Chisaka. Twenty-two or -three men from Osaka, Fushimi, other places in and around the capital, and Nara are heading to Kyoto with the same mission."

"Thank you. Now, we'll let you go."

Koemon untied the sword strap binding his wrists and pushed him away. The shamed Sakubei cast back a cold look before the darkness swallowed him.

As the two men descended the stone stairs to the Bishamondo gate, Matanojo took out and read the paper Kimura Johachi was holding. Kuranosuke carefully disguised himself to obscure his comrades' work. More importantly, he didn't expect all the men, Horibe, Okuda, Hara, and Otaka, to abruptly do something drastic and succeed. On the contrary, if he put pressure on Kozuke no Suke, would it be a mistake to drive him deeper into Yonezawa Castle? While engrossed by these thoughts, Matanojo called, "Koemon."

"What?"

"I'm suddenly worried about the chief retainer's safety on his trip. We know nothing about this man called Juhachishaku. There's a slight chance Kuranosuke will be harmed on the boat."

"I didn't say anything, but I've been having premonitions for a while and can't shake this foreboding. Listen, if twenty or so spies have infiltrated the Kyoto region, they may be waiting for us to make the first move."

"I heard he's returning by boat. It'd be better to meet him along the way. It would be awful for the chief retainer to get hurt. Should we protect him?"

"Will you come with me? I'd like to go home and get my father's advice."

"That's a good idea."

They dashed off and ran into Takebayashi Tadashichi in front of Yamashina Gobo monastery at Honganji Temple. He was coming from Osaka on business. Unaware Kuranosuke was away, he visited an empty house and was on his way back to Osaka.

Tadashichi surveyed them and asked, "What are you two up to?"

After Koemon told their story in detail, he said, "That's no good. Why did you release a guy backed by Chisaka Hyobu?"

"So he'd go back to Edo and give a candid report to Hyobu without exaggerations. If we wished for revenge, we wouldn't release spies to return home. That's what we want Hyobu to think."

Tadashichi rejected Matanojo's justification.

"On the surface, that plan looks ingenious, but how would that plan calm the famous Chisaka of the Uesugi? He was ordered to spy, penetrate their rival's plan, and return home. He doesn't intend to report the unvarnished truth of his failed strategy. Instead, he will exaggerate our actions, and these tales will reach Hyobu. As for releasing him, compassion is our enemy. So now, I will hunt him down and kill him."

"You know what he's dressed like? And looks like?"

"Where does he live?"

"He may be living in a house with the head plasterer Matsu Goro. It's in an alley four or five blocks from the workers' teahouse."

"Are you two going to Terai Genkei's home now?"

"No, we're going to see my father, Junai."

"Then I'll see you there later."

"You're going to kill him?"

Matanojo seemed to mull over Tadashichi's ideas but also knew, as did his comrades, speaking out was not allowed.

"I heard that that sort of man can't be taken lightly. Please wait at Junai's home, I'll be there later with his head."

Tadashichi melted into the darkness. The sounds of his fast-moving zori sandals went silent. After he disappeared, Ushioda and Onodera walked toward the far-off lights of town. Was Takebayashi right? Had they handled the situation correctly? They lost all faith in their decision.

THE STORY OF A SONG ON A NIGHT BOAT

69

THE BACKSTREETS OF TERAMACHI

"**W**HAT? **YOU TOLD** Takebayashi Tadashichi what happened, and he chased after Kira's spy? That fool."

Onodera Junai left the two young men in the waiting area and went into a dark, cramped room to put on a half-length haori coat. He emerged tying his belt and asked, "Why didn't you stop him?" He sat with his narrow knees forming a perfect square to wait for the answer.

His son Koemon tried to explain, "Stop him? We didn't try."

His father didn't listen and shook his head furiously.

"Oishi-dono always says to be careful. It's a meaningless use of force."

Ushioda Matanojo, who came with Koemon, was also reprimanded and kept his head down in shame.

Where was Junai going? He neatly placed his wallet, tissue paper, and tobacco pouch laid out by his wife into his pocket closed by the collar.

"This alley of ronin homes transformed into a wastepaper man, an ointment dealer, an umbrella shop, and various other businesses. There was no end to the days when suspicious-looking fellows constantly showed up to look around and were too interested in every detail. They were carrying out some plan. I'm not worried and will bend like a willow in the wind."

"But Father," Koemon felt bad for Matanojo and spoke cautiously. "It's not only that, if it goes well for them, they may harbor a plan to first assassinate Oishi-dono and then kill his closest allies."

"Who among us could be easily killed by a Kira or a Chisaka spy? You worry too much."

"But according to the note we seized tonight, the man named Juhachishaku tracked Oishi-dono when he went to Ako for the memorial service for the first anniversary of the lord's death. We'd like to go and protect Oishi-dono. We stopped here on our way to get your advice."

"Not going would be best," he said curtly, then inside his mouth muttered, "That blundering Oishi-dono."

Junai stood and announced he was going out to play a scheduled game of Go at Terai Genkei's home. His wife readied his sandals at the door. Junai slipped them on. When he placed his hand on the lattice door, he noticed a figure under the eaves.

"Onodera-sama?" the visitor asked.

"Yes. Chikara-dono?"

Had an emergency brought Chikara, Kuranosuke's son, from Yamashina? He said he broke the seal to an important letter because his father was away, and his mother Riku ordered him to bring it to Onodera Junai.

"Oh," said Junai and took the letter.

"Ah, the father and son, Kayano Shichirozaemon and Sanpei. What has happened?"

He cocked his head and called inside, "Koemon, bring the light," and went back in.

70

COMINGS AND GOINGS AT THE
RIVER POOL

A FTER SANPEI RETURNED home to Kayano village in Sesshu, he cut off communication with his comrades. He was a quiet melancholy youth but intense. Last year at the time of the catastrophe at the lord's house, he was the first fast messenger to report the Edo incident in Ako. Since then, his health suffered.

"Why not spend a little time back home to restore your health?" advised Kuranosuke.

"It's not serious," Sanpei said when friends expressed concern. Until now, he traversed the familiar Kyoto and Osaka regions where he had the geographical advantage and became a valued comrade.

However, around the middle of January, Yoshida Chuzaemon and Chikamatsu Kanroku went back to Edo accompanied by Kayano Sanpei and were to stay there until the success of the revenge. Sanpei returned to his hometown one time to, in a roundabout way, say goodbye to his parents.

"That's good, you go. Even if the situation changes, we can wait a day or two," suggested Chuzaemon and

Kanroku, then they left for Sesshu. They heard nothing from him since January.

"Sanpei probably made a clever exit from the alliance in the style of Takata Gunbei."

"No, not him," said Onodera Junai shaking his head.

After Yoshida and Chikamatsu reluctantly left for Edo, no news came from Sanpei. He finally joined the fellowship of men who changed their minds and was erased from the faces of the comrades.

"Dammit!"

When he finished reading, Junai spoke in a near moan and looked up with a pained expression under the lantern light.

"Regrettably, a precious young man is dead."

"What?"

Chikara and Koemon swallowed hard. Ushioda Matanojo watching the paper tremble in Junai's hand said, "Kayano's dead?"

"Yes, he killed himself."

"How?"

"The letter doesn't say. Kataoka and others intend to go to Genkei's home tonight, I will announce it there. You two, go to Sanpei's father Shichirozaemon in Kayano village in Sesshu. Convey our condolences and prepare a funeral offering."

"Yessir."

"Goodnight," said Oishi Chikara and went home.

Junai followed him out.

"I'll go with you."

Yoshida and Chikamatsu watched them leave.

"I can't believe Kayano Sanpei is dead."

"We better get going."

Koemon went inside to tell his mother. Kayano village

in Sesshu wasn't far. If they walked through the night, they'd get there by tomorrow afternoon.

The skies were partly cloudy. As a precaution, they carried bamboo hats in their waterproof capes. The two left the ronin house on Nijo-dori boulevard in Teramachi.

"Hey, Ushioda," someone called out.

He turned to see Takebayashi Tadashichi who left them earlier at the gate of Honganji Temple.

"Look at this," he said and held up his hand gripping a round object, a severed head. The head of Sekiguchi Sakubei, Chisaka Hyobu's spy freed by Matanojo, dripped blood.

"That spy chosen by Chisaka put up a helluva fight. Look at this scratch," said Tadashichi turning over his elbow to show them. Both Ushioda and Onodera were frowning.

"Elder Junai took us to task for our unworthy actions. Throw that thing in the temple's grove."

"Elder Junai? He's ahead of the younger men on many things. With his strong backbone, no man outdoes him."

"But he said bothering with each enemy nuisance shadowing us is an unwise strategy and warned us and you to show restraint."

"Oh, he did?"

Like the head he gripped instantly gained weight, Tadashichi looked for a place to dump it. He hurled the head from the broken fence of the temple. It landed with a thud in the bamboo grove.

"Where are you two going?"

"We're leaving on an urgent trip."

"To see Oishi-dono?"

"No, a letter came saying Kayano Sanpei committed suicide."

"Kayano? … That Sanpei?"

Hearing this, Tadashichi said he would go with them. They hurried to the river pool and arrived in time to catch the night's last boat and covered themselves with straw mats to sleep. When shaken awake, it was already morning. A little sooner than expected, they arrived at Kayano Shichirozaemon's residence in Kayano village.

"We are former vassals of the Asano clan and old friends of the son Sanpei. We've heard about the unforeseen misfortune. We wish to see Sanpei-dono's father Shichirozaemon-dono."

They stood in the entryway, and each man gave his full name.

Inside the house seemed hectic. They later found out that day was the one-hundredth day since Sanpei's death.

"This way, please."

They entered a house that looked like the home of a provincial samurai in an old clan. Shichirozaemon, a gaunt, elderly samurai, sat with drooping shoulders in the dimly lit, small tatami-mat room. He spoke the moment he looked up at the three figures.

"I heard your distinguished names from my son. If there's a matter you wish to discuss, I have no honor as a father."

Shichirozaemon placed both hands together in apology to the three men for the loss of his son.

He spoke through tears. "It happened on January 14. My son Sanpei came at the end of the year and spent New Year's in this house. He seemed at peace but used his sword to kill himself."

Earlier, Sanpei seemed sick with melancholy. He shut himself up in the study and, except for mealtimes, seldom interacted with household members.

The reason Sanpei gave him was to protect the oath with his comrades and strictly maintain the secret objective for going to Edo by not breathing one word to his parents or relatives. He only said he would seek government service. Shichirozaemon believed him but told Sanpei he could not allow him to leave the province.

"If I serve the government in the future, why can't I inherit the family estate with the consent of my elderly mother and father?"

Sanpei was in agony.

Exposure of this important matter would betray the pact with his comrades. If he turned his back on his father, he would not be a dutiful son.

Sanpei had a feeble constitution but was an honest man with integrity. He thought deeply about these two duties and was unable to conceive of a suitable life. Around dusk, he went alone to the grave of his mother in the back hills. He reflected on the pleasing sounds of the flute, stopped playing, sat on the grass, and disemboweled himself.

"It's a shame," the three men repeated. Guided by Shichirozaemon, they climbed the back hills to the grave. At the grave of their kind friend, they burned incense as an offering for the one-hundredth day.

"No, Sanpei is not dead. He'll die on the day we die. His pure heart is in our blood, so do not say your son's misfortune was a dog's death. I'm sorry we can't tell you the details."

Matanojo and Tadashichi consoled the solitary father and left. He kept them from leaving many times, but all their hearts were wounded and they couldn't bear staying any longer. They went to a teahouse with benches in Shibamura. They ate lunch, asked about the schedule for the return boat to Kyoto at the river pool, and napped on the folding benches inside.

A *sanjukkoku-bune* passenger boat traveling from Osaka

to Kyoto rode the river waves in the bright evening calm and neared the harbor at Moriguchi. The passengers named Ushioda, Onodera, and Takebayashi mixed in and boarded with the other travelers.

Onodera Koemon sat at the stern. "Isn't that?"

"Oishi-dono is here! Oishi-dono is—"

"Sh! … Be quiet."

Ushioda shook his head to curb Koemon's surprise.

Takebayashi noticed, too. He did not call out. He only watched. Kuranosuke was among a crowd of passengers in the hull. He traveled under his new name Ikeda Kyuemon and was accompanied by many mysterious traveling companions.

"It's better to act like you don't know him. The chief retainer averted his eyes. Oishi-dono would have said something if it were okay?"

Matanojo whispered from the side.

Tadashichi snapped his tongue."

"Are all those women the chief retainer's companions?"

"It looks that way."

"Who are those women and men clinging to his side?"

"Young kabuki actors."

"I know they're kabuki actors but—"

"The passengers are straining to see them and whispering 'Isn't that the famous Segawa Takenojo from Kyoto's theaters?'"

"Is that Takenojo of the underworld? The chief retainer has no discipline!"

A sullen Tadashichi spat into the water in disgust and pretended not to look."

71

———

THE RICH DRUNK

FOR SOME TIME, rumors circulated about Kuranosuke's excursions to Shumokumachi in Fushimi or hours of pleasure spent in Kyoto's Shimabara. Other gossip reported the increase in his sake drinking when he went back to Edo last year. His comrades were worried.

"Has the chief retainer been acting a bit strange lately?"

That may be best, thought Onodera Junai, Terai Genkei, and other senior colleagues who agreed but only smiled.

However, exacting men like Otaka Gengo and Tominomori Sukeemon and the young men said things like, "He's building a house and buying courtesans. He never initiates serious discussions on revenge. I don't understand the chief retainer's courage at all."

Seeing his debauchery, a faction, including Ushioda, Takebayashi, and Koemon, was dejected and sometimes sounded dissatisfied. They said nothing but turned their disgusted faces away from one spot in the hull.

The other day, March 14, was the first anniversary of

the lord's death. Kuranosuke was on his way home from the Kagakuji Temple in Ako after he conducted the memorial service as the representative of the surviving retainers.

Where did he take off his traveling clothes? No one in his family in Yamashina or Kyoto knew where he cast them off. Wasn't he a little too flashy wearing a haori jacket made from black silk crepe, the soft clothes worn by a tea master like Rikyu, a pricey, garish obi sash, and accessories?

Was he playing hide-and-seek? Despite being onboard a sanjukkoku passenger boat, he was accompanied by five whores, Segawa Takenojo from Kagema, and a parlor maid. They joined the trip at Sonezaki in Osaka and occupied seats in the hull. People tried not to look at the gaudy party.

"Oopsie … The sake is wobbling in the cups … Why is this boat swaying? Ha, ha, ha, is the shore moving away, or is the boat moving away? What do you think, Tsuya? Tell me."

Kuranosuke's tongue was twisted. While wiping up the sake spilled on his knees, the parlor maid Tsuya said, "Is the boat moving away? Is the shore moving away? Is that a riddle?"

"Yes, yes. To whoever solves the riddle, a full cup of sake."

One whore said, "I've had enough sake."

"In that case, we'll embrace and sleep."

"Goodness! Squire-sama, you are the naughtiest client in the world."

"What? The naughtiest in the world? The world should have no room for men who hate women or women who hate men. Anyone who says so is nothing but a liar. That's certain."

When does the sake drinking start?

Everyone was a little tired.

Kuranosuke propped up his head with his fingers and leaned over the side of the boat to look down.

"Squire-sama?"

"Squire."

"Are you feeling ill?"

"I'll be dead drunk long before we reach Shumokumachi."

Takenojo placed Kuranosuke's head on his lap. "Would you like water?"

"No. Sake, sake."

"Oh, you're already poisoned."

"Some poet said sake is poison. Others said it's the best of all medicines. No poet writes odes to poisons. Living a long life and amassing a fortune is the one thought of those who live long lives in this world. A man wants to pass through this life surrounded by beautiful women and intoxicated by delicious sake. We are alive in this world. The next world is empty."

"Please get up. You're a nuisance to the other passengers."

"Oh, of course. There are others on this boat. Pardon me," he said while scrambling to shift his legs to the side.

"Have we reached Fushimi?"

"No, not yet."

"I can hardly wait. Can we dance and sing on the water? Fushimi, hurry up and get closer."

"What are you saying?"

"Forgive me. A journey is paradise, the essence of Kyuemon. If I return home to Yamashina, I'll be greeted by the melancholy faces of my wife and children and receive bothersome visits from debt collectors. What am I to do? I won't stretch out and relax."

"You're joking," said Takenojo and giggled.

"No, it's the truth. If I must, on my way home from Ako in Banshu, I'll entertain myself with the courtesans Hanaurushi of Minatoya in Tomonotsu and Ukihashi of Sasaya in Sonezaki and Fushimi in Naniwa, and drink and drink. I'd like to ask for a delay in our arrival in Kyoto by one day. Ah, saying that makes me want to see her right away. Ukihashi may be getting jittery as she waits for me. I'll send a fast messenger from Hyogo to tell her the day we are to meet."

"Is this about your love affair again?"

"It is not an affair. It is real."

"Ha, ha, ha. Stop it!"

"Takenojo."

"Yes."

"My shoulders are stiff. Loosen them a little, please."

"Like this, Squire?"

"Ah, yes. That feels good. You're useful for amusement and stiff shoulders."

His fellow passengers included those unable to buy tomorrow's rice. Others wore dark faces and came to sell their daughters to brothels in Kyoto. On that day, like many others, traveling peddlers were weary after a night's sleep on rented beds in cheap inns.

For some time, they stared with envy at Kuranosuke. Whispers began soon after Kuranosuke passed out a second time in the lap of the kabuki actor Takenojo.

"Where on earth is that rich guy from?"

"I don't know, but he said Yamashina."

"Yamashina? Isn't that man Oishi Kuranosuke, the Ako ronin?"

"Maybe."

"He goes to Shimabara a lot for a good time."

"He has that kind of money?"

"He was the clan's head chief retainer in the province and probably hoarded a lot of gold during the turmoil."

"With that sort of chief retainer, their ruin was inevitable. Who's surprised?"

"Today's samurai, not just that chief retainer, are a different breed from the past. In the flashiness contests in dress and swords and the extravagant entertainment in Naniwa and Shimabara, wealthy townsmen like the daimyo's caretaker, the bureaucrats, or the town police sergeant never reach their heights."

"At least, the Kira clan has nothing to worry about."

"You're right. I heard some strange rumors, but they sound true."

Everyone chuckled at the sight of Kuranosuke's sleeping face snoring on Takenojo's lap.

"…"

With their narrow shoulders hunched together, Ushioda Matanojo, Onodera Koemon, and Takebayashi Tadashichi never raised their heads and only stared at the dark surface of the water.

A corner of each man's mind was occupied by the death of the pure-hearted Sanpei and the hardships of their many comrades.

72

A SONG BY ME

"SQUIRE? SQUIRE."

"Go away. Let me sleep a little longer."

"Please get up. We've arrived in Fushimi."

"No. I want to sleep."

"Are you going to Kyoto like that? Aren't you going to see Yugiri-san?"

"What? Yugiri is here?"

"No, we're in Fushimi."

"Hmm, Fushimi? This is important. If I don't see Yugiri this time, it may kill me. I'm coming."

"Oh, watch out."

"Takenojo, carry me please."

"Impossible. Lean on my shoulder."

"Tsuya, get on my left."

"Ah, the boat is swaying. Captain, please keep it steady."

Supported on both sides, Kuranosuke went ashore.

"What was that?"

"He's a mess."

One by one, the passengers remaining onboard ridiculed him and stretched over the empty seats in back.

"Glad to see him go!"

"But it'd be better if he left behind the Sonezaki geisha."

"Ha, ha, ha."

A townsman jumped to his feet among the laughter. He looked like a shrewd traveling gambler wearing his travel rain cape, hand and wrist coverings, leggings, and taut straw sandals.

"Eh, I fell asleep. Is this Fushimi, Captain?"

"Yessir. This is Fushimi."

"I'm getting off."

His rain cape fluttered when he leaped onto the shore.

"Are we getting off?"

"Yes."

Ushioda, Takebayashi, and Onodera followed.

They signaled with their eyes and became shore dwellers.

A young man held up the paper lantern of the Masuya Brothel next to the palanquin from Shumokumachi there to meet them. Kuranosuke's drunken eyes watched the courtesans board the palanquin.

"What is this? Ride in a palanquin? Until I see Yugiri's face, I will spend this pleasant spring evening being entertained in the parlor," said Kuranosuke as he walked away teetering but keeping time with a folding fan.

The parlor maid, Takenojo, and the Masuya paper lantern surrounded his shadow.

"Squire-sama, are you walking?"

"That's obvious. My drunkenness would go to waste cramped inside a palanquin on this night lit by a hazy moon. Takenojo, sing like a shamisen."

"What shall I sing?"

"Let's do *Ryutatsu-bushi*."

"Better than that, sing the song you wrote, Squire-sama. *A Scene in My Hometown*."

"Yes, yes, but can we practice? A private rehearsal."

Takenojo mimed playing a shamisen to accompany him.

Adorned for the quarter in the coming
    darkness,
At odds with the evening light and fire, he
    sleeps.
Invite a storm to scatter the flowers in
    dreams.
A man lured by the bedroom to be her
    companion.
A sorrowful farewell.
At daybreak, back and inner doors open.
The loose obi sash of the departing figure
Boxwood … a boxwood comb fights hair
    tousled by sleep.
Unexpected tears fall onto a sleeve.

"Squire-sama."

"What is it, Takenojo?"

"The harmony is slightly off, start again from 'boxwood'."

From the side, Tsuya said, "No, Takenojo-sama, your playing is worse than the Squire's singing. This time I'll accompany him."

"Oh, do you play the shamisen? Sing the rest."

Tears of grief fall onto a sleeve
Melancholy tears fall onto a sleeve

73

A MAN OF PLEASURE OR MELANCHOLY

"**W**ONDERFUL! YOU DID it."

As Takenojo applauded, the man from the boat wearing a traveler's cape and trailing the endless stream of shadows appeared to slip toward the side like he became entangled, pulled a dagger hidden under his cape, and lunged toward Kuranosuke's body.

"Ah! No!" Kuranosuke staggered and clamped onto the man's wrist. "Who are you? You've made a big mistake."

The man said nothing and shook free. The young Masuya servant dropped the lantern and dashed off. Takenojo and Tsuya shrieked and collapsed onto the roadside.

Takebayashi and Ushioda witnessed the attack and, starting from a distance away, chased the man at full speed.

"Who are you?"

They surrounded the caped figure on three sides.

"Damn you!"

The man panicked and flung his dagger at Onodera Koemon's face. He ran with terrifying speed from the nearby bare ground into the forest of some shrine.

"Hey. Tsuya, Tsuya."

Kuranosuke leaned limply against a row of cherry blossom trees. His escape from danger left him dazed.

"Where are you, Tsuya? What was that? A bandit?"

Takenojo and Tsuya were still face down on the road. In front of Kuranosuke, three ronin looking fiercer than the caped man scowled while adjusting their sword sheaths.

"Chief Retainer!" Ushioda Matanojo spoke first.

Next, Tadashichi yelled, "Kuranosuke-dono."

Koemon scolded, "Oishi-dono."

Finally, Kuranosuke squinted at the three.

"Ah," he said with a smile. "I was wondering who that was. Matanojo, Tadashichi, and Koemon. When did you come?"

"You knew?"

"What an unfortunate thing to say. I can still see."

"That townsman who tried to stab you was Chisaka Hyobu's spy. He's a strong spy who goes by the pseudonym of Juhachishaku. How well can you take care of yourself while enjoying yourself? It is your body, but don't you think it's not your body until a certain time?"

"What are you saying, Matanojo? Did you come to scold me?"

"Probably guided by the late lord, we happened to see you on the boat. Did you attend the first anniversary service in Ako?"

"Yes, I went," said Kuranosuke, lowering his head. "A grand memorial service was held at Kagakuji Temple. Even the townsmen, the beach inhabitants, and the peasants of the domain who will never forget their origins came with incense to pray at the shrine. I didn't expect to cry."

"You may have visited the shrine for the first anniversary, but why are you not going home to Yamashina but partaking in recreation? It is grotesque."

Tadashichi trailing Matanojo said, "Will you return with us to Yamashina? During your absence, various matters you must hear about and matters requiring consultation piled up."

"Now, now, young men don't speak so crudely. I came here with friends including my favorite Takenojo and Tsuya from Sonezaki. Why should I return home? This evening, I must drop everything and go to Masuya."

"Is Masuya that important?"

"The fun is for appearance's sake and duty. They call me The Squire of Yamashina ..."

"Disgusting!" said Tadashichi biting his lip.

"Who is this rich man called The Squire? Oishi-dono, what is your important duty in the red-light district? Does the solemn oath you made to us matter?"

"Dammit!"

His widened eyes looked at Tadashichi.

"What are you saying? The solemn oath was to Yugiri. On this return trip, I will certainly visit and present souvenirs from Ako. Now I believe sending a messenger was a mistake. All the souvenirs were taken in Sonezaki. At least, I must show my face."

"It's better to tell us! We're used to hearing that sort of nonsense."

"The taste for play looks fun to anyone who lacks courage that hides in a melancholy heart. Without speaking so inelegantly, Tadashichi, would you consider going to Shumokumachi with me?"

"I refuse. We just came from the grave of our late friend Kayano Sanpei. I breakdown in tears thinking about his death. Under these circumstances, Sanpei in the other world regrets his death without honor."

"Sanpei died? How did Sanpei die?"

"You're too drunk, and that conversation is not for the roadside. But I will say one thing. The compassionate and pure-hearted Kayano was trapped between his pact with his comrades and his aged father. He committed seppuku."

"…"

Looking at the hazy evening clouds or staring at the treetops of the cherry blossom trees, Kuranosuke leaned his back against a tree, turned his face up, and cast his eyes down.

Kuranosuke clapped to keep the rhythm and chanted.

Tears of grief fall onto a sleeve.
Melancholy tears fall onto a sleeve.

"In this world, there are men with brief lives. Matanojo, Tadashichi, and Koemon, you'll be better off seeing the unknown world soon. So you won't come? Tonight, I will be introduced to a licentious life. That'll be everything. No, the night will be late when I reach the bottom of the cup."

He staggered off and gestured with his folding fan to beckon the shadows of Takenojo and Tsuya.

PART X

A CLOSER LOOK AT THE FUSHIMI QUARTER IN KYOTO

74

———

A MOTHER AND WIFE IN DESPAIR

THE TIME MIGHT have been the last days of spring. An old bush warbler cried out in the village of Yamashina.

> *Aaay! Aaay!*
> *Ooooh!*

Spirited shouts to inspire and the sounds of wooden swords punctuated the silence. They came from the Oishi residence boasting newly planted garden shrubs and elegance designed from many stones and large lanterns.

Without fail, a passerby turned to look at this luxurious construction by a man born under the rays of good fortune to enjoy the rest of his life in this fleeting world.

The kings of gorgeous flowers bloomed and competed with peonies in beauty in the garden of trees and flowers. The dazzling sun rays of May bounced off the new ceiling made from Yoshino cedar in the study.

"Riku, water, water please," said Kuranosuke then lay down and fell asleep.

351

After returning home that morning by palanquin from a Gion teahouse, he kicked aside the bedclothes his wife Riku readied for him and snored loudly beneath the collar of the haori coat covering his head.

Aaay! Oooh!

As if trying to wake their father from his torpor, his two eldest sons Chikara and Kichichiyo engaged in dedicated fencing practice behind him.

Kuranosuke woke up and licked his lips dried out by his hangover.

"Riku!" he said and clapped his hands.

"Yes," came her distant reply. In time, her figure came running in short steps. She sat, placing both hands on the floor.

"Oh, you're awake?"

"What are you doing?"

"I was busy in the kitchen. Forgive me."

"If the kitchen is short-handed, hire more servants. Don't worry about the cost. You still think we're poor. Bring me water."

"All right."

After a night spent in the red-light district, the husband was always in a foul mood and quick to anger.

In one gulp, he drank the water Riku poured with great care.

"Are Chikara and Kichichiyo making that racket?"

"Yes, they are."

"They woke me up. Tell those noisemakers, their father says to stop the needless yelling."

"…"

"Why are you scolding me with your eyes?"

"You say that, but like an older brother, Chikara

instructs Kichichiyo on how to hold a *kendo* sword at odd moments. Praising them would be better. Why would a parent say 'stop the needless yelling'?"

"Riku," snapped Kuranosuke and sat up on his knees.

"Yes."

"Please leave me in peace today. You should go to your family home in Toyooka."

"What?" Riku caught her breath. Doubting her husband's words, she paled, drew close, and pointedly asked, "But for what reason?"

Kuranosuke stared into her eyes and, showing no emotion, said, "You are not in harmony with the ways of this family."

"If … you … If I've misstepped, please forgive me. Whatever it is, I will change."

"How old are you?"

"…"

"It's not an age where one changes when corrected. I've grown weary of having to scold. Since leaving Ako, I changed my name to Ikeda Kyuemon to live as an ordinary townsman in an interesting and fun world, and told you so. From now on, my land and home more than the bow and arrow and the abacus more than the way of the samurai will be important to me. I demand that for the education of Chikara and Kichichiyo. Your encouraging the children to play kendo in the shadows makes your future as Kyuemon's wife uncertain. Again, you are not in harmony with the ways of this family."

"Is that how you feel?"

"Obviously."

Riku bowed down on the tatami, said no more, and cried.

"Please, get ready to leave now. You may take clothes, household items, anything you wish with you."

"But ..."

She clung to his knees. "Aren't you being too severe? I'm of no consequence, your wife who bore many children, Chikara, Ruri, Kichichiyo, and Daisaburo. I do not understand why you're sending me away."

"What do you mean by 'of no consequence'? A woman not in harmony with a family's ways will bring about the family's collapse, which is important to the Oishi family. You do understand that you cannot stay here one more moment. Get up and get out now."

His mother's crying and father's yelling made Kichichiyo stop his kendo practice and jump into the room with dirty feet. Cowed by his father's behavior, Chikara slipped in from behind and respectfully shrunk into a corner of the study.

The glum older brother was quiet and waited. Alone, Kichichiyo bowed with both hands on the floor before his father.

"Father, please forgive her. Mother will correct her flaws."

"Child, this does not concern you. Your mother ..." Kuranosuke stared and patted Kichichiyo's bangs.

"Your mother ... will leave the Oishi family today. I will no longer scold her."

"No ... Father, please let Mother stay in this family forever."

"Do you love your mother?"

"Yes."

"In that case, you will become your mother's child."

"I also love you, Father. Mother and Father will live together forever."

"No, we will not."

He gently pressed his son's shoulder. Kichichiyo turned around. Riku forgot about herself and said, "Oh, don't cry

Kichichiyo. Your father's a tad cranky today. By tonight, your usual father will be back with his smile."

She moved closer to his knees and wiped his crying face.

"Not tonight. That day will never come. Only the eldest son Chikara will stay by my side. You will go immediately with the other children to Toyooka. Riku, that is an order."

"I will speak to my uncle Koyama-sama and cousin Shindo-sama. It's all right, Kichichiyo."

"I've spoken to Shindo and your Uncle Koyama, so I will not hear from you again."

"What? You've gone that far."

"Uh-huh."

Kuranosuke gave a long, deep nod and looked hard at her as he spoke.

"Years ago when I brought you here to be my wife, I believed if I ever fell into the circumstances of a townsman, you would no longer be in harmony with the family's way and have to leave."

Riku broke down. Unlike his words, distant thoughts filled with mercy in her husband's eyes were as clear as a lake with an unseen bottom. Still, there was so much she could not fathom.

"It can't be," said Riku, her hands dropped to the tatami. Her husband only nodded. It was a sorrowful time. As a woman and a mother, thoughts more painful than death pierced her heart.

She only trusted her husband. No, until today, Riku never held the tiniest doubt about him. Why was this conviction erased from her heart in an instant?

While scolding and encouraging herself, she wiped away her tears and stood. Daisaburo, cradled by his mother, had woken up and was crying for a breast.

Like rocks pushing onto his knees, Chikara's hands supported his neck and shoulders bent low.

"Father!"

He raised his damp eyes to look at Kuranosuke's face.

"Chikara," his father asked, "Do you hate your father?"

"No," answered Chikara while shaking his head. Tears rolled down his face.

"A life of debauchery has consumed me. Is there anything you want to say to me?"

"No. Do what you like. I will enjoy life."

"Uh-huh. You are my son. Come here, Chikara. You are also the son of a wealthy man from Yamashina and must understand matters concerning tea."

75

THE BITTER IDLE MAN

Fuwa Kazuemon stopped on a bare-earth corner of Tenma Oimatsucho. He touched his hand to the brim of his braided straw hat and scanned the people walking down the side street to make sure suspicious shadows were not following him as he passed under the eaves of the row houses. At the fourth row house, he peeked inside and asked, "Does Soemon live here?"

The reply came after a short time. "Yeah," said Hara Soemon out back. "I'm in the garden. Kazuemon, come to the inner garden."

He pushed open the broken wooden door beside the house and stepped over a fallen rotting bamboo gutter beneath the eaves.

"Oh, you have a garden?"

"I'm poor but have a four-acre garden. It's a little early, but I'm thinking about building a fence this summer for morning glories at the scaffold for vegetable gourds. Today, I'm preparing the seedbed."

"I'm impressed."

"It is impressive. I don't know who'll cool off under the

gourds or look at the flowers. People cannot live and do nothing. An idle life is bitter."

"People unlike you also live in this world."

"They do?"

"Some of them are our close friends."

"What? Oh, like Ono Kurobei."

"No, no, that man is no mystery and is not angry. You haven't heard, Soemon-dono?"

"Heard what?"

"About the debauchery of Chief Retainer Oishi.

Soemon spoke as he washed his hands over the fence in the water basin while keeping an eye on the edge of the neighboring house's veranda.

"Keep in mind, that's gossip. Before dew could dry on the morning glories, the men scattered. Oishi-dono, a man in his prime, lazily gazes at and savors this spring and this world where you can't be born twice. And—"

"You have to be clever to deceive Kira's and Uesugi's spies. I observed his actions and found them laudable."

"From the beginning, you said to trust Oishi-dono. Now, I'm starting to believe it was all a ruse."

"Why?" Soemon asked and sat with a thud on the veranda. He reached for an ashtray in the drawing room and gripped a tobacco pipe at an angle.

Soemon was young at fifty-six and free of gray hair. As commander of the foot soldiers, he best appreciated the spirit of the young and might have possessed a youthful spirit, too.

"If the plan is for his amusement, discretion must be paramount. Oishi-dono emerged recently, not with a few bad points but has behaved shamefully, like a complete fool. He goes where the wind blows to Shimabara, Gion, and Shumokumachi and throws away money. I can see that he takes pride in being gossiped about as the wealthy man of leisure called The Squire."

"Is that true?"

It was not true. Soemon polished the pipe's metal bit between the teeth of a forced smile and looked at the dazzling sun of late spring.

"He's a fool. I can't describe each incident. The hot-tempered Takebayashi Tadashichi will rage like fire. And Ushioda and Onodera Koemon are furious he hasn't been tossed out. What's going to happen? I don't want to abandon him. Soemon-dono, you must go to Kyoto."

"To do what?"

"To calm the younger men and keep their dissatisfaction from erupting."

"I'm not the right man for that job. After what you've told me, how can I quiet them when now I feel heartsick. Maybe, we should both go. Even if that doesn't happen, Horibe, Okuda, and other comrades in Edo recently send frequent appeals. That's reasonable. The last time he left the capital, Oishi-dono pledged to take decisive steps next year in April. He looks like he's forgotten it all and delays taking action day by day. He has tried the patience of Horibe and some others."

"Waiting for Oishi-dono to act may last ten or twenty years. Or, he may have no designs for revenge at the bottom of his heart."

"My fear is if Kozuke no Suke hides deep in the Yonezawa castle, it's all over. That's why I'm itching to act."

"We must start."

"How?"

"First, we will go to Kyoto and try to bump into Oishi-dono one more time."

"Yes."

"If he remains indecisive, we will know that is his true

motive. We will throw out that sort of man and alone we will— "

"Who will? Do what?"

"In Kyoto and Osaka, Otaka, Ushioda, and Nakamura Kansuke have been with us from the beginning. Okano and Onodera's son are not duplicitous. In Edo, Horibe and his son, Okuda Magodayu, Tanaka Sadashiro, Kurahashi Densuke are our undisputed allies."

"That's twelve or thirteen men."

"Yes. More than one hundred cowards, but if we assemble ten men with iron will—"

"Wait," he said to curb Kazuemon's excited words.

"For now, we'll take a casual trip to Kyoto to confirm the chief retainer's true intentions and set up an emergency plan. But there's one unfortunate matter." Soemon stopped and went inside. "Today my wife is visiting relatives in Sumiyoshi. Maybe, I should write a farewell note? Kazuemon, excuse me for a short time."

Soemon sat at a small desk in the adjoining room. He slumped forward and was writing something at the end of a paper scroll. They listened to the quiet sounds of oars on the Tenma River. A sleepy taiko drum flowed in from Shibai Yagura in Dotonbori.

Under the calm April sun rays and buffeted by the warm southeastern winds, Kazuemon realized he probably shared Soemon's feelings such as wanting to enjoy stealing life's small accomplishments.

"It's no surprise men like Ono and Oishi in important positions are that way. But no matter how another man lives, I will follow my path. Yes, I'll follow my path."

76

PASSING IN THE NIGHT

OEMON AND KAZUEMON went to Kyoto to visit Onodera, but both the father and son were away. They visited Otaka Gengo, but he had not returned home the previous night.

The comrades rarely communicated with each other. This splintered inactivity angered Soemon.

"As the days pass, men's hearts naturally fall into impatience. In this state, how will the vengeance of one arrow be delivered to Lord Kira?"

"Some may be in Yamashina," said Kazuemon, trying to calm him.

"I'm exhausted. This has been hard work. If we go to Yamashina and they tell us he's not home, we'll have reason to be angry."

"I'll hail town palanquins."

"My recent poverty makes me reluctant to part with the fare, but we'll ride."

The two rode to the foot of the mountain and walked from there in the pitch-black night. As they walked away from their palanquins, two just arriving from the top of

Yamashina ran past them heading the other way. They turned to watch their lantern lights.

"I think one carried Oishi-dono. Was there someone else?"

"No, it looked like a local court lady. I heard a baby crying in one palanquin."

They continued walking, unconcerned. Even on this moonless night, they could see the walls of the newly built Oishi home.

As they neared, someone stood hunched over in front of the gate. A youth was crying into the chest of an itinerant priest wearing a wicker hat.

"Isn't that Chikara-dono?"

Startled by Soemon's voice, Chikara jerked away from the priest and hurriedly rubbed his sleeve over his eyes.

"Yes!"

His sharp answer came in his usual voice.

"Hara-sama. Fuwa-sama."

"Is your father home?"

"Unfortunately, he's not."

"Is he in Gion or Shumokumachi?"

"Uh?"

Chikara looked hapless. His dried eyes flooded again with unstoppable tears.

"What happened?"

Soemon slapped his shoulder, causing his eyelashes to separate and a white ball to roll down his cheek.

"…"

Chikara didn't answer, but the unfamiliar, itinerant priest in the wicker hat greeted them from the side.

"As always, your coming is fortunate."

"And you are?"

"I am Yukai of Enrinji Temple in Ako."

"Oh, the priest?"

"At the command of Oishi-sama, I came to Edo to make contacts concerning the appointment of the lord's younger brother Daigaku-sama as the head of the clan. Despite running all around, my scant ability achieved none of the desired outcomes. The truth is I've had no success and came here a short time ago."

"Was Chikara crying out of disappointment with your results?"

"No, there's another matter."

"Another matter? Is it serious?"

"A trivial family matter. Don't concern yourselves."

"But a family matter can't be overlooked. We have an inseparable bond with Oishi-dono. Please tell us."

"All right. When I arrived a short time ago, two palanquins were preparing to leave. The master's wife Riku and three of the children—Kichichiyo, Ruri, and Daisaburo—were crying about a trip somewhere. It appears, today, Kuranosuke-dono sent his wife back to the home of her father, Ishizuka Gengobei, in Tajima, Toyooka."

"They're divorcing?"

The two turned around reflexively to look into the darkness and recalled the palanquins that came down the hill and passed them a while ago.

"That's a shame. Kazuemon, you mentioned hearing a baby crying."

"I never imagined that was her."

"Why would the chief retainer divorce? I have a hunch, but if we ask, a deeper reason will emerge. We'll see. Don't cry, Chikara-dono. I'll ask your mother to return home."

Soemon was about to run off, but Chikara grabbed his sleeve.

"Please don't."

"Why?" asked Soemon with an accusatory look.

"Aren't you sad your mother is being divorced and driven back to Tajima? The feelings of you four children about her being sent to her distant family home resemble mine. Even though I'm an outsider, this is tearing me up inside."

"No, no. Please let it go. I don't want my mother to cry anymore."

"She'll be called back, and she and your father will talk."

"There's no point."

"Hmmm. Are you drained of love or filled with hatred for your father?"

"…"

"This evening the fancy quarter will be boosted by the wealthy Squire. Kazuemon, even if it takes all night, we're gonna find Oishi-dono."

The two men strode away. Chikara could not stop them. Bewildered and despondent, tears darkened his rosy cheeks. Charm vanished from the light of a home without a mother and a father. Only the dreadful loneliness of spring was there.

"Well, if he returns home, please tell Kuranosuke-dono, I stopped by tonight. The letters from Ako contain the details," said Yukai and walked off. He took a few steps, stopped, and turned.

"Chikara, it's getting foggy. You'll catch a cold. Go back inside. A trip to Tajima may be difficult, but going back and forth to Fushimi or Gion is not easy. The body of an itinerant priest is truly a waste," said the mumbling shadow shrouded by the black evening mist of Yamashina.

77

THE RICE-WASHING BASKET

"**I**s **it ready?**"

"Not yet."

"Now?"

"Just a moment."

A wobbly drunk dressed in a costume staggered out from behind a partition screen.

"Bwa, ha, ha, ha."

"Hew, hew, hew."

"Ha, ha, ha, ha."

The party of clients and prostitutes fell out laughing at the unusual sight. They pounded their hands, clutched their sides, and could not stop laughing.

He hid his head under a rice-washing basket and held a wooden pestle pilfered from the kitchen by a maid. His sleeves were tied back by a patterned, red tie-dyed waistband sash coaxed from a prostitute.

From inside the rice-washing basket, he asked, "What's wrong?"

"There's only laughing and no dancing. Han, Toyo,

Shige. Hurry and play the shamisen and the drums. Shall we play a folk song?"

"Yes, let's!"

"We'll dance to *Son-in-Law*."

They began a lively accompaniment playing ancient and modern instruments, a recent popular trend in Gion and Fushimi.

The voices of the maid, the prostitutes, the rakugo performer Tokusai, and the young kabuki actor Segawa Takenojo competed to sing.

Is marriage only for the pretty face?
A homely face is a widow's.
Will hair grow on that bald head like your
 father's, if you eat yams?
Hey, son-in-law.
Will your hair grow?

The drunk sporting the rice-washing basket danced like a buffoon to the song. He looked sophisticated and stylish, as well as, experienced in every possible licentious act. Elegant hand gestures accompanied half of his frolicking.

Will eating a goblin grow that flat nose
 from your father?
Son-in-law.
Will eating a doctor lengthen that short
 haori jacket from your father?
Son-in-law.
Oh, will it get longer?

The place was the parlor room of Sasaya Kiemon, a first-class Fushimi teahouse. Not just in that room, lights of flamboyance and extravagance competed in rooms upstairs and downstairs.

Without a guide, two swaggering men strode around the garden at Sasaya. The two loutish samurai peered into the rooms from the garden and noticed the dancing hands of the rice-washing basket.

One pointed and said to the man behind him, "Kazuemon! There he is."

These men were Hara Soemon and Fuwa Kazuemon. They recently arrived from Osaka, made frequent visits to Yamashina and Gion, and visited the homes of comrades. Without revealing their objective, for the past half a month, the two exasperated men hung around Kuranosuke's haunts.

"Please stop!" said Kazuemon in his congenitally loud voice and leaped onto the veranda.

"This is foolish, an insane spectacle. Women, get back!"

Soemon passed between the maid and the prostitutes watching him in shock and stuck his vacant-looking face next to the face of the man wearing the rice-washing basket and holding the wooden pestle.

"Chief Retainer. I am Soemon."

"..."

"I had no idea you've become so skilled in this art in this short time. Is it impressive? Is it praiseworthy? Surely, you've heard the public's opinion. Ha, ha, ha, ha. If I might say, you've changed quite a bit."

Soemon's sarcastic critique was joined by tears rolling down his face. Kazuemon said if he had discovered him, he would have smacked him. He came here to see him, but it might have been better not to have come. The resentment in his heart paled and hardened his face as he suppressed his trembling shoulders. If he mistook this man for his superior Kuranosuke, he looked irrational and capable of violence.

"Chief Retainer," said Soemon and drew closer. "We can't talk here. Shall we go to your home in Yamashina?"

"Aha, ha, ha. I am not the chief retainer. I am not The Squire."

"What? You're not?"

"I'm very different," the man said and removed the rice-washing basket. "I'm Onodera Junai."

"Ah!?"

Both men were stunned.

"Elder Junai?"

"Did you see me dancing? How was I?"

"Aren't you ashamed being seen? Junai-dono, even you, even you …"

"Why are you here? Kazuemon, you are terribly misguided. You came to this pleasure quarter, but your face pales and you foolishly barge in here. Well, even an uncouth fellow like my son Koemon is learning somehow."

"What? Koemon is here?"

"Not only Koemon, Naka-sama, Sho-sama, Suke-sama, and Tansui-sama."

"Who are Tansui-sama and Suke-sama?"

"Junai and Koemon are the names of brutes and not spoken in the quarter. Sho-sama is Otaka Gengo; Tansui-sama is Muramatsu Sandayu; Suke-sama is Tominomori Sukeemon; Shige-sama is me; and my son Koemon is Hobotan-sama. We are all popular with the ladies of the quarter."

"Let's go," Kazuemon urged Soemon and kicked a seat.

"Wait," said Junai, "Come join the party and we'll talk. You can't leave without having a drink. Sit. Girl, bring a cup."

He forced the cup into Kazuemon's hands.

"Junai-dono."

"Why such frightening eyes?"

"Please tell this to the chief retainer, too. We'll never meet again."

"All right. If I must, I will tell him."

"I'm done."

Kazuemon witnessed a catastrophic downfall and filled with resentment. The cup of sake on his knee shattered in his grip.

78

THE SINGER

THESE DAYS, the pleasure quarters in towns and villages prospered. Like a communicable disease, when night fell, singers popped up and were heard on every street corner.

The first popular songs and dance circles, called *Nagoya Ondo*, came from Nagoya. Capitol Ondo appeared in Kyoto. *Dounen* dancing emerged in Fushimi. The men and women of the quarter wore delicate garments, adorned their heads with hand towels or braided-straw hats, held fans, and drew dance circles.

> *Saa-sa, dance!*
> *Dance!*
> *The world of people*
> *Summer nights growing short*
> *Little cuckoo*
> *Ya-yo*
> *Little cuckoo cry*
> *Saa-sa, dance! Dance!*

From a bench set out on a street in Nakacho in the pleasure district, a singer tapped a fan on his head and sang. A middle-aged man dressed in a padded *tanzen* kimono, a maid from the teahouse, an attendant, a towns-man, a youth with square bangs, a maiden, a monk, and a good-humored samurai danced with hand gestures and moved their legs in time to the dounen ditty and slowly drew a circle around the bench supporting the singer.

"Sho-sama! Sho-sama!" called a maid from Sasaya. She cut through the circle to the singer and whispered to him.

"Oh, oh, is that so?" he said and nodded.

"Suke-dono, Tansui-dono, a little emergency has come up. We must go," he said and leaped from the bench and ran off.

He was Otaka Gengo. Both Tominomori Sukeemon called Suke-dono and Muramatsu Sandayu called Tansui-dono left the dance circle and followed.

"Is there a fight?"

The others turned around, but the men's shadows had vanished.

As they went out the main gate of the quarter, someone asked, "Is everyone here?"

"Yes."

In the dark shadow of the willows, they glimpsed Onodera Junai raising his arm to call them over. He whispered something to them.

An alarmed Gengo asked, "What should we do?"

"Follow them and report back."

"We'll find out everything," said Gengo, as he looked down the road.

"All right, where do Fuwa and Hara live?"

"I don't know. It shouldn't be far. We'll split up."

"Good. I'll go this way," said Suke already running.

Gengo and Sandayu split up to pursue Hara Soemon and Fuwa Kazuemon.

The Sasaya maid ran up again.

"Are you Shige-sama?"

"Yes, what is it?" said Onodera Junai.

"The Squire is awake and wonders why no one is there. He's irritated and wants you to come right away."

"What? He's awake? He's full of energy."

When he returned to the parlor in Sasaya, Kuranosuke, The Squire, was resting his body on the lap of his lady friend Ukihashi and surrounded by the rakugo performer Tokusai, Segawa Takenojo, and a jester.

"Are all of you lonely? I'm lonely. Only strangers are having fun."

He looked like he just woke up but already held a sake cup.

"Even in a dream, have you ever seen making merry this lively?"

"Who's in that noisy group in the Azalea Room?"

"Yodoya's guests."

"Yodoya? Oh, the rich man known in Kyoto, Osaka, and Edo. Is The Squire contemptible before the glimmering gold of Yodoya?"

"Envy is unusual for you."

"Who is Yodoya? Ukihashi, let's call everyone and scatter gold, the gold not lost in the inner parlor."

"Oh my."

While she watched, Kuranosuke slid out a purse from the pocket hidden in his untidy lapel.

"Here!"

He scattered oval *koban* gold coins, nuggets, silver, and gold under the lantern light.

Women's and men's hands brawled over them. Kuranosuke clapped and laughed like a madman. The Squire only stopped clapping when overpowered by his rush of laughter. He drank bottoms up and recklessly poured for others. Everyone knew holding back was unacceptable. The teetering Squire stood out. He clumsily waved his arms around but seemed acquainted with Noh dance. The older geisha praised his precise kicks. A dounen dance learned by watching was said to be The Squire's favorite performance.

"Ah, I'm floating. I'm floating."

The rakugo performer Tokusai rose next.

"I'm floating, too," said Takenojo and rose.

More guests streamed in.

"Where's The Squire?"

"Ah, The Squire is there."

One man blindfolded Kuranosuke with a hand towel and scattered the others.

Hands clapped.

"Squire, over here."

"Squire, over there."

Kuranosuke's mouth hung open like an idiot.

"It's so dark. Very dark."

The party answered.

"It's too dark."

"Come to my hands."

"Over here, Squire."

The rhythmic clapping gradually moved away. Meanwhile, the maid slipped out to run errands. A prostitute whispered to the others to hide in the other parlor.

"It's dark. Too dark."

Kuranosuke patted the wall and unknowingly left the room. He explored the long tatami-mat passageway.

He touched cool silk. The captured rival held his

breath and let Kuranosuke's hands move over his body. Kuranosuke's hand felt something and pulled back.

"You foolish ronin!" thundered the samurai who didn't recognize Kuranosuke and shoved him back.

"Damn fool!" He glanced back as he strode away.

79

DEFIANCE

IN **THE DEAD** of night, large raindrops struck the window bamboo. The rainy season ended and June began. The tatami they napped on was not chilly, but five drunk bodies shivered from the marrow of their bones.

Where's that child?

A baby cried in a secret place.

The cries sounded like the baby's bowels were irritated. Despite being far away, the crying grabbed one's ears. The eyes of the drunk Kuranosuke unconscious on the dark tatami popped open and stared at the ceiling.

He wondered, Is anyone going to feed him?

Gloom marked late night in the pleasure quarter. The unspeakable wretched loneliness after pleasure descended on him like a silent graveyard.

Sounds resembling a whimpering voice rose from the ground. Where's the baby? Kuranosuke was wide awake.

His wife Riku, who returned to her parents' home in Tajima, had given birth to Daisaburo that year. How is Ruri? Is Kichichiyo all right?

The thought of his wife also nursing a baby came to mind.

The partition was stealthily slid open. Kuranosuke kept his eyes shut. Clothes did not rustle, but other signs revealed someone's approach. A hand patted his shoulder.

"Wake up … Squire … Squire. Please wake up and go to Ukihashi-sama's room."

He knew she was the maid, but groaned and rolled over. The window bamboo swayed, stirred by the wind. It looked like her hand was trying to rouse him but was searching his sleeve and deftly pulled something out. The maid went to the window.

"Tokusai-san."

Someone hushed her from outside. Kuranosuke spied the shaven head of the rakugo performer Tokusai hiding among the bamboo leaves.

Kuranosuke was not wearing anything that would impede drawing his sword. He found this strange but looked unconcerned as he rolled over again.

The white legs slipped out of the room. That was alarming! thought Kuranosuke. He understood why this world was called decadent and why he had to stay on guard.

Both the Kira and Uesugi clans had money and men. The quarter where money talks is the best place to act.

I'm living in that world. Right in the middle of the enemy and danger.

He slept on the bedding of a naked sword.

Even if this never happened, a warrior's body is that way at all times. A lifetime of fifty or sixty years is spent above or below a bare sword.

If he were living in the remote Ako countryside in safety and idleness, he would not give a moment's thought to a life steeped in tension. Through joy and sorrow, he relished the humanity of the life he experienced over the year since the incident in March more than a lifetime of one hundred, no, one thousand years.

"…"

Kuranosuke pushed aside the silk bedding entangling his legs and sat up.

The baby cried from time to time throughout the night.

Like a detached stranger, he reflected on his complex self as a father, a samurai, and a man. He was amused by the people of the world and perhaps saddened.

It's nothing.

If a person is born, this complex life can be savored. If one is not born, there's nothing. The virtues of being born must be contemplated.

I've heard people say the pleasure quarter should be despised but do not feel the slightest bit of that righteousness. Kind people also inhabit this world.

The feelings, experiences, and pleasures of life have, at this moment, elements that are unnatural and immoral in the enjoyment of a simple life.

It's simple … when the cherry blossom petals fall … act or don't act. His muscles tensed at that thought.

If it all ends without taking action, the Fushimi and Gion pleasure quarters are good places to return to the debauchery of dissolute rogues. Everyone has a history of lies and misdeeds.

Kuranosuke, however, could barely see the summit ahead. The arduous journey so far had been formidable, but he was confident. More than the enemy, despair moved the spirit of the inner circle.

He also feared himself. Although his conviction hardened each day, the emptiness that rattled his conviction frightened him.

Thoughts of nothingness inhabited his spiritual void.

When he saw a crack, he raised his head and said in contempt, "I'm an idiot!"

He said to himself, "What is my name? What will be my name after I die? It's transience. This phenomenon advances time and carries time away. Spring comes. Summer comes. Fall leaves and winter comes. Only that repeats. What is life without fun?"

The crying child has not been given his mother's milk. The wife loses weight in lonely contemplation. Her duty is fulfilled by that sacrifice. Is that all right? As a father or a man? Well, I will enjoy this life not only now but forever. It's a waste for a man who has difficulty being born a second time.

Only Kuranosuke nodded in agreement with the principle and spirit of the path taken by Ono Kurobei. He well understood his impulse to go that way. He believed his personality was nothing like Kurobei's. Like an objective observer, Kuranosuke now saw his own complex nature, his strength of not easily bending.

The falling of the cherry blossoms is a cherished time. Life is short. Of course, there will be regrets and disgrace. For himself, there shouldn't only be living alone and vanishing. There are also ancestors and descendants. He thought, I am the link in a chain that does not rust.

"No, that is small."

He shut his eyes and ran a dress rehearsal in every corner of his mind. He was sensitive to and surprised by his feelings. Defiance. That has been a part of me from the beginning and will make me act. Defiance seems to boldly lie dormant in people who appear to lack it.

Born into a humble samurai family, he simply lived by the way of the warrior. He was not unhappy about this and did not think about living in an irrational and unnatural society. However, dissatisfaction and melancholy are not forbidden in the ways of the ordinary world in this age of Genroku. People too often witness *inhumanity* that cannot be ignored. Much of that is misgovernment by the shogunate. The gaudy clique that built a nest inside power sang the song *Spring in Our World*. The pompous men of the Fujiwara clan brazenly sang, "This world is our world." That song was the childishness of men who still pursued a dream as a dream.

The lower classes of society were never sacrificed as much as they are by the current crowd in the inner palace surrounding the Dog Shogun Tokugawa Tsunayoshi, the deceitful retainers, and the mad monk. They have no ability, only coarse extravagance and insatiable consumption. The freedom of the common people was never stolen as it is today.

Given his genuine samurai character, Kuranosuke could not abide by the two worst policies of the shogunate: the trick of salvaging good money from law-abiding citizens and replacing it with newly minted bad money and caring for the esteemed dog in the *Edicts on Compassion for Living Things* that proclaimed humans to be inferior to domesticated animals.

The recklessness of bad money pitifully pushed the honest living of the lowest rung of society down to rock bottom and provided ample capital for more pleasures to only a portion of high-ranking shogunate officials. People in the distant Ako countryside knew that much. The ripples were far-reaching, and the situation in Edo was replicated throughout the country.

The edicts on the esteemed dog caused problems throughout the countryside. There, its application was more extreme than the central government, and strict prohibition was common. If fond of an esteemed dog, a poor man faced the destitution of his family. He had to endure feeding white rice to a dog and starving his family. A sick child received no medicine, but a dog doctor examined a sick dog. If the dog died, a list of the residents in the landlord's row house had to be delivered to a government office, and a respectful funeral held. If negligent in these duties, the punishment was banishment, one hundred lashes, long imprisonment, exile, or in the worst case, death.

This situation was repeated in every clan. The edicts of the Dog Shogun were the law of the land. Despite room for discretion by the lord of the domain and the locality, competition between clans was brought on by fear of false charges lodged by a neighboring clan. This edict strictly enforced the inferiority of human beings to dogs. Even the children of peasants ignorant of the current shogun's name, Tsunayoshi, heard of the Dog Shogun. The sight of a stray dog walking toward a person would illustrate the grander existence of a dog than a human. Stray dogs barking at crossroads or empty lots were members of the extended family of the Dog Shogun. Thus, all humans on Earth lived resigned to their lower status as animals than dogs.

For the time being, the man called Oishi Kuranosuke Yoshio found it impossible as an exceptional man to live under the current system. Simply, he knew he was not beneath a domesticated animal.

Kuranosuke heard about an assessment in the writings *Sanno Gaiki* by the contemporary Confucian scholar Dazai Shundai and obtained a copy from a bookseller in Osaka. When he read these writings, he was moved to tears of pain under the lantern light for the solitary man in this world.

The heir to the shogun is mourned before the Shogun Tsunayoshi, and no child is born again in the inner palace. Monk Ryuko of Goji Temple offers advice. The lack of an heir during his life is his punishment for taking many lives. If the shogun desires a true heir, the killing of living things must be forbidden.

During the twenty-third year of the sexagenary cycle, the shogun was born. That year belonged to dogs. The strongest belief is dogs must be loved. Shogun, this is certain.

The empress dowager, Tsunayoshi's birth mother Keishoin, renewed her devotion to Ryuko. Both preached and never stopped appealing for the edict. Shogun, order the government ministers to prohibit the killing of living things. Today, you shall hand down the edicts on beloved dogs.

These *Edicts on Compassion for Living Things* cited in *Sanno Gaiki* were issued as a law in January of year 4 of the Jokyo imperial era. Over the fifteen years until year 14 of the Genroku era, a countless number of people, like pebbles on the shore, experienced the misfortune of the death penalty, exile, and banishment in violation of the edicts of the Dog Shogun.

When this extraordinary law was issued, everyone was doubtful and confused. However, word of the first recorded violation traveled to Ako. Mizuno Touemon, the head of the shogunate's guards, together with subordinate police, was ordered into exile or placed under house arrest. A cook named Amano committed seppuku. A person in the house of Akita Awaji no Kami was severely punished. People cringed over and over at the rumors.

This law created a new system of posts such as dog doctors, dog inspectors, and dog magistrates. If dogs passed on a main road, a daimyo's procession often shied away from the esteemed dogs and did not advance. The pandemonium of dogs filled the world. Their feces were handled with extreme care. In a world that seemed unreal, people lived under great pressure, but, in time, grew accustomed to the idea of being inferior to domesticated animals. If uncomfortable with this idea, they lived in a world they could not live in for one day.

People who were conscious of the stipulation of inferiority to animals were at peace and believed it to be common sense. They worked to become people who advanced one step and were no different from dogs. The faces and figures of chief dog retainers suited to serving the Dog Shogun, dog chamberlains, dog townsmen, dog ronin, dog prostitutes, and dog anything endeavored not to change into animals but to resemble them. Anything like money, false reputation, greed, dishonesty, immorality, flattery, wickedness, and sycophancy were used to gain the advantage. And they ran around and searched with their sense of smell. But to the end, these ideas of silly people were met with contempt.

80

PROCLAIMING HUMANITY

O
F COURSE, EVERYONE did not agree. People were people, and some took pride in being superior to animals. These two types of humans formed two tidal currents. Like cold water fish and warm water fish, they inhabit the same ocean but cannot switch places.

For example, Kuranosuke thought of the incident as a situation between strangers.

The difference between Asano Takumi no Kami and Kira Kozuke no Suke and their misfortune were nothing more than destiny beckoning them with the chance to act on the provided stage dressed in worthless costumes on that fine ceremonial day. If Takumi no Kami had not been the one, in time, someone else would have been.

Takumi no Kami was well aware of Kozuke no Suke's behavior toward lords, his daily life, and his philosophy of life. He wasn't naive about the world or lacked common sense. Instead, many allies probably shared his thoughts. Most people in this world would not see a crazed man. The post of the chief master of ceremonies was lower in rank and appearance. His stipend was pitifully low. He did not earn enough to allow him to live in an extravagant home in the city and socialize with uncommon ostentation.

Being in Edo at the center, he used his official authority and the occasional ceremony to make easy money and ventured to make small amounts of money between ceremonies. He only thought about profit. But when people viewed him as the lord of the fief inherited in Yokosuka in Sanshu and the region of his hometown, they saw a good lord who loved the people of his fief, was attentive to public undertakings like flood control and cultivation, and was a fine man who enjoyed being respected as the benevolent lord of the fief.

There, he was an upright man. However, when the dog prime minister and the dog daimyos met at the knees of the Dog Shogun, Kozuke no Suke became the best dog master of ceremonies. If he hadn't, he could not have built the prosperity and the family life he enjoyed. He also possessed cunning not found in future generations. Sometimes, the master of ceremonies functioned as dog fangs capable of bringing chief retainers and daimyos to their knees.

Once a year, imperial envoys visited Edo. On this occasion, the master of ceremonies lost the ability to make money. What could become the perks of being the master of ceremonies? Watching Kozuke no Suke's mouth fill with the drool of desire meant this was more than natural to him.

On reflection, Takumi no Kami's psyche was the polar opposite. He did not understand time or the undercurrents of human life. He fully believed in the customs of military families in effect since the Genna era and was unnerved by the opposing thought of showing the polish of the ordinary military mind this autumn when he accepted the unexpected formal imperial order. Takumi no Kami was not alone; ordinary samurai shared this thought. What he didn't know was the world was not so pure.

After the imperial envoys left the capital and solemnly welcomed with ceremony and dignity, as mundane men, they enjoyed the generous gifts from the shogunate more than anything. The men accompanying them shared his feelings. Master of Ceremonies Kira was not alone but joined by the entire shogunate to greet the envoys and anxiously wait for the overflow from all ceremonies as extra profits and perks. The transient world becomes a celebration of life that involves mutual dependence, exchanges, and enhancements to the moral duty of the Imperial Court and the Shogun. The world tacitly understood the common sense of filling another's wallet.

Later, Kuranosuke's regret was, What if I had been in Edo?

If my post had been the chief retainer in Edo, I would not regret bringing about many changes in the lord's thinking. The gifts to Kira were trifling. Pleasing that good-natured old man would have been simple.

If Takumi no Kami had spent one one-hundredth of the 53,000 koku household wealth, that old man would have brushed the dust off of his hakama trousers. Usually, dispensing flattery drop by drop was a simple matter to a retainer.

Also, various duties involved teahouse sake, the business at hand, and often offered women in the preferred cosmetics. Why didn't hands grab handfuls of gold coins and nuggets and scatter them? He thought, If I were a low-ranking samurai in Edo, I would look very much like a dog among dogs while having a wonderful time.

In this world of esteemed dogs, if the two swords of a samurai, one long and one short, can't be grabbed, they are only discarded. The daimyo abandons being a daimyo;

the samurai quits being a samurai; the government official stops being a government official. Beyond the fields and the mountains, men model themselves after the sage Xu You and his companion, Qao Fu. The virtuous hermit Xu You washed the filth of the world from his ears after being asked by the emperor to take the throne. Qao Fu rejected those contaminated waters, too.

Was this good? Is the best path only for people to stay above the vulgar world?

Kuranosuke pondered these misgivings for a long time. No, he agonized over them.

His melancholy, as useless as a lamp lit in daylight, became a habit a dozen years ago, beginning on the day of the official announcement of the system of human inferiority to dogs.

We will reluctantly walk without spirit, depending on the time, we become humans or become dogs. As an ancient said, "The paths of generations are the same." If the decree is to crawl or walk this generation's path, then I will go by crawling or walking. This conclusion in his heart calmed Kuranosuke.

Therefore, a faction in the clan always whispered about misgovernment or criticized the shogunate, but the lanterns lit in daylight were always napping. The chief retainer in the province looked like a proper lamp wick, but this lamp wick was sparked.

The sad news brought by fast palanquin from Edo last spring struck a severe blow to his napping.

Kuranosuke had to swear to be different because his creed was *Our generation's path is the same.*

This action of Lord Takumi no Kami flew far outside the bounds. His action was not solely his action but became the actions of an ensemble of people, including the wives and daughters and the young and old in the Ako clan, and led to the call for the clan's extinction and scattering in their lives. Takumi no Kami was linked to the actions of the group, but he alone held the greatest responsibility.

Thus, Kuranosuke was obligated to carry out this task. He had to give meaning to the late lord's actions and search for meaning in following their tragic fate. Although the public reduced Takumi no Kami's action to a passionate temper; his fiery temper opposed the tenor of the times. His defense of humanity opposed the contemporary canine evils exhibited by Kira Kozuke no Suke.

"Damn these dogs. I'm not a dog!" barked Takumi no Kami in the palace of the Dog Shogun surrounded by dog vassals. Beneath the unemotional blade, he ignored the terrible laws of the current world. These thoughts brought joy from the depths of Kuranosuke's heart. If that lord was a pure-hearted daimyo who acted so foolishly, no one like him lived now.

We are not less than dogs. We are human beings.

He would give life to the late lord's will. If we don't eliminate the corrupt government of the current shogunate, without clan or connections and the misfortune of being banned from the world, our sole measure must be to walk a path, even if we know previous generations did not follow that path.

Public opinion was a mixed bag. The public's eyes saw things differently. In the simplest terms, the word revenge was the watchword to ignite interest in our future. But Kuranosuke did not humble himself that much. How should he strike at Kira, a good-natured man over sixty? What would it mean?

At least I am greedier for my life, Kuranosuke laughed at himself. By examining several earlier instances of revenge through the simple human affection of unsophisticated people, the past, and the results, he knew ending an important life as one's life's work was not straightforward.

If you strike, you will be struck. If you judge, you will be judged. Glory or death. Prosper or wither.

This cycle of life is a cosmic principle humanity has no power to change. The cycle applies to each person like the perfect promise of the four seasons. That lesson must be learned by the man brandishing a short sword.

However, during the brief life of Shogun Tsunayoshi, the generation of people destined to live below animals must be erased. People will be shamed until the last generation. The late lord being shamed by the elder Kira was unrivaled. Isn't all of human history shameful?

We become human. We are not dogs, even in the Genroku era.

Kuranosuke believed he found far-reaching justice within his objective. What will the public call that? The meaning will not change. Revenge is fine.

He had no pointed comments on the results achieved by his comrades. Each man should be free to minimize the significance of ambition and to think big. As Priest Ryousetsu said to him, "The code of the samurai is not rigid. The samurai life is vast." In the future, a broad swath of ronin with a broad range of ideas will end their lives without regret.

Today, drunk vassals stayed in the pleasure quarters of Kyoto and immersed themselves in naked desire and passion. Without being showy, without restraints, and in the company of ordinary people, each man's decision came by free thought. There's no need to drill down to the foundation of one's final decision and reveal it. Instead, the lies in the truth will be seen. In time, each man will find the answer to the questions, is it a lie? or is it the truth? This may be what makes the world interesting. To the comrades who asked him to lead them in their search for how to live, it may be the best place to die.

In this sort of incident, chance does not always have dramatic elements. In March when the flowers bloom, the place became an opulent stage of the shogunate's Matsu-no-Ma stateroom in the shogun's castle. The actors dressed in the classical costume of a kimono with a large daimon pattern and eboshi headgear when the lord slashed Kozuke no Suke. Taking the broad view, doesn't this more closely resemble the opening curtain of a scene in a drama more than a dramatic incident in society?

If we're lucky to be born, awful as it may be, we appear on the stage of this lived drama. Each one considers becoming a supporting player or the protagonist and takes on the mission of acting in destiny as an actor. This is not a simple matter.

What was in the spirit in space? Were the people selected for Earth ordered to give this performance?

Humans are not inferior to animals. When so directed, countless people placed below animals are the audience and, whether they like it or not, will be handed a scenario based on divine will. Will I no longer continue to act out this transient life in multiple acts?

These were Kuranosuke's musings. The reality that evening was a farewell with hard sake drinking. During a dream, the notion of a game is fully harnessed. How many times did he turn over in his sleep until the small window was faintly brighter?

In the pleasure quarter at dawn, a hush like the dead of night settled on the roofs. Kuranosuke buried himself deep inside the bedding.

81

A LONG STAY IS FORBIDDEN

Y ODOYA'S PARTY WENT home, but The Squire did not.

Today, too, he stayed at the brothel to romp with the whores until sunset.

"Enough. I'm exhausted."

The proprietor Sasaya Kiemon looked a little tired of this business.

"Master," said a flustered parlor maid.

"What?"

"Please come with me."

"Where?"

"It's The Squire. He's always trouble. I don't know what to do."

"What did he do?"

Kiemon hurried off with the parlor maid.

"Oh, no!"

Looking up at the ceiling of the new parlor built this spring, he saw the Squire standing on a tower of kotatsu quilts, holding a writing brush, and writing on the ceiling. One courtesan held the ink stone, while another supported his hips. Nausea rose in Kiemon. He tallied the cost and labor to repair the ceiling.

"Please Squire, a little mischief is fine but ..."

From atop the quilt tower, Kuranosuke looked down at Kiemon's reddened face.

"Ha, ha, ha, you're mad, Proprietor."

"Wouldn't anyone be?"

"It's all right. I only wrote this much. Write. I must write."

Then he wrote the final verse.

"Read this, Proprietor."

"..."

"If you don't like it, I will compensate you with gold. Don't get mad. I'm the one with the complaint."

> *Today again, I pass the hours with*
> *courtesans.*
> *What happens tomorrow?*
> *Perhaps forlorn, a quick sweep of my*
> *sleeve and I return home.*
> *A long stay by a patron of pleasure is*
> *forbidden.*
> *I will not stay two nights.*

Kuranosuke finished reading and collapsed in laughter onto Ukihashi's lap.

Onodera Junai happened by.

"Have a look."

He stood transfixed.

A piece of white paper dropped from his hand onto Kuranosuke's chest. Kuranosuke read it and twisted it into a paper string. Something had happened.

In an instant, Sukeemon noticed, Ushioda Matanojo

noticed, everyone noticed in the early evening twilight and cheered up. Kuranosuke said, "I think I'll be going home."

He told the maids who stopped by frequently after the proprietor wounded their feelings earlier, "I just remembered Karu. The poor thing. I must see her occasionally, but ..."

He was speaking of his amour. Karu was the younger sister of Jirobei of Ichimonjiya on the corner of Nijo-dori and Teramachi-dori boulevards and known to everyone in Fushimi. People who did not know her knew about her beauty. Kuranosuke's excessive promiscuity led his cousin Shindo Genshiro followed by his uncle Koyama Gengoemon to advise him at the house in Yamashina.

"If you're interested in that woman, you should stop fooling around."

Kuranosuke loved Karu, but Fushimi was fun, and he did not curtail his excursions.

"He doesn't know the bottom," his uncle and cousin said in despair.

"This behavior seems to be what Kuranosuke has come to be."

Many of his comrades supported this belief. Previously, the headstrong court adviser Okuno said, "I've given up." Hearing this, feelings of isolation stabbed Kuranosuke's heart.

He said, "I'm going home," and moved with his usual speed. "I want to see Karu's face. If I tire, I'll come again."

"Oh, please let go."

"If I let go, I'll fall over."

He clung to her shoulder as he staggered toward the large shop curtain of Sasaya.

"Let's go to that palanquin over there."

"A palanquin. I hate them ..."

Kuranosuke walked out into the dim brightness of

evening. Led by the proprietor, many flattering voices saw him off. A wave of relief washed over the people seeing them off and the people being sent off.

A dance ring was beginning. Someone invited Sukeemon to dance. A dog barked at Kuranosuke. Sukeemon threw a rock at it.

From time to time, Onodera Junai got closer to Kuranosuke and whispered to him. Kuranosuke looked like he wasn't listening but nodded, then whispered, "Behind us."

When they turned, the rakugo performer Tokusai with his haori coat covering him from his head trailed them. Sukeemon and Junai exchanged eye signals and hailed a palanquin for Kuranosuke. They said, "We'll see you tomorrow," and left by another road.

The moment Kuranosuke entered the palanquin, he no longer looked like himself. Tokusai's pace quickened after the swaying palanquin passed the mouth of the Kamogawa River. Kuranosuke didn't notice when Tokusai's shadow grew to two, three, and four shadows. Among them was Kimura Johachi, a trusted confidante of Chisaka Hyobu who went by the name of Juhachishaku.

"Who's in the palanquin?"

"I'll find out," answered the excited man, who looked like an on-duty samurai guard, tossing in a red-lacquered sword sheath.

"Everyone hide."

"All right, go find out."

Shadows sporadically hid in the twilight dusk. The performer Tokusai and the on-duty samurai were confederates directed by Kira and Chisaka.

"Hey you! Hey! Stop!" called the deep voice of the man with the red sheath as he approached the front of the palanquin. The startled bearers fled, but tranquil snores continued inside the discarded palanquin.

"Traitor, are you awake?"

A leg kicked away the straw curtain of the palanquin. Kuranosuke's gasp slipped outside, and he tumbled to the ground.

"Who ... Who are you?"

Kuranosuke's still sleepy eyes glided up the man's large body. The man with the red sheath raised his arm.

"Nobody. I'm a warrior."

"A warrior ... Uh-huh ... of course."

"Do you understand, you samurai dunce? No, you're a traitor. Do you know what kind of man makes a true warrior?"

"Tell me your name. Who are you?"

"Telling my name to a dog samurai like you would defile me. I am a warrior from another clan with no connection to the Ako clan, but it would be too much to say I'm furious. You're a disgrace! Are you the former head chief retainer at the Ako castle?"

"Are you mad about that? I'm sorry. Please overlook that."

"Overlook what? All you do is babble like a coward. Disgusting. A stupid, old retainer."

He placed his foot on Kuranosuke's shoulder and made sudden jerks to crush Kuranosuke like stomping on a frog. Kuranosuke slipped his hand under his face to keep it from being scratched by the dirt.

"Listen to me. The men among the rank-and-file of the Ako clan are struggling with resentment about the late lord and talk about Kira's head. But you, who during the lord's life stood at the top of the clan and was spoiled by a large stipend, instead of seeking revenge, you collect mistresses at brothels and go out to romp with whores. What kind of warrior are you? Don't you hear the dirt said about you?

You're a disgrace to warriors. You coward! Are you a man?"

"Ouch … Ow!"

"If you understand pain, you probably have a little character. If you feel regret, stand up and fight."

"You … you're absurd."

"All right," he said and spat on Kuranosuke's face.

Kuranosuke reached for his awakened face.

"It's your choice. That's it."

Kuranosuke placing both hands on the ground brought laughter from the wide-open mouth of the red-sheath man, then he railed. "You have no honor!" His eyes signaled the human shadows lingering nearby and then disappeared in a few strides.

Mysteriously, Kuranosuke's heart was bright. His miserable face and rumpled hair lay on the ground, but serenity filled his heart. He was even amused with himself.

Kuranosuke easily discerned a Chisaka spy in that on-duty soldier and guessed the performer Tokusai and the thuggish Kimura Johachi were there to observe his words and actions.

"Chief Retainer!"

Tominomori Sukeemon and the elder Junai who left earlier raced toward him.

Sukeemon rushed to brush the dirt off Kuranosuke's back. Junai took hold of his dirty hands.

With tears in his eyes, he said, "You did well."

"What? I'm still in service to the lord."

For the first time, Kuranosuke's words escaped in his usual monotone. Ushioda Matanojo returned with the palanquin bearers who bolted. The three ronin delighted in learning the tenacious Chisaka sent out spies who will now report back to the Kira clan.

"We will show this forbearance like this huge rock to

Horibe, Okuda, Fuwa, Hara, and the others. No, this evening, they are meeting at Terai Genkei's home. We will join them in their deliberations. Goodnight."

The three once again left the palanquin and hurried down different roads.

82

THE HEART OF AN INCENSE BURNER

T**HE SOUNDS OF** a koto rang deep inside.

On Kuranosuke's return home in Yamashina, Chikara greeted his long-absent father.

"Welcome home."

This spring, Chikara celebrated his manhood ceremony and took the name Yoshikane. He was a fine young man.

"Were there any visitors while I was gone?"

"Hara-sama and Fuwa-sama came often."

"Uh-huh, I know about them."

"And Horibe Yasubei-sama from Edo."

"When did he come?"

"On the twenty-ninth but came again yesterday to see you."

"That's it?"

"The rest aren't important."

As he walked inside, the loneliness of a wintry field enveloped Kuranosuke. He didn't hear his wife's voice or smell mother's milk. An unbearable emptiness chilled every room.

"Who's playing the koto?"

"Karu."

"Oh."

Chikara watched his father's back enter the room in the corridor to the annex and returned to his desk; he thought the koto music stopped.

"Karu, are you sad?" Kuranosuke sat down. "Tea, please."

"Yes."

Kuranosuke stared at Karu, facing the kettle for the bath in the next room. Her beauty stood out in a home with no wife. An unusual calm rippled through his spirit.

"I hope you like it," she said and timidly put down the tea. Her fingertips had a brilliant color not seen on the women in Gion or Fushimi.

"It's good."

"Especially when you're tired."

"Do I look worn out?"

"No."

Unknowingly, he caressed her face. What feelings drove her to come here? She might have been carefully instructed by her older brother Ichimonjiya Jirobei, Koyama, or Shindo and no longer bore the slightest anxiety or fear. She seemed at peace. Perhaps during his absence, she heard hints about his personality or the family's situation from Chikara, and felt like a true caretaker in his absence.

"I'm about to fall asleep. I dozed in the palanquin on my way here."

"Please wait a few moments."

She went to the bedroom.

During her absence, he shut his eyes and slept with his clothes on, using his arms as a pillow. He imagined Karu's white collar, her round eyes, and the searching look from those eyes.

"I laid out the bedding."

"Thank you."

Karu followed him to the bedroom. A palanquin lantern was set up in a far-off corner. Unlit incense smoked in the incense burner on the floor. The incense smelled like plum flowers and mingled with the faint scent of her rustling clothes.

"Is there anything else?"

She found it hard to leave and sat down. The shadows of the dim light from the side floated into the darkened lines of the virgin.

"Well," he could not answer for a time.

Kuranosuke closed his eyes. Blood like a young man's pulsed. Why was he lying to himself? The fluttering in his chest became desire flickering in his heart. But when he looked at Karu's beauty, he wasn't so blind he could ignore her future happiness or misery. A moment later, he gathered the strength to break away from eternal confusion and said, "There's nothing else. You should go to bed."

83

THE SOGA DANCE

W**ITH A CHUCKLE,** Horibe Yasubei told Tadashichi that soon after they became ronin, he embodied a ronin.

"It's true ... that's what they say. Everybody changed."

"Especially me."

"The only one who did not is the chief retainer in Yamashina."

"He will not. His warrior's soul is lost."

Yasubei came from Edo to Kyoto and took off his straw sandals at the ronin home of Otaka Gengo, but his presence there today was amazing.

He was sunburned and sweaty because he was constantly on the move visiting Hara Soemon in Tenma in Osaka, meeting with Fuma Kazuemon, visiting Nakamura Kansuke, and searching for Ushioda Matanojo.

He made brief stops in Yamanashi but never mentioned Kuranosuke in later conversations with his comrades. In the pit of his stomach, Yasubei had already given up on him. All of Edo gossiped about Kuranosuke's debauchery. He hated to recall the foolishness Kuranosuke dragged around to this day and too disgusted to speak about a man not worth mentioning.

Action would be soon and quick.

Yasubei's determination drew the immediate response, "That's right," from Hara and Fuwa.

From the beginning, Takebayashi and Nakamura never objected. This was connected to Okano Kujoro. Yasubei seemed to delay leaving for Edo by one day and waited to speak with Onodera's son Koemon and Ushioda Matanojo.

If Okuda Magodayu and his son met with Sugino Juheiji, Kurahashi Densuke, Maebara Isuke, and a few others in Edo, fifteen or sixteen would run to join. That would be enough. Would the opportunity pass by in vain despite Kuranosuke's calm and patient wait?

"Gengo has not returned."

"He's been spending a lot of time with The Squire, too, and his bones may have softened."

"I'm bored," said Yasubei and lay on his side.

"I've spent this month traveling and was sent out restless. I'm having a hard time moving so little. Takebayashi, shall we drink?"

"Sake?"

"You don't drink?"

"There's sake in the kitchen."

"There is?"

As he sat up, someone opened the gate and entered.

"Gengo, is that you?"

He went out and did not see Otaka Gengo but Muramatsu Sandayu.

"Oh, it's you."

A smile escaped Sandayu, but sour looks stayed on Yasubei's and Tadashichi's faces. He decided to join the pleasure-seekers happy to be in Fushimi and broke away. Eyes filled with contempt fell on Sandayu's face.

"Where's Gengo?"

"He's out."

"The others?"

"What do you want?"

"We split up and I walked here to bring an express message from Yamashina."

"Thanks for taking the trouble" was the curt reply.

Unfazed, Sandayu entered without hesitation. The heat spurred the cicadas to chirp. He shut the shoji screen tight.

"I have something to tell both of you."

The two looked uninterested in anything he had to say, but when Sandayu began to speak, they looked shocked and blushed.

That morning, an express message from Edo was delivered to Yamashina. Kuranosuke said the time had come to abandon any hope for the success of the campaign he waged privately through the actions of Yukai from Enrinji Temple to have the late lord's younger brother Daigaku appointed head of the clan.

Two letters from Yoshida Chuzaemon and Okuda Magodayu in Edo reported the confiscation of the Kobi-kicho mansion where Daigaku Nagahiro lived alone. He was demoted and relocated to Geishu in Hiroshima. Demoted and relocated. All hope for the clan's restoration was gone.

"Kuranosuke said as much. Like the pledge he made several times to each man, his mind focused on the sole path of revenge."

As he spoke, Sandayu's brow rose.

"What? Is the chief retainer ordering us to begin?"

"He'll vacate Yamashina soon and started making arrangements to travel the Tokaido Road to Edo."

"Really?"

"Who jokes about this business?"

"Tadashichi!"

Both men took his hand and looked on the verge of tears.

Gengo returned.

Unlike his normally quiet demeanor, he brimmed with excitement. He told everything he learned at Terai Genkei's home.

"I'm sorry. Forgive me."

Yasubei said he would head to Yamashina to be put to full use. The following morning, he planned to pay his respects at Yamashina. However, he was not interested in an abrupt change in his comrades' behaviors. Gengo's view was to remain steadfast until they received orders.

ON THIS DAY, Yokogawa Kanpei received Kuranosuke's secret orders and left for Edo.

On the designated day, the comrades living in Kyoto gathered in the dormitories in Maruyama and Juami. Everyone who came suspected nothing out of the ordinary. The men who didn't think about going, as expected, were not seen. The mutual fondness fostered over the past year was no longer a lie. Those who lived the lie did not appear on this day.

They numbered nineteen.

Unlike in the past, this meeting was focused and serious. Free of the disputes of the past, suspicions and doubts were swept away in the search for mutual courage.

Kuranosuke said solemnly, "All of you have waited for a long time. I've made my decision."

Hearing this, the men recalled what made their blood boil and felt the weight of their grudge lifted.

Kuranosuke announced his decision.

"Our remaining business in Kyoto will be wrapped up by the final weeks of September. Around the beginning of October, we must head to Edo. Until then, I implore you to move discreetly."

Hara Soemon and Yasubei respected and obeyed the order.

"This makes me happy. The happiest time will soon come. So far, it's only been hardship."

These men itched to snatch Lord Kira by the collar. They thought about the previous year and a half and recalled many incidents and difficulties.

Sake made its rounds, and the men filled each other's cups with good cheer. Around the time their ears grew hot and red, a clear, young voice rang out.

"Ah, a drinking party is inevitable in a gathering of warriors."

Onodera Junai beat a tambourine and sang.

"Let's dance."

Hara Soemon snapped open a fan, stood, and performed the dance honoring the avenging Soga brothers.

A chance to hunt on Fuji. A chance to hunt.

Kuranosuke watched with a smile. A pile of cups grew on the front of his tray.

AROUND TOWN IN MATSUZAKACHO

84

THE RETURN OF PAPER SCRAPS

T HE ROADS OF Kuramaguchi were scorched white. Ants swarmed the corpse of a large brown cicada in the crushing heat.

Otaka Gengo waited in the blazing sun as the soles of his zori sandals baked. In time, he spotted Kaiga Yazaemon returning from the leaf tea shop and asked, "Do you know where it is?"

Yazaemon nodded and walked ahead without speaking a word. Sweat blotted the back of his hemp summer kimono. He turned abruptly at the earthen wall of the Buddhist temple and saw the crepe myrtle flowers.

"Here," said Yazaemon, pointing to the nameplate on the gate.

Nagasawa Rokurozaemon. There was no mistake. They opened the beautiful gate to visit what looked like the retirement retreat of a town samurai. The cheerful voices of women inside stopped. The wife who looked to be forty and wore light makeup emerged from the shadow of a fine bamboo door. She gasped at the sight of the two guests grimy from the hot weather. After a courteous greeting, she went back inside.

"Oh, this is a surprise!"

Next, they saw their host Rokurozaemon who appeared holding a waterproof fan.

"Come in. Come in."

He hesitantly guided them to the second floor. Before stepping on the ladder stairs, they glimpsed a group of women plus a priest and a townsman who muscled into the circle to play a popular card game.

"Play is for later."

Their host stiffened and delivered a more formal greeting that erased all lightheartedness from his guest Gengo.

"Sadly, we've both failed to keep in touch. We're interrupting your leisure time."

Rokurozaemon looked miserable. His hand nervously rubbed the back of his neck.

"Well, I'm sorry. Ha, ha, ha, you saw? Spare time bothers a fellow called a ronin. We men of the pact will no longer serve as officers of the government but will live awful lives in which the world watches our every move."

"The truth is ..." said Kaiga Yazaemon and took a note from his pocket. "Our visit today concerns that matter."

"That matter?"

"Oishi-dono's thinking changed about the blood oaths we exchanged, while we shared the same state of mind in Ako Castle. We came to return your blood oath."

"Oh?"

Rokurozaemon frowned in disbelief and stared at his blood oath held out before him. At the height of the siege of Ako Castle, this man burned with righteous blood and was the man who shouted, "I will die in defense of the castle." The plan changed from a siege of the castle to a revenge attack. The daimyo's retainers committed to that plan numbered one hundred twenty men.

"We are returning this to you."

Yazaemon stood. "Gengo, shall we go?"

The host Rokurozaemon hurriedly opened the oath sealed with blood. This was the note he wrote last April inside the crucible of excitement in Ako Castle. The blood of his thumbprint pressed at that time had dried to the color of lacquer.

"Wait a moment ..."

Rokurozaemon raised his shoulders and with a chastened look, said, "I've heard rumors in town about Oishi-dono's debauchery but has he changed his mind completely?"

"It seems so. We are disgraced messengers. Oishi-dono is not the only one to change his mind. As the days pass, a man's heart inevitably changes with his circumstances."

"So, revenge has been abandoned?"

"As usual, conflicting arguments abound. The other day, a group of elders gathered in Maruyama. The outcome should be in line with our feelings at the time of the incident and the world's expectations of us. However, many harbored second thoughts about calling off a revenge attack when the heat subsides. In the end, the secret pact will unravel."

"So that's why you returned this?"

"And now, we must walk to over a dozen more homes. For too long a time, we've wasted many days like fools doing this and that."

"That's outrageous!" Rokurozaemon stuffed his secret pact into his sleeve and looked disgusted. "A man's blood oath is simply collected, and the offer is rejected. I thought this might happen, but it's ridiculous."

"Kuranosuke invited every participant in the secret pact to discuss the difficulties. An apology for his immorality would have been in order, too. But some didn't come to the Maruyama meeting. I guess Oishi-dono is ashamed to face them now."

"When you get back, please tell the chief retainer, Rokurozaemon has lost courage."

"I understand."

Hiding their sour smiles, the two hurried out the crepe myrtle gate."

"Kaiga. On this walk, the human spirit will be interesting. We will see the front and back in two mirrors."

85

THIS ROAD OR THAT ROAD

"**W**HERE TO NEXT?"

"Haikata Tobei in Kitano."

"That's good because he knows nearly everyone's address. How many are left?"

"Probably seventeen or eighteen."

"Returning the paper scraps of the secret pact will take five days including today. Walking is fine, but despite my deep sense of relief, Rokurozaemon's posturing when he took back his oath was disgraceful."

"Otaka, Haikata's home is on this street."

"What a rundown row house. This'll be a problem because I lent him money a while ago. I'll return this oath alone."

Gengo jumped over the board covering the ditch and peeked into the row house.

"Does Tobei-dono live here?"

"Who's asking?"

"Gengo."

In this heat, Tobei slept naked under a faded, raggedy mosquito net. He rose onto his elbows.

"Yah, Otaka-san? This is a surprise. The mosquitoes are out now, so make it short."

"Okay, you're fine there."

"I don't have a summer kimono, so I'll stay under the netting."

"I'll just sit here," said Gengo and sat on the edge of the veranda to explain, in the same words no matter where he went, his mission to return the blood oath.

"Oh, okay," Tobei said frankly, looking like a burden was lifted. "Well, I'm glad to hear that. Around the time of the ruin of the lord's house, my blood was boiling. The world was watching, and a part of the clan looked for a hero's death in defense of the castle. But after we scattered, I've thought about a lot of things."

Gengo nodded. "Indeed."

"Back then, I thought Ono Kurobei was a coward, a brute, and a joke of a man, but now he looks like a great man."

"I guess so."

"No longer surrounded by the atmosphere inside and outside the clan, proof of his goodness came out. He lives in the Saga area and, from time to time, lends me a bit of money. He looks fairly comfortable."

"I don't believe the rumors at all."

"They say he has mistresses. I'm jealous. When I went there, I was too honest. Looking at this blood oath makes me want to blow my nose."

"Ha, ha, ha, that's terrible and a change."

"Can't I change? When revenge was in the air, I sold off all my household goods and extravagant possessions dirt cheap and have spent all the money. I can't imagine when an attack on Kira will come. Before revenge comes, I'll shrivel up. During Kuranosuke's extravagance, his children had me deliver their innocent letters to him a couple of times, but he never replied. He treats people with contempt. It'd be a good idea to bring that up with Ono Kurobei in future talks. The samurai code was always on display at a seat in Ako Castle. In Ono's presence, fake samurai, who are lowlifes by nature, are reviled and cannot go even if they bow their heads—"

Before he finished, Gengo said, "Anyway, this time, you'll profit. I'll see you again."

When he moved to rise, Tobei said, "Wait a minute …"

"What is it?"

"This is hard to say, but do you have a little spare change? The truth is, I hocked my summer kimono and can't get a loan."

"Money? Unfortunately, it's also tight for me."

"What? You don't have that vital money either. But anything you can spare …"

Gengo pulled a few coins from his purse.

"It's not much."

"That's fine. The evening is saved."

Gengo went out to the road but wasn't interested in talking to the waiting Yazaemon. He thought, Have people sunk so low? Not their finances but their spiritual decay. Why didn't tears build up in his eyelashes?

Gengo reflected, How would the late lord feel if he knew this?

After careful planning, Kuranosuke ordered Otaka and Kaiga to return the blood oaths to the men who didn't attend the Maruyama meeting the other day. They went house to house every day. The pair now understood Oishi-dono's power of observation. They realized Kuranosuke's elaborate preparation had two or three levels but could not penetrate them.

They finished their business that day and went to

report back. Only Gengo visited Kuranosuke at the Bairin-an temple on Shijo street.

His other work in Yamashina of building stone and digging a fountain was finished soon after the Maruyama meeting and already passed to the hands of others. Items required by Riku and the baby among his household goods were sent to Tajima by the town doctor Terai Genkei. But he sold off most of his property.

The officiating priest at Bairin-an saw Gengo.

"Ah, the unlucky Otaka-sama. Kuranosuke-sama went to visit Genkei's home."

"Okay, I'll head over there."

Gengo turned to see Kuranosuke and Terai Genkei and his son pouring drinks for each other in the inner room.

"Good, you've come."

Like reinforcements just arrived, Genkei said, "Gengo-dono, please put in a good word for me with the chief retainer."

86

KARU'S HOME

IN YEAR **13** of the Genroku era, the year before the Asano clan invited catastrophe, Genkei became the physician on retainer in Ako for a stipend of 300 koku.

His days of service were short. His role was a physician, but his spirit matched that of a clan retainer. Kuranosuke trusted Genkei and, after coming to Kyoto, consulted with him. These consultations began with inquiries about the illnesses in his comrades' families and selling off household goods hard to part with by a retainer; then moved to the purchase of weapons, fire-fighting equipment, and uniforms to be used in the revenge attack; and the disclosure of financial details. Genkei did not betray his trust. However, when he asked to accompany Kuranosuke to Edo, he was rebuffed with the simple reason of "I've postponed the trip."

"Please tell me, Gengo-dono. Is my dissatisfaction unjustified, or is Oishi-dono's excuse reasonable?"

"It's weak. To be honest, I understand the reason for Oishi-dono's refusal."

"Why?"

Genkei jerked his white eyebrows and squared his shoulders.

"In the samurai's way and the physician's way, a difference exists in how a man must exhaust himself to carry out his duty."

"I know! Long ago, a physician in China called Kada yearned for the favor of the warlord Kan'u and stood on the battlefield. When a poison arrow struck Kan'u, Kada treated his wound. In duty and hardship, how can you say there is a difference in the duties of the warrior and the doctor when we go together with little power? I don't understand the refusal."

Before Gengo appeared, he pressed Kuranosuke with this argument. Gengo understood his feelings but looked troubled.

"Well, how can we make this work? In my foolish plan, I ask the chief retainer to take the middle road and Genkei-dono to compromise."

"I'm listening. What's your plan?"

"Genkei-dono, you will stay in Kyoto."

"And ..."

"Your son Gentatsu-dono will go to Edo in your place."

"My son?"

Genkei was a little dissatisfied and could not back down from his third plea to Kuranosuke who recently took the seat of honor at Bairin-an, which Genkei also attended.

"Gengo, that's a great idea. If his son is asked to go, he will be asked to treat the wounded on the night of the revenge."

Until that was said, Genkei's old bones could not be moved. The promise was made.

"Oh well, the senile old man will be left on the shelf."

Next came banter and drinks.

The aim of Kuranosuke's visit this evening was to

prepare for his upcoming trip to Edo. Without asking, before his farewell, the last bit of business was received from the hands of Genkei. It was a loan of money.

At that time, Kuranosuke had little money. Many of his comrades gradually making their way to Edo had scant traveling expenses and lacked travel preparations. The allowances received at the time of the surrender of Ako Castle and whatever funds they had on hand were already gone.

Kuranosuke used all of his money to order a hood with a metal visor, clothes, a haori half coat to be worn in the raid, and other items from Kinuya Yahei, one of Genkei's patients. He spent every last coin but had a plan.

A distant relative of Kuranosuke worked as the chief retainer in the Konoe clan. His name was Shindo Chikugo no Kami Nagatomi. Kuranosuke had a pupil of Genkei take a letter and collateral to this relative and requested a cash loan of 100 ryo.

The collateral was a sealed *nagamochi* clothes chest Kuranosuke filled with treasured objects. But his messenger soon returned with a reply.

"Notwithstanding the importance of this request, presently, the Shindo clan has pressing obligations of unexpected expenses making it impossible to satisfy the request in the letter."

"Thank you for your hard work," said Kuranosuke and slipped the pupil a bill and gave him a drink. The chest he entrusted to the Shindo clan was filled with relics to be parceled out after his death and accompanied by a paper assigning each item to the full name of the gift recipient.

It was late when Kuranosuke and Gengo left Genkei's house. Their legs moved aimlessly through the cool moonlit summer night. They appreciated being wrapped in mosquito netting for a short drunken nap.

When they reached the corner of Nijo-dori boulevard, Kuranosuke said, "I'm going to stop in at Ichimonjiya. Will you join me for a cup of tea?"

Gengo was tired but promised to see him tomorrow and left. He turned to see a lighthearted Kuranosuke turn down Teramachi-dori boulevard.

"Is she in?"

"Hey, it's me."

The people of Ichimonjiya stared at the unexpected guest who appeared at an unexpected hour. He was welcomed in a cool inner room in the building.

This was the home of Karu's older brother. When the Yamashina mansion was emptied of household goods, Karu returned to her family.

What an extraordinary secret visit, observed the Ichimonjiya family members and left their seats on purpose. In time, Kuranosuke seemed to get his wish. The sounds of a koto escaped Karu's room.

> *The light darkens.*
> *A beautiful mistress weeps a river of tears.*

Karu's singing voice seemed filled with heartless tears. The family members were far away but listened quietly until a laughing voice shattered the silence. It was Kuranosuke's. His usual drunken mood overtook his voice.

"What is this, Karu? Are you crying? Like I said in Yamashina, when I go to Edo this time, I am determined to search for a fine lord, fix my poverty a little, and restore my spirit. If I enter the service of a good daimyo there and arrange for a mansion, you will be welcome. Ha, ha, ha, ha. The strings of your koto are dampened by tears. I'd like to hear another song. One without tears."

Leap over the seven-foot folding screen.
Your fine twill gauze sleeve snags but
doesn't rip.

From the sky in the alley between the high walls of the houses, the apathetic face of the summer moon watched the veranda until late into the night.

~

Kakimi Gorobei, Chamberlain of the Hino Clan of Kyoto

THESE WORDS WERE STAMPED onto two nagamochi chests. A short time ago, Kuranosuke's life made a clean break from the short dream in Kyoto, and he started down the Tokaido Road to Edo. That day was October 17.

His attendants were Ushioda Matanojo, Chikamatsu Kanroku, Hayami Tozaemon, and Mimura Jiroemon. Two young low-ranking samurai attendants accompanied them. Terai's son Gentatsu led the way. Oishi Chikara visited his mother in Tajima before he went with his father on a pilgrimage to Hachiman shrine in Otokoyama. From there, they began their journey to Edo.

Okano Kin'emon and Takebayashi Tadashichi left the previous month. One after another, Yoshida, Mase, Fuwa, Senba, Onodera, and Kubisu, left the Kyoto area. They were all men Kuranosuke painstakingly screened, like straining through a silk cloth. Each was contacted in secret after extensive preparation and sent deep into Edo.

These final days of autumn received the mildly cold winter of year 15 of Genroku.

87

MY NEPHEW'S ON THE SECOND FLOOR

IN THOSE DAYS, the haberdashery Zenbei in Honjo Futatsume was a new, small shop hanging a dark blue *noren* shop curtain out front.

"That haberdasher is quite friendly." The excited women would tell the man who often came around with his back burdened by a load of hairstyling oil for men and pine oil for women's hair to hawk until summer.

From the steady stream of special customers in Honjo, despite being a small store, it grew in popularity and looked like the harbinger in trade with women in a household of men.

"Oh, is that you, Kume-san? Excuse me, Kira's Kume-san."

Zenbei who always sat properly at the storefront and became the archetype of a haberdasher was Kanzaki Yogoro.

The woman he called to stop was a parlor maid around eighteen years old. This servant of the Kira clan in Matsuzakacho was rushing in short steps past the shop curtain. Kume seemed to be waiting to be called. She blushed and said from the shadow of the shop curtain, "What is it, Zenbei-san?"

"Where are you off to, so prim and proper?"

"To my parents' home."

"Your parents' home. He, he, he. To suckle your mother's breast."

"Not at all. My father is feeling poorly."

"You pass in front of my store, turn away, and march by while showing no interest. You hate me."

"What? I didn't turn away."

"Oh, I understand."

"Understand what?"

"It's because you only see me at the shop today. My nephew Emoshichi is not here."

"Oh, Zenbei-san, your suspicions are wicked."

"This is a problem. I'm a jealous man. Why not come in? It's fine if you don't. If your friends Suzu-san and Saeda-san come to shop, I'll have a lot to talk about."

"What? What do you mean?"

"Emoshichi."

"Ah! I have nothing to do with Emoshichi. You are hateful," Kume said and walked in as her sleeve raised to her shoulder like she was going to slap him.

"Ha, ha, ha. I'm joking. It's a joke. Just a joke."

He offered her a small cushion seat.

"Don't get angry. Please sit and be sociable."

"Zenbei-san, everyone says you're truly a charming but horrid man."

"That's no good. Which should I be?"

"I prefer the horrid man."

"For you, it has to be Emoshichi."

"That again."

"Oh, you'll spill the tea. Have a sip."

"That's why you're horrid. Well, I came to buy a nice *negake* ornamental comb."

"Would you like to see the tortoiseshell combs?"

"Don't be ridiculous. I'd like to see the ones suitable for a parlor maid."

"You'll buy one to tease Emoshichi. He's a relative and once in a while comes to me for a little help. He's from a good family in the country and in the enviable position of never being short of pocket change."

"You're terrible."

"But Kume-san, I do want Emoshichi to buy it for you. Today, he's upstairs on the second floor. Kume-san, you've gotten very quiet and are listening closely."

Kume placed several combs on her knees and pretended not to be listening. Her blood stirred, flushing her neck at her collar.

"Listen, I have a better idea. Go upstairs and talk to him. He said he has a slight cold today. He's bored and reading picture books."

"But …"

"You have to get back to the mansion?"

"No, I'm fine there. I'm off until tonight."

"In that case, it's all right? The shop over there makes delicious sweet bean porridge. Earlier, Emoshichi said he was hungry, so you can keep him company."

"Is Emoshichi really sick?"

"It's nothing serious."

"Well, what if I drop in to see how he's feeling? But he's alone up there—"

"It's fine. You're exasperating."

Zenbei took Kume's white wrist and helped her up.

88

THE BABY BIRD'S CAGE

THE INSTANT A cat shot out like an arrow from under the mud stove to flee inside, the kitchen shoji screen door illuminated by the setting sun rattled open.

"Thank you again for your business. I'm from the rice shop on Futatsume in Aioicho."

From the store, Zenbei replied, "Ah, the rice merchant?"

"Yes, where should I put it?"

"Please wait a moment. A household of men has to balance the front and back. I'll be right back."

After opening the store, Zenbei looked at the shop curtain with calm eyes, climbed the ladder to the quiet second floor, and then went out to the kitchen.

"Gohei-san? I appreciate your hard work."

Six months before the haberdashery opened, a rice merchant named Gohei was running a shop near Futatsume. This shop sat catty-corner not far from the back gate of the Kira residence. This rice dealer was Zenbei's comrade Maebara Isuke.

Straw scraps covered his grainy, dry face. Yogoro's Zenbei forgot about himself and was struck in the chest by an indescribable feeling.

Gohei looking indifferent said, "Do you want me to weigh this here?"

"What? You run an honest shop, and your measurements are accurate. There's no need."

"Everybody says so and that I'm a hard worker."

"Open it there. The tea is warm, and would you like a smoke?"

"Thank you. Ah, the sun is shrinking. Excuse me, Master, do you have a flint?"

"Here, let me do it."

He shut the lower part of the shoji screen. Zenbei approached from the far side, lit the tobacco in his pipe, and touched the necks of the pipes."

"Maebara, has anything changed?"

"Yes, but that—"

He tapped hard to expel the ashes.

"Yoshida Chuzaemon-dono from Kojimachi, Mouri Koheita from Hayashicho, as well as Horibe and Sugino will come tonight. Are you coming?"

"To your house?"

"We'll be in the rice granary out back."

"I'll be there. Have you heard any news, good or bad?"

"Well, I'm trying to get closer. The vigilance of the Kira clan and the extent of the precautions are beyond what you can imagine."

"Days are no good."

"What have you heard? Lately, on Edo's streets, I often hear disturbing rumors like many Ako ronin recently infiltrated Edo; Kuranosuke-dono has come from Yamashina; or the revenge attack will be soon. Kira's defenses are obvious."

"Not only do they rouse us to action, similar rumors often circulate about Kira. Because Uesugi Danjo Daihitsu is ill, Kozuke no Suke moved with nurses to an Uesugi residence or has been shut away in the home province of the Uesugi clan and guarded by the Yonezawa clan."

"The cheering from bystanders is awkward. Their intuition that something bad is about to happen is helpful, and minor matters are exaggerated. The impossible becomes possible. But we can't get careless."

"I'd like to verify the situation inside Kira's residence soon."

"That's it. The problems discussed the other day at Yoshida Chuzaemon's ronin house in Kojimachi were finding out when Kozuke no Suke is there; getting drawings of the residence, the interior layout, his bedchamber, any escape routes; and determining the type and number of guards. Each man will rack his brain and pursue various angles in this quest, but tight security keeps us from making progress and Oishi-dono from making headway. For our plan to be executed without a hitch, we will lay the foundation by eliminating these questions."

"The truth is." Zenbei leaned forward and pointed his pipe toward the second floor. "That plan has already begun and is going well, but now is a tense time."

"Who's upstairs?"

"Kira's parlor maid, a girl named Kume. She seems like a lovely girl."

"Oh."

"It's rather amusing. She often comes here to shop for unneeded items."

"Uh-huh."

"It seems strange but understandable. Yato Emoshichi drops by once in a while. She saw him and in no time fell in love."

"Emoshichi? ... That's not surprising, he's a nice-looking guy."

"Unfortunately, he's so naive. And he's seventeen and she's eighteen. After much fretting, she went up to the second floor today, but I fear Emoshichi will not make a move."

"It's a good beginning. I'd like a small bird that can't escape to get used to its cage."

"Too bad I can't use sorcery to switch places and help him."

"Ha, ha, ha," Gohei laughed without thinking.

Zenbei silenced him with his eyes.

"Ah, it's getting dark. I should prepare the lanterns."

Zenbei peeked into the cupboard marking the boundary between the store and the private area and took out the stands for the paper-covered lanterns.

Gohei went to the kitchen, leaving traces of white bran on the tatami. He put on his zori sandals.

"Thank you for your hospitality, Proprietor. If you find the time, even if it's night, come and we'll talk."

Thumping footsteps echoed like someone was tripping down the ladder steps. Still holding the kick plate of the shoji screen, Gohei turned to look inside. It was Kume.

She came down the stairs and stood gripping her sleeve in the shadow of the papered sliding door. She was pale and cowering. Wondering what was going on, the surprised Zenbei looked inside.

"Kume-san? What happened?"

Kume stared like she was quieting her pounding heart. Eventually, she told him. When she went upstairs, Emoshichi barely spoke and looked uncomfortable. He opened the second-floor window a crack. The two were back to back. Emoshichi was looking at a book. She watched the people coming and going below and noticed someone. She spied a samurai wearing a braided straw hat. He lingered in the shadow of the shop curtain and peered into the shop.

She imagined Zenbei was tending to business inside, getting ready for the evening, and the shady, vagrant ronin was watching the store's cashbox. From the second-floor window, she was worried and instinctively shouted at the man, "What's your business?"

The man set his hand on the brim of his straw hat, looked up to the second floor, and said nothing. She closed the window and shouted.

"Oh no!"

She could no longer stand being there. Without a word to the staring Emoshichi, she stumbled downstairs in a daze. She trembled like she had seen a supernatural creature of the twilight.

Zenbei calmed himself and asked, "Who is he? That ronin wearing a straw hat and standing at the storefront."

Kume's face stayed white from fright as she spoke.

"He's Shimizu Ichigaku-sama from the samurai barracks in the mansion. What should I do? What if he returns to the mansion and says that I was here on the second floor?"

Her lashes held back tears.

Unnerved by his failure to remember, Zenbei blurted out, "What? Shimizu Ichigaku?"

"Ichigaku-sama was standing there? What's the problem? Ha, ha, ha. He often passes by drunk and singing little ditties on his way home late at night. He's a fun guy, isn't he? It's all right. There's nothing to worry about. I'll lend you my wisdom and tell you what to say."

Looking up the ladder, he said, "Emoshichi, could you come down for a moment?"

His eyes glanced to the side. Gohei was standing

outside the kitchen looking uneasy. Neighbors passed through the alley carrying water buckets, so he left in a hurry while brushing bran off a bag of rice.

89

KUME AND TSUYA

Emoshichi's loud voice dropped from the second floor.

"Yessir."

As he came down, he saw Kume lingering in the shadow of the ladder steps and flushed pink.

"What is it, Uncle?" he asked Kanzaki Yogoro's Zenbei.

"Go look out front."

"In front of the store?"

Emoshichi went beyond the shop curtain and scrutinized the area.

"Everything looks normal. What is it? Did something happen?"

"Kume-san said Shimizu Ichigaku-sama, a vassal of Kira-sama, was standing out there and looked up at the second floor."

"She probably mistook someone else for him?"

"Perhaps."

Zenbei looked at her wilting figure and reassured her.

"Kume-san, no one's out there. If you return to the

mansion, nothing will happen. Would you like an escort to the back gate?"

"No."

Kume shook her head and did not budge from beneath the stairs. It was already dark. She had to return to the mansion but wanted to stay by Emoshichi forever.

"…"

She gripped both her sleeves and let the tracks of teardrops stain her pale face.

"Listen to me," said Zenbei. He placed a hand on her shoulder and looked at Emoshichi in the shop as he whispered, "Are you thinking about him? If you truly love him, as his uncle, I also have a few ideas."

"Zenbei-san, are you lying or joking?"

She collapsed into sitting.

"I just may be. Sometimes young people become overexcited but eventually come to their senses."

"I have a favor to ask. I may be that woman, please let me be with him. I will spend the rest of my life as his wife," she said, as her lovely spirit dampened her eyelashes.

This is a crime, he thought. Yogoro's Zenbei was on the brink of darkening her weak spirit.

It's a sacrifice for a great cause!

His eyes looked away as he throttled his tiny conscience. Without warning, he clamped onto her wrist.

"If what you're saying is true, you will be with my nephew Emoshichi. It can happen soon, this year. And when spring comes next year, he will part the shop curtain of this haberdashery and run this business."

"Is that true?"

"Yes, but," said Zenbei, staring into her eyes burning with the spirit of her heart. "The oath of a married couple is the destiny of a lifetime. If you have a change of heart, as an uncle, my stance will not change. I'm not motivated by doubt, but I want a written oath to be upheld. No, your spirit is fine."

"I'll write an oath and prick a finger. Zenbei-sama, I'll do anything."

"Your father is a master carpenter. Emoshichi told me."

"He does jobs for Kira-sama, and I became a parlor maid there."

"Well, this spring, the storehouse was repaired, the bedchambers were rebuilt, and other construction took place at Kira-sama's residence. Your father probably worked on those jobs."

"Yes, he's worked there for a long time."

"So any renovations there are probably unique. In fact, at a mansion I serve, my client says that Kira-sama is famous for his refined tastes. According to him, construction is Kira's pastime. What could be the floor plan of the living quarters? If there's an interior drawing of the residence, I'd like to see it. Kume-san, would your father happen to have a carpenter's drawing from that time?"

"I … I don't know. Maybe. Sometimes he does. When a job ends, the drawings are probably returned to the mansion."

"Yes, that makes sense. What to do? If you find an opportunity to get your hands on one, would you please bring it to me?"

"What?"

"I know, that's asking too much. Would you feel uncomfortable doing that?"

"I'm not sure …"

"Look, it's easy to say we'll write an oath and prick fingers, but I'm asking this of you for Emoshichi's sake. Are you already having second thoughts?"

"No, it's not that. There are whispers in the mansion about threats from the Ako ronin. Security is strict."

"I think you may find a chance, but we will find a way to guide you from outside."

"If I steal it, it's for Emoshichi's sake?"

"As I said, the retired life of the former retainer is devoted to construction. I long for a glimpse of everything from the garden to the floor plan of Kira's home. Showing loyalty in this matter is also the character of a merchant nowadays. If you have the drawing delivered from Emoshichi's hands, you'll gradually gain favor. If he marries you and has a business, I see a bright future for you two. But your reluctance is inevitable."

"…"

"Kume-san, don't worry. The request is not unreasonable or something you have to do."

"Zenbei-san! But does Emoshichi-san really want me to be his bride?"

"My nephew is bashful. Maybe, you don't truly love him. Even with my consent, Emoshichi may have doubts."

"So … you want the construction drawings?"

"You can bring them to me?"

"…"

Kume's eyes said yes.

Those eyes no longer had tears, only a strong readiness for love that will gamble her entire being.

The heart of Yogoro's Zenbei was scarred by guilt. He used Emoshichi, knowing he would not go along, as his lure to deceive this naive young woman. He wondered how unhappy this young lady's life would become as a result.

Now, Kume was eager. She said she would return to the mansion and bring out the drawing tonight. Zenbei cautioned her not to be too rash because she may not find it right away. But she knew the carpenter's shed contains everything used in construction. She assured him she could bring out the drawing board and toss it over the eastern fence of the mansion at whatever time he gave her.

"Well, are you sure?"

"Yes."

While they agreed on a time, Emoshichi, working as a shop assistant, peeked inside and sounding upset, said, "Uncle, please come here."

"There's a customer, Kira-sama's Tsuya-san. Please come, Uncle, I don't know the price."

90

THE BAT HAORI COAT

Tsuya was Kume's fellow parlor maid at the Kira residence. She was around twenty years old and often shopped at Zenbei's haberdashery. This pretty woman with a slim waist was two years older than Kume, cheerful, and wise to the ways of the world.

"From the looks of it, retirement never ends," Tsuya often said in jest.

She sat on the top step at the storefront and drew nearer to the stacked boxes made from paulownia wood to select a negake ornamental comb.

"Welcome," said Zenbei, rubbing his hands together and offering a sitting rug.

"This one, please. How much is it?" asked Tsuya.

"The price is the same as always. And that's part of a pair."

"Then I'll take both of them," she said and peeked inside the shop.

"Is that Kume-san?"

"Ha, ha, ha. At last, you spotted her. Right over there is

a shop that makes delicious sweet bean porridge. You two should rush over and enjoy a tasty meal."

"I should have come sooner. Kume-san, do you have to go back?"

"I was just thinking about leaving."

"This is a perfect opportunity, please join Tsuya-sama."

"Today is our one day off and we should have fun."

While hiding her thumping heart, Kume said, "But I was going to go home."

"Don't you always say 'spoil yourself and have fun'? … Ha, ha, ha. You're afraid to have fun."

"Tsuya-san, you haven't had a break from service in four or five days either."

"That's right. I came here to buy this comb for my future fun."

Kume watched for a break in the parade of people. She hurried to put on her sandals and looked anxious after slipping out through the shop curtain.

Her eyes said goodbye. The women walked to the nearby side service gate of the Kira residence with the *tateya* standing arrow bows of their obi sashes side by side.

"Emoshichi, bring the curtain pole."

Zenbei removed the shop curtain hanging from the eaves.

He soon closed the shutters and locked them with a key from inside. With their faces hidden, the two men emerged from the back door, headed to parts unknown.

Despite rice in the rice chest, a household of men often eats out for the evening meal. They'd either stop at a stall selling dishes from Ryogoku or a boiled rice shop in Yagenbori.

They would drink but not for too long and miss Kume at the promised time, wander back to Matsuzakacho, and later that evening, would attend a secret meeting at the home of Maebara Isuke, a.k.a. the rice dealer Gohei.

"Emoshichi, never let your guard down. I'll watch your back."

Kanzaki Yogoro's Zenbei made Yato Emoshichi go first and stayed sixty feet behind him.

Yogoro wore a hood. Emoshichi wore a haori short coat that covered him from his head and sported long sleeves resembling a bat's wings. They walked at night wearing the long and short swords of a samurai and carried themselves like samurai. Even neighbors who passed them did not recognize the haberdasher Zenbei out with his nephew.

"There. Over there," said Yogoro's hushed voice from behind. Emoshichi stopped and looked up at the high wall circling the Kira residence. The tall chinquapin tree was the meeting spot. Emoshichi didn't move for a while.

If she easily found the carpenter's drawings of the interior of the Kira residence, they'll have a rousing time at tonight's meeting with the comrades at the rice dealer's shop. It will be a hand-clapping good time. Emoshichi imagined their radiant faces and his heart pounded. He could only pray the carpenter's drawing would be tossed by Kume's hand over the wall and drop down to him.

The quiet night was broken by the barking of three or four stray dogs attracted to his bat haori coat.

"Shh!"

As his fist swung up, from the darkness, Yogoro whistled to call the dogs. Unfortunately, the dogs gathered around him, tails wagging, and waited for food to be thrown.

Lingering too long in the same place would draw suspicion, so Emoshichi walked away from that spot and returned several times. However, the pebbles from Kume he eagerly awaited to bring news never came.

91

A STRATEGIC BATTLE FORMATION

THE FORMER AKO samurai hiding out in Edo did not see the detailed work with sights set on the target day and the steady advance in preparations that missed nothing.

October came. Oishi Kuranosuke's party from Kyoto arrived in Kamakura, met in secret with Yoshida Chuzaemon's group in a farmhouse in Hirama-mura in Kawasaki, and stripped off their traveling clothes.

Tominomori Sukeemon had been holed up in the home of Karube Gohei, a peasant in the village of Hirama-mura in Tachibana-gun, Bushu. He welcomed Kuranosuke who tracked him down in no time from his connection to the writing practice books he received from the village's children. Horibe came. Kataoka visited. Yogoro and Emoshichi showed up three or four times.

Using the pseudonym Kakimi Gorobei, Kuranosuke went to Edo and often visited the home in Shinkojimachi 5-chome of Yoshida Chuzaemon's Taguchi Ichigaku who put out a signboard as a teacher of military strategy.

438

The Edo comrades gathered at the night course to learn the military strategy of Sun Tzu. However, this soon attracted attention.

Kuranosuke, in particular, sensed danger. Swordsmen of the Uesugi and Kira clans were rumored to turn up frequently.

While he examined the opportunities and the means for carrying out the raid, who could be certain no rival would launch a surprise attack?

While he targeted the head of Lord Kira, how could a rival assassin be prevented from snatching away Kuranosuke's life?

Chuzaemon worried all the time about that possibility.

Alarmed caution was visible among the enemy Kira, but scrupulous vigilance was demanded from the Ako ronin, too.

A short time later, Kuranosuke moved from Hiramamura to a rented house on a back street of Kokucho-ura.

Several comrades trailed him on his outings, but Kuranosuke complained. "My life is not yours." His comrades forced their protection on him.

Shinkojimachi and Kokucho became the de facto headquarters of the Ako men hiding in Edo. Terai Genkei's only son Gentatsu stayed at Shichimonji-ya in nearby Honcho. "I'll assist as a doctor." He promptly treated anyone falling ill with a cold or any other ailment.

"The long-cherished plan will be carried out within the year." They hoped.

No one set the group's objective, but it existed nonetheless. The hand of Chuzaemon reported each man's daily actions to Kuranosuke. Sometimes, he knitted his brow; other times, he clapped his hands. He cheered, "Good news. Good news," in celebration.

Weapons, uniforms, and other items procured before leaving Kyoto were disguised as baggage and transported by boat to the hideout chosen because it was close to the Kira residence. Horibe Yahei and Okuda Magodayu were responsible for moving everything to the hideout.

The plan progressed in steps. However, two problems remained unsolved. The interior layout of the Kira residence and the movements of Kozuke no Suke were unknown to the outside world.

"A year will have passed." They worried.

Horibe Yasubei and others were impatient for good reason. No matter how ingenious they were in changing their names, the world knew about the Edo incident and the fifty or so comrades hiding out in Edo.

Another reason was the lack of money. Every comrade who left Kyoto and other regions to come to Edo struggled to pay ruinous traveling expenses. They sold household effects and personal belongings, and most of the men led a solitary existence. The men with a little extra lent money to the men with no means of support. But that money soon ran out.

The poor men laughed with each other, but the laughter stopped when their revenge became far from certain. They were driven to lives of subsistence or doing their best to stave off hunger.

In this backdrop, scandalmongers probably said, "They'll end up struggling in poverty and live desperate lives."

Yasubei said that was happening. The once one hundred and twenty comrades dropped to fifty-five. Most cocked their heads and left for economic reasons. More deserters would emerge in time. Defections would grow; every man had weaknesses. No one blamed the men who left.

Chuzaemon lamented, "This situation makes the military strategy vital."

No matter how impatient they were, the unresolved problems were immovable lines. The floor plan to give a satisfactory understanding of the interior of the residence and Kozuke no Suke's whereabouts were unknown. Random guesses about these critical matters would be reckless, and Kuranosuke would not budge.

"We'll turn into spies."

"Then we'll search for them ..."

These searches consumed most of their energy.

Joining Maebara Isuke's rice merchant Gohei of Aioicho 2-chome, Yogoro's haberdasher Zenbei, and his shop assistant Okano Kin'emon and employee Kurahashi Densuke, more than fifty men changed their names and their professions to become doctors, swordsmen, tea ceremony masters, day laborers, and merchants. They pursued every acquaintance and opportunity, and focused their attention on the wall in Matsuzakacho, never missing the smallest detail about Kira.

Yato Emoshichi looked up at the chinquapin tree from the edge of the ditch near the wall. He considered sneaking in but didn't.

He thought he could not stop that failure alone. All his comrades could do was pray for good news in their hearts and share a plea for the promise made in vain by Kume.

"God have mercy."

Several flowers fell from the chinquapin tree, then a small pebble dropped behind Emoshichi.

"Ah! Kume? She did it."

He snatched up the pebble and threw it to the top of the chinquapin tree.

He guessed that was the signal. From inside the wall, Kume tossed over a drawing panel. This wood panel was the floor plan showing the rooms drawn by the carpenter in the black ink of an inkpot. The panel bounced off a corner of the stonewall by the ditch and split in two.

92

KIRA SAMURAI

"**T**HANK YOU! THANK you so much!" Emoshichi shouted from his heart to Kume on the other side of the wall.

He reached to grab the broken drawing panel. A hand clamped onto his bat haori coat covering Emoshichi from his head.

"Gotcha!"

"Eeyah!"

"Who are you?"

When the man yanked his coat, Emoshichi dropped one piece of the broken drawing panel into a ditch. Unfortunately, his rival's strength kept Emoshichi from getting free of his coat. His head was covered, and the two arms tightly encircling him from behind felt like an iron hoop. He struggled in vain.

The seventeen-year-old Emoshichi had a weak constitution. The man, who looked to be around thirty, was the opposite and twice his size. He wore a red-lacquered sheath for his long sword. A grim, scraggy beard grew on his angular face.

"Where are you from, ronin?" asked a bullying voice reeking of sake, while he executed a move to twist Emoshichi's body.

Emoshichi knew the man enveloping him was a Kira ronin. His heart screamed, What a mess! He grabbed his rival's wrist to toss him over his shoulder, but his technique barely budged his hefty opponent.

"Dammit!"

His rival's arm struck him with a throat attack. The two bodies formed an arc and staggered backward. Emoshichi was mute.

Yogoro almost flew like a bird from his hiding place and ran behind them, unknown to the interloper. Yogoro slapped the man's earlobe hard. That slap hurt more than a fist. Hurt as if his eardrum ruptured, the man released Emoshichi.

"Eeyow," shouted the man and dodged him.

Yogoro's hand shot to the back of the man's neck. No one saw the throw that splashed muddy water from the ditch.

His body rose like a muddy ditch rat. The man shouted from the bottom of the ditch.

"Stop, you bastards."

He crawled up to the road and chased after the two fleeing shadows.

"Guards! Guards!" he called out while never slowing down.

He came to the corner of the firewood dealer beside Ekoin Temple.

"Is that you, Niimi?"

"Yes, Shimizu."

"What happened?"

"I'm after those two."

"Those two?" he said with a mocking smile.

Shimizu Ichigaku seemed to be on his way home. A braided-straw hat concealed his face. Not just Ichigaku, the party of ronin living in the residence and crucial to protecting Lord Kira needed to disguise themselves from the Ako ronin. They wore bamboo hats when going out and took on various appearances when out and about in the neighborhood.

"Yes, dammit."

Niimi Yashichiro was the man's name; he was one of the eleven swordsmen chosen from the Uesugi clan in Yonezawa to come here.

He stomped the ground as he inspected the crossroads.

"Did those stinking rats escape while I was calming down? I know they're Ako men."

"Aren't you the one who stinks?"

"This is no time for jokes!"

Niimi scowled at the ditch mud covering his body and said, "I went with Osuga and Saito to Futatsume for drinks on the way back. I'm sober now. But something bad has happened."

"Where?"

"Under that chinquapin tree." He stopped and walked back. "Someone threw something over the wall. Don't be careless or let your guard down, Shimizu."

He looked at the ditch and picked up the broken drawing panel.

"Here it is," he said, holding it out to Shimizu Ichigaku.

"This is from inside the residence."

"Mmm. I have to ask, whose handiwork was this? Looking at this, there's no room for doubt about the Ako ronin."

"They were a little too eager."

"The supply of provisions may be hard. They're

desperate. People don't understand what starvation can do to you. Where there's smoke …"

"Well, hurry home. A bath, even in well water, is good. It's a problem for whoever's talking to you."

The wicket back gate was ajar. Lantern light swayed inside. What noise did the low-ranking guard hear? Everyone in the residence was on edge. Four or five men would investigate the source of any unexpected sound.

93

GENROKU STYLE

"**W**HAT'S GOING ON, Ushi?"

"What? What'd I do?"

"You said the way I shook my dice bowl was fishy."

"Hey, Tatsu, enough of your whining. It's not just this gambling house, aren't you famous all over for cheap tricks?"

"Stop lying."

"Serves you right. I hit a sore spot."

"Get out. Go outside."

"Why should I leave?"

"You won't go? Coward!"

He grabbed the dice and blindly flung them at his opponent's face. His rival was not defeated. Chaos reigned. Tobacco pouches, bowls, and teacups flew.

Ushi and Tatsu stood up to wrestle and exchange blows. The men around them tried to break them up. Huge shins kicked lamp stands. The objects on shelves crashed down.

"Gohei-san, Gohei-san, please come down. Hurry."

He came from the second floor of the rice shop.

Neighborhood men, including a samurai footman, the proprietor of a cheap candy shop, a packhorse driver, a low-ranking guard from the guardhouse gathered every night to gamble but not for high stakes. Everyone knew money for sushi was handed over to the guard. Tonight again, a fight broke out when the gambling started.

"The second floor is empty, use it any time, but please no fights or fires," warned the rice merchant Gohei. He opened this place to them without charge. Once in a while, he provided a feast of rice crackers and buckwheat noodles. In return for this kindness, fighting was the height of rudeness. The group's boss reasoned with them and vowed men like that would be kicked out.

Usually, the proprietor Gohei entered in the back of the storehouse for unpolished rice to pound rice and sift bran. Tonight, however, a class on mutual finance was being held from evening until daybreak on the second floor of the storehouse.

"What's going on down here?"

Ushi, Tatsu, and the others looked at Gohei's face and were subdued by shame.

"What? Just a little misunderstanding."

"That fool Tatsu doesn't understand much."

"What? You're the one who knows nothing."

"Stop it now. Don't worry, Sir. We'll be here for a little while longer and will be quiet."

Maebara Isuke's Gohei looked at each man's face and smiled although peeved. He couldn't hate those faces.

"Very well. There's no hurry, but don't make too much of a racket. Even the guard can't be silenced by sushi."

"That's true. If we disturb you, just wrap a rope around our necks and strangle us."

"The mutual finance course will go on for some time,

so there's no hurry," said Gohei and went back to the storehouse.

Sacks of polished and sifted rice were tightly packed downstairs. He went upstairs to the room with a straw mat covering the sixteen-square-yard floor, paper-covered lamps, and a brazier boiling tea.

The guests surrounded by flickering firelight were silent until Gohei returned. They were Otaka Gengo called Wakiya Shinpei; Horibe Yasubei who went by the pseudonym Nagae Nagaemon; Kurahashi Densuke, Gohei's shop assistant; Isogai Jurozaemon called Naito Jurozaemon; Muramatsu Kihei, the physician Ryuen; and Kataoka Gengoemon called Uedaya Genbei. Also present were Okajima Yasoemon, Takebayashi Tadashichi, and Onodera Junai's son Koemon.

"I'm sorry for the interruption," said Gohei's Maebara Isuke, weakly smiling as he returned to his seat and described the commotion of no consequence in the main building.

"Ha, ha, ha, ha, what nonsense."

They were all drawn into laughter. Yasubei picked up a cracker from the tray, snapped it in half, and asked, "No one has seen Yato or Kanzaki?"

"That's right, although they've gotten closer than anyone—"

Everyone exchanged looks.

"Maebara, did he say he was coming?"

"He said he'd be here, but that was in the evening."

"What's happened to him?"

"Should I go see?" said the shop assistant Kurahashi Densuke and stood.

"Can't we wait a little longer? It's not a good idea to have too many people going in and out of this storehouse," said Muramatsu Kihei.

Others nodded. They met at this storehouse twice a month to talk with each other about their searches concerning Kira's residence. They conferred on the current situation and future plans.

However, from summer to the end of fall, these searches unearthed nothing. They were so close they could hear a shout right outside the back gate of the Kira residence. Not being able to verify what was in front of their eyes was painful frustration more than impatience over the distant object.

"But Kuranosuke warned us against rushing ahead recklessly. The revenge of Okudaira Genpachi at Joruri-zaka was a catastrophe because they never tracked down a detailed layout of the interior before rushing in."

"To that end, Yoshida Chuzaemon is probably the best prepared. He's inclined to consider military science the foundation of any matter. Every day, centered on Matsuza-kacho, he walks the belt of Honjo from Ryogoku and steps each foot on all the hilly back alleys, empty lots, and loca-tions with wells, and seems prepared to take advantage of the terrain in case of emergency."

"The other day, Kuranosuke praised Chuzaemon's humanity. If Chuzaemon does not apply pressure, the Edo samurai will break things as Edo samurai do. The men in the Kyoto region may have lost their resourcefulness."

Kataoka Gengoemon leaned forward.

"Okajima"

"Yes."

"The other day, you confirmed seeing Lord Kira's face at the gate in Hibiya. Is that true?"

"Yes, I glimpsed him."

"Why?"

"Not one of over fifty comrades knows what Lord Kira looks like."

"It's necessary to know on sight the master of ceremonies and the daimyo's retainers."

"So at the time of the revenge, we may miss him and raise another man's head. I've been thinking about this for a long time and watching the comings and goings at the Kira residence but haven't had a good opportunity to see him."

"Okay."

"Another time, we passed Kozuke no Suke's palanquin on our way home from Kojimachi after the lord's introduction. The samurai in the retinue of attendants would remember that palanquin. I thought my heart was on fire and devised a plan. When I saw it again, I ran ahead of his palanquin to kneel and place my head on the ground."

"Of course."

"If he meets a relative of one's lord or a familiar lord along the way, samurai etiquette demands sliding open the door of the palanquin to greet them. When he saw me, Lord Kira opened the palanquin door and asked who was my lord."

"All right, he did it."

"When I told him I was a vassal of Matsuura Hizen no Kami, Lord Kira asked for my full name. I gave myself away but spoke in a way no one heard my name, and I easily got away."

"Ha, ha, ha. Are you sure you saw Lord Kira's face?"

"No, I couldn't see him. I intended to calmly look up, but the palanquin's door only slid open a crack for a short time. I only saw a white satin collar flash near thin side locks of gray hair. I noticed the white hair on his neck and anger flared in my heart. I wanted to lunge at him. Thinking about it later, my memory is fuzzy."

"Where was Lord Kira going?"

"To a mansion used as an emergency safe house by the

Uesugi clan. I tailed him again on the way back to Honjo. The palanquin looked empty."

"This is a dangerous plan. If you think he's there, he's not and vice versa."

"But we have no one inside to search."

"Isogai has little confidence in the future but still hasn't said anything with any certainty."

"Juroza?"

Everyone's eyes turned to him. He said nothing but looked like he may or may not be at the edge of his seat.

94

THE GRIM DUO

I SOGAI JUROZAEMON WAS a conscientious young man whose good looks were admired by all.

He was a handsome, stylish man of the Genroku era. His eyebrows seemed to be made from jet-black lacquer. Red lips graced the white complexion of his oval face. Although slim, he was not frail.

He possessed a handsome face and grace, but his most appealing feature was his seriousness. He was reserved and, more importantly, passionate. His elder comrades often talked about his devotion to his parents.

"That's news to me, Juroza. Whether it's good or bad news, isn't the aim to uncover something soon?" said Takebayashi Tadashichi beside him. He like so many others frequently asked about the objective.

"I can't say now," said Juroza with his shy eyes cast down. "If that's the aim, I wish to know even one day sooner."

"Since you're a prudent man, what are you going to do? Oh, I think I get it. I understand," said Maebara Isuke like he remembered something and faintly smiled. "Juroza, should I tell them?"

"No, please don't."

"I want to tell them. There's nothing wrong with it."

"Why don't you drop it?" Juroza said enigmatically to Isuke and blushed like a virgin.

The group heard and wanted to hear more. They demanded Isuke tell them.

"Well, I'll tell them because, by nature, I can't keep a secret. The truth is a beauty named Tsuya is a maid in service in the Kira residence. She's become friendly with Juroza and fallen in love."

"Oh, with Juroza."

"Although only a thought in my head at the beginning, at some point, she fell in love."

"Good work," praised the unsmiling, 62-year-old elder Muramatsu Kihei.

"Juroza, you did it," said the elder to the conscientious youth to encourage him. "Women … ah women. I paid no mind to women. As I aged, I made mistakes in that realm. In whatever matter, not taking women into consideration is a mistake. Military strategists like Yoshida Chuzaemon remain ignorant in this area.… Juroza, you've done well! Excellent. But why are you so bashful?"

The clapper hanging at the downstairs entrance rattled. The startled men swallowed hard, and their eyes brightened. Onodera Koemon peeked down the ladder. "Kanzaki-dono?"

From below came, "Yes, Yato's here, too," said the haberdasher Zenbei's Yogoro, climbing up ahead of Emoshichi.

"My apologies for being late."

"We were worried and a little edgy. Kurahashi was about to find out what happened to you."

"We had pressing work this evening."

"At the store?"

"Business at Kira's."

"What was that?"

"Yato, show them our souvenir."

Emoshichi displayed the broken half of the drawing panel under the light.

"This is Kira's residence?"

"Yes. Unfortunately, we lost half. It doesn't show the interior of Kozuke no Suke's bedchamber to the inner residence but shows the area from the nagayamon gate to the front of the residence."

"Kanzaki, how did you get this tonight?"

"A lovely thing named Kume, a lady's maid from the Kira household, often shops at my store. She has fallen in love with Emoshichi, and I concocted this crime. For a noble cause, I misled her into believing marriage was their fate and convinced her to steal it."

When tonight's success was added to the discussion, the elder Muramatsu Kihei slapped his knees and let out a yell so loud his voice leaked outside the storehouse.

"What! A woman did this, too? Stolen by a woman's hand? Unfortunately, I'm not twenty years younger. Even if I enraged my wife, I would try to make her bring out the other half of this drawing."

Only Yato Emoshichi and Isogai Jurozaemon failed to smile at his exuberance.

PART XII

LORD KIRA'S BARRACKS

95

AN AUTUMN ON EDGE

THE SOUNDS OF the hooves of spooked horses scrambling to their feet echoed from Kira's stable housing eight animals. Five or six horses were always hitched there.

When one horse became restless, all the horses jumped at their hitching posts. The sounds of the clamor traveled inside.

Kira Sahyoue no Suke, Kozuke no Suke's heir, was the most sensitive person in the mansion to noise. His nervous eyes glistened. He laid his book on the desk and went out and stood in the corridor.

"Who's out there?"

"Is anybody here?" He called for the guards. "Magohachiro! Toshiemon!"

"Yes, Prince."

Souda Magohachiro and Torii Toshiemon rushed from the office separated by the corridor and hurried to place their hands on the ground. Sahyoue's complexion paled to the color of paper. His pounding heart turned his voice raspy.

"What's that racket in the stable?"

"That jumpy chestnut is in there. He probably upset the other horses and caused the disturbance."

Confident in his sixth sense, Sahyoue shook his head and said, "No, that's not it."

"I sense a difference from the usual neighing and agitated horses. Check on them."

"Yessir."

This day did not start like an ordinary one that usually evoked indolence and peaceful yawns. Every day and night, life was spent tense and alert.

Souda Magohachiro slipped on his zori sandals and ran out. The wooden door passing from the stable to the attendants' waiting room beside the entrance was ajar. He was soon outside the front gate as if jolted by the shadow of an evil spirit shooting past his eyes.

Someone called to him.

"Souda, where are you going?"

"Ah! Is that you, Johachi?"

"What's the emergency?"

"Not now. I'll tell you later."

Magohachiro's anxious eyes scanned the road. He ran to the end of the long fence of the neighboring Honda residence.

Dusty white autumn winds dried up the town in the afternoon. Traffic was unusual at the crossroads. The back of a samurai's attendant plodding away caught his eye. Sadness flowed like a song of mourning, even from the taiko drum of the candy seller.

"Where'd he go?"

Remarkably, Magohachiro could not find the mysterious human shadow. He could not understand how a touch of magic slipped out the wood door of the stable, passed through the small gate, and melted into this traffic.

He stood for a while. At last, the world was deep into autumn and leaves were falling. The eyes and whispers of the world, showing interest in the Kira clan versus the Asano ronin, were also distracted by the leaves on the trees. Magohachiro noticed his presence attracted the neighbors' eyes and his guilty self-consciousness returned.

With no one to catch, he went back through the front gate. Kimura Johachi stood there waiting to inquire about his odd behavior.

"Souda-san, who are you looking for? Who?"

"No one, the prince's words alerted me to the open door of the horse stable."

"Uh-huh, did someone enter the work area of the residence?"

"I don't know. I'll ask the men out front."

The two went to the entrance and called over to question the petty samurai on duty as gatekeepers and the men in the business office. All of them insisted they saw no signs of any intruder. However, one guard said a samurai's attendant came with a letter from a vassal of the Makino clan and sat in the waiting room for a time to wait for the lord's reply, and left with the reply.

"Now, I remember!" Kimura Johachi shouted, surprising himself.

"I brushed past that attendant moments ago at the crossroads. I thought I'd seen him somewhere but couldn't remember. Thinking about it now, I'm sure he was the Asano ronin Katsuta Shinzaemon. I'm sorry."

"What? The attendant who was here?"

The gate guard and the staff official blanched. The envoy came with a letter apparently from the Makino clan, so no one was suspicious. Now, they grumbled about their lack of vigilance.

A difference is natural in the standpoints of the target

and the man taking aim. Today's incident can be said to be an inevitable force. Nevertheless, the workers at the Kira residence were disturbed by the ever-changing, intimidating behavior of Asano ronin who entered this mansion by impersonating the attendants of other lords and vassals. Their skin chilled and they shuddered.

"It'd be best not to inform the young lord of this incident. It would be like pricking nerves with needles. This stays with us," Souda Magohachiro whispered to the other men. He turned to Johachi and said, "I'll see you later," and vanished inside.

96

THE PAPER MEMORIAL TABLET

S HIMIZU ICHIGAKU, KOBAYASHI Heihachiro, Osuga Jiroemon, and others lived in the guard barracks that filled one block in a corner of the Kira residence and was a row house in line with the entrance.

Johachi peeked into Ichigaku's home.

"Are you here?"

During the afternoon, Ichigaku usually returned to the row house to rest. He answered from his prone position.

"Kimura? This is a surprise," he said and sat up.

The two exchanged letters endlessly but had few face-to-face meetings. The last time was last year when they met in the Hazu district in Mikawa, the fief of the Kira clan, on the way home from Ako. They enjoyed country soba cooked by Ichigaku's elderly mother in the thatched-roof home of his birth and talked the night away.

"It's been a while."

"Well, you look fit."

"I'm not. I caught a cold in the fall, and it kept getting worse. I've been in my sickbed for about two months."

463

"You're better now?"

"I could finally get up and walk here."

Was this why Johachi's cheeks looked hollow? His build also looked different. For some time, he wore the topknot of a townsman and furtively walked the environs of Ako and Kyoto. Today, his loose hair tied back in his sickbed was styled again in his previous samurai topknot.

"And you, how are you?"

"As you see," said Ichigaku extending his hands to his knees, "I'm in good shape."

"It's good you can drink."

"If I don't have sake, I'm very bored."

"How can I help?"

"There's nothing for you to do. Except for the swordsmen from Yonezawa here at the residence, twenty or thirty newly employed ronin and other attendants bring the number of men to over one hundred."

"That many?"

"The lord's wife returned to her family. The children and grandchildren are gone. Only Kozuke no Suke-sama and his son and heir, Sahyoue-sama, live here. So the only work done here is done by the one hundred or so staff members for themselves."

"What about the night?"

"The shift changes each night."

"That wears on the mind."

"What?"

Ichigaku shook his head, looking sad.

"Mental fatigue comes from feeling useless. Among the newly employed swordsmen with no purpose, how many would throw away their lives in a crisis? They don't have the heart."

"I see."

Johachi agreed. He cast his eyes down and was silent for a time. Then he jerked his head sideways and peered into the dimly lit room next door. His wary eyes looked at Ichigaku's face.

"Who died?"

"What?"

"Isn't that the smell of incense sticks?"

"A messenger came this morning. My mother died ..."

"Oh no! Your dear mother who cooked soba dishes for us?"

"Yes."

"That's too bad."

"No, I'm ashamed because when I received that message this morning, I started feeling better. The day news springs from here for the countryside is not far away. Her passing before mine is unfortunate, but I have no regrets."

"You're that prepared?"

"Of course. The coming attack clashes with the inability to avoid it. Only in defense, I've committed countless dishonorable acts. I'm a bad actor, but others don't know about my bad side. I only want to die as a full-fledged samurai."

"..."

"Kimura, men like you, me, and Kobayashi Heihachiro are few, but don't you believe we are true vassals of the Kira clan? Even if the number of men increases, we will engage in a struggle to the death with Ako. My mind will be at ease no matter how many gather at this residence. Since that is what I see, I'm not concerned about mundane matters. I believe the highest level of loyalty is to drink sake, store up power, and wait for that day."

"You've said a lot."

Kimura Johachi flushed red in his once again healthy face.

"I will die, too." He bit his lip. Aware of being heard outside the barracks, he quieted his powerful voice.

"To be frank, I thought Chisaka Hyobu-sama's determination sat with you. As you said, despite praying for no attack and guarding as best we can, the future is like a cloud in a swift wind soaring in the sky. This storm can't be avoided."

"Do you see it that way, too?"

"I sensed weak factions among them while I spied on them in Ako, Kyoto, Yamashina, and other places. However, all the men who never left Kuranosuke to this day will relish dying. That's frightening. There's no stronger rival."

"That I understand. Given the education hammered into us from childhood, that result is natural because of the beauty of moral principles in society until yesterday. Men who seek to outwit the desperation of men who hate the enemy in vain and lost their stipends and men who act to gain false reputations do not understand the extreme beauty of the samurai way in which the cherished wish is to die. Right now, I feel I am there. It's a mystery to me, too. The day of my death is not the least bit horrible to me. I feel that even in this dreary mansion. If many Ako ronin come to this mansion's gate, it will be the same as being at the gate to a peaceful death and Buddhist paradise preached about by the priests. When they climb in here, they will truly live."

Johachi realized everything he came to say had been said by Ichigaku. Chisaka Hyobu, who gave him direct orders and was always a close confidant, observed his mental readiness was close to Ichigaku's. During the summer, he came to agree with Hyobu's sentiment that the final calamity was unavoidable.

The Uesugi clan must devise a more aggressive plan. The world speculated Kozuke no Suke would move to Yonezawa, take refuge in the daimyo's main Edo mansion in Azabu, and assassinate three or four of the Ako leaders in a counterattack.

"It must be done!"

If someone proposed plans like that, Hyobu shook his head no. Senior vassals in the Uesugi clan in a calm state of mind said to leave everything to divine will at the bottom of his deep will and to take no action that would endanger the sovereign Uesugi clan in an attempt to save the Kira clan. These two beliefs resembled sitting like a rock.

Kimura Johachi left his sickbed after returning to Edo. The work did not aggravate him as much now. All the seniors and newcomers in the residence were frequently upset and fearful. Their nerves were pricked by the rewards for Ako spies, the sounds of wind, and the comings and goings of dogs.

"Kimura, our talks tend to fall into reason. Would you like a drink?"

"Yes, we have matters to discuss. We'll talk as we drink. But before that, shall we pay our respects?"

Kimura Johachi saw the light of the incense sticks on the desk in the gloomy room and kneeled before it. This house lacked a woman's touch. The offerings on the desk were a cup of water and a few flowers. The miserable display appeared to be the work of Ichigaku's hands. The votive light was missing. There was no memorial tablet, but a scrap of paper was stuck to the wall in front of the desk. Johachi recognized the handwriting and was hit with melancholy. He placed his hands together and kneeled again in worship.

> *Mother - Died October of year 15 of Genroku*
> *Shimizu Ichigaku - Died the same year*

The mother and son were together on the memorial tablet.

97

A LOVE THAT IS NOT

THE HIGH-PITCHED WAIL of a woman about to cry rose. The clattering sounds of footsteps heard below a window of the barracks might have been someone tripping and tumbling down. A woman screamed and pleaded for help.

"I don't know! It wasn't me! Please forgive me! Somebody, please help."

"Why are you screaming? You're hardheaded!"

This yelling voice was muddied by a Yonezawa accent. The voice belonged to a low-ranking samurai attached to Sahyoue named Niimi Yashichiro.

"Lately, you've been acting strange. Talk. Tell me the truth. If you don't, you'll be arrested and fired."

"I don't know. What am I supposed to say? I—"

"Shut up. You know nothing, so why did you go into the carpenter's shed?"

"I don't remember going in."

"Well, whose comb is this?"

"That's—"

"An attendant picked it up in the shed. We kept quiet

about this for four or five days and watched. She didn't show her face today, but someone, maybe a maid, was hanging around the carpenter's shed. And now here you are hiding in the shadows of a tree in the back garden and writing."

"It's a letter to my father," answered her trembling voice. She was young and confused, and her excuse was infantile against Niimi's hounding. This lady's maid was Kume.

Inside the barracks, Ichigaku and Kimura Johachi were pouring each other drinks and enjoying a side dish of dried sardines Ichigaku happened to have. They lowered their voices and set aside their drinks to listen.

"We could do without that ridiculously thorough investigation," whispered Ichigaku and swallowed a dried sardine. Johachi drank a cold drink.

"What's that about?"

"Nothing important."

"Is that woman with such a tearful excuse being accused by a menacing look that could kill?"

"A panel drawing of the renovation to the residence went missing from the carpenter's shed. Someone stole it and threw it over the wall to an Ako man. She's probably a suspect?"

Ichigaku spoke like it wasn't his problem, poured another round of drinks, and suggested they relax and enjoy their drinks.

"Poor thing. What does that young girl know? No matter how big the secret, some shrewd man from Ako knows about the residence. He'll find a way to ferret it out. It's discouraging because only a man who worries about the smallest matter knows how to prepare an impregnable fortress."

"Shimizu."

"Yes?"

"Go out and see what he's doing to her. Isn't she crying in despair? He may be roughing her up.... And the sake's not good."

"I'll go because he sounds a bit hateful. I'll mediate."

"It'll be an act of mercy."

"I guess so."

Ichigaku stuck his head out the window at the entrance to the room.

Niimi Yashichiro clutched the back of Kume's neck and was dragging her to the big paulownia tree. He tied her to the base of the tree and wrenched up both her hands.

"Cry all you want. Tell the lord, and later scream as much as you like. Confess your crime right now or after you feel the pain. It will end in the same way. Your refusal to speak leaves me no choice."

"Help me, please.... Somebody, please come. Mother! Father!"

"You idiot!" he said and kicked her. "Who will come? You must confess. You have no choice. Call for your parents. What good is that?"

"Aah ... forgive me! Please forgive me."

"Will you talk? You stole the panel drawing and carried it out."

"I ... I don't know."

"Isn't your father the master carpenter? I suspected the carpenter's daughter would steal that panel."

"That makes no sense. I don't know."

"Show me the letter you wrote while hiding from people's eyes."

"I lost it. I was going to send the letter to my father."

"Why were you hiding in the back garden to write a

letter to your father? If you find it, you'll rip it up and eat it."

"No. No."

"Damn, you are stubborn."

When a second kick knocked her turned-away face, Ichigaku slipped on his zori sandals and walked up behind Niimi Yashichiro.

"Hey, Niimi, aren't you a little loud?"

Yashichiro looked back and loosened his grip.

"Oh, Shimizu-dono?"

Kume lost color, startled by Shimizu's voice.

The other day, she was alone with the man she loved, Emoshichi, on the second floor of the haberdashery of Azukiya Zenbei. Without thinking, she poked her face out a second-floor window to see a man in a braided straw hat standing in front of the shop curtain and looking up at her. He was, without a doubt, Shimizu Ichigaku.

Only Ichigaku probably understood her love for and closeness to the haberdasher.

This man won't save me.

Her surprise crushed her urge to escape, and cold resignation lodged in the depths of her heart. She believed she would call out her lover's name at the moment of death.

"What are you doing?"

"Did you hear me?"

"I heard."

"This is connected to the other night. I've accused her because she's been behaving suspiciously. Do you want to help?"

"Don't be ridiculous!"

Ichigaku smiled and said, "Stop wasting time on her."

"Why?" Niimi's anger was sparked. "Why is this a waste?"

"She's just a woman."

"But women …"

"Our rivals are the Ako ronin and not women or drawing panels. Isn't Ako the opponent? Pretending paper is pasted to the shoji screen doesn't keep out the cold wind. It's already winter. Niimi, release her."

"No, I'm questioning her."

"Enough of your brutish talk. When off duty, do you frequent the Tatsumi or Okabasho pleasure district? Or is she a respectable woman? Aren't there women wherever you pass through? She's forbidden to form liaisons with men in the residence, but this girl seems to have a fiance or a sweetheart. She probably wrote a letter to him in secret."

"But what about the drawing panel?"

"What could anyone do with that? How many times did the carpenter change the layout of the rooms during construction?"

"It doesn't matter if they're accurate. She stole the panel and is dangerous. How can you allow her to stay in the residence?"

"You're too loud. Niimi, keep it down. It's better if the lord doesn't hear. The lord and his son already live in fear. If this trivial matter brings needless distress today, it will make it a day of disloyalty."

"It's the opposite of what you're saying."

"What you're thinking is backward. Let's stop this endless argument. Wouldn't it be best if you leave this naughty parlor maid alone and quietly withdraw to a lodging house?"

"Why are you defending this woman?"

"The truth is … Niimi … I'm a little embarrassed, but I've fancied this girl for a while."

"Stop joking."

"I'm serious. For a long time, I've been thinking about

what could I do if I weren't inside the residence. So I more than anyone should understand this girl's behavior and temperament. She's certainly not a woman capable of a bold act, disloyalty, or greed. If I'm wrong, I'll take full responsibility. Leave today's matter to me."

"All right. You say you're sure."

"I'll take full responsibility.... Ha, ha, ha. Isn't my indulgence of women the same as yours? Kimura Johachi is visiting, and we were having drinks. Why don't you join us?"

"Enough!" Niimi turned away his enraged face and left.

The next day, Kichigoro, a master carpenter and father, was surprised to receive a letter from the Kira clan summoning him.

Your daughter Kume's services are no longer needed.

He went to fetch his daughter.

Before leaving the residence, he asked, "Did you do something unforgivable in this house that has blessed me for many years? You have disgraced your father."

His scolding never stopped. From a window, Ichigaku glimpsed the hand of her enraged father jerk the dejected Kume through the back gate.

"Hey, Kichigoro, Kichigoro," he called to stop him.

"Oh, Master? I don't want to be seen today."

Kichigoro tried to hide his daughter behind him like she was something hideous. His nose stopped up, and he bowed his head to the window.

"I thought an angry man was passing through. Are you mad at your daughter?"

"Yes. She got herself fired from the mansion."

"Don't be too hard on her. Better than that, go now and look for a good son-in-law."

"I don't deserve your kind words. My behavior was improper, and I apologize to the people of the mansion. When I get home, I'll be sure to find one for her."

From behind her father, Kume pressed her palms together and raised them to the window of Ichigaku's room.

98

WINTER WINDS

NOVEMBER BEGAN. A restless Niimi Yashichiro visited Kichigoro's home near Takabashi in Fukugawa. He immediately told Kichigoro the reason for his visit.

"A little time has passed, so I've come to investigate your daughter one more time."

"Why?" Kichigoro looked surprised.

"It's not another problem but is more serious than before. This is not about the missing drawing panel. A copy of the grounds allotment drawing delivered to the Imperial Court and a copy of the room layout of the residence disappeared from the library near the lord's home."

As he listened, Kichigoro's face swelled with rage.

"There's always a disaster with her, but why do you want to question my daughter about this?"

"She's still a suspect in the earlier matter."

"Yes, but why are you accusing Kume of stealing the other documents?"

"I have no other suspects."

"You're kidding. It's been half a month since I dragged her home. Is she going to be blamed for stealing everything that disappears after she left? I went to the trouble to fetch her and bring her home. I'm disgusted, too. If you must question her, please go to her upstairs because she never comes down or goes outside."

"In that case, I'll be careful."

When Yashichiro got up, "Master," said Kichigoro, rising to grab his sleeve.

"It's all right for you to question her, but when you're convinced she didn't do it, what will you do?"

"What? Nothing in particular …"

"Master, you're also a samurai, but I'm an Edo townsman. Because of her inexcusable behavior at the residence, as her father who tossed her in a room on the second floor, questioned her, and found her guilty, I have no reason to ask you to not speak to her and go home. I can stand it, but for her sake, please understand she didn't know how to behave while living there."

Yashichiro placed his hands on the ladder stairs and looked up. A dim gloom hung over the confined space like a prison cell. He reflected on this father who still asks forgiveness from the residence that gave his daughter an apprenticeship and is carrying out this harsh punishment. Yashichiro was aware of his slight hesitation caused by the words of Kichigoro, who could not be called a townsman.

"Well … no … Everything you said wasn't just about Kume's behavior. It's not good to come here with suspicions beyond your duties."

He pulled back the leg stepping toward the second floor.

"Excuse my intrusion. I'll be going."

He rushed to put on his sandals in the dirt-floor entryway and went outside the lattice.

"What a pest," muttered Kichigoro.

"Come the day before yesterday," chanted his sole

apprentice, while sprinkling salt to drive him and evil spirits away.

He looked up a Kichigoro and said, "Master, if he likes Kume-san, wouldn't forgiveness be best?"

"Yeah, but that won't happen. The truth is I'm not sure what's going on. He's like her lover."

"That's it."

"You talk such nonsense. Stay alert when I'm not here."

The apprentice and the servant boys pitied Kume on the second floor. If they heard about a lover, they pitied her too much.

Kume was gaunt. She slept with a medicinal jar placed at her bedside. The past half month took a toll on her. Unlike her time of service in the mansion, she was free to think about whatever she wanted.

"Emoshichi-san ..."

When she whispered his name, the white face of that young man with bangs poked out from the ceiling and beamed a smile at her.

"I long to see you."

The memories pained her.

"I wonder if his hands caught the panel drawing I threw?"

She wanted to know but had no way to contact him. The ladder stairs creaked.

"Who is it?"

"It's me," said the junior servant Take bringing her gruel and slowly poked in his head.

"Kume-san, don't you want to go outside?"

"Go outside. No, not at all."

"You're lying. You want to go to him."

"..."

"Your father's gone out. He said he was off to see a regular customer in Koamicho. It'll be night before he returns. You can go and be back before then. I'll take the blame if you don't get back in time."

"Really?"

Kume got up from her bed.

In a short time, she covered her head with a hood and left the house. Her legs that had not stepped on the ground for a long time were blown by a biting, cold wind of winter. She looked feeble, almost unable to walk; and she was not happy.

She did not see the familiar dark-blue shop curtain at the haberdashery across from the back gate of the Kira residence.

"Oh? He's probably out?"

She looked up at the second floor. The storm shutters were closed and a crooked white For Rent sign hung down.

"…"

Standing under the wall of the Kira residence she served until last month, Kume stared at the rental sign for a long time. She looked at the shutter where she once quietly sat with Emoshichi.

A flood of white tears flowed down her cheeks. Leaves fell like rain from the top of the paulownia tree and covered the roof of the Kira residence. She cried and beat on the door and eaves of the empty building displaying a For Rent sign.

PART XIII

A PICTURE OF THE PEOPLE OF THE GENROKU ERA

99

A TWISTED CORD

YAMATE, A TOWN of mansions and many trees, was buried under fallen leaves and glazed by the November frost. The few remaining days of this year were slowly counted. Humanity's winter amid this unhurried feeling penetrated dreary breasts.

"This frost is awful," groaned Okado Denpachiro standing on the veranda. The frost's whiteness seemed to stab the eyes. His expansive residence in Omote Yonbancho was abandoned with no upkeep during the winter storms.

Amid the flapping sounds of a flock of small birds flying from the trees, the cocky voices of samurai laughed and traded jokes as they walked down the small road right outside the wall. They had emerged from the gate of a neighbor, the retainer Torii Nanigashi. Until a little after midnight, Denpachiro heard hand clapping to keep time for risque songs or musical pieces. The figures of bath-house girls, unbecoming in a neighborhood of samurai residences, came and went. Perhaps the group corralled women from a pleasure bathhouse in town to drink the night away, and now, they were on their way home.

"Damn, it's cold. My nose is about to snap off," said one man as they passed by.

As if walking through a field, he called ahead, "Hey, Imamura … Are you on emergency duty today?"

"Yup. I'm on duty. I'm not off even when I'm off. I hate days like this and don't want to go."

"Are you going?"

"Where?"

"To Bunnagashi."

"Wherever you go in the morning, there are no tatami rooms."

"Is it close to the north quarter?"

"A little further away. Why don't we drop in on Ren, Cho, and Fuji who came from Choji Bathhouse last night?"

"A bathhouse? I'd like a bath. What do you guys think?"

"Sounds good."

"What about the rest of you?"

"What would be the objection?"

The last man answered with a stanza in the language of kabuki, causing small groups of several men to burst into laughter.

When the sounds of footsteps disappeared, the small birds quietly returned to the treetops and sang. The dull winter sun shone between the rain shower clouds on the bright red persimmon leaves.

"Master, please gargle."

In this morning ritual, the elderly servant placed items like the mirror, the water bucket, and the portable kit of hairstyling tools, and assisted by holding Denpachiro's sleeves from behind. Denpachiro moistened the comb's teeth then combed his recent spectacular growth of salt-and-pepper hair.

"Uncle, who were those noisy idiots?"

"That group often gathers in Torii-sama's or Suzuki-sama's mansion. I think they held some event last night. It was a cheerful racket."

"They were too rowdy, not only at night but in the morning and afternoon, too."

"When we were young, morning meant the sounds of bowstrings at the target range; and night, voices reading and hushed silence."

"Things have changed."

"For the past few days, the sounds of a shamisen rang…. They don't speak too loudly, but flashy fellows who look like gamblers or gangsters go in and out. Maybe, the mansion has become a gambling house."

"These are terrible times. They say men, such as relics like us, idolize the old-fashioned ways of the Keicho and Genna eras and prize the spirit of the Kan'ei era in the warrior's way and have gone stale in the head. Why did the powerful Yanagisawa only blame a low-ranking petty official for that situation?"

A parlor maid appeared far below the veranda.

"Everything is ready."

"All right."

Denpachiro nodded and went down to the garden where a small Shinto shrine was erected. Every morning, he kneeled, clapped his hands, and recited his morning prayer. Next, he went to the family altar room to greet his ancestors. Eventually, he ate and, on a day of attendance at the castle, he put on his service clothes and sat for a time in the library to steady his spirit before leaving."

"Master, an unfamiliar ronin left this object a moment ago while you were changing. He kept saying it was an expression of thanks and left," said the petty samurai who always accompanied him in the palanquin to the castle and presented him with what looked like a box of cakes. What was this friendship gift? The exceptionally guileless Denpachiro frowned.

"Who was it? And what is this?"

"I asked for his full name. He only said he was Yoshioka Katsubei, an Owari ronin. He said a letter was attached, and he was only the courier."

"Why did you accept it? Haven't I said not to respond to callers if I have not given permission to accept friendship gifts or presents from visitors?"

"Yessir."

"No, not yessir. Go after that man and tell him this gift cannot be accepted. I must give it back."

The panicked petty samurai bolted out of the gate from the side entrance. This happened moments ago. An exasperated Okado Denpachiro pushed the box of thin wood before him to the side.

He realized what his hand was touching and looked at the wrapping paper around the box.

Ako Specialty - Cherry Blossoms
Baked salt made by Banshuya

"What? … Ako … He wondered about the Owari ronin and his gift of Ako salt"

The vivid calligraphy of the letter's characters attached below the decorative twisted paper cord struck Denpachiro's eyes. He flipped it over.

"Oh!"

This is what he read.

Kataoka Gengoemon

100

THE TWILIGHT OF HIS DAY

THE INCIDENT FELT like an event from the distant past or just yesterday. But when accurately counted, it took place in the spring of last year at twilight on March 14.

Under the trees with blooming flowers in the evening on the estate of Tamura Ukyo-dayu, by order of the shogun on that day, Asano Takumi no Kami Naganori committed seppuku.

> *Like cherry blossoms scattered by inviting*
> *winds,*
> *Forever gone.*
> *With sorrow, I bid farewell in the*
> *springtime.*

On that evening, he chanted the hated death poem, then the fresh blood on his sword stained his white kimono.

"Oh, those moments ..."

I will never forget! Okado Denpachiro could close his eyes and vividly draw that twilight on his eyelids.

Accompanying Chief Inspector Shoda Shimousa no Kami and his assistant Okubo Gonzaemon, he, as the deputy envoy, was entrusted with the role of post-mortem examiner and observed the event to confirm the seppuku of Takumi no Kami. Many memories crossed his mind, from each step the lord took to the seat of his death in the dim garden to the movements of a gentle breeze playing with his hair at the instant of death.

That's how it was. He recalled a fine samurai who looked about thirty-five or -six years old, had distinctive eyebrows and a sturdy build. The retainer of Takumi no Kami named Kataoka Gengoemon was on his knees to a figure in the garden to get permission from the Tamura residence.

"May I see my lord in his last moments when he departs this world?"

He pleaded like he was going to rip open his intestines.

The lord and followers of the Tamura clan and the senior envoys of the chief inspector were unmoved and rejected his request. However, when they drank in his spirit as warriors, they granted permission even if their posts were put in jeopardy.

"You will see him."

Those words pleased him. The droplet of light on his eyelashes that spoke of neither misery nor joy had a value he would remember his whole life.

The proceedings on the Tamura estate were not the only ones in progress. In Edo Castle, those seated in deliberation decided nothing in the confusion following the incident, Denpachiro believed he alone expressed the argument that fearlessly criticized superiors and bravely described the official misconduct of Kira Kozuke no Suke and the unfair decision of seppuku on the same day by the shogun's Council of Elders.

This appeared to weaken the strong convictions among the senior retainers, particularly, Yanagisawa Yoshiyasu, despite his deep relationship with the Kira clan. But by evening, he received a reprimand.

Okado, you are exceeding your authority and ordered to show restraint.

He understood the reprimand. His superiors in the shogunate's leadership were aggravated by Okado Denpachiro's existence. Failures continued to emerge. The mood among the leadership responsible for creating the current situation in the world could not penetrate his hard bones. His integrity would turn into sadness in his later years.

But Denpachiro regretted nothing. Rather, he pitied those anesthetized to their humanity by a moment of vanity. He only grieved the coming erosion of the nation. The people of the Genroku era enjoyed Genroku and died. That could be called the privilege of being born. Although the nation is eternal, the lifetimes of those alive are not. The shogun families do nothing more than receive sovereignty from the emperor. The mold from a spoiled culture bloomed on imperial land that glittered since the nation's founding. Does the source of the calamity of the country's ruin remain in the eternal subjects of the emperor and our descendants? If we live our brief lives selfishly, our nation can be no other way.

From a personal perspective, how long do momentary pleasures and self-indulgence drained to nihilism last in a lifetime? That collision is bound to end in a hole of destruction. Light and the happiness of human life are deeply felt.

"I've brought him back," said the gasping petty samurai at the next edge of the papered sliding door.

"Ah!" Denpachiro's brow in deep thought rose at the sound of his voice.

"Did you catch him?"

"Luckily, I caught up to him at the foot of the fire lookout tower."

"Very good. Now, please return this." He stood and held out the gift box of Ako salt. "No … wait, wait…. I almost forgot. I know this man and wish to see him. Please be gracious and show him to the room over there."

101

WARRIORS' SALT

"DAY AND NIGHT I yearned to visit unannounced to thank you for your kindness at that time and am ashamed of my pursuit of a wandering life. Please forgive my crime of silence," said Kataoka Gengoemon. His eyes were filled with great appreciation and looked with nostalgia at Denpachiro. His eyes expressed what his words could not, especially, the fellowship between warriors.

"What?" softly said Denpachiro but was happy with the thought that his good faith impressed that man today, over a year later.

"You say gratitude, but I'm ashamed. After the change in your master's house, each rumor indirectly wounded me. But it's good to see you in good health."

"You too, Sir," said Gengoemon forgetting his hands planted on the tatami. "When I saw you looking as you did, the garden lights in the twilight and the scattered cherry blossoms at that time came to mind."

"I share your thoughts. The year has already passed to a second."

"By your good offices, the lord's farewell note and

death poem were delivered to the home province. Everyone from Kuranosuke on down appreciated your bringing together the former clan warriors and grateful for your goodwill. Please pardon the absence of news on the circumstances of the other men after the scattering ."

"Where are you living now?"

"I'm sorry to say I'm renting a house in Hayashicho in Honjo and living the miserable life of a ronin. I hear nothing from government officials and spend my days doing nothing."

"Days with nothing to do—" he was about to ask a question but was stopped by Denpachiro's nod and look.

"Thank you for the gift."

"It's a small gift. I recently received it from a friend in Ako."

"It's perfect. I could only hope to have what people called the salt of the Earth. Warriors' salt, Ako salt, is prized."

Denpachiro raised the box with reverence to his head and placed it in the alcove.

Morning came. Aware a long stay would cause problems, Gengoemon left. He didn't intend to see anyone, but this encounter brought unexpected happiness. Denpachiro wanted their talk to go on but knew it was time to go to the castle. He saw Gengoemon off at the entrance. "If you have the opportunity, please come again."

Gengoemon almost spoke his thought, This may be our farewell in this life.

He sensed this was the only man he could reveal clues to his true motive but casually said, "Yes, when I have the time," and left through the gate.

102

THE MAN SPEWING GRIEF

WHILE TRYING NOT to look villainous, a man wearing a braided bamboo hat took a sharp turn at the crossroads of Kokucho.

"Hey! Oishi-dono," called out a man from behind and quickened his step.

The man wore hakama trousers with sharp pleats; a greenish-brown half-length haori coat with a crest; and zori sandals with twisted white paper straps over white tabi socks. The slender man, who looked a little over thirty, wrapped his pale face in a dark blue hood and seemed weak like a Kyoto samurai, but his features were solid and eyebrows, bushy.

"Excuse me for bothering you, but aren't you Oishi-dono?"

Inevitably, Kuranosuke slowly turned his bamboo hat and said, "Uh, yes," like he was regaining consciousness.

"And I believe you are Kada Azumamaro."

"Yes, yes, in this unexpected place."

"What a surprise."

"How long have you been in Edo?"

"Well, in my situation as a ronin with no appointment, the days mean nothing."

"Where are you staying?"

Kuranosuke couldn't dodge this question. "Nearby."

"Oh, with your son?"

"We live solitary lives."

They talked for a long time but could only afford cheap tea. Azumamaro and Kuranosuke met last year in Kyoto but were also old friends from their school days.

Kada Azumamaro was the pseudonym he used for his poetry and literary works. His real name was Hagura Itsuki. Even as a young student, he was at the level of the literary greats. While in Kyoto, he received the patronage of Minister of the Right Ooi no Mikado and was a Shinto priest at the Kyoto Inari shrine. Kuranosuke's intellectual and ideological connections to him began when he attended his literature course and occasional exchanges such as revisions to poems. He never imagined running into this man in Edo.

"Forgive this cramped room."

He brought Azumamaro to the ronin home on 3-chome Kokucho, served tea, and tried his best to draw out gossip about poems and literary men.

"In Kyoto, I heard about your life of luxury, but this is a simple life," mumbled Azumamaro, looking at the walls and the horizontal beam of *nageshi* wood running the length of one wall.

"I met Nakajima Gorosaku soon after I arrived in Edo."

"Gorosaku. Oh, the rich man in Reiganjima? I was introduced to him in Kyoto. However, because of my fall in this world and no leisure time, I held back on visiting him."

"Gorosaku told me you moved here."

"So you knew I was here?"

"Whether I knew or not, your coming to work in the capital sent powerful echoes throughout the world. The kingfisher changed treetops to see the fish …"

"That's funny. Who?"

"Oishi-dono."

"Is that a riddle? Well, it's idle speculation. In the pursuit of spare food and clothing, I must live in the world."

"During your time here, have you been to Yoshiwara?"

"Death in battle in Gion or Fushimi turns into failure in Edo. As you see, the quiet and simplicity of the ronin house are not conducive to those adventures. From now on, quiet and simplicity will come to life, and I will conduct the tea ceremony. But these days, I need money for tea."

"Have you observed the high and low customs of Edo?"

"Not yet. You need money for those delicate, gaudy creatures to do anything. This is a world of gold and only gold."

"This literature is said to be fully mature, but when will it come into its own and shine?"

"That's hard to know."

"I think both the high and low pursue loose women and pleasure and don't open their eyes to the deplorable conditions in society. So is some sort of divine punishment taking place? It's painful but people are fearful today. We have no choice other than to be lower than the esteemed dogs and subordinate to beasts. The crime is the human body. The esteemed dogs themselves know nothing."

"Well, it hurts to hear that truth."

"No, no, it's not only you. More than you can imagine, cabinet officials, townsmen, and samurai have decayed. They all forgot the way of the warrior during the Kan'ei and Genna eras. Only gold has influence, and merchants control that gold. The dying off of virtue was a surprise, and only ego and hedonism saw a tenacious rise in human thought. Today's society scorns human compassion and virtue.

"The self-destruction of humanity is coming. Hearts will ache. Will true human beings, whoever they are, emerge and rebuke them? No, people today do not listen. Things will not go well if those people don't show themselves. If no force strikes me to live as a true human being ..."

Kuranosuke listened without interrupting, but his expression showed no focus.

In contrast, the ears reddened on the young literary man and poet, Kada Azumamaro, out of fear of the times. This was not simply the emotions of a scholar. Anyone could feel the power rising from his companion's intestines. Despite Kuranosuke's placid expression, he spewed grief and rage over a conviction that made him tremble.

103

THE MOMENTS WAITING

AFTER THEIR MEETING, Kada Azumamaro often visited the ronin house in Kokucho. Kuranosuke's trust in him grew each time they met, but he never divulged his true motive of revenge.

Before Kuranosuke realized it, Azumamaro and Horibe Yasubei he met there formed a closer relationship.

Azumamaro spoke of his enthusiasm and grief over the deplorable state of the world with Kuranosuke not knowing how he would react. When he met and talked to Horibe Yasubei, the surprised Azumamaro thought, Well now! You think so, too? Yasubei's answer spoken with violence through grinding teeth intimidated Azumamaro.

"You are an agreeable man."

"You're also a scholar of literature and have a certain strength."

Each man met his kindred spirit.

When asked, "Where do you live?" Yasubei said, "At the Kinokuniya store in Hayashicho, Honjo."

Azumamaro said, "I'm at the lending shop of Nakajima Gorosaku in Sajikkenhori in Kyobashi. Please come by when you have time and we'll talk."

An unforeseen secret emerged from an unexpected place. Despite no success in the struggle to uncover good or bad news, he heard unexpected bits and pieces of information.

Yasubei saw Azumamaro a few times and discussed various topics, mostly the tea ceremony. In time, details about the Kira clan leaked out.

One time, Azumamaro mentioned that through contacts with court nobles, he went twice to tutor Kozuke no Suke's son on classical literature.

Yasubei's face reddened, and he celebrated victory in his heart.

From then on, his friendship with Azumamaro became his sole endeavor, and he frequently visited Sajikkenhori.

During that time, another gem dropped into Yasubei's hands. He successfully obtained a hunted object. The retainer Matsudaira Noborinosuke was the prior occupant of the mansion in Matsuzakacho where Kozuke no Suke now lived. His secret mission targeted the Matsudaira home of the former renter to obtain a drawing of the mansion.

That was close to perfect. However, his comrades theorized the rumors were true. Kira's side missed nothing and rebuilt most of the important locations and added extensions.

"Of course." Yasubei did not insist on his view.

Meanwhile, Isogai Jurozaemon presented a current map of the Kira estate.

"Here it is."

He leaped for joy like a young man in his first battle who took the head of a general.

"How did you get your hands on that?"

He was asked about this miracle and praised for his outstanding service.

"It was nothing special."

He was not being humble. Juroza blushed and hid without saying a word. The reason was vaguely understood only by the men gathered on the second floor of the storehouse of the rice dealer Gohei. Juroza had a little secret with Tsuya, who worked deep inside the Kira household.

"Don't ask," said the laughing haberdasher Zenbei's Kanzaki Yogoro.

Yato Emoshichi received Kume's love and pieced together the panel drawing carried out with her heart and soul to the one brought by Juroza. The sizes and room arrangements inside the Kira estate, the row house, and other locations were estimated.

"Excellent. They fit."

Outside the Kira estate, Yoshida Chuzaemon measured the widths of the roads, the gutters, the relationships to the neighboring houses, and the open spaces and temples near Ryogoku.

"In case of emergency, I left nothing out and investigated the number of men sent out by the Uesugi clan, the place where the party will withdraw, and other concerns."

He reported his findings to Kuranosuke.

All weapons and uniforms had been smuggled by boat to Yasubei's ronin house. Preparations would be finished in a few days. For some reason, only one final search yielded no results.

When they reached this point, the party's impatience grew. The outwardly composed Onodera Junai was restless and went out walking every day with his hood pulled over his forehead. The young men were jumpy.

The last obstacle was not knowing what days Kozuke no Suke would be at the residence.

If a rare blunder ended in failure, all the hardships endured until that day, and their spirits would be destroyed in one stroke.

Not only would they become laughingstocks for one hundred generations, the reviled townsmen would criticize the former Ako clan and even the late Takumi no Kami. This dilemma made taking the first step terrifying.

When all the other battle plans were arranged, the younger comrades—Horibe, Takebayashi, Hazama, Katsuta, Yato, Isogai, and Sugino—couldn't wait any longer and said he was there.

Sometimes they confirmed insignificant hearsay from around town, the comings and goings at the gate door, and showed signs of breaking the dam and taking immediate action.

Over the past few days, Kuranosuke's eyebrows moved with great sensitivity. He made Chikara change disguises and often visited the ronin hideout. Above all, he abstained from drinking and did not act wildly or accidentally start a fire. He used all his abilities, took meticulous notes on matters concerning the townspeople and the guardhouses, and paid close attention in the public baths and on the streets.

"Do not act."

"Tighten the noose and wait."

The men living incognito in different parts of Edo were silent.

The news, "Mouri Koheita deserted," echoed among them.

There were a few more deserters. Some of the men who came this far through hard work didn't know when human feelings would crumble or waver. These men numbering close to fifty covered a wide range of ages. The younger ones were around sixteen to eighteen years old, and the older ones, sixty to seventy. They held an assortment of former ranks and a jumble of ideas about life and training. Despite being difficult to achieve in this society, this group became one in mind and body and focused on one purpose for a short ten days of their lives.

This place is like a battlefield. Man returns to his original brutal nature. What he hears and sees is insignificant in events engulfed by echoes of carnage.

The world was filled with drinking songs, women's rouge and powder, the luxury of the Genroku townsmen, the showy quilted silk kosode robes of samurai, the influence of dog doctors and dog inspectors, and everything dazzling and unbelievable. Men who wet hand towels at the public bath in the morning and cook on a small *konabe* pot were there as the men who ride on sightseeing boats in the middle of the Sumida River to view wintry scenes amid muted sounds flowing from a shamisen. Every night, haiku poets met in Edoza. The tea ceremony was also trendy. The fires in the unlicensed pleasure district thrived with the presence of humanity. Violators of the decree on pet dogs were arrested as criminals. Groups of vagabonds were seen loitering under bridges. No matter where one looked, the world of Genroku was stained by the two colors. One was the development of animalism for living, playing, and satisfaction. The other was the exact opposite, paupers who were more like filth in the gutters.

At last, December neared. Without waiting for spring, the old and young spirits of forty-seven men would congeal into one and die. Everyone in today's society was enveloped by deep pleasure rather than clinging to slight pleasures. Those deaths will be so enjoyable blood will surge toward their ribs.

104

LISTENING

"I'VE HEARD UESUGI Danjo Daihitsu-dono, the biological son of Kozuke no Suke, is ill."

"With the love of a father for his son, Kozuke no Suke frequently visits to nurse him."

"That's not true. Many retainers and relatives of the chief retainer came and went from Matsuzakacho, but Kozuke no Suke never stepped off the Uesugi estate."

"The rumor is he's already hiding in Yonezawa Castle."

"That's a lie. The shogunate will not be notified."

"He's here! In Matsuzakacho."

"No, he's not."

The nerves of the group were sensitive to the glut of information. They cracked like a ceiling crossbeam on a dry winter night.

Yoshida Chuzaemon from Yamate in Kojimachi and Kuranosuke from the lowlands of Kokucho closely watched the expansive encampment. Only these two did not leave the kotatsu foot warmer.

Except for emergencies, the comrades refrained from

meetings. Wherever anyone went, the residence had a clear connection to someone.

After a long time with no contact, Horibe Yasubei often thought Kada Azumamaro would become suspicious and visited his home unannounced.

"Is he in?"

"He is. And you're Horibe-dono?"

"I was in Zaimokucho."

"Come in."

Azumamaro passed through to the study filled with Chinese and Japanese writings. The scent of ink wafted in the air. He was settling in to write and encircled by scattered colored papers.

He picked up a hawk's feather on the desk, dusted off the guest table, and placed tea utensils on it. Yasubei saw books in the alcove. The moist-looking splashed ink of the five characters of Tenshoko-daijin were visible. As Azumamaro poured the tea, he noticed where Yasubei's eyes focused and said, "Amazing, isn't it?"

"A work by Hosoi Kotaku Sensei?"

"Yes. I heard your respected father Yahei and the sensei are close."

"You also know."

"In that case, this will be a good meeting."

"Aha, but I don't know how friendly. You and Kotaku Sensei are close."

In his heart, Yasubei knew he must avoid careless talk. Early on, Hosoi Kotaku knew the group's intentions and was confided in with no fear of leaks. Perhaps Azumamaro heard of their friendship.

Yasubei considered asking Azumamaro for help because he had been inside the Kira estate once or twice but feared revealing his true intentions. He felt it necessary to harden his courage.

"Ooh, yes, yes, it was this morning. I just remembered while pouring your tea. Nakajima Gorosaku met with the lord of this house."

They probably conversed about the world's trivial matters. Yasubei picked up his teacup.

"Gorosaku. I think I've heard Kuranosuke-dono mention him."

"Yes. Gorosaku boasts like a rich man. He said he'll soon receive an invitation to a tea gathering hosted by Kira Kozuke no Suke."

"What?"

While the startled Yasubei scolded himself for his reaction, he asked, "Is Lord Kira enthusiastic about the tea ceremony?"

"It seems so. He often holds gatherings."

"I see."

Once again, breath burst from his chest.

"Is Gorosaku close to Lord Kira?"

"No. Yohouan, Gorosaku's teacher of the tea ceremony, is a master called Yamada Sohen and a retainer of Ogasawara Sado no Mori, a member of the shogun's Council of Elders. Lord Kozuke no Suke also studied tea following the school of Yohouan. Gorosaku was probably invited to accompany Yohouan. He was ecstatic and seemed to be honored."

"Ha, ha, ha, ha. Can you believe the master of ceremonies invited a rich man like Gorosaku?"

As he tried to look nonchalant, Yasubei was aware his awkward sounding words and oblivious to the taste of the tea. Great joy somersaulted in his chest, and he tensed with anxiety.

Unable to calm down, he left Azumamaro's home before a coherent topic emerged. He waved his hand at the crossroad and shouted, "Palanquin!"

105

YOHOUAN'S CALENDAR

A FEW DAYS earlier, three men moved from Honjo through the back streets of Minami Hatchobori. They were from the households of Kataoka Gengoemon, Kaiga Yazaemon, and Otaka Gengo, the trio known as the Owari Ronin.

Without warning, Yasubei appeared at the gate.

"Hello."

Otaka, on his way out and putting on his footwear, stopped and stared.

Otaka Gengo manipulated the heft of his thickset, muscular body. He had a darkish, lightly pockmarked complexion, and the habit of bending his neck, perhaps the fault of a somewhat short and thick neck.

Many would say at first glance Otaka looked ugly and dimwitted, but peacefulness would wash over a companion sitting opposite him as they listened to the knowledge he gradually shared, looked into his eyes, and observed his demeanor. He was a genius at haiku, writing under the name Shiyou, meaning an embryonic leaf, and more accomplished than most in the tea ceremony. He was a warrior who understood and could write about pathos and was suspected of avoiding the spirit of bravery and martial arts.

"Where are you going?" asked Yasubei, a little out of breath.

"Today's poets' meeting at Kikaku's home."

"Can they wait?"

"Elegance … like the wind, like the water, what should I do?"

"I'm sorry to trouble you."

"I have to go and have no welcome for you."

"Oh, I'm not here to see you," said Yasubei and sat. "Are Kaiga and Kataoka in?"

"No, they're not."

"Well Otaka, I'll quickly tell you."

"All right?"

His big eyes flashed in the lightly pitted face. Yasubei moved forward on his knees and gave a detailed report of what Kada Azumamaro said.

"Well? What do you think?"

"It may be true."

"I can't believe it's a lie."

"Very well, I'll find out."

"I knew this task would be too hard without your help, so I came here before reporting to Kuranosuke-dono. When will you go?"

"I'll need to prepare a little but soon."

"Better than going as a haiku master, wouldn't he find you more believable disguised as a wholesaler from Kyoto?"

"Yes, of course. But I don't have the time to get ready today."

"Tomorrow is not too late. It'll be important to put on airs."

Yamada Sohen's home was located in the Takabashi area of Fukugawa. The river encroached on the back garden to create refined charm. He looked up at the Yohouan signboard at the gate to the tea ceremony cottage. As he entered the gate to the silent moss-covered path from the thick growth of secluded shrubbery, the only sounds were the fallen leaves.

"You wish to learn about tea?" asked the aged Sohen.

"Yes, I do," Otaka Gengo answered and bowed. Lately, this tea master had seen many men of refined taste who shared this interest.

Gengo was dressed as a townsman. His clothes and accessories gave the impression of the generous proprietor of a large store. He spoke softly.

"I am Nishijinya Rihei, a textile wholesaler from Kyoto. The fact is I've been engaged by a daimyo and frequently visit this area. I don't know what to do with free time during my short business trips here. I've always admired you and came to seek enlightenment."

"Well, you do have a little understanding."

"I wouldn't say that."

"Learning will be fine."

"Thank you so much."

He presented a gold-leaf paper with *1,000 gold coins* written on it as the entrance fee.

"A thank you for your consideration."

The envelope was accepted with ease.

"First things first," said Otaka Gengo patting his chest in relief. The gift of a gratuity was presented at each future visit. He sensed indifference to gold and silver in his companion and little by little observed the style of a tea gathering at the Kira residence.

Sohen was delighted to have another pupil. From the first meeting, their growing genial relationship was amusing. If all went well, Gengo would ask to attend a tea gathering at the Kira residence and accompany Sohen.

However, burdened by the lives of his forty comrades, he stepped onto thin ice. If he saw a crack, the destruction would be complete.

"This is the heart of the tea ceremony."

He braced himself, threw away his readiness to learn about tea for the secret plan, and faced Sohen to immerse himself in tea from his spirit. After that, Sohen opened up.

But the chance never came. The calendar advanced to the days of December.

PART XIV

THE RAID BY SUN TZU OF THE KOTATSU HEATER

106

A LOSS OF NERVE

K URANOSUKE WAS SENSITIVE to the cold. His visiting comrades often joked, "He must have been born in the hottest days of summer."

He admitted he whined much more than others about a chill in the air.

"When winter comes, I'm like a toad sleeping underground. I have no pride. Please forgive me," he said, sitting by the kotatsu heater. To his left, a bookrest held a book, and thick silk wadding stuffed behind his back made him look hunchbacked.

The ronin house in Kokucho was ready for winter. When he opened the shoji screen, he could see the redness of the southern sky beyond the veranda. He looked up at the icicles that never melted hanging like swords from the rain gutters in the shade.

"I'm back."

It was Chikara.

"Is it done?" asked the voice from the kotatsu.

"Yes, I asked everyone to help."

"Thank you all."

A letter announcing tomorrow's meeting made the rounds. The secret code gradually became known and rapidly spread. Still, it was always a struggle to transmit the will of the nerve center in a short time to more than fifty men scattered throughout Edo.

The leaders squatted around the kotatsu.

"Chikara, there seems to be a gap over there. Close the door tightly."

"It's shut."

"Wind is slipping in somewhere."

"Today, the cold is bone-chilling."

"It's probably colder outside."

"December starts today."

"Uh-huh."

"Father, a detestable comrade has surfaced among us. Nakamura Seizaemon took the name Suzuta Juhachi."

"Another deserter?"

"We trusted Nakamura-sama. On the night Takumi no Kami-sama's body was sent to Sengakuji Temple for burial, he cut off his topknot before the corpse and vowed revenge."

"I see ..."

Kuranosuke's ear facing the shoji screen looked painfully cold. After hearing this news, he laid that side of his face on the kotatsu quilt and narrowed his eyes like a sleepy cat.

Was he listening?

Chikara's shoulder muscles, two times stronger than his father's, tense involuntarily.

"He's not the only one. Tanaka Sadashiro and Nakata Riheiji vanished without a trace. You don't want to hear the worst one, Father."

Kuranosuke turned up his face.

"Oyamada?"

"Yes, Oyamada Shozaemon."

"I've heard."

"Who told you?"

"While you were out, Fuwa Kazuemon stopped by and told me."

"Isn't he outrageous? To this day, that man ..."

Chikara's cheeks burned with the emotions of an indignant young man. This happened yesterday, the last day of the month.

He told an unbelievable tale. His comrades believed the serious and unflappable Oyamada Shozaemon had a change of heart on his way to visit his aged father Ikkan. He entered Kataoka Gengoemon's home and ran off with three ryo in gold and a padded silk kosode kimono.

Chikara heard and came in from outside with his blood boiling. He vented his despair to his father.

"No, he was prone to losing his nerve. If I'm honest about myself, I possess every human weakness, such as cowardice, regret, whining, and confusion. Chikara, this is not a problem of other men."

"Yessir."

"Be careful, you talk a little too much."

"Yes, I'll be careful."

"Faces will be missing from tomorrow's meeting. When the hard work of our comrades is about to bear fruit, some fish will flee, and the waters will muddy. But that's all right."

107

THE PLOVER LECTURE

THE PRETENSE OF the gathering was a mutual finance association.

It was December 2. Men in the varied dress of doctors, Confucian scholars, merchants, soldiers, and monks appeared among the faces trickling in for the lecture in the teahouse in front of Fukagawa Hachimangu Shrine.

"It's been a while."

"How long?"

The attendees casually greeted each other at the gate. No one suspected a thing at the teahouse.

This sort of meeting was not uncommon. They settled into their seats, chatted for a while, and called for tea. Kuranosuke gauged the time.

"We'll begin now."

He faced the group and straightened his sitting position.

"I thank you all for coming. As you know, the day will be here soon. Will this great secret unfold as a matter of course? From the start, we were of one mind and body. From here on, there is no reason for differing views. Now, the renewal of our written pledge to god will further solidify our unity, and I don't believe it's meaningless. If there are no objections, I ask you to seal them with blood."

"Yoshida-san," he said and signaled with his eyes.

Yoshida Chuzaemon and Hara Soemon worked through the previous evening to write the pledge. Chuzaemon pulled it out of his pocket and handed it to Soemon.

"I appreciate your hard work."

"You're welcome," said Soemon and straightened his posture. "I'll read it now." The vow had four points.

Here is the first.

*Out of respect for Reikou Inden-dono, the samurai agree on
the goal of killing Kira Kozuke no Suke.*

Cowards who changed their minds kept emerging. The remaining men were warned about the need to solidify the all-important unity. The soul of the late lord would witness their agreement.

For the second point,

*The date of the raid shall be pledged.
There will not be unequal acclaim for meritorious deeds. All
the conspirators will share in the success.*

In the third point,

Discipline and temperance.

In point four,

If Kozuke no Suke is killed, his partisans will not be driven away.

The fourth point ended with:

If we fail in this solemn undertaking, we will be exactly like cowards who run away.

Soemon read that part a second time.

"Pass it around please."

The written pledge moved from hand to hand. Each man wrote his full name and sealed it with blood. The oath circulated in silent solemnity, undisturbed by even a cough. The names totaled forty-seven, everyone present that day.

Until the previous month of November, the comrades numbered fifty-five. By the last day of the month, the number decreased by five. A short two days later, three more men fled forever.

Chikara's heart remembered his father's words yesterday, "Is this how it ends?"

His father sat pained by the cold but seemed oblivious to it. Like the rich man who delighted in major construction as he watched the framework being raised, his eyes were serene.

"Are you finished?" he asked the man beside him.

"We're done."

Soemon rolled up and put away the signed secret oath.

"Now, read this," said Kuranosuke and pulled out a letter from inside his kimono.

Memo of Understanding of the Participants
Rendezvous point on the day of the raid and the appointed time.
Handling of the raising of Kozuke no Suke's head
Rules followed en route to Sengakuji Temple.
Caution when the head of his son Sahyoue is raised high.
Treatment of wounded allies
Signaling by whistle blows
Gong strike for a full withdrawal

Withdrawal route decided at the back gate.
The pursuit attack, Uesugi force, and behavior during a clash

Various details were written down.

"As expected, you anticipated your leader's concerns."

The men recited from memory, copied, and stored the details deep in their bodies.

"Chief Retainer." Horibe Yahei looked at him from a party of four or five men in front.

"Now, the entire plan will be prepared, but what has just been presented missed one point."

"Please speak up if anything concerns you. Go ahead, Elder."

"I see another problem. If an emergency arises, like an official of the shogunate hears a rumor or the government summons an ally, what should we do? With all the gossip swirling around Edo, we can't say that would not cause unexpected harm."

Kuranosuke slapped his knees.

"I never thought of that, an oversight by a careful man. Elder, I truly thank you."

Kuranosuke mulled over this serious problem.

"In the rare event this happens, we will privately request a full inquiry. Given the circumstances since the surrender of Ako, we have no other option but to be forthright."

"Yes, that's reasonable."

Chuzaemon and Hara Soemon agreed. The group was of the same mind.

Dusk fell and the sky was overcast. The charcoal fire was kindled, but the cold penetrated to their bones.

"That seems to be all."

"Any other issues?"

"No, everything's been covered."

Kuranosuke called for sake and, for the first time, relaxed. The business of the mutual finance association was addressed in the small talk. In time, each man finished his rice topped off with green tea and left.

Scattered frost whitened the road. A tenacious plover flying off the coast frequently cried in the darkness.

108

A YOUNG LADY IN THE RAIN

ON THE NEXT day, December 3, Horibe Yasubei was alone in the hideout in Hayashicho, Honjo. He went over to an ink stone box and stamped what looked like a memorandum. The note listed the weapons brought here in small quantities over the past six months. Not written clearly originally, only Yasubei could read it.

The list began with 12 spears, followed by 2 each of *naginata* pole swords, battle-axes, bows, and short bows.

More items were listed.

Bamboo ladders
    Hammers
    Crowbars
    Levers
    Large saws 2
    Clamps 60
    Lock-picking rods 16
    Pine torches 1 for each man
    Dark lanterns 2
    Gong 1

Whistles 1 for each man

"These whistles are a surprise."

He went out to the narrow porch and stepped down into his footwear. The shed looked like storage for pickled vegetables or sacks of charcoal on the dirty space in the back. Yasubei entered and inspected a large basket covered by a straw mat.

"Anyone here?" a voice called out from the front.

He hurried to cover the basket.

"Who is it?"

"It's me."

Outside the lattice, he glimpsed Otaka Gengo, now the proprietor of a haberdashery in Kyoto.

"I'll be right out."

"I'm in a hurry. I'm coming in."

Gengo opened the wooden side door and entered the back. Beyond the thicket, he could see the narrow river coated with a thin sheet of ice.

"Horibe."

He lowered his voice the moment he saw Yasubei's face.

"I'm pleased to bring good news."

"What is it?"

"Today, I attended my usual practice for the tea ceremony with Yohouan. After the lesson, as I was preparing to go home, I casually said I'd come for my next lesson on the morning of the sixth."

"Uh-huh."

"Then Sohen said the sixth would be a problem. He has plans to attend a tea gathering at the Kira residence on the sixth and told me to pick another day."

"You did it!" shouted Yasubei, without thinking.

Whether asleep or awake, he prayed to hear this. They

uncovered proof of a day Kira Kozuke no Suke would be at the residence. If the tea gathering will be held on the morning of the sixth, then, without a doubt, he will be at the residence during the evening of the fifth.

"Kuranosuke must be told soon."

"Yes, immediately. The morning of the fifth is the day after tomorrow. We must prepare now."

"We have to be ready at any time."

"How will we enter and leave the Kira estate?"

"I'll take care of that. You must go to Kokucho right now."

"Then I'll leave it to you," said Gengo and left.

After locking up, Yasubei rushed from the Hayashicho hideout.

The nerves of his silent comrades concealed all around were strung tight on this day. They spent the day waiting for a man to fly in with written orders from the Kokucho headquarters and anxious to get ready.

However, the fourth passed with no news.

Not one man budged from his position. If he were out and missed the call to action, he would trigger a breakdown in discipline and be disgraced by his late arrival.

On the morning of the fifth, cold misty rain fell.

Kanzaki Yogoro contacted Yasubei in Hayashicho and then put on a sedge hat and straw rain cape. He got drenched watching Kira's residence in Matsuzakacho.

"Good. I have a clear view."

This neighborhood was dangerous ground for him. Until this fall, he hung out a shop curtain as the haberdasher Zenbei and was acquainted with many people in the neighborhood. But the world forgets.

He brushed by several familiar faces but said nothing. Yogoro even passed the home where he used to live.

"Ah, it's still vacant."

He looked up at the closed door on the second floor and was struck by sadness. For a short time, his thoughts changed with each moment.

"Oh ..."

He stopped in his tracks. A pretty young woman stood dripping wet under the canopy rotting in the rain. Why was she standing under the eaves of the vacant building with no haberdasher's shop curtain hanging outside?

While stroking the storm shutters, her soft voice said, "May I see the ornamental hairpins? ... There are none.... Well, do you have hairstyling oil?"

109

———

HEAVEN'S WILL

THE COLD DRIZZLE beating down was driven by endless gusts of wind thrashing the door of the vacant building.

The young woman seemed oblivious to the cold. Her fawn-colored satin obi sash was saturated and dripping.

Knock, knock, knock.

Her white fist tapped on the door.

"Emoshichi-san, Azukiya Emoshichi-san ..." she whimpered and pressed against the door.

"Are you asleep? Please, I'd like to buy hairstyling oil. Open the door. Please Emoshichi-san."

Frozen in place in the rain, Kanzaki Yogoro watched her. All the blood in his body congealed. The only warmth in his body pushed against his eyelids.

"That's Kume."

I have no excuse for my crime. If this were simple fate, Kume's lover Yato Emoshichi would be with him and that soaking wet figure would be taken somewhere for a warm embrace. He wished to make this sweet first love bear fruit.

His apology was only to himself. Kume no longer

behaved as she did in her normal state of mind. She would not understand any joy given to her now.

His sole thought was I'm so sorry. Only an apology filled his heart. He thought about taking off his rain cape and making her wear it but hesitated, fearing unwanted attention.

Three or four carpenter's apprentices, looking like wet mice, ran up.

"She's here. She's here."

"Kume-san is here."

"You came here again?"

"Why do you come here every day?"

They yelled as they surrounded and guided her home.

Yogoro glided past a muddy puddle and was too scared to look back. He finally returned to his senses after the wall enclosing the Kira residence was far behind him, and the endless waters of the Ogawa River reflected in his eyes from the Ryogoku shore.

He stayed in the area for some time and kept a sly watch on the back gate of the Kira residence as he walked the streets of Matsuzakacho. A painted palanquin exited the gate accompanied by six foot soldiers and two low-ranking samurai guards.

It looked like an ordinary outing. However, about seven samurai wearing sedge hats, straw rain capes, and straw sandals followed about sixty feet behind. They appeared to be the guards for the palanquin they trailed.

That may be … ?

Intuition struck, and Yogoro followed them under the eaves of buildings to the vicinity of Shinohashi Bridge. The number of waiting attendants kept growing.

That's Kozuke no Suke! He was sure.

In time, the palanquin arrived at the back gate of the Uesugi residence.

Peering from the shadows of trees, Yogoro glimpsed a head of gray hair worn in a knot resembling an oak silkworm and a kosode kimono bearing a hollyhock crest. That confirmed what he saw.

It's him.

He ran, oblivious to the splashing mud, to Kokucho to report to Kuranosuke then returned to Matsuzakacho to watch for Kozuke no Suke's return. He kept close watch like he was studying a nest of spiders, and was ready to raise the alarm in nearby vacant lots, eating and drinking establishments, and shadows of the temple gates.

Night fell without the return home of Kozuke no Suke's vehicle.

Each moment brought a report to Kuranosuke who never left the kotatsu.

The hot-blooded crowd grew impatient. One came, then another, and in no time, a crowd packed around Kuranosuke's kotatsu.

"Chief Retainer, we must act."

"If the gathering is tomorrow morning, Kozuke no Suke will return home, even if it's midnight."

"If we miss this chance ..."

They pressed for decisive action.

Some burst out in anger and kicked the tatami when they saw indecision cross the thoughtful face at the kotatsu.

He sat up straight when an ally said, "We will wait."

The men's will compelled only by a force ready to erupt heated up to rip open the Earth's crust.

Others were sickened by suppressing that force and losing patience at the sight of Kuranosuke.

Seeing this, Horibe Yasubei said, "It's no good," and came in looking disappointed. "I visited Nakajima Gorosaku to fish for answers. He said Lord Kira had a problem with the sixth, and the morning gathering was canceled."

Yogoro said, "He'll probably stay at the Uesugi residence tonight."

Their reports were consistent. The news forced the younger contingent to back down.

Frequent reports stated Kozuke no Suke would be in his residence on the eleventh. Kuranosuke forbade action that night and began to lean toward an attack on the night of the eleventh.

Also on that day, the shogun would visit the mansion of Matsudaira Ukyo no Daibu, Master of the Western Capital Office. As a consequence, the fire watch and security would be strict throughout the city. Somehow or another, every man understood this would complicate their serious mission.

Why is our luck so bad?

But as impatient as they were for a chance, their blood seethed, and their bones shook. Not one more deserter emerged.

110

LEAVING THE KOTATSU

N O ONE KNOWS where heaven makes connections. No one knows when heaven's will will emerge.

Not far from the homes of Yasubei and the others who lived undercover in Hayashicho, Honjo was a grimy old temple squeezed between the blocks occupied by craftsmen. Yokogawa Kanpei visited often in his leisure time.

"Is Mouami-san in?" he called toward the narrow abbot's quarters.

"Yes, he is," said a voice mimicking his own that belonged to the Buddhist priest who appeared. He was a jocular man of fifty.

Kanpei did not know this priest's name, but he overheard the local people calling him by a name that meant blind masseur. The priest did not seem to object. As his name said, this priest was blind, unable to see colors.

Yokogawa Kanpei worked as a guard of the gunpowder storehouse in Ako and took an interest in firearms. The priest learned about single-shot gun technology before his vision failed and often discussed taking life with Kanpei. At some point, they became friends.

"Yes, yes, if you came, I thought I'd let you have a peek. Again, I hate to impose, but I have something I'd like you to read?" said Mouami like he just remembered. This was the usual favor he asked. Kanpei never looked annoyed and scrutinized the document.

"Is it a letter?"

"Yes," said Mouami while his hand searched the top of a small desk and picked up one sheet. "Please read this to me."

He glimpsed the name of the sender of the sealed letter.

From: Saito Kunai
To: Kira-sama
Inside the gate of Matsuzakacho

"Oh?" quietly slipped from Kanpei. Saito Kunai! He was a retainer of the Kira clan. Kanpei's hand was shaking. He felt like he was holding a secret treasure able to destroy his sight.

"Uh-huh ... This?"

"Yes."

"When did it arrive?"

"A few moments ago."

He thought about the day. It was December 10.

Kanpei broke the seal as he quieted his leaping heart. The text was simple.

The evening gathering will be held on December 14. Disregard all previous arrangements.

Mouami nodded as he listened.

"Oh, all right," said the priest, untroubled.

"Do you have a response?"

"Yes, if it's not too much trouble."

"My pleasure," said Kanpei and wrote the concise and detailed acknowledgment instructed by Mouami.

Seeing that no servant came, Kanpei said, "If you like, I can deliver this to Kira-sama."

"Don't be ridiculous," said Mouami shaking his head. "I can't ask you to write and act as the messenger in place of the servant."

"We are friends, so why are you so reserved? I have business that takes me to Ryogoku." He lightheartedly added, "Mouami-san, is there a letterbox at poor temples?"

"Excuse me. Even a poor temple has a letterbox."

"Well, give the letter to me and I'll drop it in the box and be on my way."

When Kanpei left by the stone steps, he spontaneously looked at the vast sky.

"Thank you. Thank you," he said under his breath.

Kanpei carried himself like a servant when he entered the Kira estate.

He soon left. His legs were already leaping into the air on their way to the Kokucho headquarters.

"The fourteenth!" said Kuranosuke with unusual power. This piqued his senses. His face lit up.

He's dead. I have Lord Kira's severed head. His heart spoke of this intuition. The fourteenth was a marvel. It landed on the anniversary of Takumi no Kami's death.

At that moment, an express letter arrived from Otaka Gengo.

On the fourteenth of this month, at the invitation of Dayu Omino-mamori, a tea gathering will be held. The tea master Sohen of Yohouan will also be in attendance.

At last, the time has come! thought Kuranosuke.

A delay like before was a slight possibility. They neglected nothing and did their best in pursuit of the enemy.

"Yokogawa."

"Yessir."

"Return to Matsuzakacho. Whisper this news in their ears of the men hiding and watching that area. Do not miss one man."

"Done."

When Kanpei left, he called toward the other room, "Chikara. Chikara."

"Get ready. You will go to Yoshida Chuzaemon's home and then return here."

"Yes, Father. And you?"

Kuranosuke muttered, "I'll also make rounds," then said, "My work here is done," and rose from the kotatsu.

PART XV

THE SEASON OF THE MOON, SNOW, AND FLOWERS

111

THE ROOKIES' WOODEN BOWLS

UNUSUALLY HEAVY SNOW fell that year. Even long-lived old men opened their eyes wide and gazed outside. Snow began falling on the eleventh. Large heavy snowflakes did not drop down; the wind whipped around silver slivers resembling shaved ice. Dawn on the twelfth came with snow. The thirteenth ended with snow. On the fourteenth, greater Edo was rounded hills and valleys of snow. At the end of the day, the world was mostly silent of human voices.

He could hear the clopping teeth of geta sandals in the snow. An old man of seventy-six years covered by a kotatsu quilt rested his rounded back against a pillar and propped up his white topknot.

"Granny, did you notice any activity at the gate or see any guests pass through?"

The old man with the remarkably loud voice was Horibe Yasubei's father, Yahei Kanamaru.

Just inside the part of town entered when traveling west from the banks of the Ogawa River, the elderly husband

and wife set up a temporary hideout in Yonezawacho in Yanokura.

His wife's reply from the bustling kitchen was prompt.

"Yes, I did."

The kitchen at twilight filled with the aroma of stew and food simmering in broth. Yasubei's wife Sachi was busy giving instructions to a relative's daughter who came to help and the servant girls.

"Sugaya Hannojo-sama and Hayami Touzaemon-sama came together."

The sixteen- or seventeen-year-old relative wore her obi sash tied perfectly, looking like today's gatekeeper. She placed both hands on the ground before Yahei at the kotatsu and gave her report.

"They went to the second floor?"

"Yes."

"For the guests who arrived late, if a group of unfamiliar faces shows up, tell your aunt or me immediately, but usually few pass through."

He remembered his unfinished letters and put on his eyeglasses. Five or six letters caught his eye. After finishing them, he wrote two more. He said to himself, "These are mainly farewell letters, so I'll hold nothing back."

Before long, the cheerful voices of the guests and the sounds of people moving around bounced off the room's ceiling brightened by lantern light.

"Well, I've seen enough."

He took off his eyeglasses, looked at the ceiling, and broke into a wide grin. From the cupboard in the next room, his elderly wife asked, "Grandpa, would you like to eat?"

"I'm fine," he said and rose from the kotatsu.

"I wrote these letters to people in the home province

and family I have no way to see. Please send them by express messenger after I'm gone."

"Yes, I'll do that."

"When can you bring the trays upstairs?"

"Any time is fine."

"Thank you for all your efforts. It's probably chilly in the kitchen on a wintry day like this. To think we've lived together for forty years. Today, I will eat the evening meal prepared by your hands with gratitude. You have been a great help for so many years."

Their niece interrupted.

"Uncle, Kakimi Sanai-sama of Kokucho and Senboku Ju'an-sama are here."

"Oh, they've come?"

Yahei went out to the entry. The two guests were taking off their snow capes. Kakimi Sanai was Oishi Kuranosuke, and Onodera Junai had changed his name to Senboku Ju'an.

"Good evening."

"Good evening …"

This evening, their usual warm greetings with their eyes brought home the gravity of the situation. The guests climbed the ladder behind the master Yahei to the open space on the second floor. On the twenty tatami mats covering the floor, except for twelve feet, were nearly twenty guests in idle conversations. The only seats left were the formal head seats in the alcove.

They spotted Yoshida Chuzaemon beside the empty seats. Kuranosuke's eyes met his.

"Excuse me," said Kuranosuke and sat.

"I told Chikara, Ushioda, Chikamatsu, and Mimura to hand over the vacant house in Kokucho to the landlord and to settle any loose ends and not stop by here but go to Hayashicho. We will see them later."

After Kuranosuke apologized to his host, Yoshida Chuzaemon said, "Although my son Sawaemon accepted your kind invitation, please excuse his rudeness in going earlier with Fuwa Kazuemon and Terasaka Yoshiemon to Maebara's home in Aioicho."

The men made themselves at home and never changed the conversation as evening fell. Yasubei's wife, Sachi, and the servant girls brought up and placed the trays before them. Kuranosuke began his greeting and raised his cup.

"Elder, I wish to express my deepest gratitude to you."

"My pleasure ... It was nothing," said the elder Yahei, serving as host to the young group of samurai in the lower seats. "Now that this spread has eaten up my fortune, there will be no holding back out of politeness. Leftovers would be a waste. Please eat and drink to your fill."

However, the young men showed restraint that night. As they faintly flushed, they quietly poured each other drinks. Each tray held a bowl of vegetable and poultry soup with dried chestnuts and kelp. Yahei picked up the chopsticks and said, "This is Granny's way of congratulating each of you on your departure and leaving your mark on this world. But remember this, the old men will not be defeated," then he sipped broth from his bowl.

112

A DIFFERENCE IN AGE

I N A SNOWSTORM big enough to stop palanquins and carriages, the men's movements went unheard in the world. With speed and no sound, they methodically made their way to this evening of December 14. Everything unfolded in the short time from yesterday until today.

The fourteenth as the date of the year-end tea gathering at the Kira estate was certain. Kuranosuke, who stressed being careful, was painstakingly cautious on this day. He had a comrade deliver a jar of tea to Yohouan Sohen in Fukagawa Takahashi. He asked Otaka Gengo, disguised as the textile wholesaler Rihei, to observe Yohouan-sama's discerning eye for tea and monitor the day's events.

Yohouan's assistant told him that his master was attending Kira-sama's tea gathering but allowed him to leave the jar of tea.

The team of scouts watching Matsuzakacho reported Yohouan's palanquin passed through the gate onto the estate.

There's no mistake!

Tonight, Kira Kozuke no Suke will sleep in the mansion in Matsuzakacho. By coincidence, a deep layer of snow blanketed greater Edo on the anniversary of the death of the late lord.

Beginning the previous evening, his comrades busily wrote letters home and packaged keepsakes for mothers, wives, and friends. The man who rented the house and known as a secondhand goods dealer closed up the house. He apologized to the landlord for leaving for a distant province and said he would spend the night at a relative's home. Neighborhood debts and shop leases were promptly settled.

Everyone awakened to the lightness of his body at peace. They would break away from the bonds to relatives and the troubles of the world. The deep emotions they harbored were not from their lives. From now on, no other thought would occupy their minds. Not one was conflicted over participating or deserting. These men, freed from all cares, calmly thought about one important matter.

"The smoke from the tobacco is thick."

When the trays were taken away and replaced with tea, Yahei had the shoji screens to the veranda opened wide. The fire of the charcoal or the stale smells of so much humanity fled from the eaves in a purple haze.

"Ah, the moon."

"Has it cleared up?"

"Look at the waves on the Ogawa."

A part of the river shimmered whiter than the snow under the moonlight between the roofs of the townhouses on the Yanokura shore. A couple of lights flickered in Ryogoku on the opposite shore.

This place was separated from the mansion of Kira Kozuke no Suke by a road five or six blocks long. The town was silent. Was Kozuke no Suke nestled under his quilt for the night?

"Ah, it's a good wind."

A few of the young men blew pure white breaths. Their cheeks flushed from drink were exposed to the cold air.

Kuranosuke huddled with senior retainers, like Yoshida Chuzaemon, Onodera Junai, and Hara Soemon, to search for consensus on the steps to take.

The matter seemed to be money. Kuranosuke informed the elders that the spending of the public money he had at hand and ledgers detailing the income and expenses left his hands yesterday and were delivered to Elder Ochiai Yosaemon in the clan of the lord's widow, Yozen'in.

The total amount of public money held by Kuranosuke was just 651 ryo. The interest on the money lent to buy Yozen'in's make-up totaled about 90 ryo.

If the clan had been restored and Takumi no Kami's younger brother, Daigaku no Kami, appointed as its head, that money would have been the first deposit allotted to restore the Asano clan. However, Kuranosuke's hardship went unrewarded. And the money was spent in ways he disliked.

During the more than 650 days since they scattered from Ako, the living expenses of the ronin have been used on military expenditures for revenge. This resulted in a deficit of seven ryo as the last figure.

The young contingent had nothing to do with money. With no freedom and too much poverty, the suffering in the hearts of Kuranosuke and the elder group led them to spend money they did not have. Even now, talk of money was kept far from the younger men.

Hayami Tozaemon asked, "Won't the rest of us leaving together raise suspicions in the guardhouse?"

"Yes, we'll trickle out a few at a time and scatter," Kura-nosuke calculated, and the younger men left in small groups.

A short time ago, Hayami Tozaemon wondered why he did not see the landlord and elder, Yahei. He went downstairs and to ask Yasubei's wife Sachi where to find her father-in-law.

"I'd like to thank him."

"It's the fault of his age. He could be called spineless but left the gathering before it ended and is resting in the room over there."

Hayami Tozaemon slid open the door to the room she pointed to and peeked in. Yahei was on his side with his legs under a kotatsu warmer covered by a futon. In his role as host, this evening, he heartily dipped into the sake and was sound asleep snoring loudly like a young man.

"He looks ready," said Tozaemon, his voice revealing admiration as he stared at the big-hearted old man resembling a warrior of long ago. Sugaya Hannojo standing behind him looked back and said, "As I see it, there's only a difference in age."

113

LEAVING YANOKURA

IT WAS PAST midnight.

The many guests were gone. Clanking sounds of long-cold earthenware rang from the kitchen. After everything was put away, silence filled the house. The sounds of cracks ran through the roof and ceiling beams buried under snow in the late night.

"Uncle!"

Yahei's nephews Sato Josaemon and Horibe Kujuro dashed in and stopped to scan the house. Sachi slipped down from the second floor and watched them for a few moments.

"He's in there asleep," she said.

"What? He's sleeping?"

Looking doubtful, the two barged into the elder Yahei's sitting room.

The raid is tonight! In a breath on this night, the struggle mounted over more than six hundred and fifty days of the Ako ronin would be swept away. The red blood of the retainers will be given to the soul of the late lord!

Yet, weren't they listening to his contented snores?

The two couldn't say he was a hopeless old man but stood and stared at the foot of the lantern. They could not understand how anyone could sleep under a kotatsu at a time like this. His wife, who was about to turn seventy, massaged the legs of the seventy-six-year-old man with all her might. Concern drove the nephews to his side.

"Uncle. Uncle," said Kujuro.

The old couple lifted their faces together.

"Oh? What is it?"

Josaemon said, "Your comrades already departed for the three rendezvous points of Yasubei's home in Hayashicho, Honjo; Sugino Juheiji's hideout in Tokuemon-cho; and Maebara Isuke's store in Aioicho. Did you know that, Uncle?"

"Do I know? Half of them raised cups in celebration here and left. But it's still too early."

"The snow is piled high. And we can't be irresponsible and make the old man go out early and trudge through it, right?"

The listless old man was not about to docilely accept the words of his young nephews.

He swept aside the kotatsu quilt.

"Josaemon."

"Yes ..."

"I was told. And you will come with me to Juheiji's home in Tokuemoncho."

"From the beginning, I've been going with Kujuro to that neighborhood."

Meanwhile, they heard the old man shuffle into an adjoining room. He took down a spear from the horizontal beam in the unlit room. His bent hip managed to straighten like a released bow. He stroked the spear a few times.

"I've been inside a little too long. Kujuro, shorten this handle about eight inches and replace the butt end," said Yahei and passed the spear to him.

Kujuro shortened the spear handle as ordered and returned it to his uncle. Yahei struck the tip of the replaced butt end two or three times against a garden rock to make it ring.

"Yes, this is good. Very good," he said, nodding in approval.

Carrying the spear under his arm, he went out the entry gate. His wife's eyes followed the gray hairs on the temples of the ronin she stood beside for over forty years. However, Yahei looked around and saw no one.

He turned and shouted, "Sachi! Sachi!"

Sachi's sobbing voice slipped under the sliding papered door to the small adjoining room. Yahei had lowered one leg into his footgear.

"You silly woman! If Yasubei hears you, he'll despair. More than him, your father-in-law will feel shame."

Concerned about the old man's legs, Josaemon went around to face him.

"Uncle, is that footgear good enough?"

"Uh-huh. They're ready at the Sugino house."

The old man went outside and peered at the sky. He heard the squeaks from oars rowing down the Ogawa.

"Sachi, do you have anything to say? Anything to say to Yasubei?"

She couldn't answer. Then he heard Sachi's voice from a window.

"Go in good spirits. Go freely to the future because I'll be here."

"Yes, yes. You should say that to Yasubei, too. All of you, live happy lives."

Sachi and Yahei's wife could hear the crunching of the

three men's footsteps on the frozen solid snow for some time. The women could not quite believe the men left with the promise of never returning home.

114

FRAGRANT ATTIRE

T HIS WAS NOT a soba noodle shop, but anyone who'd like a meal of soba would order out and eat the delivered meal here. It was a teahouse called Kamedaya across the way in Ryogoku.

Boisterous laughter burst from the second floor. During the day, it was the amusement quarter. Many stores stayed open until late at night in this area and the men's presence didn't raise suspicions.

Kaiga Yazaemon looked outside from time to time.

"Hayami and Sugaya are passing by," he whispered to Otaka Gengo.

"Get them."

"Get them?" asked Okajima Yasoemon near the stairs and rushed down.

"The snowy scene looks nice."

When Okajima returned with the two, the teahouse's proprietor followed carrying a slip of paper on a dirty counter ink stone.

"You gentlemen look cultured. Will you compose a haiku verse to finish this?"

Kataoka Gengoemon stopped eating to say, "Proprietor, it's best if you don't ask. This bunch will happily scribble all over a papered sliding partition or a folding screen you didn't ask for."

"What? Don't worry. They're not valuable."

"Do you write haiku, too?"

"Yes, when business is slow. I'm in a crown verse writing competition, so a shoddy fake is fine."

"That's funny.... What do you have so far?"

"This poem's opening phrase *How does* came from a master yesterday, but no one added a good last part to the verse."

"In that case, have that man add it," said Gengoemon, indicating Otaka Gengo with his eyes. The proprietor swiftly pointed the ink stone box and writing paper in his direction and approached.

"What? You want me to add the crown verse."

Otaka Gengo picked up the brush and below *How does* wrote

a mulberry bow pass through a rock?

The eyes of the men eating their cups of soba read the poem in silence then laughed. The teahouse master went downstairs without understanding it meant the force of will focused on a goal will bring success against overwhelming odds.

Two in the morning approached. The fires were out in the back streets of the unlicensed pleasure district, home to women who wear white face powder. Seven or eight men streamed outside and closed the door at Kamedaya and acted like they were waiting.

"It's time."

"We'll go in a little while."

They split into two groups at the crossroads and took different routes.

Three or four men, including Otaka and Kataoka, ran at a faster pace to the home of Horibe Yasubei in Hayashicho, Honjo.

It's coming!

They were filled with hope. This evening, Yasubei hosted another celebration of the raid in his home. After everything was readied, the men gathered in Yanokura. Others who waited for this night in scattered locations began arriving at the rendezvous point.

In the back garden, they opened the packs, boxes, and straw bundles storing weapons, apparel, and other gear for the raid.

Guards hid in the shadows along the road in front of the house and at the crossroads.

Preparations took little time and effort. The men cast off their usual dress and changed into firemen's uniforms for the raid on the cloudless night.

"All of you look transformed into fine warriors."

The men were impressed by the appearances of their comrades, especially, Yoshida Chuzaemon who was tall with muscular shoulders and striking features. White horizontal leather stripes were inserted into black leather on his *kabuto* helmet. A *Hachimanza* hole pierced the helmet's top. Its visor was scarlet. The curved *fuki-gaeshi* side projections were white woolen cloth. The gauze *shinobi-no-o* chin cord was tied deep under his chin.

His undergarment was two layers of pale blue *habutai* silk padding under chain mail and stitched to a black tea-colored quilted, short-sleeved kosode jacket with a short-ened hem. Both arms were thrust through mismatched unpadded gauntlets. A large braided tasuki cord tucked back the sleeves. And he wore chain long underpants and military-style straw sandals.

On a sleeve was written *Yoshida Chuzaemon Kanesuke*.

A poem of his last words in this world was bound to the back of the neck plate armor of his hood.

> *My thoughts gather for you.*
> *Morning winds through the pines scatter*
> *the deep, white snow.*

Everyone in this squad, except Oishi Kuranosuke, looked up to this man as their deputy commander.

The younger men chose gaudy braided tasuki cords, scarlet crepe cords, or purple leather cords.

A matching metal visor was inserted on the inside of the fire hood. Some preferred figured satin and others chose satin damask.

They wore gauntlets and leggings. The kosode coats all bore the crest and had bleached cloth sewn to both sleeves. These were the fellowship marks of the allied comrades. Each man wrote his full name, province of birth, and age on it, and his full name on a golden leather tag then sewed it to the back tasuki. Some wrote a farewell poem or haiku.

The tasuki cord was a mix of a braided cord, scarlet silk crepe, and leather, and a chain was twisted around it all.

At the end of a string hidden in the sleeve was a whistle. These would signal the raising of Kozuke no Suke's head or the retreat.

Under their sleeves, three or four men concealed special daggers and ropes for tying up people.

Chuzaemon carried a new white fan for sending messages to the authorities and one other item, the baton carried by the second in command.

A respiratory drug and a stimulant were tied with thread to his collar to put in his mouth during a hard fight.

A small amount of a blood-clotting drug, rice cakes, and fried rice rode at his hip.

And each man received one ryo.

All of these preparations were aimed at the goal and the necessary actions. However, everyone prepared only one item unrelated to the night's objective. What was that? A fragrance was placed inside of each man's clothing and the neck plate of his hood to be relished after death.

115

SNOW ECHOES

THE ROAD FROM Hayashicho in Honjo to Matsuzakacho was a little over half a mile. The snows and the winds ceased, but snowy whirlwinds swept through.

The men in front kicked up the snow. A hazy silver light beat down on the men's figures trailed by blackness.

When they came to Futatsume-bashi Bridge, someone said, "There's the bell!"

"It's four in the morning," said Kimura Okaemon almost shouting.

A hand opened to pick up whatever fell from Kanzaki Yogoro's neck as he swiftly moved forward.

"Yogoro, you dropped your farewell poem."

The man scooped up the tag and read it aloud as he ran, before handing it back.

> *A catalpa bow*
> *As spring nears, snow on the back of the*
> * gauntlet*
> *Scatters like a blizzard of cherry blossoms*

Hazama Kihei jumped in with his farewell poem.

> *The shameful world of the warrior.*
> *Questioned by the seagull.*
> *He knows or doesn't know.*

"Wonderful! Here's mine," said Onodera Junai raising his voice.

> *Perhaps forgotten.*
> *Over a hundred years pass.*
> *Mercy on you with generations of service.*

The first squad to cross the bridge followed the river-bank and pushed forward like crows in the moonlight and the snow's luster. After getting this far without stabbing and shaking blood off their swords, a leap into the air of their entire bodies was not enough; they had to shout.

Kimura Okaemon's white breath chanted his poem sewn to the inside of his hood.

> *East of the deep blue sea*
> *The body nears floating clouds.*
> *In a world forsaking duty for ages,*
> *An unsettled grudge from the month for*
> *   viewing cherry blossoms*
> *Creates winds scattering trees and grasses*
> *   at dawn.*

It was no longer the dead of night but just before dawn. The bell at four in the morning heard on the bridge was the signal to rendezvous.

At the crossroads in Matsuzakacho, the Tokuemoncho

Squad of Sugino Juheiji and the Aioicho Squad of Maebara Isuke formed one band and turned inky black.

"Quiet!"

Yoshida Chuzaemon waved his hand to direct the passionate footsteps. As he scanned the surroundings of the Kira residence now before him, his pores tightened and, like anyone, his feet froze to the street.

"..."

In the shadow of the chain hood's visor, unlike those of other men, Chuzaemon's eyes were sharp and in a heartbeat registered the total number of heads gathered.

"Good."

He approached Kuranosuke and whispered a few words, then divided the forty-seven men into the eastern front gate squad and the western back gate squad.

Each man's position had been decided earlier. The commander at the front gate was Oishi Kuranosuke. At the western back gate, Chikara Yoshikane was in command, assisted by his second-in-command, Yoshida Chuzaemon. The entire force fell into disciplined ranks. One went to the back gate and the other to the front gate.

As clumps of snow thudded to the ground, lively figures could be seen climbing up like monkeys from the back and front gates to the top of the wall and the treetops.

The thuds of falling snow clumps quickened. All the trees in the garden surrounding the deep inner residence of Kira Kozuke no Suke scattered snow and trembled. So far, there were no signs anyone inside the mansion noticed.

The end of the ladder propped against the front gate pierced the moon that seemed to glare at the scene. First, Otaka Gengo jumped from that light onto the eaves of the roof.

"Pardon me," he said and scrambled up ahead of Okajima Yasoemon. The second man to climb up was

Yoshida Sawaemon who made the earth ring inside the gate when he jumped down.

"Be careful, Elder," said the third man Yasoemon and stretched his hand to Horibe Yahei scrambling up after him.

The elder only said his help was not needed, rejected Yasoemon's hand, and climbed up still hugging his spear with one hand. No matter what he said, he was a seventy-six-year-old man. He watched the faces of Kataoka, Hazama, Yato, Katsuta, Takebayashi, and Hayami steadily climbing up after him as they jumped down onto the estate; their moves looked hard on the body.

"Gengo, Gengo, come here. Lend me your shoulders," he said and crawled on all fours onto the gate's roof.

"Okay."

Otaka Gengo went to help him from below.

"Here, let me help."

The elder Yahei hung one leg over his shoulder and jumped down. He believed he jumped, but on the way down his body was assisted by Gengo's powerful arms.

"Light as a feather."

As Gengo's hand let him down like a child, "Woo!" escaped the old man

He mixed in with the other young men unnoticed, he leaped inside with his spear pointed at the smashed main entryway.

The front gate force, numbering twenty-three men, was still coming down one after another from the gate, wall, and roof into the residence.

Amid shouts of "Ooops" or "Dammit," Kanzaki Yogoro and Hara Soemon slipped off the snowy roof.

No one knows when he came over, but Kuranosuke was already standing on the grounds. He brandished a huge wooden mallet and stood looking at the demolished large entryway door. At that moment, the shadow of a servant from the gate guardhouse darted, like a weasel, into the shadows of the trees.

"He's mine."

Someone spotted him and took up the chase.

"Don't kill him!" Kuranosuke warned. In no time, the tied-up gate guard was tightly lashed to a pillar of the guardhouse.

A voice from somewhere shouted, "Fire! Fire!" He couldn't tell whether the voice was friend or foe.

The noise escalated when the men from the back gate showed up. A wall running two miles from east to west and 1.3 miles from north to south surrounded the grounds of the Kira estate. The rumbling of a tornado, like the Earth's crust ripping apart, engulfed the wall.

116

PEONY SLEEVES

THEY SWARMED FROM the front gate into the library abutting the room at the entryway, a dressing room, and several sitting rooms. Those were the living quarters of Kozuke no Suke's son, Sahyoue no Suke.

The men leaping in from the back gate were closer to Kozuke no Suke's hideout. Sahyoue's living space and the hideout were linked by an inner corridor next to the inner garden.

The cascade of falling tiles suggested activities on the roof. Sounds echoed of men dashing around like demons dancing on the planks of the roof and the large eaves.

"Hara, do it now!" said Kuranosuke.

"Yessir," said Hara Soemon and ran toward Mase Kyudayu holding a nine-foot-long green bamboo pole in front of the entryway. He took a letter from his pocket and fastened it to the end of the bamboo and thrust the pole deep into the earth where the two men stood.

On the front was written *A Message from Asano Takumi no Kami* followed by the full names of the party of forty-seven men. The compelling wrath of the vassals and the lord's shame were recorded. Finally, they stated their objection founded on "our unflinching sense of justice and the position of the lord's house" to the shogunate investigator who would be standing here tomorrow.

After erecting the bamboo, Kuranosuke said, "Hayami, Kanzaki, it's clear our preparations to deal with the barracks were unneeded. Go in!"

Skilled attendants sent from the Uesugi clan appear to live in these barracks. Hayami Tozaemon and Kanzaki Yogoro carried bows. Four or five men lay prone to keep watch. The command was given despite no sign of the enemy.

"Yessir."

The squad started down the long corridor. Several layers of rain shutters were removed. Huge mallets repeatedly slammed into doors and sent them tumbling like tops into the garden. The men called out as they ran around like an attack by she-devils. Their shouting voices sounded young, hoarse, or enraged.

"Excuse this intrusion by the vassals of Asano Takumi no Kami to avenge our late lord."

"Where is Lord Kira?"

"Meet us soon and bravely give us your head."

"Your disgraced name will remain for the rest of time!"

"Lord Kira! Lord Kozuke no Suke!"

"Come meet the vassals of Takumi no Kami."

Onodera Junai's son, Koemon, shook loose his hair. A man burst from the attendant's room.

"Intruders!"

Three samurai advanced with swords in hand to surround him, became death, and crossed swords.

"Watch out!" shouted Otaka Gengo and ran to help at full speed from the library. He didn't know who, but along the way from the shadows of the sliding partition, someone shouted, "Get back, you bastard!"

A blade leaped at him like a leopard.

"What the ..."

When he swung around, his eyes burned like torches, and he held his long sword high.

His challenger was all bark and no bite. As he leaped to the side and was about to flee down the hall, the spear spike of an Ako warrior forced him to jump, and he flew off the veranda.

The sight of Gengo convinced two of the men surrounding Koemon to scurry away. Gengo chased and killed one.

Gengo's uniform was brilliant. He carried a long war sword that resembled a halberd. The deep red sleeves looked like fire beneath his black kosode jacket. The crazed whirling of his long sword seemed to sketch the purple peony on the back of his sleeves.

Koemon struck down the last enemy.

"Well done!" Gengo praised him without thinking.

A smiling Koemon turned and darted toward the alcove in the hall. Where was the enemy? Gengo watched him swing his sword and sever bowstrings hanging in a line at the twelve-feet wide alcove.

"Ah!"

In a hard fight, anyone could lose an ear. Like cutting a koto with one hundred strings, the bowstrings rang out different tones as they snapped.

"Good. You spotted them!"

This praise from a raspy voice probably came from an elderly ally confused in the shadows.

KIRA'S LOYAL RETAINERS

117

THE FRIEND WITH A GOOD SENSE
OF SMELL

GIVEN THEIR USUAL cautious behavior, only tonight, Kira's side was unexpectedly lax in their preparation and response to emergencies. Many slept soundly believing they were inside iron walls.

Perhaps the snow was to blame. Were they unable to imagine an unforeseen terrifying incident that would shatter the peace a moment after they lay down on warm, thick, cotton beds on a winter night as they thought about the deep snow on the highest ridge of the roof covered by the ashes from beautiful charcoal fires? Even premonitions deceived the heart. Men sometimes rejected common sense. Surely, not on a night like this.

Another reason was their concern over the tea gathering held that day. This gathering with many attendees, who included vassals of the Kira clan and their attendants, always caused headaches. Especially, when Kozuke no Suke held a gathering at his residence, they hustled to retrieve and return various items from the storehouses, rehang pictures, prepare the tea ceremony, plan meals, and hold the reception on that day. It was not an ordinary affair even for a man of leisure.

"Where's the enjoyment? How can a tea ceremony be held under this security?" asked some attendants from the Uesugi clan. Others said Kozuke no Suke now living in seclusion had no joy other than entirely forgetting these stressful days by making tea. That explanation made sense to them.

The vassals and the attendants shared sad empathy for the daily lives of Kozuke no Suke and his son.

His heir Sahyoue with his pallid, twitchy face shut himself away. His lonesome father Kozuke no Suke said, "You should have some contact with the world," and invited him to the tea gathering and a seat at the exchange of calligraphy antiques. However, Sahyoue always complained of a headache or said he wasn't in the mood and preferred his darkened room.

Sometimes, his father clicked his tongue in exasperation. Kozuke no Suke was a cheerful man who liked flamboyance. But for more than a year, he's been without joy. His elderly wife Tomiko returned to her family; his flesh and blood heir Saburo was the adopted son of the Uesugi clan and a governor and no longer felt like his son. His other children were girls who would marry into other families. Reflecting on this, the court rank and treasures around him weighed down his old bones. The love of blood relations and the familial warmth were not blessings at all. The father and son were lonely like solitary geese in a winter storm.

Watchful eyes in the barracks on the ground constantly scrutinized the lord's situation.

"This is wretched. Kozuke no Suke seen by the public and Kozuke no Suke-sama seen from here are two different men. However, the public doesn't think so. It is probably thought of as the greed of great wealth but ... it may be bad luck. That's inevitable."

Shimizu Ichigaku always muttered this to himself when off duty and drinking alone.

"If I'm glum, I drink this sake, use my hands as a pillow, and rest, but I'm still grateful."

He thought about his lord and empathized with the loneliness of Kozuke no Suke.

In contrast to his love for Kozuke no Suke over many years for plucking a big-headed fourteen year old from a peasant's cottage deep in the countryside of Yokosuka village in Mikawa Province, Ichigaku meditated day and night in his heart on the loneliness of his lord now and the feeling of dark days. On the many nights when his body ached, sleep often came by the power of sake.

From noon until evening on the fourteenth, night fell during a busy time. After the tea gathering and the guests were seen off and the utensils stored away, the time came to close the front snow shutters.

Ichigaku took a bath. Around ten, he returned to the row house.

When he turned his attention to his nightcap, he heard, "Shimizu, you're drinking. It's probably my good sense of smell. I caught the scent and now, I'm here."

As usual, Kimura Johachi, his secretly sworn friend, dropped by late at night.

118

THE SAKE MEMORIAL SERVICE

JOHACHI COULD HOLD his drink, as could Ichigaku. The bottle he brought to the kitchen door was empty.

"There's nothing left to drink. Why don't we go to the boarding house to drink like we usually do?"

Ichigaku rose and said, "I'm good. Tonight, I will show self-control because I'll be returning to the attendants' room soon to go to bed."

"Is this an unprecedented end to a good idea?"

"I'm a little worn out."

"We should go and talk a little longer."

"I'll talk, but I won't drink."

"I want to talk more than drink, too. Can I bed down here tonight? On an evening like this, I don't know whether next year will come."

"Shimizu, this is a lonesome night, isn't it?"

"The many guests have gone home, and Kozuke no Suke-sama is spending a night alone. That thought pains me," said Ichigaku and peeked into the unlit room next door.

"For two nights in a row, I've only dreamed of my late

mother. I may be getting closer to seeing her. But I've been worrying about what you've said for a long time."

Hearing this worried Johachi, too. Lamplight flickered in front of the memorial tablet for Ichigaku's mother in the adjacent room, a space lacking a woman's touch.

Not only today but on any day, after he finished his duties and returned to the barracks, Ichigaku faced his mother's memorial tablet before he did anything else.

Today again, the day passed with no harm coming to Kozuke no Suke-sama.

After this announcement, he loosened the cord of his hakama trousers.

Johachi visited Ichigaku on a visit to the country home of Ichigaku's elderly mother and spent one night under the thatch roof in Yokosuka village in Mikawa. At that time too, he saw and was deeply impressed by this mother and son's genuine appreciation for the favor of the lord of the fief, Kozuke no Suke. He had not forgotten the delicious taste of the country soba noodles made by the old woman's hands.

Since the report of her death came from the countryside, Shimizu Ichigaku has been in deep reflection in his heart. On one hand, he was devoted to protecting Lord Kozuke no Suke. On the other, he was patiently waiting for the arrival of the "situation that makes protecting him difficult."

"This has become strangely gloomy. When you and I drink sake, we always have the habit of going too deep."

"The taste of sake has value in penetrating the heart. If sake is drunken boisterously, nothing, not even a companion, is chosen. So you'll stay the night. I have no bedding, but my talking while sleeping in my clothes on a futon isn't too bad."

After hearing that, Kimura Johachi didn't get up. It

shouldn't be a bad thing to use his hands as a pillow after drinking with his friend with a forgiving heart. That friend wanted a heart-to-heart talk only on this night. His only regret was the absence of sake. If only there had been a little more sake. He craved a drink.

The heavy footsteps in the snow of someone carrying a load passed under the window.

Here's my chance, thought Johachi and stood. Thinking the same thing, Ichigaku reached the window before him and opened the snow shutter.

"Hey, attendants! Attendants."

He called, believing two attendants were on night patrol. But the man responding to his voice was not two attendants returning from the shadows of the trees and not carrying a palanquin bearer rod or a paper lantern.

"Are you calling me?"

"Oh, excuse me. You're the shogun's guard Kasahara Shichijiro."

"Yes."

"I mistook you for the patrol. I thought everyone was fast asleep and no one was walking around the grounds."

"Is there anything I can do? I'm not the night-duty guard, but I'm tired from today's work. On a snowy night like tonight, men tend to let their guard down. Instead, I thought I must be strategic. The truth is I took it on myself to patrol. If there's something I can do, please give me the order."

"No, no, you're off duty and not resting."

Without thinking, Ichigaku lowered his head to speak to the shadow in the snow's brightness.

"We appreciate your diligence. The truth is I'm here to share a nightcap with Kimura Johachi. If you were the attendants, I'd have you grab some from the boarding house. Being awake while everyone else is asleep, I'm ashamed to ask you to keep watch in this snow. I feel like I've been doused with gallons of water. In contrast to your loyalty, I feel shame. Forgive our interruption."

"Oh, you'd like sake?"

Kasahara Shichijiro smiled and nodded. Ichigaku's love of sake was well known.

"That's a simple errand. I'll go get it now."

"No, don't bother. Kasahara-dono, you mustn't," he said almost in apology and closed the shutter. A short time later, footsteps returned outside the window. When he opened the shutter, Kasahara Shichijiro wearing a red rain cape hugged a bottle of sake in his frozen hands.

"I'm sorry, but this is all there was. Is it okay?"

"Oh, thank you so much. Forgive me for bothering you."

"It was nothing."

Kasahara Shichijiro left smiling.

For a short time, Ichigaku and Johachi stayed at the window to see him off and then carried the bottle of sake to the side of the brazier. But they both looked at it disappointed.

"Johachi."

"Yeah."

"Of the more than one hundred vassals and attendants on the grounds, I always worry whether any of those men have the heart for public service. But there are true samurai. Drinking this sake would be inexcusable, in light of the seriousness of the young samurai Kasahara.

"He's the younger brother of Sekiguchi Sakubei. Although young, he's a man with a prepared mind and skills."

"Who is Sekiguchi Sakubei?"

"He was a confidante of Chisaka Hyobu-sama. Like us, he was ordered to investigate the movements of the Ako ronin around Kyoto and Osaka but was killed near Bishamon in Yamashina. Interestingly, his corpse was headless."

"My guess is his killer was an Ako ronin."

"I only understand ones like Takehayashi Tadashichi. Kasahara Shichijiro always seemed strained by despair over the coming attack by the Ako men because of his older brother's fate."

"I hear Hyobu-sama is in excellent health now."

"He's probably exhausted from worry. Before this snow fell, I went to give my usual report and visited him in his sickbed. I didn't see any other visitors."

"It's getting colder and late."

"The sake's cooling down, too."

"There's no excuse for Kasahara Shichijiro to be patrolling and not sleeping, but shall we drink this sake? Johachi, hand me the sake-warming bottle over there."

"Wait. If you don't fill the charcoal, the hot water in the copper boiler will cool a bit."

The two kept drinking and talking. When midnight came, as expected, they were quiet. A little sake remained but they had fallen asleep on their hand pillows with only their legs under the bedding.

The two men drank close to two bottles of sake. They didn't intend to get drunk but sake soaked their bowels.

Then four in the morning came.

A little earlier, Kimura Johachi was tossing and turning. The paper lanterns were out. He appeared to be groping his way to the kitchen. His throat was parched, and he searched for the bamboo ladle of the water bucket. Unfortunately, Johachi had to break through a sheet of ice to get to the water.

At that instant, Shimizu Ichigaku sat up with a start in the darkness.

"Johachi. What was that noise?"

"That was me. I broke the ice in the bucket."

"Didn't you hear it? That noise?! There. Ah, it's the front gate and the back gate. That doesn't sound normal."

"What was that?!"

The shock froze Johachi where he stood. Ichigaku moved his face toward the window to listen. His fiery white eyes glowed.

Punctuated by the thuds of snow, the dreadful sounds of large wooden mallets, and footsteps kicking up snow and running over the spacious grounds, he heard voices, raging voices, and shouts.

It's the Asano ronin. They've come for the head of Lord Kira.

"Ah! We're under attack!"

Johachi did not notice the ladle of ice drop from his hand.

"Shimizu! It's the Ako ronin!"

"Calm down."

Ichigaku reprimanded him then grabbed the neck of the sake warmer bottle to drink the last drops. What was he thinking? He went into the dark room next door and sat.

119

THE WINDS OF ARROWS AND SWORDS

I CHIGAKU DRANK A teacup of sake and informed his late mother on the Buddhist altar of his impending death. Kimura Johachi returned to his usual self when he looked in and thought, Now I have an obligation to myself.

He was a confidante of Chisaka Hyobu. After he received the military objective, he was ordered to spy in the region from Ako and across Kyoto and keep constant contact between Kozuke no Suke and the Uesugi clan.

"Shimizu, I'm going."

"Wait."

Ichigaku gulped down the sake poured for his late mother and turned to Johachi. "This is our parting ..."

"Yes."

Johachi dropped to one knee to accept the teacup. The windows and the rain shutters at the entryway rattled like they were being pummeled by hail, but those sounds were strikes by arrows shot from short bows. The tips of several arrowheads piercing the rain shutter glimmered like white stars.

Ichigaku hiked up his hakama trousers readying for the

fight, put on a headband, tied back his sleeves, and approached the door.

"Watch out! Use this as cover when you go out," said Johachi and tossed him a woman's quilted kosode robe. Only Johachi knew about the kosode robe in the closet of Ichigaku's home where no woman lived. It was the bride's kimono of Ichigaku's late wife.

"Thanks."

Ichigaku covered himself from his head with the long garment. Fusing with the moldy smell, his head was wrapped by the lingering scent of the young woman who died after giving birth in the second year of their marriage.

My wife and late mother are tired of waiting for me. They will witness the actions of the death of Shimizu Ichigaku, he thought as he placed his hand on the door.

Johachi and Ichigaku both heard voices that sounded like older men in command among the Asano ronin outside shouting the battle cry.

"Don't attack women or children. Let the women escape."

For the short time, the sounds of arrows ceased, Ichigaku flung open the door and dashed out. The coldness of the frozen snow piled high on the ground pierced him from the back of his bare feet to the core of his head.

Not only the snow, but the moon was also cold. The spacious entryway was quickly demolished, and human figures were seen breaking down the door of the study with large mallets.

Ichigaku's hair stood on end the moment he saw the black shadows of men and swords sprinting over the grounds and in the snow like night crows.

Ichigaku shouted, "Villains! A surprise attack! But while I live, you'll take no heads."

Using the shrubbery as cover, Ichigaku raced to

Kozuke no Suke's sleeping quarters. Although it was fortified, guarded, and unlikely to succumb to an ominous fate, his heart sounded an alarm. He worried about the safety of the lord and his heir.

Thick snow like cotton on the treetops scattered and dripped onto the shoulders of the overgarment. Agility unexpected under a charming lady's veil raised suspicions.

"Wait."

An Ako ronin holding a short bow came running from the shadows of the trees.

That looks suspicious!

He pulled back the arrow fixed to the bowstring and released a shot. The arrow stopped in the sleeve of the overgarment. Like a bird of paradise, the shadow ran up a man-made hill.

"You bastard!"

The ronin threw away the short bow and took up the chase.

"Coward! Coward! I'd help a woman, but you're a disgrace. An attendant living in Lord Kira's barracks shows me his back."

When he called out, Ichigaku gained a foothold and swung around.

"Ah! Who is this scrawny Asano ronin?"

"Chikamatsu Kanroku, a cavalry officer with a stipend of 200 koku."

"What a fine introduction. I am Shimizu Ichigaku, a true-born vassal from peasant stock from Kira Kozuke no Suke's domain."

"Shimizu? Our meeting is destiny. You will get your wish and accompany Lord Kira in death."

"I thought I'd seen you before. You're the traveling merchant who came to Yokosuka village in Mikawa and sold goods at my home."

"Excuse my rudeness at that time."

"A fine rival. Today, there is no escape, and we'll travel the road to death together."

"What?"

The overgarment flung by Ichigaku floated with the wind and danced toward the tip of Kanroku's exposed long sword.

He stepped to the side as he turned his face away, but Ichigaku's sword powerfully waved around with both hands in the next instant sliced through space and dropped to point right at Kanroku.

"What is this?" asked Kanroku's whole body, as his long sword was outmaneuvered. This enemy had a subtle recovery that did not give him time to attack. The pressure of the fierce winds of three or four swords continued.

"Aah!"

Kanroku's foot slipped toward the fountain water from the cliff of the man-made hill and he tumbled in.

The thin ice cracked, and Kanroku plunged waist-deep into the water. One leg in a night-assault straw sandal and a leg of light yellowish green long underpants raised high into the air.

Ichigaku did not turn around.

Where are they? Kozuke no Suke-sama. Sahyoue-sama.

His face drained of blood. Then he jumped on the slippery snow and ran down to the large garden from the west side of the hill.

A shadow pursued him.

"Ichigaku, wait! I'm the Asano ronin, Kanzaki Yogoro."

Wondering why the man sounded like he was introducing himself, Ichigaku swung his long sword behind his back and hit Yogoro's chainmail underpants. Light radiated like a rock was cut.

"Dammit."

With his left hand on the ground, Yogoro watched the shadow of his enemy make a swift escape. He received a slight wound near his thigh or knee.

Yato Emoshichi, Hayami Tozaemon, and Hazama Jujiro were nearby and witnessed the shadow of the amazing acts of the warrior Ichigaku and kicked up powdery snow in pursuit.

120

THE FOOT SOLDIER KICHIEMON

OF COURSE, THESE actions happened simultaneous to the assault by the front gate squad.

The squad of twenty-four men attacking the back gate of the Kira estate under the command of Oishi Chikara was helped by the elders Yoshida Chuzaemon and Onodera Junai who acted as sub-commanders.

Mimura Jirozaemon with a mallet launched the first revenge attack. Jirozaemon was a petty kitchen official with a stipend of just seven koku and rice provisions for two in the former Ako clan. Besides tonight's work, he delighted in thoughts of divine protection. He was at peace with death as he smashed through the enemy's gate.

Bang, bang, bang!

To get a reaction from the guts of the sleeping Lord Kira, he struck the gate three or four times. The gate's door split open with a crack.

"Go!" shouted Chikara.

Yoshida Chuzaemon held the golden command baton. Sugino Juheiji, Kurahashi Densuke, Akabane Genzo,

Isogai Jurozaemon, and Horibe Yasubei did not wait for him to wave it.

"Halt!"

Yasubei checked the surge of men, removed the bar on the inside, and hurled it a short distance with great force into the side of the guard house.

A man, probably the gatekeeper, and three or four samurai shouting inside ripped something off their heads and ran off nearly tumbling over.

Five men, Kayano Wasuke, Hazama Shinrokuro, Fuwa Kazuemon, Kimura Okaemon, and Maebara Isuke, carried bows. They lined up their bowstrings, promptly pointed them at the barracks visible in the distance, and began bombarding it with arrows to flush out the hidden enemy.

The sub-commander Yoshida Chuzaemon was surprised by flames rising from a building in the barracks. But just as rapidly, the fire was extinguished and human forms scrambled out of each window and backdoor of the pitch-black row house.

Okuda Sadaemon, Senba Saburobei, Mase Magokuro, Nakamura Kansuke, and others were outside gripping long swords and clashed with the enemy in their initial attack. A melee overtook the area. Spears flew, swords slashed, and dirt and blood were chaotically stomped into the snow.

An unseen Chikara barked commands.

"To the hideout. To the inner sleeping chambers."

The map of Kira's residence impressed into each man's brain came to life and was put to use. This back gate was closer than the front gate and next to the enclosure of Kozuke no Suke's hideout.

"The Asano ronin dropped in to avenge our late lord."

"Bring us the head of Lord Kira."

"Nonbelievers come out and see."

"Come out!"

"Come out!"

They broke through the door of the inner entryway, then the rain shutters of the study, the windows, and the kitchen door.

As many as ten men, including one cutting his way in with a nine-foot-long spear, Horibe Yasubei with his *odachi* long sword, and Sugaya Hannojo with his familiar *kodachi* short sword, rushed inside.

This scene was described in a letter sent by Onodera Junai to his wife in the home province.

The Tenma Hajun demon with the power to end a man's life would not face that incredible power.

"Chikara, Chikara, it's still bad out front."

Yoshida Chuzaemon and Onodera Junai readied their spears and peered outside. Pulled in by the power of the men rushing into the room, they checked Chikara from behind as he was about to move.

"I see them."

Chikara turned and looked at them with smiling eyes in the shadow of his headband visor. He snapped his spear to the horizontal position and glanced around for a fitting rival like his young blood couldn't stop him from acting like a warrior. A man bowed with both hands on the ground in apology before Chuzaemon. Although dressed in full armor for the raid, he did not appear to be on duty. Chikara noticed him.

"Who's that?"

The man buried his crying face in the snow. Looking harder, Chikara recognized him, a foot soldier named

Terasaka Kichiemon, he served Yoshida Chuzaemon for years.

Chikara's eyes heated up because he understood both Kichiemon's and his master Chuzaemon's feelings. Terasaka was a low-ranking soldier to an undervassal of the late lord Takumi no Kami and not allowed to join as a comrade in the revenge. His direct master Chuzaemon understood this man's sincerity and commitment but was at a loss. During his father's days in Yamashina and after he moved to Kokucho in Edo, Chuzaemon brought him along a few times on visits to Kuranosuke.

As he listened in the shadows to the words of the foot soldier Kichiemon, Chikara didn't care what the world said and wanted him to join. But his father had to refuse. He had this reason for his firm decision.

"In the revenge, warriors will invade the residence of Master of Ceremonies Kira in an act of unprecedented destruction of the public order. The addition of a common foot soldier to those warriors would complicate the issue. Furthermore, how would including the foot soldier of an undervassal affect the dignity of the late lord? It would look like the Asano clan lacked men."

However, Kichiemon's enthusiasm prevented him from giving up. He set out to persuade the comrades, one by one. Finally, he spared no effort to demonstrate his sincerity to Chuzaemon and the rest of the men.

This man seemed to have exhausted Kuranosuke's and Chuzaemon's patience. They had to say, "All right!" However, Kichiemon had to respect the opinions of men other than Kuranosuke.

He came determined in his heart to join the raid, stepped inside the gates of the enemy's residence, witnessed the actions of the men, and voluntarily disappeared from the company of the comrades. With no regrets, he hoped to at least live long enough to recount the circumstances of that night to these men's bereaved families.

121

NO MAN'S DISCIPLE

CHUZAEMON ANTICIPATED HIS feelings, so when Kichiemon came to him and placed both hands on the ground, he said, "Leave now!"

"I know this is where we part. Master, Master … Goodbye."

"Wait. Say your piece to Kuranosuke-dono, then go."

"Yes, yessir."

When he ran out, a Kira samurai with disheveled hair and bathed in snow and blood entered his path and crashed into Kichiemon's chest.

Kichiemon was knocked down, face up. The man wielding the blade hovering over his chest ran to the side. Chikara heard someone say, "He's the attendant Kobayashi Heihachiro from the Uesugi clan."

Chikara had already forgotten Chuzaemon's words. Hugging his spear, he leaped onto the porch of the study.

He called out, "I am one man with a spear. I am the son of Kuranosuke, Chikara Yoshikane."

Seeing this, the archers said, "Don't shoot Chikara-dono," and lowered their bows.

When as many as three or four men charged in sporadically to help, other men in the shade of trees beside the road composed themselves and walked out. Not a man among them had a frenzied look in his eyes. A glance revealed they were not allies, but they were too calm.

What's going on?

Is this an unexpected visit from another clan?

Seeing them roused suspicions in the Ako men, but they held back and didn't interfere.

A man came forward and went to the back gate before the standing spears of Yoshida Chuzaemon and Onodera Junai. Junai saw his defiant look and pointed the tip of his spear at him.

"Go back!"

"What is your name? Who are you?" asked Chuzaemon.

The man showed no fear. He noted the suspicious human shadows wearing chainmail undershirts and dressed in firemen's uniforms pointing spears at him behind the two men facing him. Before he took one step, he understood everything. In a voice straining to sound jovial, he said, "I may know someone in your party. I'm a trusted associate of Chisaka Hyobu, a retainer of Uesugi Danjo Daihitsu. My name is Kimura Johachi."

"What? Kimura Johachi?"

The moving spikes of the spears glimmered. If Chuzaemon's hand had not restrained them, Johachi's body may have become a beehive.

"Uh-huh," Chuzaemon backed down and nodded. He looked at the man and was amazed to see the face of this man from the shadows who went by the name of Juhachishaku and pestered his comrades from Ako to Kyoto and Osaka.

"Where are you going?"

The trace of severity in Onodera Junai's voice would depend on his answer.

Johachi looked around like he was counting the heads of these men floating in the snow's brightness. He recognized these faces in Gion, on boats from Ako, and on passersby in the towns of Edo.

"My duty will end tonight, too. I will leave matters to the attendants and vassals and return to my master Chisaka Hyobu. I will say farewell here. Our association was short, but I feel a deep connection. My long-cherished hope for years is for it to be beautiful, whether it succeeds or not. Goodnight."

Followed by the eyes of many men, he bowed and crossed a distance to go out the back gate.

The elder Junai's eyes met Chuzaemon's. Under his breath, one said, "Chisaka Hyobu raised a good man."

PART XVII

WARRIORS CRY

122

THE TAIKO DRUM VOICE

AT THE TIME of the battle inside staged by the team searching for Kozuke no Suke and the battle outside staged by the team expecting to achieve the objective as they protected their comrades inside, the Kira residence transformed into the bottom of a crucible.

The racket startled the occupants of the mansions neighboring the Kira residence. At first, they believed the noise came from thieves or fire.

Retainers climbed onto the roofs of Makino Nagato's mansion across from the front gate and Honda Magotaro's mansion to the north.

What's going on? …

They gaped in wonder at the whirlwind of flames, smoke, and disembodied shouts.

The vassals in the mansion of Tsuchiya Chikara on the other side of the wall realized what was happening. They raised large paper lanterns high and considered emergency measures given the unusual event next door.

Yoshida Chuzaemon watched Kimura Johachi of the Uesugi clan leave through the back gate of the crucible.

Struck by emotions familiar only to a warrior, he said, "Oh! Has anyone told the neighbors of our presence?"

When someone off to the side said, "No, not yet," Onodera Junai said, "That's a mistake! We must maintain goodwill with the neighbors. A horde of men disturbing the households of Tsuchiya, Makino, and Honda is a problem."

The elder ran out immediately. His quick footsteps, like he was enjoying the snow, made the slender man look younger than his sixty years.

"I am addressing the neighboring residences."

The voice of the elderly Junai echoed beneath the edge of the wall. His voice was an accomplishment forged by a samurai and described in writings on the samurai way. A high-pitched voice or a weak voice is used to introduce oneself or say something to the enemy when leaving the battlefield because dignity is involved.

The booming voices of Horibe Yahei and the elderly Junai were usually problems. The younger men called Junai's, The Taiko Drum Voice.

Junai added these words to his introduction in his thunderous taiko drum voice.

"I am a former vassal of Asano Takumi no Kami. No doubt the sudden uproar and disruption shocked you at this time, the customary time for sleep. We've paid this unannounced visit to Lord Kira to avenge our late Lord Takumi no Kami. The way of the samurai is said to be mutual sympathy. A stray arrow knows nothing. We hold no malice toward the other households; therefore, please do not interfere. In the rare event, you appear to be preparing for the slightest interference, you will become our rival and be attacked."

A hush fell over the neighboring residences, as though enchanted by his powerful voice.

They understood his intention!

Junai nodded alone. When he was about to move his legs, a Kira vassal hidden nearby shot out from the shadow of a stone lantern, waving his long sword, aiming for Junai's legs.

"Aah!" The old master leaped; his spear seemed to pierce his opponent. The enemy's body stretched out with his long sword, fell flat on his face, and turned the snow bright red.

Surprised by his skill, someone behind him shouted, "Junai-dono, well done!"

He looked back to see Kataoka Gengoemon. The old man seemed delighted to be praised, smiled broadly, and said, "It's a crime of the old."

From the same hiding place as the fallen enemy, another man jumped out and slashed wildly until he was killed. Gengoemon was no longer there, but Junai felt good. He wrenched out the enemy's windpipe with the spearhead.

The fallen man looked like the typical pious man who chanted, "Praise to Amitabha Buddha," in his final moments.

In the future, the mouth of Oishi Sezaemon would repeat this chant when he told the story recalling this night. Sezaemon running past him might have overheard the stricken man's prayer to Amitabha Buddha.

123

______

THE BEST OF THE KIRA CLAN

TONIGHT, THE HANDSOME man among the comrades, Isogai Jurozaemon, raised his sharp eyes to his metal visor. The bright drops of blood on the spike of the straight spear in his sword hand smeared down to the *hiru-maki* wrapping of the handle. His chainmail undergarment poked out at the shoulder of one of his sleeves torn by an enemy's long sword.

Mimura, Muramatsu, and Hazama burst inside. Mimura Jirozaemon brandished a large mallet and knocked out the doors, the shoji screens, and the fittings of cedar doors from the edges.

"Bastards!"

Shimizu Danzaemon, a gatekeeper at Kira's residence, emerged from the shadows of the missing cedar doors and slashed at Mimura.

"Hey!"

Mimura swung the mallet that smashed into the wall. A landslide of wall plaster crumbled between them.

"Intruders!"

Hazama Kihei's cross spear closed off the side and

destroyed Danzaemon's composure, making him tumble out into the large corridor. A sword plunged into the side of that shadow.

The enemy kept streaming outside. The mansion was huge, but how many men were crammed inside?

Isogai Jurozaemon captured a Kira samurai and was holding him by the nape of his neck.

"Help! Somebody help me!"

"You'll help. Take out the candles."

"Okay. I'll get them."

"Where are they?"

Jurozaemon dragged him slipping and sliding to get the box of candles, light them, and place them in every room.

"Juroza, you're worked up. If you don't calm down, you'll be useless. This is more amazing to watch than you as a warrior wielding a spear," said Hazama Kihei, as he helped.

With the cedar doors, sliding doors, and all the partitions knocked down, the interior of the Kira mansion became a cavern from the front to the back. Countless lights blew soot and smoke at human figures. Light from the swords mingled and flashed incessantly.

"Where are you, Kozuke no Suke?!" shouted Takebayashi Tadashichi as he entered a room with a wooden floor deep inside the mansion that looked like a dressing room.

"What? Is Kira here?"

Maebara Isuke and Okuda Takuzaemon were close and crawled over. Two older samurai escaped from the shadows of the futon room.

"No!"

"No!"

They sounded like they were tumbling over as they

spoke. At the kitchen door, Maebara Isuke was hit by a nine-foot-long straight spear.

"Oow!"

He tumbled in toward the large kitchen sink, then came out like a cat burglar and jumped from the top of the wall into a big ditch outside and hid behind Kasaya San'emon diagonally across the street.

Several elders in their sixties were present. Takebayashi Tadashichi mistook the gray-haired one for Kira, but he recognized the men behind him, vassals of the Kira clan, Souda Magobei and Saito Kunai.

"We're wasting time," he muttered in exasperation, then said, "Where's Kozuke no Suke?"

They split up and ran deeper inside.

Then Tadashichi stepped into the sitting room of the heir Sahyoue no Suke.

"Who's there?"

A thirteen- or fourteen-year-old youth lurched forward waving a pole sword with a blue shell handle. He was a good-looking novice with a shaven head.

A stunned Tadashichi quashed his surprise and stepped up.

The youth looked angry from the depths of his spirit and advanced wildly swinging a pole sword his small body could barely manage.

"Damn you! Damn you!"

He was Makino Shunsai, in training to be a tea server. Kozuke no Suke and others in the household lovingly called out, "Shunsai, Shunsai," as if he were a favorite toy.

Tadashichi pitied the poor fellow who failed to hit anything.

"Will you stop?"

After Tadashichi knocked down the pole sword with his

spear handle, Shunsai raised his heel like a *Kakubei* lion street performer wearing a wooden lion mask.

"Don't back down, Shunsai."

A page and his good friend Suzuki Sadonoshin aimed at Tadashichi from a corner of the room and hurled a *Go* board at him.

The board grazed Tadashichi's head and left a triangular dent in the pillar behind him. Tadashichi tossed aside his spear.

"I see a fine rival. Don't move."

He leaped and cut Sadonoshin straight across his forehead and down the front of his shoulder.

An assortment of white and black go stones peppered one side of Tadashichi's face. The youth Shunsai kept grabbing and hurling the scattered stones at him.

"You bastard! You rat!"

As he moved, Tadashichi thought, I must not strike this enemy. Suzuki Sadonoshin still prone on the ground after falling said, "You shit!" and swept Tadashichi's legs.

While balancing on one leg and crossing over the other, Tadashichi slashed Sadonoshin across the face during his second fall backward. The blade rang like it was cutting through gravel.

"Cowards! Cowards!"

Shunsai wildly shouted and randomly flung whatever was in reach at enemies other than Tadashichi.

Wondering if another man's blade killed him, Tadashichi left and tried to pass through a second time. This time the pitiful novice already lay dead on top of his friend Sadonoshin. A glance revealed their deaths in battle were heroic.

～

FORTUNATELY, the following was found in an old book containing a list of the loyal Ako retainers.

Alone, one youth.
Driven back but fought back.
A horde had to kill him.
All praise his spirit.
And deeply regret his loss.

After the act of revenge, Yoshida Chuzaemon confessed, "The truth is I was unlucky in battle and did not meet one enemy. However, there was a youth among the enemy. He tried hard but cut a pitiful figure. I had to take his life, but one thing I can say is he reached the zenith of courage and was the best of the Kira clan."

The premier Ako strategist Yoshida Chuzaemon claimed Shunsai, the fourteen-year-old child of a traveling merchant in Nihonbashi and an apprentice of one year and several months in the art of the tea ceremony, was the best of the Kira clan.

124

THE ATTENDANT HEIHACHIRO

AMONG THE SAMURAI and attendants of the Kira clan were men who ran outside trying to escape and the opposite, men who ran inside.

Few men were like Shimizu Ichigaku, Kobayashi Heihachiro, Kasahara Shichijiro, and Osuga Jiroemon. They believed any man who got closer to Lord Kozuke no Suke, even if only a foot or two, would die.

Someone noticed Kobayashi Heihachiro, who possessed the power to keep the enemy at bay, standing outside the kitchen door about to run in.

"Wait, wait! I don't see the retreating backs of the enemy. I have no shortage of rivals. Look, here comes the ex-Asano vassal Fuwa Kazuemon."

A she-devil wallowing in snow, dirt, and blood released a hoarse shriek and hurled a wind of long swords at Heihachiro.

"Do you want to die?"

He looked back and was hit in his chest by a gust of air stirred by Kazuemon's blade. Kazuemon raised his heel

593

and smashed through the bamboo water pipe at the kitchen door.

The icicles hanging from the eaves like several hundred swords crashed to the ground. Kazuemon exposed his back to this enemy, but an icicle struck it. The tip of Heihachiro's sword cut the neck armor plate of Kazuemon's helmet hood and near his shoulder.

If the chainmail undershirt had not saved his skin, Kazuemon's shoulder would have been severed and his arm gone. The force of the sword was extraordinary. He thought, It didn't pass through, echoed like the sharp pain from Kazuemon's shoulder bone to his backbone.

As more swords joined, the two crossed swords but never battled each other. Kazuemon was the comrade skilled in sword test cutting and practiced origami. Heihachiro was among the many attendants selected from the Uesugi clan, an expert with exceptional hands, and a man whose strength and faithfulness was acknowledged by all.

Kazuemon's only win was his armaments. Heihachiro's kosode quilted robe looked shredded, and blood spurted from every wound cut by several long swords.

Mase Magokuro and Okuda Sadaemon soon arrived.

"Hold on, Kazue. We're here."

Mase's spear thrust in from the right.

Heihachiro swept his spear away and retreated inside.

Instantly, Kimura Okaemon crossed swords with an enemy and backed into Heihachiro's back.

"Kira's man?" Okaemon asked and hit Heihachiro's hip while his blade pointed at the enemy in front of him but ended up tottering on one leg until his body slammed with great force against a plank wall in a corner.

Heihachiro slipped and fell at the foot of the large sink. He pulled in the base of Mase Magokuro's spear shoved at him, held up his long sword with one hand, and energetically bounded outside. His enemies Kazuemon and Sadaemon wanted to say, "Well done!"

However, the sword that beat the hip was rewarded. Heihachiro leaped outside but fell to the ground.

A spear to his chest, a sword to his forehead, and the blows from Fuwa Kazuemon and Okuda Sadaemon took their toll. Kobayashi Heihachiro lying face up kept swinging his long sword and working his foot techniques.

He did not stop fighting until his last breath.

The three men breathed deeply from their shoulders in relief. Exhaustion hit their bodies, not a surprise after a clash with a great man who refused to yield.

"After all that, he's not here. Where is Kira Kozuke no Suke? No one has blown the signal whistle. We must find our sworn enemy!"

Fuwa, Okuda, and Kimura grabbed fists of snow to wet their mouths. Their shoes tread on existing shoe tracks through a snowslide into the hideout.

Around that time, the battle of men inside the residence crossed the peak of violence. Between heavy breaths, they talked as they ran all around in a frenzy.

"Where's the enemy? Where is he?"

"Where are Lord Kira and his son?"

"Where are they?"

"Find Kira!"

The house search began.

125

THE LIFELONG VASSAL

T HE FIERCE BATTLE was far from over. Bounded by the corridor of the large study, one group engaged in a brief but desperate fight.

An onlooker would recognize one pudgy, sturdy young man with a round face as Yokogawa Kanpei, a guard of the gunpowder stores of the Asano clan.

Originally, Kanpei was a swordsman. The long sword suited his build.

Another man, Tominomori Sukeemon, was an expert with the cross spear. He was a master of the evening's weapons.

The enemy waiting for them was a samurai unrivaled in the Kira clan, Shimizu Ichigaku, who called himself Kozuke no Suke's Lifelong Vassal.

He held his long and short swords in his right and left hands and said, "Come on. You? You? All of you?"

His breaths were relaxed.

Everywhere Ichigaku ran Ako men were wounded, chased off, kicked down, or cut down by the power of the tip of his sword. He dropped challengers into the lake and kicked them off the veranda. Ichigaku never rested one knee on the ground. Only a light scrape was visible on his left forearm.

Was it the strength of his heart, courage, or arms?

The mental preparedness of the Ako men and Shimizu Ichigaku was identical. Shimizu Ichigaku swiftly braced himself with a mental attitude equal to that of the forty-seven ronin.

His absolute stance was "retreat is not my way of the warrior" and drew his long and short swords. His loyalty to his lord, his purity, and the culmination of his life's work as a samurai would be decided in this snow.

Yokogawa Kanpei was short-tempered. His enemy Ichigaku knew choosing this formidable enemy would not settle this evening's fortune of war but understood his aggravation would spring from his sword.

If he approaches, these two blades will open his breast, thought Ichigaku.

Echoes sounded like they were dropped to the floor by Kanpei's feet. His massive frame stomped down the corridor and bounded toward his rival.

"Dammit," Kanpei said gulping the air. He held his whole body upside down and cut into a square pillar in the room with his long sword.

Ichigaku spotted the attack and swung his long sword at Kanpei's back, but Tominomori Sukeemon's spear blocked him. Light in the shape of a cross bounced off his chin and flickered on the tip of his nose.

Clang!

The small blade in Ichigaku's left hand warded off blows. He failed to check the spear handle. He drew the spear through his hands and thrust. The same light shined again and again.

Sukeemon's tenacity annoyed Ichigaku. The instant

Ichigaku sunk down, his body, as limber as a fish's, thrust the spear into space and made Sukeemon fall sideways onto his shins. He cried out.

The chain of his shin guard repelled the blade and saved his legs, but the pain kept him from standing. Despite himself, Sukeemon groaned and sat with a thud.

Kataoka Gengoemon shouted, "I'll get behind him! Ichigaku, fresh troops are here!"

Without saying a word, Ichigaku easily extended the blade of his long sword toward Kataoka. In the moments Gengoemon shuffled back, Ichigaku leaped off the veranda into the snow in the spacious garden.

"Coward!"

The curse did not stop a smile from appearing on Ichigaku's face, burning with sweat.

"I got a foothold now. Who's a coward? Being raised in a small clan in Ako, you like cramped places, don't you? My technique uses all the directions of the universe. Come here! All of you!"

"The nerve!"

He couldn't tell one from the other. They looked like a flock of birds streaming toward him. The snow on the ground became powder and wrapped long swords and human figures in a blizzard.

Ichigaku positioned himself as usual while moving forward to receive the enemy horde, as much as possible, in a line. He slipped on the snow several times but seized by superhuman ability and unimaginable vigor, he sprung to his feet.

In no time, blood covered his body, and his hair was disheveled. Did one man's soul emanate the beauty of an end so magnificent and so impressive? The men approaching to attack him and those advancing not to kill were also unable to tell whether he was friend or foe.

The attacker's wish for a loyal soul was the only wish of the attacked man.

He was a flower. The blood, the snow, the swords, the eyes, everything became this flower of the highest virtue of humanity, the culmination of a samurai's path.

They chased him but felt this enemy was too much to handle and would never die. One man rushed in from the side to stand before Ichigaku and introduced himself.

"You're our enemy but an amazing man. True men can be found among the followers of Lord Kira. I am the Asano ronin Horibe Yasubei Taketsune,"

Horibe? Ichigaku fully opened his eyes, clouded by sweat.

"The enemy I hoped for."

"The rival I asked for."

The voices sparked a fire. The small sword held in Ichigaku's left hand soared like a flying fish into Yasubei's chest plate.

Just as Ichigaku thought the light of the sword missed his back, Yasubei's body and Ichigaku's body moved close enough to bump chests, and their fists exchanged blows.

The two tread cautiously in the snow but slipped and began drawing swirls. Each man's blade aimed in a tiny space swept away the other's kosode.

Tominomori Sukeemon's cross spear got entangled in the bases of both their collars. In an instant, Ichigaku's face turned to the open air. In his final moment, his face saw dawn in this snowy world.

Yasubei Taketsune's sword swiped across his forehead, cutting from the front of his shoulder down to his chest.

His red blood sprayed three feet.

"Eeyaah."

Grabbing for the truth of life in space as he fell like a tall tree, his short life of thirty years ended. Ichigaku had already written the date of his death on the paper memorial tablet with his mother's death. His corpse probably froze in the snow with a smile.

"..."

Yasubei, Sukeemon, Kanpei, and Gengo, sweat pouring off of them, placed their swords behind them to gaze at Ichigaku in death.

126

___

FRUSTRATION

A ROOSTER CROWED far away. Dawn was near. A voice sounding like Yoshida Chuzaemon said, "Usually, the living quarters are deeper inside than the inner garden and closer to the back than the front. Look for the back. Look for the back of the mansion."

A voice strained to give a command.

"We must find Lord Kira. Let's go!"

Yasubei and the others, each in his own time, abandoned Ichigaku's corpse and went back inside.

"Where's he hiding?"

Their frantic eyes were on a hunt.

At a corner in the central corridor, a large man bumped into Yasubei's shoulder.

Another man, a young man of just twenty, was behind him carrying a pole sword. His cowardly eyes trembled as he moved close to the wall.

Yasubei knew the large man, a steward named Sudou Yoichiemon, an expert in martial arts.

Yoichiemon looked startled, retreated one step, and moved his hand to the sword's handle.

"Bastard!"

He drew his sword, straightened his elbow, and struck in one motion.

After his rival slashed the air several times, Yasubei cut down Yoichiemon in a single stroke.

Seeing this, the young man who stuck to the wall launched his attack with panicked swinging of his pole sword. Yasubei forced a smile in the breeze created by the sword.

He may be a court noble, thought Yasubei and knocked down the pole sword and swatted his long sword with one hand. The young man let out an absurd, long shriek and dashed away.

Don't flush out people hiding.

Don't hurt women or children.

Use a short bow to shoot down anyone fleeing over the wall.

Moments earlier, Oishi Kuranosuke and Chikara shouted these ironclad rules several times to the moving fronts of the comrades engaged in battle.

Yasubei took no notice of the escaping man but picked up the pole sword he abandoned. He surveyed the blue shells on the handle, the gold fittings, the crest of the Kira clan, and the scattered crests of sycamore trees.

"Dammit! That was the heir Sahyoue no Suke."

This blunder galled him. Where is he hiding? I don't see him.

"Where is he?"

"Is he here?"

"Is he hiding here?"

These questions were asked by Hazama Jujiro, Otaka Gengo, Kurahashi Densuke, and others passing nearby.

In front of the cedar door that marked the deep interior of the residence, Chikamatsu Kanroku fought the

Kira attendant Torii Toshiemon. Hazama and Otaka barreled towards them.

"I don't need help."

That didn't stop them. They rushed in and cornered Toshiemon. Believing he was no match for the enemy, Toshiemon jumped into the courtyard and ran off.

"Get back here."

Fueled by a reserve of power to chase down and kill him, Kanroku accidentally jumped into the courtyard pond.

If Toshiemon had doubled back and swung his sword, what would have happened to Kanroku? But Toshiemon lost all nerve. He clung to a garden tree and stretched his leg to the top of the wall.

An arrow from a short bow shot from the mansion pierced Toshiemon's back. His corpse somersaulted down into the lake to take the place of Kanroku who had crawled out.

The unyielding nature of the surviving enemies remained. Of the eleven swordsman attendants sent from the Uesugi clan, including Sakakibara Heiemon, Osuga Jiroemon, and Yamayoshi Shinpachi, most were killed after putting up brave fights. In contrast, most of the hereditary vassals of the Kira clan either fled or hid. Laughably, as the stipends increased, the retainers lost all shame or decency and hid.

The most destructive force was always a momentary event. The sounds of swords, screams, and bowstrings echoing around the scene of carnage gradually subsided. In time, only isolated exchanges were heard.

"Where is he?"

"Is he here?"

"Over there?"

"He's not here!"

Eyes, noses, and lips twitched. Their entire bodies were bundles of nerves as they searched for Kira Kozuke no Suke's quarters.

They fought as long as they wanted and won. However, their last critical objective did not allow the Ako men to sing the victory song.

They already heard the first rooster crow in town. Daybreak was coming, but the key figure of Kozuke no Suke had not been found.

"Dammit … did he escape?"

Some stamped the ground in regret and sighed. A cry rose.

"All for nothing …"

Another came in tears like blood clouded his eyes and sniffed the darkness in confusion.

"What's wrong with you? It's too soon to be discouraged," an elder scolded, but his expression showed he'd lost confidence.

The search was painstaking; they went room by room.

The men raised spears to punch holes through the ceiling. They tore up the floor planks, kicked apart closets, and then used a spear or a long sword to ransack.

"Don't rush. Don't make a mess!" Yoshida Chuzaemon said to his enraged comrades.

"If we don't find him by dawn, even if it takes all day tomorrow, we will search until we find him. The well-informed among the public knew Lord Kira had been in the mansion since last night. Don't discount this evening's preparations. Without getting upset or discouraged, pay close attention to every spot in this mansion."

The men had their usual mysterious trust in Chuzaemon's words. In any situation, they drew strength from the confidence in his voice.

Where is the bedchamber in the living quarters?

Where is the sitting room? What about the tea room? These were the questions before the raid. They did everything in their power to find the answers. The floor plan was in Chuzaemon's hands. He should have had sufficient knowledge. But the rooms trampled down in frustration exposed the uselessness of the knowledge gained from the map.

Some rooms were unexpected. There was a hidden room, a tea room appeared, as well as a sitting room here, a bedroom there. They couldn't help being confused in the huge area.

Isogai Jurozaemon knew this kitchen best because he managed to carry out the map of Kozuke no Suke's bedroom and delighted his comrades with that knowledge.

"Well, Isogai-dono, where's his bedroom?" asked Oishi Chikara.

Kimura Okaemon came up from behind.

"Do you know?"

Jurozaemon's eyes lit up.

"Well?"

Okaemon shook his head and said nothing.

He entered a secluded room. The twelve-mat room was nondescript. He looked at the wall of the alcove where a wide hanging had fallen off. A cutout hole resembling the lantern opening in a tea ceremony room opened into another dark opening.

"What's that?"

"A cutout."

Air blew in through the opening. Okaemon moved closer but sensed danger.

While he wondered what was in there, Chikara glided through the hole.

Later, after Okaemon was placed in charge of the Hisamatsu clan, he answered the question, What kept me from entering the hole and Chikara climbing through first? His honest recollection was not only is there a difference between bravery and cowardice but also a difference in the quality of bravery.

As soon as Chikara entered the hole, he shouted, "This is it."

Jurozaemon and Okaemon followed him. Their feet touched a cold wood-plank corridor and faced three rooms they had not sensed from any location.

In one room, flowery bedding was laid out next to an arrangement of bedside candles. The air of a nobleman and the seductive scent of pleasure's afterglow drifted in the space. Needless to say, this must have been Kozuke no Suke's bedroom.

Near an unlit exquisite hanging lantern, a lacquer ashtray was overturned. Women's clothes were discarded in a corner, and no one lay inside the futons in any of the three rooms.

127

IN THE SHADOW OF A
KIMONO RACK

CHIKARA REACHED INSIDE the bedding. "It's still warm," he whispered.

Okaemon yelled, "It's open! Back here."

"They escaped through a secret passage."

The two hurried to the back.

Isogai Jurozaemon stayed behind as a precaution and poked and jabbed at the ceiling and closeted shelves. In one corner of the room adjoining the bedroom, he saw a lacquer kimono rack draped by a long, gold-accented blue uchikake overgarment and a pink kosode.

Then ... the rack rocked by itself and was about to topple over.

Jurozaemon turned with a start.

He pointed the white tip of his spear at the shadow of the kimono rack and quieted his breath.

Someone's hiding there!

A woman.

Probably, several guards had been in here. Why was she left behind when everyone else fled?

Jurozaemon appeared to have solved the riddle. The

eyes of the trembling woman in the shadow of the kimono rack and Jurozaemon's eyes connected for a moment like the spear was not between them. Tears filled her eyes. Jurozaemon's eyes glittered like pearls from the passion of blood and tears.

Jurozaemon said little. "It's dangerous. Stay in here."

"…"

The woman suppressed a groan with her shoulders. Her trembling shook the kosode and the kimono rack.

Others seemed to have discovered the cutout. Their footsteps and voices raised a racket.

"Oh no."

Jurozaemon panicked a bit. He might have missed the chance to say more. He spun around and leaped out into the snow light through the back door where Chikara and Okaemon exited a short time ago.

The red of daybreak was already faintly visible in the sky.

The whistle sounded to gather everyone. It was the signal decided long ago. Lord Kira is here. They found Kozuke no Suke-dono.

Four blows then five. The whistle blew the signal until every man appeared.

128

AN OLD SCAR

LIKE THE BEDROOM in an unusual place, the kitchen in the hideout was in an odd location. Inside was a coal room.

In one building, the door of the hut was locked from the outside. Nothing looked out of place at a glance.

"What's this?"

Chikara stopped. Okano Kinemon inched toward the wainscoting and pressed his ear against the wall.

Meanwhile, Yada Gorozaemon broke through a wooden door from an alley where Horibe Yasubei happened to be. Then Yokogawa Kanpei and Hazama Jujiro rushed up from behind.

"That's strange," said Kanpei.

"Open it," said the approaching Chikara. Sensing danger, Yasubei pushed him aside and placed his hand on the door.

Yada Gorozaemon hit the lock several times with the butt end of the spear. The lock popped off and the door to the coal room opened. He stepped in alone to be met by a flurry of plates, teacups, and pieces of coal and wood hurled from the pitch-black darkness.

"I see two or three men."

By that time, a considerable number of men had gathered outside. Someone said to get away from the front, then an arrow from a short bow was shot into the coal room.

From the darkness, a valiant young samurai came out fighting. Before the raid, he worked on night patrol inside the estate, intent on reassuring and protecting the sleeping lord.

"If I die …" he said, but his shout couldn't be heard. He came out holding his sword high and slashing at a ceiling of countless spears and long swords. His fresh young head with a disheveled topknot only got in the way of the men's feet.

Next, a middle-aged samurai came out to sacrifice himself. He was kicked on his bare shins, threw a sword into the group, and toppled forward. Someone grabbed him by the collar.

"Tell me where Kozuke no Suke is."

"If you don't, this should convince you!"

Yada Gorozaemon touched his spear to the thigh of the seated man. The samurai stubbornly refused to open his mouth but picked up a dropped blade.

He lunged.

"Bastards!"

"Dammit."

The men lowered their blades on him.

A queer tension surrounded the door to the coal room. One older-looking man remained inside.

Outside, they heard a series of dreadful, violent thumps. First, they thought someone else had entered the coal room, but that wasn't it. The last man seemed to be blindly moving around, determined to destroy something.

Hazama Jujiro entered. The figure saw him and ran toward the open door.

"It's Kira!"

Jujiro knew this instinctively and sent a spear to his feet. The old man took one powerful step outside and sat defiantly on the ground.

Not thinking he was Kozuke no Suke, Takebayashi Tadashichi stared and slashed his head with a long sword.

"Wait."

"It may be him?"

"Yes, yes."

"Is he Kira?"

The men weren't sure.

His hair was streaked with gray. He looked to be over sixty and wore silk nightclothes under a white quilted kosode. A search of his pockets uncovered his protectors, a statue of the Kannon, the Goddess of Mercy, and Jizo, the guardian deity of children.

"Well …"

"It's him."

Everyone assumed it was him. However, not one man had ever seen Kozuke no Suke's face.

"If he is Kozuke no Suke, he should have old scars on his face or body," said Kuranosuke.

One man inspected his hairline.

"Here's one," he said.

"There's a scar?"

"Yessir."

"All right. "

"Yes, that wound … is it an old wound on his forehead? That scar was the cut made by our late lord in the palace."

Whenever anyone spoke of the late lord, the comrades choked up. A whirlpool of emotions moved them to tears.

A couple of men groaned. The stamped-down emotions in others erupted at the sight of men bending their arms to cover their faces.

They cried out in pain and clung to each other, placing their faces on another's shoulder. In time, their wailing turned into tears of joy. The old and the young cried. Even Kuranosuke touched his fingertips to his eyelids for a moment and didn't see the dawn sky change.

PART XVIII

THE END OF WARS FOR THE UESUGI CLAN

129

THE TOFU SHOP MESSENGER

EVERY MORNING BEFORE the night ended, when a gong for a religious service could be heard behind Ekoin Temple, the husband and wife who ran a tofu shop were opening the rain shutters.

"Gisuke, Gisuke! It's me, Kimura Johachi. Are you up? Hurry. Let me in."

Although the front door remained closed that morning, the tofu merchant Gisuke and his wife were up and about. Gisuke lit the lamplight near the stone hand mill for beans while his wife drew ice-cold water from the well in the room with the dirt floor.

"Kura, someone's banging on the shop door. He sounds too excited. Open the door and tell him the people living here aren't deaf."

"It's still night. He's probably some ill-mannered buffoon. We're about to open so he can wait. He better not break the door."

The man outside kept pounding frantically.

"Are you asleep, Gisuke? It's me, Kimura Johachi. Please hurry and open the door."

"Oh, that sounds like Kimura-san."

Gisuke stepped the long teeth of his high geta clogs onto the dangerous ice near the sink and slipped.

"Is that you, Sir?"

"Yes, it's me. A serious incident has occurred. I have a request. Hurry open the door."

"I'm opening it now."

The threshold was iced over. He had to muster all his strength to slide open the door. The bright snow and moonlight dazzled his eyes.

This tofu shopkeeper did business with the kitchen at the Kira estate and was known to be an honest man. His shop became the home base of sorts of the young samurai on their nights out for a good time. Gisuke had always been friendly with Johachi.

"Come in, please. What brings you here so early?"

"Don't you know?"

"Know what?"

"A gang of Ako ronin finally raided the Kira estate."

"What? When?"

"Just now."

"..."

He listened carefully as the morning moon grew cold in the deathly silent neighborhood. Wild sounds like blowing snow echoed. For a long time, this old man bickered with the good people in the Kira household. He thought his body was trembling as he spoke.

"Kura, I'm going out. Keep the shop closed until I get back."

He ran out into the snow with Johachi who never explained the errand.

"Gisuke, Gisuke, don't turn there. This way."

"But Kira-sama's estate is this way."

"Don't worry. Be quiet and follow me."

"You're going that way, but the mansion is in the opposite direction. Master, where are you going?"

"To the main residence of the Uesugi clan in Sakurada."

"What? Me too?"

"No, you'll run to report this incident to Chisaka Hyobu-sama at the villa in Azabu Mamiana."

They exchanged shouts while running across Ryogoku-bashi Bridge. They reached the crossroads of Bakurocho where the all-night palanquins to Yoshiwara and horses for rent gathered around bonfires.

Kimura Johachi found and mounted a horse. Gisuke said he couldn't ride.

The distance to the Mamiana villa was twice as far as the main residence in Sakurada. Johachi planned to go to Sakurada to give a brief report but sent Gisuke instead.

"Well, I'll go to Chisaka-sama. Since you can't ride a horse, don't lose any time. Go by palanquin to inform the main residence," Johachi commanded as he took the reins from the horse driver. He sped off, constantly hitting the horse's belly with the end of the reins. The powder of the rapidly freezing snow turned the man and the horse white.

130

THE SWEAT OF ILLNESS

S INCE MAY, UESUGI Danjo Daihitsu had been bedridden from illness.

A fleeting look at his circumstance would give anyone the impression of a fortunate man with enviable success after being adopted from the Kira clan and appointed the governor-general of the powerful Yonezawa clan. However, Danjo Daihitsu always said, "The heir to a small clan is the lucky man. His challenge is to revive and expand. He is free to test his strengths. Doesn't a man born to that station rejoice?"

Like his biological father Kira Kozuke no Suke, he was tall and slender, but his health was nothing like his father's. From his early years, he was not educated humanely. He probably sat as the governor-general of this powerful clan and handled with care inside and outside. In an influential clan, a hereditary senior vassal or a subsidiary fief held power. Often the Danjo Daihitsu became the heir in the distinguished Uesugi clan by entering from the outside and was nothing more than a man adorned with the honorific title of Lord.

The retainer Chisaka Hyobu, a frequent visitor for many years, encouraged and consoled him. He was unrivaled in power internally and externally in clan administration and always said, "Be patient. The suffering of the common people and the hardship of being the head of a clan do not change the value of hardship. A man who succeeds in avoiding the gate of suffering does not become one of the ancients."

Chisaka Hyobu had not been in the daimyo's Edo mansion for the past several days of heavy snow. He was often stationed at the villa in Azabu.

Danjo Daihitsu apologized to him in his heart because he knew Chisaka wondered why he was often assigned to the Azabu mansion.

Needless to say, a series of problems in the Kira clan, beginning with the incident on March 14 of the previous year, engulfed his birth father.

This might have caused Danjo Daihitsu's illness. In July when Miyake Bizen no Kami was dispatched by the shogun as his envoy to call on the sick man, his condition was grave for a time.

Hyobu sat at his bedside. He filled his stern words with warmth.

"Why is your spirit so weak? Whatever it is, let this old man see to it."

Hyobu encouraged him with the words of a sage, the last words of the founder of his clan, Uesugi Kenshin.

But what Danjo Daihitsu saw over the past year was Chisaka Hyobu's hair turning completely white.

Uncle … Uncle … I'm sorry. This thought jumped into the mind of the bedridden Danjo Daihitsu when he opened his eyes.

The thuds of clumps of snow falling from the large eaves of the main residence woke him. He sat up and scanned the room. White steam rose from the large brazier. In a corner, two samurai government guards with heads dropped down had dozed off.

"What time is it?" he muttered.

"Oh?" A guard lifted his head and looked around. "I think it's about four in the morning."

"You're waiting for dawn."

"Does your chest hurt? Should I summon the doctor?"

As he shook his head no from the pillow, quick tapping footsteps entered the adjoining antechamber from the corridor.

In the antechamber were the doctor, the head page, the inner gate guard, and other guards. After a few words were spoken, one nearly shouted in surprise, "What? Is … is that true?"

"Unbelievable!"

Everyone was now standing.

They heard a shout from the corridor into another room.

"They're saying Ako ronin invaded Kira's mansion."

Danjo Daihitsu threw off his bedding and lifted his pale face.

"What? What happened?"

Before him, the inner gate guard Iwai Gorozaemon opened the sliding door and fell prostrate.

"Lord, you're awake?"

"Goroza, something seems to be causing a commotion. What is it? … What has happened?"

"It's unbelievable," Gorozaemon said, deliberately in a quiet voice.

"Just now, a merchant who does business with Kira-sama, a tofu merchant in Honjo called Gisuke, ran up to the gate. He reported that this morning a band of Ako ronin boldly forced their way into the mansion in Matsuzakacho."

"Oh no …"

Danjo Daihistu bit his lips drained of blood and stared at the white flickering of the candlestick.

"Just now? … It just happened?"

"I don't know the details, but the raid happened a short time ago. The circumstances are being verified by Kimura Johachi."

The governor-general had been ill since July and barely took one step out of his sickroom, but dressed in his white silk bedclothes, he shot to his feet.

"Damn them!"

He stumbled forward; the surprised Gorozaemon reached out to support him.

"Lord, Lord … Are you going out?"

"That's obvious," he said and waved away Gorozaemon's hand.

He roared with fury, "Bring my clothes. Guards, prepare. Prepare now!"

Beads of sweat rolled over his pale forehead.

131

THE UESUGI AVALANCHE

THE PAGE SUPERVISOR Mori and the other attendants stood crowded before Danjo Daihitsu.

Touching his sleeve to support him, Gorozaemon said, "You are ill. Lord, Lord … please rest."

Danjo Daihitsu shivered like he was suffering a convulsion.

"Ill? Who cares about illness? Although the Ako ronin have trampled the Kira estate and the honor of the Uesugi clan, if I idly remained in bed, do you think no sickness would touch me?"

"We are here. Lord, we are here to—"

"Silence. Do you have no sense of duty to me?"

"That's not so."

"Then bring what I asked for, now."

As the governor-general impatiently paced back and forth, he said, "Not a kosode, bring me a fireman's uniform. We're losing time. The Ako ronin will escape leaving only their footprints. Hurry!"

Few had ever heard such strong words coming from the lord's mouth. And the expression on his face said anyone who stood in his way would be sliced in two by the sword he wore.

"We have it."

Three or four attendants scurried in and laid the fireman's uniform beside him.

Danjo Daihitsu had already loosened and tossed away his obi sash.

The belly band, underwear, and leather socks were sorted by the attendant beside him who helped him dress.

"Daihitsu," called an elderly woman's voice from behind.

She was Tomiko, Kozuke no Suke's wife and Daihitsu's biological mother. When she left the mansion in Gofukubashi, she left Kozuke no Suke and came to this estate.

"Oh ..."

Danjo Daihitsu's heart was stirred by the sight of his mother. Tears rose and he could not look at her face.

His mother's eyes also seemed filled with tears. Danjo Daihitsu looked over the state of his preparation and became more frustrated.

"Please hurry," she said.

"Yes."

Daihitsu placed both hands on the ground and said, "Goodbye. How can I not go?"

"Be well," Tomiko said, wiping away tears.

"You. Sahyoue. I've been blessed with children ..." she was about to repeat her husband Kozuke no Suke's gloomy complaint but hesitated in front of the Uesugi clan attendants.

He sighed and mumbled to his mother, "I'll be fine. So it has finally come to pass."

"Don't worry."

A storm of footsteps was heard again in the corridor. Danjo Daihitsu shouted, "Ready the horses!"

He carried the pole sword with the blue shell handle under his arm like he snatched it from the attendant offering it and moved toward the scattered footsteps going out front.

"Ah, excuse my lateness."

Irobe Matashiro Shigemasa, the Uesugi clan's chief retainer in Edo, was late and rushing toward him. He looked deathly pale.

"I'm sure you know what has happened. Prepare for my absence."

"All will be ready in a short time."

"What?"

"As you know, the appearance of the lord is not a simple affair. First, someone from the clan will be dispatched to assess the situation."

"Silence. Is this the time for delays? Don't you understand?"

Samurai holding sharpened weapons continued filing outside. Spears and pole swords crowded the entryway and the garden.

"How violent were these stray ronin who lost their stipends?"

"I must see those Ako rogues one time."

"Don't be too undisciplined. It will impact the honor of the Uesugi clan."

"But this is an emergency."

"Should we check on the safety of the sheltering lord and his son?"

"No, eleven attendants selected from this clan will go. Surely, they were all shamelessly attacked. The men who came to protect the lord were probably not enough."

This turmoil was not unlike taking to the field in battle. Every man in the clan residence began to prepare.

Just as Danjo Daihitsu stepped out to the main entryway, a Kira clan vassal named Maruyama Seiemon came tumbling in the snow to report a sudden turn of events.

"Seiemon, how is my father?"

"He was injured."

He could not say the ronin took the lord's head.

"He was killed."

The governor-general's voice sounded tragic, shocked, and reverberated among the Uesugi clan members.

Dammit!

Some bit their lips.

Now it begins.

Oil was poured on the strong hatred of the Ako ronin.

For more than a year, the emotions of the Ako ronin and the samurai of the Uesugi clan heightened the danger, like fire and oil.

Since the days of Kenshin, the Uesugi clan was proud of its lineage in the way of the samurai. Perhaps many men inclined to passion were in the clan residence. To overlook this would offend the honor of the Uesugi clan and their status as warriors.

Their numbers overflowed outside the gate. An elder warrior followed by another kicked up snow racing on horseback to the front of the gate of the residence.

The gray-haired man was the retainer Chisaka Hyobu; behind him was Kimura Johachi.

Hyobu rode his horse into the armed retainers in front of the gate to ask, "What's going on?"

He jumped off the horse.

"Without my permission, not one man will rush to the scene at Kira-sama's. Go inside. Go back inside the gate."

"No, this is by order of the lord," someone replied.

"Silence!"

The front gate opened wide. Hyobu pushed it back with great force.

"You don't know if it was an Ako ronin gang, your actions are the actions of the Uesugi clan. First of all, when a clan possesses great force and weapons, the opinions of the subsidiary clans and senior vassals are always explained in the presence of the governor-general, then orders are handed down based on that consultation.

"For some time, the Chisaka clan together with the Hirobe and the Sawane clans were called the three branch families of the Uesugi clan. Since the time of Lord Kenshin, generation after generation, they sat in the upper seats in the council.

"I forbid taking up arms and acting by order of the governor-general in the absence of consensus among me and the other senior vassals. This will create discord for no good reason."

The truth of his reprimand sent the samurai back inside the gate. To the recalcitrant ones, he said in parting, "An order will certainly be handed down. Any man who rushes to Kira-sama's estate without permission will be severely punished."

Hyobu passed the reins to Johachi and pushed through the clan members to the entryway.

A voice resembling Hyobu's echoed in the governor-general's ears. The horse saddled with a mother-of-pearl saddle was there, but Danjo Daihitsu stood motionless. The butt of his long sword jutted toward the steps.

The lord and his follower spoke.

"Oh ... Uncle?"

"Lord."

During a brief silence, both contained their emotions ready to erupt and stood like stones.

132

REPEATING ANOTHER'S MISTAKE

HYOBU BOWED AND said, "First, I'd like to ... Shall we go inside?" and followed Daihitsu into the waiting room at the entryway. They sat close together.

"Hyobu, you've heard?"

"Kimura Johachi gave me a detailed account."

"We'll go inside and you can tell me what you know."

"Lord, there's a matter I'd like to discuss."

"Until today I've followed your advice on any matter. But today I object and will not stop."

"Then I will stop. I will give you my life."

"What?"

"Lord Irobe and Lord Fukusawa are here, but why haven't they asked the lord to stop? Even if I die, I will never let go of the hem of your trousers."

Danjo Daihitsu's suppressed emotions exploded.

"Hyobu! Dammit, Uncle."

"Yes."

"Do you intend to make me look like a fool to the world? Is there a son in this world more loyal to his father than I?"

"Of course, you are right."

"Have you lost your mind?"

Without thinking, Danjo Daihitsu raised his leg to shake off Hyobu's grip on the hem of his trousers. Hyobu's thin frame was flung toward the tatami, but he held on.

"Let go! Let go!"

He dragged Hyobu several steps as he spoke.

"The vassals delay, and the Ako ronin will melt away. The disgrace staining the Uesugi clan will not be erased for generations. Uncle, you are in the way. Release my leg and confine yourself inside."

Hyobu held tight. "Please wait."

If the attendants leap at him on the lord's order, he planned to drive them back with a howl. Chisaka Hyobu's sharp white eyes glared at those men. Not one dared interfere.

"Lord, just a little longer … please wait a little longer. I have something to show you."

"What is it?"

"The five articles of the constitution of the Chisaka clan received from the founder, Lord Kenshin. Please note the first article. It states

1. *Uesugi exists, Chisaka exists; Chisaka exists, Uesugi exists. It is that simple. The sovereign family shall be respected.*

"…"

"This is not boasting, but since the time of the founder Chisaka Kagechika, Chisaka carried the lineage in which an attending chief retainer is appointed and holds the same rights as the governor-general of the Uesugi clan to handle any serious incident related to the fate of the sovereign family.

"The words were awe-inspiring, but you and I do not differ as lord and follower but differ in age. My wisdom is how I see the world, the people, and the essence of a matter, and excel in understanding the overall situation."

"Uncle, your eloquent explanation was in vain. You were probably just stalling."

"Yes, I was. However, good will come of this, and you may come to understand my complaint."

"What good will come? Where will the honor of the Uesugi clan stand? The name of the undutiful son Danjo Daihitsu will be a joke for generations to come. And where will the military clan stand?"

"I'm sure the world will laugh. However, justice in a military clan will be ridiculed."

"You're in the way. You're wasting time. Let go! Get my horse!"

"Listen to reason!" Hyobu's voice strained as he scolded him like a child. "Have you forgotten about the lord and the follower of our powerful Yonezawa clan? The death of Kozuke no Suke-sama is consequential. Don't you value the lives of the people of the Uesugi clan?"

He sounded nothing like an ordinary vassal.

His severe tone weakened Danjo Daihitsu's legs.

"Please sit," said Hyobu solemnly and straightened his posture.

"You are quite right. I do not understand your feelings at all, but my guesses break my heart. There must be affection between a parent and a child. First, however, the lord through his experiences must always become the heart of the people as well as be the heart of the vassals. That is the principle of just rule.

"Even if acts of selfishness, ego, and little justice are proper, as the lord, you must forbid them. Your love is small justice and is not the same as the justice of the military clan. Please understand your emotions will drive you to push the clan samurai into a clash with the Ako ronin. It will be a bloodbath.

"I am guilty of having a personal struggle at your knees. The court's censure of me may be inevitable. Lord, I believe you're not troubled about battling ronin who threw away their stipends or upsetting the sovereignty of the Uesugi clan.... But do you believe that will revive the severed head of your birth father?"

"..."

"I knew this incident was inevitable and always kept you informed indirectly of my readiness. Have you reached this day without a decision in your heart?"

"..."

"Even the lord must have heard the rumors of the many wretched figures of those vassals or family members left in tears by the vile public scorn caused by Asano Takumi no Kami's recklessness."

"..."

"To repeat myself, your body is not yours. Your body is the heart of the people and the vassals and carries the great responsibility to protect the sovereignty possessed since the time of the founder. Your mental anguish is like biting the root of a tooth. You must eliminate your ego and personal feelings and exhaust your body for the sake of the people and the nation."

"..."

Danjo Daihitsu slumped into his seat and dropped his head.

While encouraging himself, Hyobu in a tearful voice said, "Oishi Kuranosuke's stance and mission as the leader of the faction are the warrior's way of a vassal. He may not understand his actions are the noblest ones in the warrior's way.

"The lord and the Uesugi clan may be outraged at the present situation and rush to confront them, but that would not be a righteous act. Heartless townsmen will laugh, but they will be the outliers. True experts and men well informed about military families will not thoughtlessly say your family was cowardly or you lacked filial devotion."

"Hyobu, … I … I understand. I hear your words as a rebuke from the founder of the clan."

"I'm sorry."

Hyobu fell prostrate and asked, "But do you understand?"

"I erred and was about to repeat the mistake of Asano Takumi no Kami."

"It's getting cold.… Lord, please let me help you up. You must take care of yourself. You are ill and should return to your sickroom."

He took the governor-general's hand and led him inside.

No one followed the two. When the door closed behind them, Danjo Daihitsu surprised Hyobu with a hug.

"Uncle.… Uncle, please forgive me."

"It's all right. It's all right."

At the threshold of the room, Hyobu's voice and body weakened. He sobbed without making a sound, and a stream of tears spilled down the governor-general's back.

"I understand and I thank you for understanding. Starting today, I will be sick, too."

The lord and his follower collapsed into their seats.

133

THE TASTE OF TANGERINES

AN ATTACK BY the Uesugi force would come.

Kuranosuke saw this first, then Yoshida Chuzaemon and the others.

Pull back!

The whistle sounded. The ronin looked around the trampled-down estate and extinguished the candles, poured water over the remaining fires in the braziers, counted the dead and wounded enemies, and treated wounded comrades.

"Go to Ekoin Temple. To Ekoin Temple."

Men streamed out from the front and back gates.

Only four comrades were wounded: Yokogawa Kanpei, Hara Soemon, Chikamatsu Kanroku, and Kanzaki Yogoro. However, the enemy dead numbered sixteen. Over twenty men had minor or serious injuries.

Around six in the morning, they came out at the main Ryogoku Road. The morning moon had changed.

From the back of the line, Yoshida Chuzaemon and Hara Soemon, dragging his leg, spoke to the young men in front.

"Don't break rank."

"We're still in battle."

From the head of the line, one man, Kanzaki Yogoro, ran out ahead.

Was he scouting?

This was the immediate thought of the anxious men, stressed by constant thoughts of the coming avalanche of Uesugi's power. Yogoro turned left at the corner of a long earthen wall and pounded on the door at the large front gate of Ekoin Temple.

"I'm addressing those inside the temple. We are the ronin of the late Asano Takumi no Kami. A short time ago, we avenged our late lord and have come from Lord Kira's mansion. We'd like to borrow your temple to rest for a little while. If it's not too much trouble, please open the gate."

After he repeated this shout a few times, a muted response came from the other side of the gate.

"We apologize for keeping you waiting."

"Unfortunately, the chief priest is away. We don't have the authority to open the gate. I'm sorry, you may not enter."

Yogoro's reply was an exasperated tongue snap.

Meanwhile, his comrades stood at the crossroads, preparing for the unlikely appearance of the enemy when they heard about the rebuff at Ekoin.

Yogoro pointed and said, "We'll rest over there. That place looks good."

It was a local sake dealer. The proprietor opened the door, casually looked in their direction, lost color, and scrambled to shut the door.

"Open up! Open the door."

Yasubei ran to him and appeared to calm the trembling proprietor. He smiled as he raised his hand to summon the group. They gathered around and handed over money.

"Proprietor, bring one *komokaburi* barrel out to the porch."

Each man held a teacup. The sake cold enough to penetrate teeth made their throats gargle with "Aaah."

Dawn faintly lit the eastern sky. Kira Kozuke no Suke's head was wrapped in a white kosode robe, lashed to the tip of a spear, and held high.

Someone said, "Aaah, delicious. It seeps into my bones."

Kuranosuke was also given a cup.

The elders expressed their satisfaction.

"Even in death, I will not forget this taste," said Junai in jest.

Otaka Gengo and Tominomori Sukeemon asked the proprietor for an ink stone, perhaps to write haiku.

"Now, let me see." Okuda Magodayu peeked and recited the poem.

"The power to wrench mountains breaks. Fallen snow piled on pines. Isn't that a verse by Otaka Shiyou?"

"Yes."

Everyone nodded.

"Now, Sukeemon's."

"The body of the winter bird is plucked."

"That was excellent."

A man carried in a box of tangerines mixed with rice cakes. He was Jinzaburo, the servant of Chikamatsu Kanroku.

"You miss nothing." Kanroku praised him and placed rice cakes and tangerines in everyone's hands.

The tangerine skins on the snow created scattered splashes of bright yellow. In that terrifying battle of swords, somehow, few of the men came out smeared with blood. The young comrades, including Chikara, Sukeemon, and Emoshichi, were telling jokes and falling out laughing.

As the sky whitened, the bloodstains on each kosode and weapon vividly reflected in their eyes.

Kuranosuke cautioned the group. "Spearmen, tear off your sleeve markers and wrap your spear points."

They soon reached the crossroads of the main street where only black figures stood. No one approached. They simply stared at the large number of men staring their way and understood the shock in the countless eyes darting back and forth.

"That doesn't look like the Uesugi clan has come here to attack," whispered Chuzaemon.

"There's Chisaka," said Kuranosuke in a low voice.

However, others were anxious. Another plan was not only the Uesugi clan but also the Kira clan would track them down to annihilate them.

The party included Kujuro, a nephew of the elder Horibe; Oishi Sanpei, a distant relative of Kuranosuke; and Horiuchi Gentazaemon, an expert swordsman. Each was accompanied by several disciples.

"It was a success. Your hope has been achieved."

Their happy words explained why they came.

"No, I see no signs of men from the Uesugi clan, from Sakurada or Azabu."

"Well then."

The ranks formed proper lines and began walking the road to Sengakuji Temple. The fifteenth was the day of thanks on which various noblemen are in attendance at the castle. They avoided crossing Ryogoku-bashi Bridge and marched straight to Kashisuji in eastern Ryogoku and climbed the first bridge.

"Aah."

The men's hands shielded their eyes from the glare. The morning sun broken by the clouds at daybreak burned red on the forty-six faces.

PART XIX

A FIRESIDE CHAT AT SENGAKUJI TEMPLE

134

THE GATE OF TIME

A s THE STORY goes, the moment the sun rose, the snow in Edo was dirtied black. Every citizen of Edo went out to the streets and stirred up a storm.

"It's done!"

The public's premonition was not betrayed. They watched the truth pass before their eyes.

They wanted to shout, "You did it! Thank you!"

Their naive excitement made them tremble. The streets at daybreak sketched an unusual scene.

Citizens from the assorted classes of society witnessed the withdrawal of the line of forty-six ronin led by Oishi. Most of the gaping eyes belonged to curious onlookers. That unsophisticated group was struck by the action stemming from the ronins' conviction. They scrutinized these human forms, beings greater than dogs, shimmering on the snow, and discovered their humanity. The faces of the scores of ordinary citizens flocking to the crossroads and the roadsides reflected a new awareness of the samurai class.

We are different. We are not lower than beasts.

With envy resembling respect, the ordinary towns-people saw off the uniformed ronin who smelled sweeter, looked more beautiful, and wore mysteriously serene expressions.

The planned withdrawal route began in an alley near the boathouse, crossed Eitai Bridge, and coursed through Reiganjima island, Teppouzu, Shiodome Bridge, Hibiya, passed before the Sengoku estate and the Date mansion, and crossed Kanasugi Bridge to arrive at Sengakuji Temple that was nearly four miles from Matsuzakacho.

Out of concern, Kuranosuke turned to Yahei. "Elder, you look tired. Hail a palanquin." In line with his nature, Yahei shook his head no, but unable to match the strides of the younger men, climbed into a town palanquin near the boathouse.

Along the way, the wounded men, Hara Soemon, Chikamatsu Kanroku, and Kanzaki Yogoro, were placed on carriers.

From time to time, tearful relatives of the ronin dashed from the crowds to grip the men's hands. Did friends and strangers glimpse this scene and wonder what they didn't know about those men? Emotions welled up from their chests to their eyes.

"Teppouzu," some men muttered. The procession of ronin stopped unexpectedly at the gate of the daimyo's mansion of the former Asano clan.

The flow of time struck them. Asano Takumi no Kami's presence there was in the past. Many vassals and family members whose lives centered on him had been carried away by the progress of time and disappeared to places far from this gate.

But now, only forty-six of those men achieved their

great ambition and passed before the gate a second time on their way to inform the late lord at the family's *bodaiji* temple of their success. Kuranosuke looked on disheartened. All of them recalled unique memories as they passed the gate.

135

THE MAN AT THE SIDE OF THE ROAD

"Juroza. Juroza. Juroza," Kuranosuke called when he reached Kanasugi Bridge and turned to look over the heads of the men behind him.

Leaving the line and coming forward, Isogai Jurozaemon answered, "Yessir."

"Juroza, Shogen-bashi Bridge is nearby."

"Is it?"

"Would you like to see her? I believe your mother lives close to this bridge."

"Uh."

"She was moved to the home of your older brother Naito Nan'emon, fell seriously ill, and can no longer sit up. I don't think you'll have another chance to see her. Go see your mother, then you'll have no regrets leaving this world."

"Yessir."

"You have my permission, we'll see you again soon."

Jurozaemon looked down, moved to tears by Kuranosuke's words.

"No, I'm staying." He was firm and stepped back into the line.

Kuranosuke did not ask why. He and every man walking with him understood Jurozaemon.

Sengakuji Temple was nearby.

Melting snow formed muddy spots. Muddy water splashed onto the backs of the ronin. At the Mita crossroads, a whisper rose.

"Look there, a stranger's coming this way."

Horibe Yasubei turned away. Okuda Magodayu also looked away, pretending not to see him.

"Who is he?" asked one after another.

"Look at that grinning man coming this way. Isn't that the traitor Takata Gunbei?"

"Sure is."

Elder Yahei appeared to have heard their whispers and stepped out to the side of the procession. He looked like he wanted to call out, "Is that you, Gunbei-dono? Hey, Takata!"

Takata Gunbei managed a smile as he approached the side of the road.

"Well, Elder, you and your comrades achieved your long-cherished plan."

"You see, Gunbei, we accomplished this through determination and are taking the head of Kozuke no Suke to Sengakuji Temple. Why are you out here traipsing through the melting snow?"

"For necessary personal reasons. Although each man will depart this world and covets his remaining time, every morning for the last dozen days, I made a secret pilgrimage to Mita Hachiman Shrine to pray for success in your goal one day sooner. I'm on my way home now."

"Oh, but isn't this the way home from the pleasure quarters in Shinagawa?"

"That's ridiculous. Anyhow, I spotted your party's grand return and was delighted."

Both the man asking and the man answering were shrewd and a little too jovial, but Gunbei looked pained. He never looked this miserable before.

However, Yahei thought the shame coming like fire from Gunbei's face surfaced only at that moment. When about three hundred feet away, Gunbei looked back and felt no remorse over his wise choice to stray from that path.

"That bunch is honest to a fault. I'm astonished they executed it as planned.... The gossip spread over seventy-five days was kindled by fleeting emotions. They threw away their unknown future lives of several decades. Idiots. My future lies in the fleeting world of pleasures."

However, no one heard rumors of Takata Gunbei enjoying the ideal future life he imagined. Did he later maintain the self-confidence of that time to spit at the forty-six men who moved in the opposite direction? Was there a day he did not feel the nothingness and spiritual poverty of his remaining years?

Whatever path life takes, the path selected by each person will be different. However, the person who seizes meaning and a life worth living will enjoy life to the maximum and be immortal. Will one's life never decay, or will one disappear into a life that is nothing more than a withered leaf? A man only chooses what he wants.

136

A WHITE WORLD

THAT MORNING, THE residents of the monks' dormitory gathered in the dharma hall of Sengakuji Temple to socialize over Zen-style ceremonial tea.

"What's going on? What's that racket?"

"This is awful!"

An acolyte raced in and quickly described the situation to the men who pricked up their ears.

The gatekeepers ran inside, leaving the main temple empty. Forty-six men came through the gate and stood. The shouts of one echoed deep into the Buddhist temple to the dharma room.

"This message is for the guardians of this temple. We are the vassals of the late Asano Takumi no Kami. Tonight, we invaded the Kira estate in Honjo to ask for the head of Lord Kozuke no Suke. We achieved our goal and came to present our offering at the grave of our late lord. Together, we will go to the family cemetery. We ask you to shut the main gate to prevent outsiders from entering when we pass through to his grave and report to our lord's soul."

The monks in the dharma room fell silent and gave full attention to his voice. Their expressions asked, What should we do? The brow and eyes of the head priest Cho-on moved first.

Guessing his feelings, one blurted, "Tell them no. They cannot enter without the permission of the shogunate."

Shoten Sokuchi jumped to his feet. He was the deputy administrator of the temple, second to Priest Cho-on.

"Wait. There may be a better way to drive them away without being so blunt. By the laws of the shogunate, a higher ranking official should handle this matter and give instructions. It must be done like a Buddhist to a Buddhist. Sengakuji Temple has been the cemetery of the Asano clan for generations and must maintain this bond. Not to mention, those loyal vassals rely on the support of this temple and from their hearts will give their offering at the grave of their late lord. Although as monks, we may have reasons to refuse them, let them pass, but tell them to make haste to the grave."

From outside, the gatekeeper who went around to the inner garden said, "Sokuchi-sama, they've already filed in and gone to the grave."

Satisfied, Sokuchi said, "That's fine. Gatekeeper, have all other visitors leave the grounds, then close the main gate for a short time."

The monks went out and saw a crowd much larger than imagined. A throng trailed the ronin from Fukugawa and Kyobashi. When they were sent out and the gate closed, they swarmed the wall and knocked down the graveyard fence. The many monks of Sengakuji were enveloped by the overpowering mood brought by the crowd, grew excited like actors in a play, and scurried about the temple grounds.

The pure, thick snow piled on the graves turned many tombstones into round snow pagodas. Nothing in the graveyard cast a gloomy shadow this morning.

At the well at the graveyard's entrance, Kuranosuke filled the bucket with water to wash Kozuke no Suke's head.

The temple priest Sokuchi, standing behind him, asked, "Is there anything you need? Anything you wish, sir?"

Kuranosuke turned. After he explained the situation, he said, "That is kind of you. I hesitate to ask but may I borrow an incense burner and three sticks of incense?"

"Of course."

Sokuchi gave the order to a servant who soon returned carrying the items.

This is it.

The forty-six men stopped and looked up at one snow-covered gravestone. Under Kuranosuke's orders, Chikara respectfully removed the snow from that grave engraved with the Buddhist posthumous name of Asano Takumi no Kami.

Reikoinden saki no shofu …

The characters engraved on the gravestone appeared from beneath the snow. They brought back the sense of having an audience with the living lord.

… Chosan Daibu Suimo Genri Daikoji

When these characters came into view, the forty-six men sat on the snow.

Incense smoke drew an unbroken purple line, like a

bloody sleeve from last night turned into smoke. Downcast eyes before the grave slowly looked up to see the washed head of gray hair placed on a triangle of plain wood as an offering.

"..."

Kuranosuke fell prostrate. Every man thought of himself in that position. The words spoken by Kuranosuke to the late lord's grave echoed their voices.

At that moment, Takumi no Kami's grave was not a cold stone to the forty-six men. Their characters were complete in both sincerity and action. The stone seemed to cry out of joy to their moist eyes and to move as it listened to Kuranosuke's report.

Then, Kuranosuke pulled out his short sword, pointed the blade at the head, and placed it on the stone pedestal. He picked up the sword and tapped the head three times.

"..."

Again, he lit incense, kneeled on the snow, spread his hands, and placed them on his knees. A long time had passed since he last sat like this, solemn and straight, in the reception hall in Ako Castle.

His eyes passed over the heads of the party.

"Hazama."

"Yessir," Hazama Jujiro answered from a distance.

"Please come forward." His voice was stern.

Jujiro hesitated. Urged by discreet whispers, he timidly moved forward.

Kuranosuke said, "As we agreed earlier, no distinction will be made in the depth of meritorious service in this undertaking. However, your spear was the first to touch Lord Kozuke no Suke, an act with divine protection to samurai. With your comrades' permission, you should be the next to burn incense."

"Yessir."

"The second sword Takebayashi Tadashichi will be next."

"Me?"

As if ashamed, both men stiffened with surprised expressions.

137

THE MEN AT THE MEMORIAL SERVICE

SENGAKUJI TEMPLE WAS the largest Zen temple in the Kanto region. It was big enough to serve meals to one hundred guests and did not lack amenities. Warmth spread from the kitchen, but smoke from the firewood penetrated the eyes and, for a time, bothered those inside the temple. The ronin entered the main temple and made themselves at home. Seated on the tatami, they wondered, Is this a dream?

Priest Cho-on asked and wrote down every man's name and took it to the superintendent of temples and shrines. He returned to calm expressions all around, like they didn't have a care in the world. His demeanor became more serene, and he went out to the main temple.

"As you know, the Zen sect has the strict rule that forbids the entry of pungent vegetables and liquor through the main gate of a temple. But you are all tired, so I ordered a cup of inexpensive sake for each of you. The kitchen is preparing gruel for your meal. Please rest."

Kuranosuke thanked him for his hospitality.

"I wondered how could I ask for drinks given the ban

on liquor in the temple. Because of your considerable kindness and little to dislike here, we will eat to our fill."

"There's no need to worry."

Each man tipped a cup, big or small at his pleasure. Redness soon outlined Kuranosuke's eyes.

A voice said, "The bleached bones in the earth were treated with unexpectedly warm hearts."

That's right. Before long, we'll be the bleached bones in the earth.

This was the shared thought of the tipsy men. They recalled the offering of sake poured on the ground in memoriam.

"Priest. Priest."

A group surrounded him.

Priest Cho-on turned to answer.

"Yes."

From among the youthful faces shining bright red, the elder Horibe Yahei said, "After the meal, we'd like you to give us last rites for departed souls."

The priest waved away the request.

"I'm sorry, but that's not possible."

"Why?"

"Why not?"

"We priests have practiced asceticism in deep meditation on the floor for thirty or forty years, cling to the teachings of our path of Buddhist devotion, and struggle with abstinence. In other words, we aim to achieve the state of mind each of you now enjoys. Even with a lifetime of training, that destination is difficult to reach. How can foolish priests guide you? Rather, we'd like to learn about your state of mind."

"Ha, ha, ha. Well, these samurai will only die alone and pass to the other world alone."

"No, as someone said earlier about bleached bones in

the earth, before long, last rites will be spoken for our departed souls."

Sokuchi returned. "The bath is hot. Anyone who wishes to enjoy one is welcome."

The men exchanged glances. Just the mention of this unexpected hospitality filled their hearts."

On behalf of the group, Kuranosuke replied, "Thank you. But our being here means soldiers commanded by the Kira and Uesugi clans will attack at any moment. This is not the time for baths."

As expected, the neighbors of Sengakuji and throughout the city said the Uesugi force would strike in a great storm.

False information echoed throughout the temple.

"Two hundred samurai are on their way from the Uesugi estate in Sakurada."

"Squads of ten or twenty scouts are active near Fudanotsuji."

"We think almost thirty Kira vassals landed at the shore in Takanawa."

The faces of the younger men, not satisfied by the previous night's activities, said "We're waiting! Any time is good!"

They inspected their blades, retied their bellybands, and inspected everything down to the cords of their straw sandals.

Chikara surveyed the furious men and said, "That's unnecessary. The best plan is to rest your bodies. If Uesugi's force aims to launch an attack, would they choose the middle of the day?"

His father Kuranosuke added, "He's right. We think alike. However, those who think differently must not boast of wisdom. The best course is to be prepared for an emergency."

An acolyte said to Chikara, "I'd like to see that. A real fight." .

"If they attack, we'll show you. You probably see an actual war as nothing more than crossing swords in a puppet show in a frontier town, but it's glorious."

Then a kitchen monk with rolled-up sleeves came in.

"Everyone, the gruel is ready. Will you eat now or later?"

"It may be gruel, but I want to eat right now."

"There's a lot of sake left."

"We'll drink that, too."

The elder Okuda Magodayu burst out laughing.

"You've been quite busy.… Everyone has returned to being human …"

Sake plunged them into drunkenness. Stomachs filled. Their fatigue from last night appeared on their skin. Some sunk down in clusters around the large hearth and lay on their sides snoring.

"Aah, it's nice and warm now."

"Emoshichi, come here for a thumb wrestling match."

"Thumb wrestling. All right. Chikara won't beat me."

Rowdy laughter erupted.

138

A PEEK INSIDE

T HE MONKS IN the kitchen cooking rice were huddled together whispering.

"Hey, a woman is mixed in that crowd."

"Don't be stupid. How does a woman mix into ronin seeking revenge?"

"Well, it's true."

"No, it's not."

"Come here and have a look."

"Where is she?"

"There … in that bunch of ronin gathered around that hearth … in the group of seven- or eighteen young fellows flush in the face and losing at thumb wrestling."

"Uh-huh, I see."

"That's not a man. She's just dressed like a man. No matter how I look at her, I only see a woman."

Everyone agreed.

Usually, the words "a woman is here" would be received coldly, but now they were out for blood. An extraordinary urge was sparked in the temple. The acolytes took turns peeking into the room with the hearth.

Disturbed by this, the head disciple, Sokuchi, marched in to patrol the kitchen.

"What are you idiots looking at?"

"The woman in there with the ronin," one cook told him.

Sokuchi went to see the unbelievable sight and returned smiling.

He laughed. "That is Xue Diao."

"Who is Xue Diao?"

"No, he may be Wei Jie."

"Who are you talking about? Xue Diao? Wei Jie? I have no idea who they are, please tell me."

"They're written about in Chinese books."

"Oh?"

"Xue Diao grew to be an astoundingly beautiful man and scholar. People called him a living Buddha. Wei Jie also became an elegant, beautiful man and went to the capital. Having heard of his reputed beauty, spectators came to see and clogged the streets like a fence. When Wei Jie fell ill and died, everyone in the capital believed their eyes killed him. He was too beautiful and was watched to death by the crowds."

"Is that a woman or a man?"

"As a woman, she's plain. He's a man."

"What? ... That's a man?"

"A man named Yato Emoshichi. He's seventeen."

Their voices probably carried a distance. From the side of the hearth, Emoshichi happened to look their way.

He noticed the crowd of monks from the kitchen looking at him and talking. Emoshichi felt ashamed. He swiftly rose and exited through the veranda on the side of the main temple. Some, sounding concerned, called, "Emoshichi-dono. Hey, Emoshichi-dono."

He glanced down the corridor to see the face seen at

the roadside a little while ago, the face of the deserter Takata Gunbei.

"Is that you Takata-dono? What are you doing here?"

"Could you be my messenger?"

"For what?" asked Emoshichi. His eyes dropped to the sake cask covered by a straw mat carried by Gunbei.

"The truth is … My friends accomplished their grand ambition. Although I broke from the secret pact, my heart never intended to abandon the group. After leaving you earlier, I wanted to share my feelings. I thought about it and brought this cask of sake as my token of gratitude. When Elders Horibe and Okuda saw me earlier, they looked disgusted. I'm reluctant to go to the main temple, so can you deliver this and give them my best? Please?"

"Please, Gunbei, I can't take this."

"Why not?"

"Can you ask someone else?"

"Please, kindly ask for me?"

He spoke tentatively. "Well …"

The instant he saw Yasubei, Emoshichi said, "Horibe-dono, Horibe-dono," and looked like he was trying to get away. Gunbei turned to leave. Yasubei spotted that sake cask sitting there.

"Hey, Gunbei."

He turned. "Yeah."

His smile was honest but could not hide the weakness of his guilty conscience.

"Is this your sake?"

"Break it open. It's a small gift to express my feelings."

"Your feelings?"

"…"

"Gunbei, I'd like to accept this item brought here by a friend. But even if I accepted sake from a stranger, I cannot drink sake from you."

"Don't get me wrong. My feelings ... my feelings will always be the same as all of yours."

139

A FIGURE IN THE SHADOWS

"Stop!" His contempt was clear. "Gunbei, the path you have taken in life is in many ways not a particularly fine way to live. Lies may be the truth to your comrades. But to mine, adorning oneself is a weak way to live. In the end, the most a man resembling scum in this world can expect is to live life free of the trivial matters of the world.... My final words to you as your friend are any path is fine, Gunbei, but it's a lie if you can't punch through and live the path you chose."

"Thank you."

Run down like a dog with its skin stripped off, Gunbei, hunched and looking down, raised his head.

"Yasubei, only you would tell me that. I won't forget. I will live with my head high and do good work in the world. But I put my spirit into this sake. Can you find a way to give it to the men?"

"You're hopeless, Gunbei, and a pain. Go home now."

"I'll leave this here."

"You fool!"

Yasubei lost his temper. His furious tone bombarded Gunbei like spit.

"You came to get permission to visit the lord's grave. If you knew you were going to bring sake to us, why didn't you sweep snow from the grave with us this morning? Your inability to deceive no matter what mask you wear and going to the lord's grave show you're still a good man. If anyone else discovered you, he would have beaten you. No more of your lip. Go home!"

Then Yasubei's words became blunt when he yelled at the monks in the kitchen.

"Close the side door at the main gate. Leaving it open allows unauthorized people with no business here to wander in. Drive off this man with this sake cask."

After Gunbei made a quick exit, the acolytes tossed his cask out the side gate.

When they went to close the gate, one acolyte's eyes opened wide and stared at a corner inside the main gate.

"What's that?"

He jogged over to it. A hooded woman lingering in a gloomy corner of the gate looked down and shrunk into the corner.

The acolyte stared like she was transparent.

"It's a woman…. She looks like a real woman."

Another monk looked like he wanted to grab her wrist and reveal her face.

"Who are you?"

He cross-examined her. "Why did you enter the grounds? Huh? Why are you here?"

She paled inside the hood. Her lips trembled.

"No … nothing. I'm …"

"You came in here without permission. You probably want to peek at the Ako ronin."

"Yes, yes, that's it."

"Please go now, outside the gate."

"Yes, I'm leaving."

"An official of the shogunate will be here soon. Please leave."

The woman was beautiful and slender with the refined scent of wealth.

She trembled as she inched toward the side gate and frequently looked with tearful eyes to the main temple where the ronin were resting. She seemed to be searching for someone.

No ONE else was in the cramped room. Isogai Jurozaemon sat alone behind a screen partition painted in the style of the Kanou school.

When he thought he caught sight of Jurozaemon, Maebara Isuke left the main temple and called him in a low voice like a dove.

"Juroza, Juroza ..."

Jurozaemon didn't answer, but Isuke found him behind the screen. Isuke had changed his name to the rice dealer Gohei who ran a shop in Aioicho in Honjo to watch Kira's movements. Until that day, they were friends with kindred spirits.

"Hey, what are you doing here? Juroza, did you hear?"

"What?"

"She came. The woman from the Kira estate. Tsuya."

Juroza looked down with cold eyes. His hair seemed to wobble like needles. Isuke looked away.

"A miserable sacrifice. Maybe, you should go and comfort her with kind words. Your feelings kept you from going to your mother's home earlier. Don't hold back. Juroza, those same lingering feelings drove Emoshichi's

Kume crazy. Now, she wanders the streets. Emoshichi doesn't understand a woman's heart and easily forgot about her, but you can't."

"Maebara."

"Yes."

"I may sound selfish, but I don't doubt you have another friend to confide in. Go back to the hall and laugh with the others."

"You're right."

"I have a headache. I want to lie down for a while, but I'll return to the main temple soon. Go back to those merry, laughing voices. Okay, Maebara?"

While speaking, Juroza gazed at the snow's bright glare and turned on his side.

PART XX

NIGHTTIME TALKS OF THE LOYAL RETAINERS HELD BY THE HOSOKAWA CLAN

140

THE RIGHTEOUS PATH OF REVENGE

"SUKEE-DONO, ISN'T this the residence of the inspector-general?"

"Yes, we should call on him first."

Tominomori Sukeemon and Yoshida Chuzaemon were still dressed in the uniforms worn for the raid and carrying their large spears. Since dawn, the spearheads had been hidden, wrapped by bleached white cloths.

Outside the residence's gate, Sukeemon said, "This is a request to the gatekeeper. We are the Asano ronin Yoshida Chuzaemon and Tominomori Sukeemon, vassals of the late Takumi no Kami. We've come to make an urgent appeal to the inspector-general, Houki no Kami-sama, and are requesting a meeting."

"One moment, please."

The rushing footsteps of the vassals disappeared inside. Meanwhile, townsmen discovered the pair. Curiosity made them want to get closer.

"Look, Ako ronin."

"The samurai who attacked."

Their eyes opened wide at the unusual sight of samurai

dressed for battle. They stared as they formed a circle at a safe distance and slipped closer the more comfortable they felt. The first man to speak up launched a stream of comments.

"Hey, Ako ronin-sama, you're finally done. Today, Edo is filled with rumors about you."

"Why have only you two not withdrawn to Sengakuji?"

"Congratulations," said a passerby.

"A fine deed."

People bowed their heads to the pair as they walked by like they were involved in some way.

Chuzaemon and Sukeemon responded to the people's kind words only with grins and smiles. Embarrassed at times, they turned back to the gate to wait for the reply.

Around that time, their comrades were arriving at Sengakuji. These two were ordered by Kuranosuke to leave the procession near Shibaguchi and come here.

The philosopher Yamaga Soko summarized the argument in his writings.

Matters of vengeance must be presented to the magistrate to clarify the relative merits and morality. His orders will be followed. This is an ancient law. The public's gossip will say informing the magistrate resembles the spirit of not completing one's mission. If after vengeance is achieved, there is no place to seek life or death, then it was all for nothing. The laws of the world are ignored, and there is simply courage. These are the words of men who do not know the way.

Without a doubt, Kuranosuke's heart held these teachings received in his youth from this deceased man. The group had an abundance of good sense. Along the way, Kuranosuke paired Sukeemon with the eloquent Chuzaemon and ordered them to go to the estate of the inspector-general. He believed it was just to make his appeal to the shogunate in advance of their orders. In other words, he stepped onto the path of surrender.

Houki no Kami surely heard about this morning's incident and gave the gatekeeper his answer.

"Let them in. I will see them."

The two came as the envoys for surrender. A pocket carried the paper explaining the reason for the raid and summarizing the key points. Houki no Kami took it from their hands.

"There will be no resistance. I will go to the castle to inform the shogun's Council of Elders and receive orders. In the meantime, you two may rest in this house."

The two passed into another room. Hot water poured over boiled rice was a kindness found in a Sengoku home for empty stomachs.

The room was an ordinary parlor. Grateful but ashamed, they addressed the vassal.

"It would be vulgar to enter wearing last night's clothes, so we'll eat here by the door."

"That's absurd. The lord commanded you to rest."

"Well then …"

The pair retied their undergarments and sashes to show the spirit of their civility and ate.

A monk came to pour tea. Both men declined.

"There is quite a lot of tea."

From inside their sleeves, they pulled out roasted rice wrapped in paper.

"I'm so sorry, but these filthy objects were carried last night in the food provisions. Please discard these useless items."

Meanwhile, Sengoku Houki no Kami spurred his entourage to action and rushed by palanquin to the castle in his role as the inspector-general.

THIS DAY WAS a day of attendance of lords at the castle.

The serious incident at dawn sent shock waves through the government. The atmosphere in the palace offices mirrored the forbearance on that day of butchery, March 14 in year 14 of Genroku.

At the time of Takumi no Kami's bloodshed, tension filled the pretentiousness of the judicial court, and dark and sorrowful shadows covered their brows. Today, the tension was the same. However, a brightness showing the light of humanity permeated the day's confusion.

"Perhaps you've heard. An ominous incident took place this morning in the imperial capital of a peaceful world."

As officials of the court, all of them lamented out loud, but their hearts upheld the truth.

They could no longer say the way of the warrior had collapsed. The code of the samurai had not crumbled in this land!

This sentiment was visible on the brows of the lords in any office.

Shogun Tsunayoshi punished Takumi no Kami at the time of the sword attack with too much speed and emotion. He listened to the report from the elders delivered by Houki no Kami. His reaction was to press his lips into a thin line.

The officials were notified, and one after another gathered at the government office. The appeal from the priest of Sengakuji Temple was submitted from the hands of the superintendent of temples and shrines. An imperial hearing was sought independently by the Kira clan, the Uesugi clan, and the town magistrate.

Inspectors rushed to the Kira residence. Houki no

Kami received the court's intentions and raced back to his estate.

> *Instructions will follow on the punishment of the ronin. Until then, the ronin shall be split up and placed in the custody of four clans.*

The shogunate handed down an immediate order to Sengakuji Temple.

> *Within the evening, Kuranosuke and his comrades shall be removed from the temple, be taken to the home of Inspector-General Houki no Kami to receive instructions in private.*

It rained that evening. Showers followed the snow and turned the roads into muddy fields.

When night fell, the statement "the Uesugi force has taken to the field" became plausible and put many on edge. On that rainy night, there was no need for anxiety over "What if it happens tonight?"

141

A NIGHT IN A DOWNPOUR

THE FOUR CLANS of the Hosokawa clan of Higo, the Matsudaira clan of Iyo, the Mori clan of Nagato, and the Mizuno clan of Mikawa assembled nearly 1,500 men.

From dusk until eleven-thirty at night, they stood soaking wet in the shadows of the wall and across the street centered around the front gate of Houki no Kami's mansion.

"Not yet?"

"Not yet."

"What are they doing?"

"I have no idea what's going on in the mansion."

The rain seeped through their rain capes. Arms and legs numbed in the cold.

The shogunate ordered the forty-six ronin in custody to be assigned to the four clans as follows.

Hosokawa - Etchu no Kami Tadatoshi: 17 men
Matsudaira - Oki no Kami Sadanao: 10 men
Mori - Kai no Kami Tsunamoto: 10 men

Mizuno - Kenmotsu Tadayuki: 9 men

Only the Hosokawa clan mustered close to seven hundred men and was ready for any possibility.

The shogunate ordered the Hosokawa clan to take charge of the prisoners. Around two in the afternoon, the entire clan assembled and reached Sengakuji Temple by evening. Because the shogunate switched the order to hand over the prisoners at the estate of Houki no Kami without warning, they pressed forward in the pouring rain to Nishikubo and endured until past ten at night. No news came as the rain worsened.

The other three clans did the same. As their bellies shrunk, the cold closed in, and the night grew late. Rain poured down black on the snow accumulated over the past several days. Viewed from the darkness outside the residence, countless lights shined inside the walls, and streams of rain appeared to light the sky.

"It looks like they forgot we're here. Why is the Sengoku clan taking so long? Is there any way to speed them up?"

The voices had reason for their dissatisfaction. They tried to cover the paper lanterns to keep them lit but found that impossible in rain and wind blowing sideways.

Intent on calming the ranks, Hirano Kuroemon, the head page in the Hosokawa clan, said, "Be patient. I asked a man from the Sengoku clan. He said Houki no Kami-sama planned for them to be running behind schedule."

"They're late on purpose?" The dissatisfied voice sounded angry and rose in pitch.

"Yes, it's on purpose. I was pleased when I heard Houki no Kami-sama's reason. He said the forty-six Ako ronin who entered this estate may never see each other's faces again in this world. The day of punishment is still in the future, but tonight they will be divided among four houses and held in custody. There are fathers and sons, like Kuranosuke and his son, uncles and nephews, and long-time friends."

Not everyone heard, but everyone nodded, shouted, and blinked while rain pounded their faces.

"I get it! So that's what he's thinking."

"I'll wait as long as he wants. If the parting of those men is delayed by each moment I wait, then nothing else matters. Not the rain. Not the cold. Nothing."

As midnight approached, the chief retainer Miyake Tobei and a steward Kamada Gunnosuke of the Hosokawa clan were called into the estate.

The time has come, thought the men, drenched and frozen since the afternoon but determined to endure. More than compassion, the final parting in this life of family and friends stung their hearts.

The Hosokawa clan's seventeen prisoners included Kuranosuke, Yoshida Chuzaemon, Hara, Hazama, Kataoka, Onodera, and the elder Horibe but not Chikara.

Chikara's name was listed among the prisoners of the Matsudaira clan.

Kuranosuke on the verge of leaving called to Chikara somewhere in the shadows. "Chikara, this is our parting in this life."

"Yes, Father. This is the last time I'll see your face."

"Remember what I've always told you."

"Don't worry, I haven't forgotten."

"Good. Very good ..."

The father's eyes reflected his joy. Would the father with his deep love different from a mother's love hold back hot tears at the depths of his soul and rise from his seat? A little later while being transported to the Hosokawa residence, his body swayed while his mind drew the face of Chikara he left moments earlier.

The allotted number of ronin was taken in turn by the Matsudaira clan, the Mori clan, and the Mizuno clan. For a little while, a heavy show of guards by each clan stood in the rain before the gate of Houki no Kami's mansion and created excitement that resembled going to war. A step ahead of the other three clans, the more than seven hundred samurai of the Hosokawa clan left in a procession of paper lanterns followed by cylindrical lanterns, riders on horseback, palanquins, and foot soldiers. Only a powerful clan worth 540,000 koku put on such a display.

The daimyo's Edo mansion was in Takanawa. The seventeen palanquins carrying the prisoners and the throng of men entered the estate through the Meguro Gate. The time was two in the morning.

A voice from outside called to them occasionally.

"I am Horiuchi Den'emon. Ronin, if there's anything you wish ... anything, please shout it out. If it's too hot in there and you'd like the door opened, just ask."

That kindness was not chivalry flowing only through the men of this clan. The governor-general Hosokawa Etchu no Kami stayed up to await their arrival.

That action was out of respect for the order handed down by the shogunate. When the seventeen ronin fell prostrate in the reception hall of the estate, Etchu no Kami came out and took his seat.

"You are all probably exhausted." Out of concern for Kuranosuke and the others, he said, "I am a bit in awe of your actions. It's the middle of the night and you should stretch out and rest. If there is any matter my vassals can assist you with, don't hesitate to ask."

The prisoners had violated the nation's laws. Beginning with Kuranosuke, not one of them ever dreamed of this courteous treatment. They had doubts about this kindness exhibited by a governor-general worth 540,000 koku.

The seventeen prisoners answered, "Yes … Yessir," but not one man hurried to raise his head. As Etchu no Kami's considerate words sunk in, they could not find words to express their gratitude.

SPRINGTIME IN INCENSE AND FLOWERS

EARLY IN THE morning of the sixteenth, a man in traveling clothes stormed through the gate of the Nanbuzaka residence of the Asano assistant master of ceremonies. A bamboo-shoot hat obscured his face.

The gatekeeper looked past him unconcerned while thinking he's probably the messenger, just a little earlier than usual. The man in the bamboo hat handed a sealed letter to the petty samurai who came out to the entryway step. Without waiting for a reply, he went back out the gate.

A diminutive old man strolling through the garden stopped in front of the stable next to the side entryway.

"Wait a minute. That was ..."

He ran out to the side of the gate and raised his hand and called, "Hey, Kichie! Is that you? Kichie! Kichie!"

The figure was too far away. The old man tilted his head and said to himself, "That's odd. It looked like him. Was I mistaken?"

The gatekeeper, who was around the same age and a

good friend, asked, "Saida-san, do you know the man who was just here?"

"Yeah, I haven't seen him in a long time, so that may be a stranger who looks like him. But I'm sure he was Terasaka Kichiemon who served as a foot soldier to the Ako ronin Yoshida Chuzaemon-sama."

"Isn't that strange for him to come as a messenger to pass something to the gatekeeper and go? Kichiemon's your friend, Saida-san?"

"My nephew serves Honda-sama of the Himeji clan. Relatives of Yoshida-sama serve in the same clan. The connection is not close, but he's had tea and been a guest at my nephew's home. If that's Kichie, they probably want to tell the full story of what the Ako ronin did the night before last."

Near the entryway, the attendant, Ochiai Yozaemon, was waiting. He held the document with the great seal received from the gatekeeper.

"Wait. Where's the messenger who brought this."

Both men turned around.

"He's gone."

"He's gone? ... I have many questions for him. Yozen'in-sama will be disappointed, too."

"He was probably a messenger from the Ako ronin."

"Zuiko-in Temple in Kyoto was written on the front of the envelope, but sealed inside was a letter addressed to Yozen'in-sama from Kuranosuke-dono. What does that mean? If he were Kuranosuke's messenger, he may have hurried here with detailed knowledge about the raid."

Yozaemon lamented this missed opportunity but was struck by an insight.

"A thoughtful man like Kuranosuke-dono was probably resolved to not implicate this family or the widow Yozen'in-sama. All of you must understand and reveal this to no one," said Yozaemon and went back inside. He slipped into the dowager Yozen'in's chilly room where she would spend the rest of her life.

"Excuse me. It's me, Yozaemon. A man left a letter from someone at Zuiko-in Temple in Kyoto. I opened it and found this letter addressed to you from Kuranosuke-dono."

"What? From Oishi?"

Yozen'in turned and had her maid Tae retrieve the letter held out by Yozaemon in the adjoining room. She opened it.

Twenty-one months had passed since Takumi no Kami's death. During that time, all hope vanished from her face. Her hollow cheeks and sharp shoulders looked pitiful on a figure once deemed a young beauty.

She heard about Kuranosuke's tattered reputation. He alone possessed unique strength, but was no longer reliable, doubted humanity, and might have hated his own life. He knew nothing about the widow beyond his help who agonized under the curse of the cold shackles of life deep inside the daimyo's residence.

But yesterday morning, like during the bygone days before her husband's death, she prepared her favorite weak tea infusion and sat for her morning prayers.

The usually composed Yozaemon misstepped and tumbled at the sliding door.

"My Lady! I have wonderful news! The Ako ronin … Lord Kira … finally. Lord Kira is …"

As he tripped over his words, for an instant, she thought, He lives!

She trembled with joy, doubted Kuranosuke's heart, and looked with malice at this human world. Shame overwhelmed her.

I'm so sorry, she thought then consoled her husband's

spirit. Your retainers succeeded. Your castle in this world did not perish for no reason. No, even at the end of generations among the souls of people in this world, no one knows the importance of one's role.

That day she recalled many memories and cried tears of joy.

Not only in her room of incense and flowers but also on the servant's side of the mansion, yesterday, faces changed to cheerful. The maid Tae, who continued to serve after they left the Teppouzu mansion, clutched the widow's hands. Tears melted away the melancholy of the last year and a half.

Another message came that morning. This document from Kuranosuke was thicker.

What could this be? But more than doubt, nostalgia pressed her bosom. Although a retainer, in the lonely Yozen'in's heart, Kuranosuke's presence in this world embodied a great life worth living.

However, the writing taken from the sealed letter was not simply news. The ledger of numbers was alien to her heart. In the account book titled *Cash Accounts Ledger*, Kuranosuke provided in painstaking numerical detail the personal use of public money since leaving Ako. It was a report on the cost of the revenge.

She wondered if a letter with more news was enclosed, but there was not another word.

"…"

Yozen'in was robbed of her spirit. Why should she care about these essentially trifling numbers for Kuranosuke and the former vassals? Rather, his honesty was forbidding and saddened her.

Kuranosuke, where is your humanity? What sort of man are you?

She still did not grasp the deep emotion in her breast

awakened by the reality of yesterday. She couldn't help feeling the impossibility of understanding the man Kuranosuke. Was he too multi-faceted? Were his formidable and lesser traits the same in any man?

Before the incident, Kuranosuke's short stature and listless demeanor led people to judge him to be an inept vassal and a useless lantern in daylight. After the incident, when the world thought they knew him after observing him indulge in the pleasures of Gion and Fushimi, he swiftly moved to his final aim and shocked them with the reality of the attack.

Is he a vessel of ingenuity, a passionate samurai, or the owner of the sharp mind capable of the meticulous calculations in the *Cash Accounts Ledger*?

A warrior rich in compassion and fervor lacks a calculating mind. A man bestowed with a genius for calculations does not decide to go forward and leap into the jaws of death despite his understanding of justice and loyalty. He is not brave and usually lacks the ability to take action.

A cursory look at the numbers in the cash accounts ledger left Yozen'in surprised by his discipline.

She thought, This deception of the world for so long a time was not an easy task. He gave considerable attention to detail.

For him to do this much, she thought. She believed a few words written by Kuranosuke to explain the circumstances of the former vassals would have been heartening news. But as Yozen'in read a few pages of the *Cash Accounts Ledger*, she soberly corrected her shallow notions.

The title was nothing more than *Cash Accounts Ledger*, but when she read the uses of the money noted in each detailed entry, she saw vivid images of the lives over the past year and a half of the forty-seven comrades who took part in the revenge. Depending on the reading, these were not mere numbers but a diary of the life of revenge of the former vassals.

Yozen'in welled with tears soon after she began reading. She compared her life resembling that of a nun, a life resented for being the unhappiest life possible, to the vassals' lives. How selfish I've been. Without thinking, she placed her palms together.

Perhaps Kuranosuke sent this *Cash Accounts Ledger* to simply report the numbers or to illustrate his integrity. Did he wish she would read this and learn of the miserable living conditions for over a year of his comrades?

If she read his spirit, more than a long letter or hearing about it in person, this ledger provided a detailed account. Again Yozen'in compared the sensibilities of men to those of women and concluded women's sensibilities cannot be fathomed in the thoughts of men who keenly sense objects with depth, height, and width.

She lamented over why her eyes had to be opened to the respect held for her late husband and imagined he could not have been better served.

143

THE CARRYING POLE DEBATE

A**T TWILIGHT ON** the sixteenth, heavy evening rains washed pebbles from the streets. A young monk carried a paper lantern bearing the name Sengakuji Temple. Another young monk struggled to carry a heavy package under one arm.

"Shoo! Go away!"

He shook his cane at a stray dog trailing them and continued to trudge down the dark road.

"Why are there so many stray dogs in Edo? I guess we'll have to put up with all these barking dogs."

"You can't avoid them at night."

"He's coming back. What should I do?"

"Nothing works. He'll keep coming back. Ignore him. We'll speed up."

"Why is he following us?"

"It's definitely the smell. Dogs have good noses."

"Oh, yeah," said the monk hugging the round case and gave his burden a disgusted look. "Oh, I see. The head is sealed in a bucket, but the dog knows it's there."

"You can say the dog has earthly appetites."

"That's true! We're getting close to Eitai Bridge, but Honjo is still far off. The sky looks brighter over there. Are those the theaters in Sakaicho?"

"I think so. I can just make out strains of music. The night travelers include messengers carrying severed human heads."

"The world is a mixed bag. I wonder what the Ako ronin in the custody of the four clans are feeling tonight?"

"We've heard rumors at every corner along the way. They're still in the custody of the shogunate that has not decided their punishment. Their act was committed out of loyalty. Because loyalty is the spiritual foundation of the nation, some say they should be given clemency. They may have stepped onto the path of loyalty, but they also trampled the basic laws of the nation and will be punished. Some see a punishment more severe than that of their lord Takumi no Kami. What will be the shogunate's judgment? If done poorly, lords, scholars, and public officials will be joined by townsmen and peasants and erupt in backbiting and slander. Mocking poems will pop up everywhere."

"Yeah, that will be a sight."

"Based on this one judgment, the true essence of loyalty will be defined. The many daimyos who stand for the way of the samurai are the shogunate and cannot carelessly carry out the punishment."

"Ah, there's Eitai Bridge. At last, I see the sky over Honjo."

"We still have a little ways to go. Boy, a human head is heavy. Since no one is traveling along the riverbank, push your cane through here and help me carry this."

"All right. Like this?"

The bamboo cane pierced the knot of the wrapping cloth bundle, and each monk grabbed an end.

These monks from Sengakuji Temple were Ichidon and Sekishi.

The superintendent of temples and shrines from Banshoji Temple, the bodaiji temple that cares for the dead of the Kira clan, negotiated to have them "transfer the head of Kozuke no Suke-sama." The chief priest ordered them to deliver Kozuke no Suke's head in the temple's custody to the Kira residence. Now, the two were on their way to Matsuzakacho in Honjo.

"Ichidon, what do you think?"

"About what?"

"Should the Ako men be spared or punished?"

"Isn't it obvious? They're loyal men. There is bushido. The way of the warrior. Public order in the nation is also maintained. Isn't a new spirit of humanity putting a squeeze on depravity, the sign of the times of the Genroku era, and being built stronger on the lifeless spirit? If these courageous warriors are killed, bushido will be lost."

"At the Shibaguchi teahouse where we rested earlier, a man with the air of a scholar said this to the townsmen. 'The act committed by the ronin was certainly an act done in the spirit of loyalty. But the nation's laws state they committed a grave crime.'"

Ichidon replied, "They probably violated the shogunate's laws, but is it proper for this shogunate to lecture the common people about fair play? I'm delighted. People are not lower than dogs and beasts. I couldn't bear the happiness I'd feel to see the laws of the shogunate crushed, but their way of the warrior is fine. This is a meaningful heroic deed to all human beings."

"That's true, too."

"Sekishi, are you saying laws are more important than spirit?"

"Well, aren't laws important? Think about it, the

nation's laws are hard to violate. Any disruption leads to a breakdown in societal order. What is the correct reason for compassion?"

"Wait a minute. You said compassion, but I'm not going to argue from puny personal feelings. You have to think about it from the perspective of a dignified nation. How does a nation of human beings rule that people are less than beasts? Laws must not be violated, but authorities who abuse that right are criminals who are breaking the laws of humanity."

"That's a bit extreme …"

"Are you stupid? What's extreme? You don't understand because you are trained on the floor of a Zen temple. If you explain the spirit from the perspective of Zen, the questions become what is there? and what is the point of life?"

"If you want to fight, I'll fight. I can't stand being barked at by an esteemed dog or a traveling companion."

"This isn't a fight. My friend, I'm irritated because you talk about the law like a peddler selling housecleaning services."

"What? I'm not saying to kill the Ako ronin, am I? That argument's been made on the streets."

"That's fine but …"

They became aware of the pole's weight.

"I wonder what looks our little talk put on Lord Kira's face."

The two laughed.

144

A RECEIPT FOR A HEAD

Fʀᴏᴍ ᴛʜᴇ ʙᴇɢɪɴɴɪɴɢ, Sekishi and Ichidon, young monks practicing in a Zen temple, looked offended by the attitude of the Kira clan.

They understood the confusion and the absence of help, but not one cup of tea on a brazier was offered; no elder vassal came to greet them; no monk from Banshoji Temple appeared to take possession of the head bucket.

Their trip home would be long. The night was growing late, and their legs tingled the longer they sat.

"Hey, Sekishi, can you ask again?"

"I asked for a receipt for the head. I think I'm getting weaker."

"No matter how weak you get, we came here as couriers on an important mission and can't return without a receipt."

"Unlike an ordinary object, we must get a receipt for the lord's head in writing even if it's from a spineless vassal because this is unprecedented among warrior families. Try clapping your hands for tea."

"Still no tea. Would you like tea, too?"

"My throat has been parched for some time. But as we sat in this room, a terrible odor hit my nose. Now, I feel ill and lost all desire to drink."

"I feel nauseous, too. What's that smell?"

"Isn't that blood? It smells like blood. Look over there at the sliding door. Those look like stains from splattered blood."

Looking ashamed, the chief priest of Banshoji Temple entered.

"I'm terribly sorry to have kept you waiting."

Wasting no time, Sekishi asked, "Chief Priest, there seems to be a strange odor in this compound. Don't you think so?"

"You are right. The truth is sixteen corpses are laid out in the adjoining room."

"What? Sixteen."

The monks looked at each other and swallowed hard.

"That many died?"

"Yes, beginning with the attendant Kobayashi Heihachiro-dono and the guard Shimizu Ichigaku-dono …"

"And more were wounded."

The chief priest's voice broke with grief.

"Twenty-two were wounded. The stroke of a sword brought a heartbreaking death to a young man, a fourteen-year-old novice."

Ichidon and Sekishi were oblivious to sitting up straight. The realization that the foul odor sprung from loyalty struck them. The Ako clan was not the sole possessor of loyalty.

In front of the late lord whose head was being returned, the elder vassals were delayed for a long time inside in deliberation. Their fatigued faces looked reluctant. The document was held out for the two visitors to read.

To the Monks of Sengakuji Temple
Monk Sekishi
Monk Ichidon

Note

This receipt is for the following items.
- Head 1
- Paper scroll 1

Kira Sahyoue
Souda Magobei
Sato Kunai

"Is this acceptable?" asked Chief Retainer Souda Magobei. A white cloth wrapped the left wrist of the chief retainer, evidence of a minor wound. He looked odd. Neither his expression nor his bandaged wrist moved.

The two monks faintly smiled.

"Thank you. This is fine. We failed in our duty to conduct a memorial service. Goodbye."

They went out, released sighs, and looked up at the stars in the night sky.

145

THE MAN WHO JUDGES ANOTHER

E VERY DAY SINCE the raid, the crush of people in front of the gate of Sengakuji Temple made it look like a holiday. Not only military families and townspeople, local peasants, and even travelers on the Tokaido Road stopped their palanquins and horses there.

Although the forty-six Ako ronin were in the custody of the four clans, the public wanted to see the weapons they left behind, visit the grave of Takumi no Kami as people do today, or seek a meeting with a priest or an acolyte.

"How did the loyal retainers carry themselves the day after the raid?"

"What stories did they exchange?"

"How old is the man Kuranosuke-dono?"

"Is Chikara-dono as handsome as they say?"

Were warriors asking these probing questions?

Townspeople came carrying clothes, writings, and food.

"Can a temple worker give this to the loyal retainers?"

The people in the temple had no way to deliver these items. However, if given this explanation, the visitors would reject it. The temple could no longer bear the disruption and closed the gate.

Then anonymous satirical poems lampooning Kira or Uesugi were stuck to the gate. Many contributors plastered the gate with songs praising the loyal retainers.

Among them, someone placed a large patchwork of paper filled with bold characters.

Pray with respect.
Wise officials do not execute true warriors.
Heaven and Earth offer divine protection to brave and coura-
geous warriors.

Agent for the People of the World: Jonan Inshi

These posted papers were discovered at the crossroads of other shrines. From the day the citizens learned of this incident, voices and rumors grew over the next five to ten days. Day and night, all topics related to the actions of the loyal retainers and the opinions presented by the people in various provinces and clans dominated the conversations of ordinary people and added to the turmoil.

The public was most interested in how the shogunate would treat the loyal retainers.

The idea of the *loyal retainers* was a new phrase created by the public over several days. Loyal retainers were interpreted as a reference to the Ako ronin.

The bad guys were the townsmen who bet on whether the loyal retainers in the custody of the four clans would be given clemency or the death penalty. Frequent reports were heard of squabbles among the zealots.

Conflicts weren't confined to the ignorant masses. Warriors were prone to arguments about the way of the samurai. The philosophical choice became whether the code of the samurai or the law would prevail. In contrast, the positions of educated men easily polarized between two philosophies based on different schools of thought.

Scholars jumped into the whirlpool of public opinion. Muro Kyuso and other leading Confucian scholars of the day and high-ranking officials in the shogunate embraced the following sympathetic opinion.

Not punishing them is akin to punishing the sages. The way of the sages disappears. Justice for our lord disappears. And the government is bereft of insight. How are the original meanings and the dignity of the nation's laws preserved? The laws of a nation that ignore the way of sages merely become unbridled power.

Many refuted this sympathetic view by employing political and legal arguments.

In short, the spirit of justice is a selfish action to turn oneself into a hero. It is the belief in one's life. An opinion that disregards the law based on the claim that a selfish act is loyalty and fulfills filial piety must be called a personal opinion. When filial piety becomes theft, carrying out the punishment through tears becomes one's official duty. If personal opinions warp the nation's laws, a future world will have laws, but they will be worthless. No one knows how the complex sentiments of society will evolve.

However, both sides were aware of a space left untouched. This surely touched on the laws protecting animals based on the order of the Dog Shogun for the past dozen years, in other words, human abuse laws. However, they preferred arguing. The philosopher Ogyu Sorai, in particular, was the main advocate for punishing the loyal retainers and represented one scholarly faction.

The lords' opinions were divided. The course of opinions among the high and the low in year 15 of Genroku focused on the treatment of the loyal retainers. Anyone from the lowly peasants to the highest-ranking shoguns thought, Why not give my idea a try?

Churning in the background of this problem, secret maneuvers disconnected from theory to advance various wishes from the Kira family line and from people related to the Asano clan swayed the senior vassals of the shogunate.

A hundred arguments emerged. A theory could not afford to be vague. Theories on the conduct of the loyal retainers and theories on revenge were endless. Assorted gossip and vulgarities were tossed in. The shogunate appreciated the gravity of the issue and could not easily render judgment. The shogun did not search his heart. He appeared to avoid addressing the dilemma until asked to render a verdict.

The end of the year approached. No matter what was going on, the towns of Edo bustled with New Year's markets, colorful *hagoita* paddle markets, and the sounds of a world preparing to wait for spring.

146

THE WOMAN SEEN A SECOND TIME

ORIUCHI DEN'EMON WAS an elder. He was a hereditary vassal and public servant with the role of a commander in the Hosokawa clan. After the seventeen men, including Kuranosuke, were brought onto the clan's estate, he was appointed a host.

Since he lived in town, he went home at night on horseback and returned the next day to the clan residence.

"Heisuke, will it be snow or sleet tonight? I'm chilled to the bone. That's quite a crowd over there. They're probably writing satirical poems or some other nonsense. Please have a look."

The groom and footman Heisuke sped toward the crowd at the wall at the crossroads then returned to the side of the lord's horse."

"I'm back."

"Is it satire? What did it say?"

"The waters of the Hosokawa and the Mizuno flow clear but …"

"Okay, and the rest …"

"It's muddy offshore in the open sea."

"Ha, ha, ha, ha. The observations of the townsmen are frightening. Of the four clans who've taken custody of the loyal retainers, the Hosokawa and the Mizuno have shown compassion, but the Mori and the Matsudaira cringe before the shogunate and are cheerless and inhospitable. That seems to be the poem's meaning."

Den'emon went out to the side of the estate and started the climb up Sakanokoji road at the Meguro Gate. He called, "Wait, Heisuke," pulled the reins, and looked back, nearly burying his body in the horse's mane.

A thin veil of the white haze of dusk settled on the road from the forest on the cliff running along one side. Den'emon wasn't sure but, from time to time, a woman seemed to linger outside Meguro Gate and wander by as if searching for a peephole in the wall.

"Oh, it's that woman again, the woman in the purple hood. Heisuke, what is she up to?"

"I don't know."

"I've seen her several times. She's acting strangely. Arrest her. Ah, she's spotted us. Hurry Heisuke, get her."

The instant Heisuke took off running, the woman's shadow flew off like a little bird and escaped into the clump of trees on the cliff.

Den'emon followed him. "What happened?"

The humiliated Heisuke returned alone. He couldn't find her and said she ran like she was being hunted.

"No, that's not it. If she had done something wrong, why would she come to a place of young samurai in a clan made up like a woman from Shinagawa? She's embarrassed but respectful of us who have custody of the loyal retainers.… That said, I was young once and did a few things. Ha, ha, ha."

Den'emon left the horse with Heisuke and disappeared inside the residence. The loyal retainers had a mysterious pull on this elder. The clan lord Etchu no Kami sympathized with Kuranosuke and his comrades and applauded the forty-seven warriors; thus, not one vassal spoke against them. But in their hearts, some men in the residence disliked Den'emon's opinion and attitude toward the ronin.

A total of nineteen men was selected from the clan to act as hosts to the prisoners. All were the appropriate ages and held important positions in the clan. They crammed into a front room, while the loyal retainers stayed in two sizable interior rooms.

Den'emon peeked into the rooms. His face tensed and he marched into the office. A petty samurai carrying something inside caught his displeased eyes.

"The day before yesterday I ordered braziers for their rooms. I look inside now and see none. Why haven't they been brought out?"

The samurai moved closer to the wall and began a faint-hearted apology.

"We retrieved the braziers from the storehouse as you ordered, but Miyake Toubei-sama said it was an outrage to give them to prisoners of the shogunate."

From a nearby room, Miyake Toubei overheard Den'emon and the samurai talking and appeared.

"Den'e-dono, you ordered the braziers?"

"Yes. Why did you rescind it?"

"It's obvious. Leaving aside the braziers, there is no need to converse with criminals who broke the nation's laws. Given your exceptional discretion, I allowed for the provision of writing materials, combs and other articles for the bath, and medicines. Those items were listed and provided after making inquiries at the shogunate. But the braziers overstepped your authority."

"You ... you don't understand." Den'emon muzzled himself like he would be unlawfully arrested.

"Understand what?"

"Do you believe they are only prisoners?"

"If I count the crimes of that faction, the crimes of the weapons and the crime of killing a prominent man, five fingers aren't enough. The men who committed these grave offenses against the nation's laws are, without a doubt, criminals."

Unexpectedly, Den'emon's eyes blurred. He wanted to argue against that stance, but Miyake Toubei was a chief retainer, and he was a low-ranking commander. Den'emon said nothing but could not avoid Toubei's glare.

He broke his silence. "Chief Retainer, from the beginning, the public dubbed the samurai, the loyal retainers and the flowers of the warriors' way. I don't know how far that nobility has penetrated the public mind."

"Silence. Handing out nicknames to criminals has a deleterious effect on the public mind. This gives rise to an atmosphere that ignores the law and disrupts the nation."

"Chief Retainer,—"

"You have more to say. Disregard for the law will melt away the clan's governance."

"Your words do not know the heart of a warrior. If I am a warrior, I cannot obey."

"You will disobey."

"Yes."

"Den'e-dono, you said you will not obey."

"Yessir."

"At your age, the mood in the streets shouldn't dazzle you."

Then Den'emon spoke without pausing.

"It's regrettable you've adopted such flippant ideas. Can you not see the signs of the times? Where is the way of the samurai? Where is the honor of the lord and his vassals? The way of a warrior's wisdom is to accumulate money, count mistresses from stipend to stipend, be absorbed in singing and dancing, be charming, and be well dressed. The men who banished those days can be called wise men.

"A fine model is the complicated affair between Lord Kira and Lord Takumi no Kami. If the customs of military families had not died out, that sort of incident would not have happened. The actions of the Ako ronin established their righteousness and led to soul searching about the rotten state of the world today and the public mind, and at the very least, has altered contemporary views.

"That outlook does not only brush away your complaint, the law does not touch the great love between a parent and a child demonstrated by the public, the beautiful friendship, the stoicism, the integrity, and the execution of a necessary goal. Can the thoughts that solemnly resulted in the surrounding actions be questioned by the law?

"Although they were reluctant to act within today's laws, wasn't this the rare reasonable act unseen in previous generations? Your absolute belief in treating them like simple prisoners leads me to question whether you are a samurai."

147

REDDER THAN FIRE

T OUBEI SMIRKED LIKE he took pride in his cool-headedness.

"Your fervor is a problem. It is wrong to violate the dignity of the law. The braziers are inappropriate. Page! Return these braziers to the storehouse."

"No, stop. Leave them."

Unlike his usual self, Den'emon quashed the order.

"I am also a host. If this is a mistake, I will slit open my belly."

"That would be a fine end for you alone, as long as the lord's house is not implicated."

"I will take full responsibility. Tears will not be shed in the public mind, and tears are not shed by men. The way of the samurai will die out. As a host, I will gamble my life. I will not obey a command, even from the chief retainer, if it is cruel."

"You're hopeless. What has happened to you? Page! Page! Put them back now."

"Ignore him. Take them into the sitting rooms over there."

"I am the senior officer giving you an order."

Den'emon did not back down.

"I am acting out of loyalty to the lord."

Their voices rang in the ears of Kuranosuke and the other ronin. The Ako men pricked up their ears and noted deep in their hearts the name Horiuchi Den'emon, a Hosokawa vassal. Some cried hot tears seeping up from the depths of their spirits in gratitude.

Soon the voices stopped, Den'emon with his always-congenial, smiling face stepped inside to give orders to the storehouse page and direct where to install the braziers.

"Put one there.... And one over there."

Each large bronze brazier was topped with a metal mesh. No fires burned in the broad upper and lower rooms. After several braziers were set out, Den'emon breathed easily like he was also warmed.

Four or five days earlier in a chat with Den'emon, Tominomori Sukeemon in the lower room mentioned Kuranosuke's weakness to cold in the winter months. Some imagined, without proof, that was the source of this incident. More than the glowing redness of the charcoal fires, Den'emon's compassion warmed their hearts.

"That's better."

Den'emon made the quick decision to have small crimson futons brought in and hung over the metal mesh of the braziers to create makeshift kotatsu warmers.

He muttered in the direction where Kuranosuke sat in the front of the upper room. "Now, you all should be fine when night comes or sleet falls ... especially Oishi-dono."

Den'emon smiled, thinking about giving him relief from the cold.

From a distance, Kuranosuke bowed his head cascading with emotions. The gratitude filling his eyes was reflected in Den'emon's heart.

"Den'e-dono, I appreciate your kindness, but we have been convicted by the shogunate and are undeserving. Please take away the braziers."

"Ha, ha, ha, ha. Our earlier conversation outside leaked this far. What a shame."

"Sukeemon gossips needlessly. The problem is not the cold."

"Don't worry. Senior officials have minor disputes. The lord sent an official notice to visit Atago Shrine tomorrow. The lord has reason to pray.... What will he pray for? ... You understand. The ruling of the shogunate has troubled the lord the entire time. The braziers are no problem at all. When the senior vassal Miyake-dono heard about the shrine visit, he had reason to withdraw without another word.

"There's nothing to worry about. You are reserved, and people hesitate to approach you. Please accept the kindness of the Hosokawa clan and make yourself at home."

148

THE ARCH OF A FOOT

DAYBREAK CAME THEN a night and another night.

Brightness from the candles set up in the two rooms threw dim haloes onto the darkened coffered ceiling.

Ushioda Matanojo and Tominomori Sukeemon each read a borrowed volume of the epic historical novel *Taiheiki*. Some men wrote letters. One group huddled in conversation, while Akabane Genzo cleaned his ears beside them, trying to act like he wasn't eavesdropping.

The seventeen men were divided into two groups: eight in the upper room and the nine younger men in the lower room.

Many older men, the oldest being Horibe Yahei, were in the upper room. His companions included the quiet-spoken but frightful-looking Yoshida Chuzaemon, the silent Hazama Kihei, Onodera Junai who occasionally recited poetry, Mase Kyudayu, and Hara Soemon. Some-times they told jokes.

Kuranosuke took a seat in the alcove with both hands always shoved inside the small crimson futon. His head was tilted up, his eyes in boundless contemplation. He seemed to not be thinking about anything. His eyes looked distracted and unfocused at the young men in the adjacent room and vacantly at the ceiling.

He passed each day with no sense of boredom. When spoken to, he answered with a smile. His small stature and relaxed shoulders resembled the back of a hunching cat. He sat serenely like his body was where it should be.

People adapt with ease. I've grown accustomed to the exceptional graciousness of this place. This is excessive and too much of a divine blessing.

His mind constantly asked and answered questions. Deprived of nothing, they were given food, clothing, and objects for everyday use. In one leap, life became too easy. For that reason, he felt ill at ease.

Afraid to comment on the excessive kindness yesterday, Kuranosuke made this request to the generous Den'emon.

"We have lived as ronin for a long time and became accustomed to wearing coarse clothes and eating simple foods. The full-course meals we receive day in and out from this house are superb, if not a bit heavy. It's ungracious for ordinary men to tire of luxury. But from here on, I'm requesting simple fares of soup and no more than two vegetables or salted-rice bran soup for both the morning and evening meals."

Yahei, Junai, and Soemon also spoke up in jest.

"Yes, absolutely. That's what we want."

"To tell the truth, mouths accustomed to poverty came to enjoy, just a little bit, the daily feast."

Den'emon laughed. "So you're saying we're spoiling you."

"Yes, that's it. We will occupy ourselves writing letters and reading."

"I understand. However, the lord recommended the

fine cuisine. I cannot reduce the rations on my own. And the cooks brag about bringing joy to your palates and cook to the best of their abilities every day."

"I'm weakening."

"It's a good idea to move your bodies a little because you belong to the shogunate. If a fire breaks out in the neighborhood, everyone will be guided to the garden because the rule is for everyone to gather there."

"Well, I'll wait for the fire."

Everyone burst out laughing.

The taciturn Okuda Magodayu surprised them with a few words.

"It may be the fault of not getting enough fresh air, but I'm bothered every night by the arch of my foot drying out."

"You are right," said Den'emon.

"The clock has struck. Well, I'll say goodnight."

He left but soon returned. "I'm sorry, but I forgot one matter. Starting tomorrow, carpenters will begin work in the officials' office. To avoid misfortune, pay them no mind."

He seemed to choose his words carefully. The group fell asleep, appreciating his words.

A small folding screen stood at each pillow.

Kuranosuke slept wearing a brown silk crepe hood. The younger men in the next room were soon asleep and quiet. In the upper room, however, the hacking coughs never stopped.

Ushioda Matanojo was often teased for grinding his teeth. One night, the elder Yahei, as the oldest man who would turn seventy-seven the next year, shouted in his sleep, "Aiee! Eeyaah!" like he was killing someone. All the younger men in the other room leaped up together. When they realized the shout was from a half-asleep elder, a roar of laughter rose in the middle of the night. Inside this monotonous life, sleeping provided the greatest pleasure.

They were taken into custody after the raid. For two or three days, they shut their eyes on their pillows. The white snow and the white blades glimmered in the darkness. They all felt the same.

Like a nightly routine, deep thoughts about their oncoming deaths attacked them every night. The younger men experienced more furious thoughts and were weary from a restless sleep. Night after night, the older men could not fall into a deep sleep despite their tenuous attachment to life. The coughing stopped and breathing quieted when they recalled their lives until this day like enjoying a picture book over and over.

However, the problem of avoiding sleep and thinking obsessively emptied their heads. Death becomes a commonplace idea like staring at the word on white paper. The breathing of all the sleeping men was soon tranquil. Behind the small folding screens surrounding each pillow, they embraced thoughts of wives, brothers, children, and comrades in the custody of the other three clans. The souls did not wake up but fully enjoyed their thoughts until the morning light.

149

NO, NOT YET

SPARROWS CHIRPED. THE early morning light bounced off the frost. Anyone seeing the sun's glare would think, I'm still alive. Strong emotions drifted over each man's brow, but not one talked of his dreams.

Some said, "This year is coming to an end."

Others said, "The winter sunshine is wonderful."

Death may come tomorrow. But some men's hearts absorbed and savored today, a day in the few remaining days of their lives. Other men ground ink stones in meditation. The happy-go-lucky men laughed. The days changed, but the daily routine stayed the same.

As on every other day, Den'emon seemed to stay smiling.

"Beginning today, smoking is allowed. I've brought tobacco. Please light up a pipe."

This was a surprise. They appeared to have forgotten that craving. Most of the men liked tobacco, but Governor-General Etchu no Kami of the Hosokawa clan hated it and banned smoking throughout the clan. Nonetheless, Den'emon gained the lord's permission.

"Ashtrays have not been set out, but anytime you wish to smoke, just ask."

One said, "Well, I …"

"Please, enjoy," said Den'emon as he offered a pipe.

They thanked him but could not find the right words. More than being happy, the comrades were solemn. The methodical Okuda Magodayu blinked. Elder Yahei turned away to blow his nose into a tissue.

"You are spoiling us with your kindness."

Hara Soemon took a kiseru pipe and raised it to his head out of respect. However, he did not smoke first but was acting on behalf of Kuranosuke.

"Since it's his favorite, Oishi-dono should be first."

For a short time, purple smoke wafted through the two rooms. Out of nowhere, Hayami Tozaemon asked, "Are the repairs done? I didn't hear the carpenters' chisels yesterday."

Den'emon was about to answer but shut his mouth, then said, "In early spring, you can move into the officials' room. This place is dark. There will be a sitting room, and you'll be able to look out at the garden and the sky to brighten your spirits."

The year came to an end. After New Year's, a few days into the spring of year 16 of Genroku, everyone moved into the renovated officials' room. They delighted in the view like children.

"I can see the ocean."

"I can see the clouds."

If a ronin wrote a letter, Den'emon would deliver it on his way home and wait for the reply. Everyone heard the rumors floating around town. However, Kuranosuke was troubled by their divine blessing and worried particularly about the young men in the custody of the other clans and his son Chikara. He wasn't worried about harsh treatment but feared they would get too comfortable with these easy-going days and hold different feelings than their convictions before the raid.

He thought, If I have the chance to see a new spring … If I'm alive, I will see the plum blossoms next year. If I leave this world, I will be poorer than I am now but my days will be freer.

The sudden awareness of his thoughts frightened Kuranosuke.

News of the successful raid led the world to believe the ronin were satisfied. In Kuranosuke's heart, however, one action remained. Until that was done, his work could not be said to be finished. His fervor until that day hung on its completion. He would cleanly and sensibly reach this destiny. In the rare event, he were unable to achieve this fate, he would simply end as a villainous criminal who violated the nation's laws. This thought preoccupied him as he waited impatiently each day. To the end, he considered the kindness and favorable treatment by the Hosokawa clan to be an ordeal.

Also, the public's opinion irked him. They heaped praise on the ronin, but he thought differently.

I am not that sort of man. I am definitely not that man. The praise is unwarranted. What is in my mind is identical to what Ono Kurobei thought. The drunken spirit of Gion and Fushimi was not a strategy. It was nothing but intoxication from the spirit and pleasure from the spirit. Perhaps I was carefree and enjoying nature's beauty in Yamashina. I'm sure I'm that sort of man. But an unexpected repulsion in my blood to that was the force enveloping the warrior spirit.

The praise is not because I am a great man but because my grandfather and father were great. A man's character is not created in his generation. The creation spans at least the three generations of his grandfather, his father, and himself. To praise oneself is presumptuous, but, for now, I will say it's my blood. I merely trained that blood a little.

The force that brought me this far without stumbling on the path to the goal was the force of that training. I can't brag about my abilities. Beginning with Yamaga Soko-sensei, teachers came with the teachings of the ancestors, but that is overrated by the world.

But if appreciated this much by the public, I will not betray that promise. A good part of the public mind throughout the country made impassioned appeals for clemency. So that I don't betray the hope in that popular support, I must now betray the world's expectations a little sooner.

His belief did not waver. Not just him, the other forty-five men must keep the final act secret until the deed was done.

With no effort being made now, nothing would happen. His spirit enjoyed the spring winds skimming over the garden. He could only wait for that day. He thought, Come one day sooner.

150

GREAT MERCY

AFTER THE FIRST week of the New Year and the pine decorations were taken down, the problem of *the punishment of the Ako ronin* heated up again in the halls of government and the court of public opinion. The people split apart and battled over clemency versus conviction.

The fourteen members of the shogunate's supreme court all signed and sent a fiery opinion entitled *Ronin Clemency* with the following key points to the cabinet ministers.

> *They undertook a heroic deed. The virtue of the lord and his vassals culminated in this action. Taking their lives is identical to killing morality. Their actions do not upset the spirit of even one article of the Laws for the Military Houses. This faction cannot be said to be violent.*

This could be said to represent the public's opinion but was also suspected of being that of the shogun Tokugawa Tsunayoshi.

The unyielding opposing argument came from Ogyu Sorai.

Respect for the law must never be violated, not even a little. The law is perverted, and the nation becomes ungovernable.

The cabinet ministers could not agree on a judgment. The shogun received their opinions. He would sanction the road to be taken.

Sorai's argument championed by Yanagisawa Yoshiyasu impressed the shogun. The touch of humanity in Sorai's words brought forth this sound legal argument.

They committed a crime and paid homage to samurai. A fitting punishment would be seppuku.

The shogun gave the final judgment to all opposing arguments.

"I order the forty-six men to commit seppuku."

He was the supreme legal authority in the nation. This man of absolutes did not allow an iota of will to influence the law through emotions. He could say nothing else.

Coincidentally, Priest Rinnoji no Miya of Nikko visited the castle for the beginning-of-the-year meeting. The priest was the shogun's close friend. After the formal meeting, they chatted for hours. At one point, Tsunayoshi sighed and said, "On the whole, no one suffers as much as the man who takes on the politics of this world. At times, human beings are entwined in compassion. Even a criminal who considers the importance of human life will have the urge to help. But the importance of the nation's laws is evident in that case. When willed by the law, the will of Tsunayoshi cannot be imposed."

"..."

The priest only listened.

The conversation changed, but Tsunayoshi repeated the same words as if remembering and sighed. The priest only nodded. Later, he left the castle by palanquin. At his temple, he told the following story to the attendant *Bokan* priests.

"No day has pained my spirit as much as today. The shogun touched on many topics and brought up the Ako ronin matter twice. Obviously, if the shogun spoke to me about clemency, he spoke in confidence.

"However, he said the grave action taken by Kuranosuke and his party was both right and wrong. For generations, many people have accomplished rare acts. Even if men of ability appear, an opportunity may not, then an event will never transpire in this world.

"Because I respected that idea, in my eyes, their actions did not create the loss of eternally new and beautiful light like those of the sun and the moon. If the judgment is clemency, when they die of old age, the hearts of those forty-six men will be as heroic as they are today.

"If one man brings dishonor, the entire party will be disgraced. Instead, if tears are swallowed now and death is given to those men, the light of their lives will be the same as the sun and the moon. How will this world change? How will people's hearts harden? The spirit of truth will always be a great force and a light shining in the hearts of the people of this nation.

"Looking at how one lives, he thought giving them death in a world of short, transient lives is great mercy. Until I left, I was unable to answer the shogun. I'm sure he viewed me as a heartless man."

151

SWEET SAUCE AND SAKE

THE JUDGMENT REMAINED a secret for a time. Even the Hosokawa and the other clans believed the arguments favored by the public. They all thought the ronin would be saved and knew in their hearts the shogunate wanted to save them. No matter what, they leaned toward that view.

The entire Hosokawa clan knew the shogunate's decision would be announced soon.

They imagined the following scenarios: 1. a pardon, 2. banishment to a remote island, and 3. the death penalty, a remote possibility. To not be taken by surprise, they prepared for the worst.

Of the three, Den'emon thought the last punishment, the death penalty, was unlikely.

The men in the sitting rooms were suspected of going crazy with thoughts of death. The fault might lie in the new year. But every night, spirited laughter filled the rooms.

"This place is as lively as ever."

"Ah, Den'e-dono, please come here."

The young crowd treated him like a favorite uncle. He relished that.

"What's so funny?"

"Please sit and we'll tell you."

The free-spirited Kataoka Gengoemon said, "This guy Chikamatsu Kanroku is not himself. He's talking about love."

"Well, unusual incidents have been happening. What is this love affair?"

"During my days in Edo as a low-ranking samurai, I went to Yoshiwara, was entertained by the first courtesan I saw and failed to return home by curfew. Oh, her face—"

Kanroku pointed and said, "You're lying," and waved his hands around.

The others were amused.

"A samurai changes his story. Right after Den'e-dono sees it—"

"Ah, ha, ha, ha. Something like that happened to me, too."

"Den'e-dono, will you tell us about your love affair now? It must be splendid."

"Ah, it's here. What will I have? How about the rare treat of tea over rice."

Covered earthenware dishes were brought out. Inside were red peppers and dried anchovies in boiled soy sauce.

"Oh, sardines."

"What? Sardines."

The group stretched to see.

"This is a rare treat."

"It smells good and is delicious."

"Ouch. I bit a pepper."

The noise became too much for Yoshida Chuzaemon in the upper room.

"Den'e-dono, your favoring the youngsters is becoming

a problem. Come up here and chat with us."

"Please, excuse my rudeness."

He grabbed the dish of dried fish and stood. The young ronin rolled with laughter.

When he changed seats, Hayami Tozaemon in the lower room said, "Den'e-dono, there's another funny story. Not about a sweet love affair, but a gossipy one. The youngest and the best-looking fellow down here is Isogai Juroza. Last night, he was talking in his sleep, and Gengoemon-dono was listening."

The handsome Juroza beside him tried to muzzle him.

"You're a liar. Den'e-dono, he's joking."

Gengoemon was tickled.

"Hey, it's not a joke. I heard it and I don't lie."

Den'emon joined in the teasing.

"Ha, ha, you may be outnumbered. From your looks, Juroza, I believe the rumor. Okay? Now, tell it all."

"Here it goes."

A somber Juroza turned to Gengoemon.

"Please stop this cruelty."

"But I can't lie."

Den'emon said, "Gengo-dono, I'd like to hear this. What did the fine-looking Juroza say in his sleep?"

"Well, Den'e-dono, he said … a woman's name."

Juroza turned red.

"Please stop talking about that! It was my mother's name."

"I don't think so. I know that wasn't your mother's name."

Kuranosuke looked at him and smiled. Juroza couldn't bear this any longer and hid behind Akabane Genzo. The rumor was confirmed.

January passed in a flash. An incident occurred on the evening of the second day of February.

Kuranosuke noticed Den'emon seeing to some business matter and called him over, a rare event. He spoke in an unusually cheerful voice.

Den'emon looked over to see sake being held out in a friendly gathering. The non-drinkers with a sweet tooth, Akabane Genzo, Yoshida Chuzaemon, Onodera, and Mase, exchanged cups of *amemizore* sauce.

They looked more relaxed than usual. Even the silent lay Buddhist Okuda Magodayu beamed that night.

"A toast to Den'e-dono."

"A toast to me? I am honored."

Den'emon emptied his cup and poured a drink for each man. When he came to Isogai Juroza, he was waved away.

"I've had enough."

Chikamatsu Kanroku said, "Isogai's a coward," and poured a cup.

The seldom playful Kuranosuke said, "Den'e-dono, Juroza is a sweet-looking man but a hard drinker. He has no choice."

"Look at that. He's trying to escape."

"I'm sorry. Excuse me."

He stood and tried to flee, but Den'emon grabbed him and made him drink. Onodera Junai said, "The young Atsumori dies in battle again!"

His comrades roared with laughter.

Den'emon felt a sudden odd shift in the usual atmosphere but was unconcerned.

However, late that night, a messenger appeared out of nowhere.

Advance notice of the verdict on the ronin was being shared confidentially. Messengers were heading to the other three clans. The confidential ruling by the shogunate showed the strict nature of the law.

The forty-six men shall commit seppuku!

152

TELL THEM WITH A VASE OF FLOWERS

"**I**S IT BAD?"

Den'emon lost the courage to leave the guard-house and the energy to speak. As a groan rose from the pit of his stomach, he said, "This is splendid. Magnificent."

He gathered a few thoughts in his mind. January was a month of many ceremonial days. The Kagami Biraki ceremony was held in Nikko on the first day of February, a day to avoid bad luck. He understood that before they were freed from their bodies, drinks would be poured to mark their parting.

Logically, many letters were written on the second and the third. The men also seemed to be tidying up their appearances.

Despite many of the men having peered far into the future and prepared their minds, Den'emon could not bring himself to tell the ronin of the shogunate's decision.

A disappointed Etchu no Kami shut himself inside. The ronin had to be told. It was already the morning of the third. In a day or two, those laughing voices and unique looks would be gone from Earth forever.

Den'emon settled his mind by flower arranging. On the morning of the third, he set an arrangement in the alcove of the upper room. The flowers were set up in a room housing criminals.

Those insightful men would solve this puzzle without being told.

"Has the day come to finally show flowers to these men?"

Den'emon's eyes stayed cast down when he left the vase. He wasn't seen again until night. He couldn't bear to look at them.

His concern prodded him to visit during the night. Most of the men in both rooms were sleeping. Oishi Sezaemon, Chikamatsu Kanroku, and Tominomori Sukeemon were still up and saw him.

"Ah, you came at the right time. Come here."

"But you're resting."

"No, we're just on our beds. You're blinking too much. I'd like you to see something."

"What is it?"

"We know that before long, the absurdity of this world will be over for us. We'd like to express our gratitude. Please watch our performance as our farewell."

A small folding screen was held out. Hidden in its shadow, Sukeemon and Kanroku mimed playing the old song *Ryutatsu Bushi* on flutes. A solemn Oishi Sezaemon danced a Kabuki dance from the theaters of Sakaicho in Kyoto.

A humorous sight was created by the two buttocks poking out from the shadow of the folding screen and Sezaemon's hairy shins keeping time. The snickers leaking from inside futons were replaced by bursts of laughter. Den'emon also doubled over. Tears spilled and he shook with laughter.

Now was the time for Juroza's revenge. He raised his head from inside a futon.

"The troublesome adults never sleep. Den'e-dono, please thoroughly investigate this matter tomorrow."

"Of course, I shall do so. And you will no longer talk in your sleep in retaliation."

"Oh no, not that again …"

Juroza disappeared into his futon.

"Ha, ha, ha. Goodnight."

"Goodnight."

"A goodnight to you, too, Den'e-dono."

With nothing left to be said, they extinguished the light.

153

LIFE WITHOUT DEATH

DEN'EMON LOOKED EXHAUSTED. Since it appeared nothing would happen until noon on the fourth, he left for home by horse for his usual nap.

The townsmen had no inkling of the shogunate's will, but Den'emon, who knew, sensed an aura of gloom on this February afternoon.

Around the time his home near Kyobashi came into view, he turned, startled by the sounds of hooves coming fast from behind. It was his colleague Hayashi Heiroku. "Den'emon, come back! The envoy! The envoy has come!"

"He's at the residence."

"He came at last. The inspector Araki Jusaemon-dono and the envoy Hisanaga Naiki will conduct the post-mortems. They arrived around two, accompanied by seven foot soldiers and six junior inspectors, and disappeared into the officials' office!"

"Ah! It will be today!"

The horses' muzzles were side by side as they scattered sand racing back to the clan residence in Shirokane.

Den'emon's mind was a dreamscape as he galloped

into the compound. This place already looked different from the morning. The seventeen ronin had finished their final meals. They wore the gifts from Etchu no Kami, spotless pale yellow kamishimo robes with white sleeves. Tabi socks and obi sashes were nearby. In silence, they were preparing to die.

Ah! Den'emon glimpsed them and lingered in confusion between the corridor and the antechamber for the post-mortems.

"What should I do? This will be hard to watch."

He went in the guardhouse, gulped down water, and went back outside.

Instead of giving advance notice, the appearance of the envoy meant the seppuku was imminent. A crowd of people was present. The seventeen ronin had to die, one after another, before dusk.

Etchu no Kami was quietly present. He seemed to be watching from the grand study. Den'emon looked away from the courtyard, the place with the white curtains and the white folding screen.

The preparations were done. What did he see when he looked toward the sitting rooms? Dressed in white and pale yellow for death, the seventeen sat in a row facing the garden. Den'emon watched through burning eyes and inexplicably could see the nerves of the energized but composed men.

They seemed to be aware of his presence. He glimpsed the eyes of several men saying goodbye to this world and saw eyes filled with smiles in the soft light of a spring day. In response, Den'emon's eyes failed and flooded with tears.

One of the ronin said, "Den'e-dono, we ate very well today but still no tobacco."

"Oh, it'll be there soon!"

This upset the men who would not die. All the

Hosokawa men rose to their feet. The novice assigned this duty scrambled to bring the tobacco.

When Hara Soemon stroked his head and said, "Grow up to be a good man," the tears returned.

Each condemned man received writing paper, an ink stone, and a brush to write a death poem. Some wrote, others did not.

During that time, Den'emon exchanged a few words with the men. He heard Kuranosuke, the last man to speak.

The time came. Tension turned the faces of the envoy and the inspector into masks. The hushed silence experienced in a cavernous temple hung over the residence. The sounds from throats swallowing saliva could be heard. Then a voice calling for the first death echoed from the courtyard.

"Oishi Kuranosuke-dono! Come forward!"

Den'emon saw a figure stand among the sea of white and pale yellow. With only part of his body visible, he seemed to glide away. For an instant, one doubted he was human. He looked like a being higher than the humans who will remain in this world.

A moment quieter than midnight came. After Kuranosuke gave his respect and his figure became a shadow on the white folding screen, painful pounding thrust out many chests, then an extraordinary sound struck the ears.

A ringing blade shook the air. Faces lost color, and mouths dried up.

"Kuranosuke-dono is dead. Yoshida Chuzaemon! Come forward."

The official's voice sounded parched now.

One after another, each name was called.

The names of the comic dancer Oishi Sezaemon from the previous night and the twenty-four-year-old Isogai

Jurozaemon who longed to see a certain woman were called.

Shadows came over the courtyard as the cold, bleak night fell. The sunlight filtered by the trees seemed to smell like blood.

Den'emon's temples throbbed. He didn't know whether he was an evil demon or a human being. He attached a nametag and a number to each burial article and the clothes of the deceased for eventual delivery to their families and stacked them in a corner of the room.

While doing this, he remembered Isogai Juroza's clothes. He didn't need to fold them. Juroza had already done so. He meticulously placed everything—old obi sashes and personal possessions—on top.

"He was so young."

Den'emon released a long sigh. He picked up the clothes, pressed them against his cheek, and thought the faint warmth of the young Juroza lingered. Something dropped out of a sleeve.

"What's this?"

He picked it up and stared. A dark reddish-purple piece of silk wrapped a small object. He accidentally opened it. A pick for a koto harp fell out. Alone, deep inside this piece of purple cloth was a single koto pick.

"Oh, so the owner of this pick is ..."

An image of the woman Den'emon used to see near the clan residence floated into his head. Now he remembered with regret. He suspected the joking words of Gengoemon the other night were not a joke.

The courtyard was in shadows. Juroza was no longer there or anywhere in this world. Without a word to a soul, Juroza snuck away leaving this riddle in his harmonious figure of good looks and a stout heart.

An extreme of love is secret love
The scent of a warrior's love is faint.

These words, seen somewhere and now flitting across Den'emon's mind, were for Juroza. Is that love in the way of the warrior?

That appeared to be another obligation of their important work left in this world. This flower bloomed beside the way of the samurai. The love destined for a man was as distant as the sun.

The night stars in February were brilliant. The darkness that night carried the faint aroma of plum blossoms in a quiet breeze. Somewhere Kuranosuke was at peace. As the white folding screen in the courtyard of the Hosokawa estate was being folded, white screens were being folded in sixths at the Mori, Matsudaira, and Mizuno estates, too.

Den'emon could say it had been a good day. Kuranosuke died to live for all time and was truly at peace.

Unlike the miserable laws of the times, the righteous men of humanity were on display.

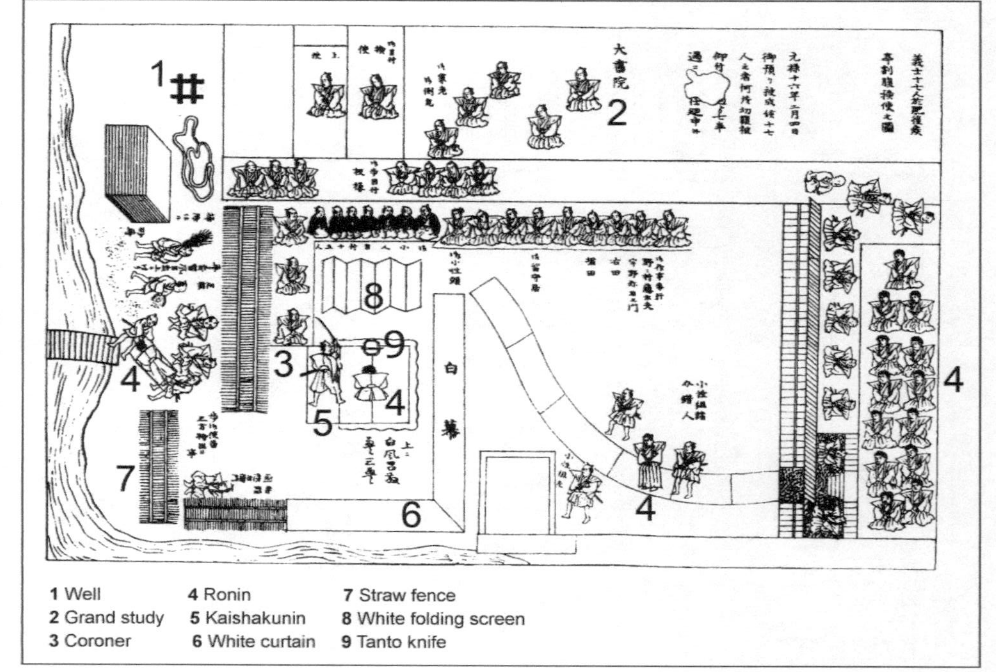

Seppuku in the Hosokawa Courtyard

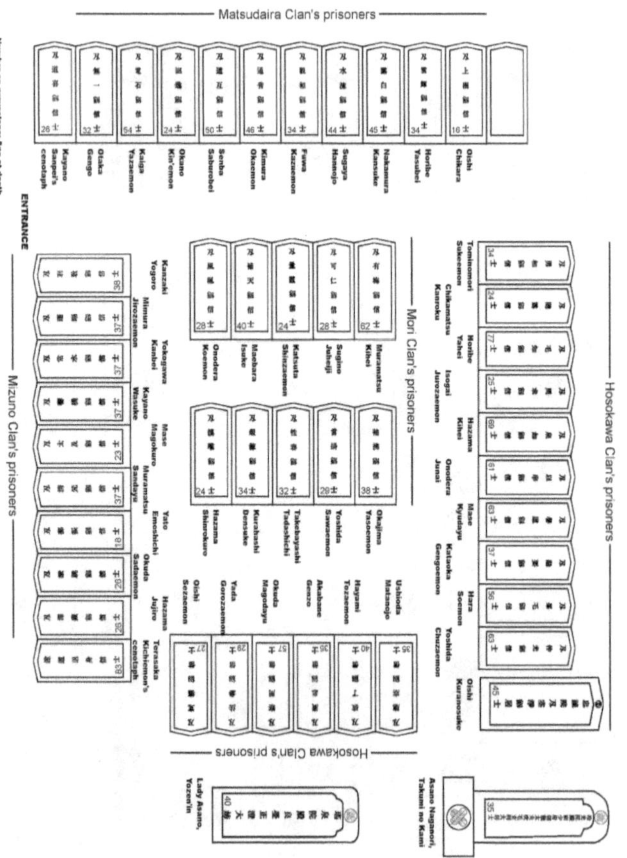

Graves at Sengakuji Temple

ABOUT THE AUTHOR

Yoshikawa Eiji (August 11, 1892 - September 7, 1962) was a Japanese novelist and master of the historical novel. He was born Yoshikawa Hidetsugu in Yokohama, Japan. His father Yoshikawa Naohiro was a former samurai in the Odawara clan. After working at a variety of jobs, he gained fame as a popular writer with the serial publication of the novel *Naruto Hicho* [The Secret Record of Naruto] in Osaka Mainichi Shimbun (August 11, 1926 - October 14, 1927). He gained a wider following with Miyamoto Musashi, published serially beginning in 1935. A prolific author, he received the Order of Culture in 1960 and the third Mainichi Geijutsu art prize in 1961. In his honor, The Yoshikawa Eiji Prize for Literature was established in 1967 and The Yoshikawa Eiji Prize for New Writers in 1980.

From the Japanese Wikipedia page for Yoshikawa Eiji (https://ja.wikipedia.org/wiki/吉川英治
    Accessed February 6, 2019).

CREDITS

Japanese source text:

Aozora Bunko. Yoshikawa, Eiji. The New Chushingura (新編忠臣蔵), Hinode, January 1935 to January 1937. Accessed July 27, 2018.

Input by: Yuki Hiroshi

Revised by: Kitagawa Matsuki

https://www.aozora.gr.jp/cards/001562/files/58019_65472.html

Cover image:

National Diet Library Digital Collections. Reprint of *The Ako Loyal Retainers Attack the Kira Estate* (赤穂義士復讐吉良邸討入之図) by Isshunsai Yoshikazu in *Edo-e Nihon-shi* (江戸繪日本史). Tokyo: Sato Kyuta, 1900. Accessed November 16, 2019.

https://dl.ndl.go.jp/info:ndljp/pid/9369964/25

Asano Clan Crest:

National Diet Library Digital Collections. Mishima,

Sousen. *Ako Gishi* (赤穂義士). Tokyo: Jidou no Tomosha, 1943. Accessed November 26, 2019.

https://dl.ndl.go.jp/info:ndljp/pid/1169890

Ashikaga (Kira) Clan Crest:

By Shelley Marshall using GIMP-2.8

Uesugi Clan Crest:

Mukai, CC BY-SA 3.0 <https://creativecommons. org/licenses/by-sa/3.0>, via Wikimedia Commons. Accessed July 24, 2021.

https://commons.wikimedia.org/wiki/File: Japanese_Crest_Uesugi_Sasa.svg

Seppuku in the Hosokawa Courtyard:

National Diet Library Digital Collections. Nishimura, Yutaka. *The Families of the Loyal Retainers of Ako: Oishi Kura-nosuke* (赤穂義士家庭：大石内蔵助). Tokyo: Seikeido, 1913. Accessed June 8, 2021.

https://dl.ndl.go.jp/info:ndljp/pid/945242

Illustrations of the 47 Ronin and the Graves of the 47 Ronin:

National Diet Library Digital Collections. Color Print Collection of Soga's Chushingura (曽我忠臣蔵錦絵并番附集). Vol. 2. Accessed July 20, 2019.

https://dl.ndl.go.jp/info:ndljp/pid/2591881

Epitaphs on Tombstones and Asano Clan Crest:

National Diet Library Digital Collections. Tsuji, Iwao. Collection of Epitaphs for the Ako Loyal Retainers (赤穂義士碑文集). Kobe: Tsujiko, 1922. Accessed June 8, 2021.

https://dl.ndl.go.jp/info:ndljp/pid/1182186

Layout of Tombstones:

National Diet Library Digital Collections. *Ako Seigi Sanko Naishodokoro* (赤穂精義参考内侍所). Tokyo: Kinshodo, 1887. Accessed July 2, 2021.

https://dl.ndl.go.jp/info:ndljp/pid/782803

Asano Takumi no Kami's Grave:

National Diet Library Digital Collections. *The Incarnation of the Extraordinary Kuranosuke in Bushido* (武士道の権化快傑内蔵助). Tokyo: Chukokan Shoten, 1917. Accessed July 3, 2021.

https://dl.ndl.go.jp/info:ndljp/pid/955998